Charlotte Hardy was born in Brighton. After training as an actress in Bristol, she spent fifteen years in the professional theatre before beginning work as a London tour guide. In 1982 she was awarded a Ph.D for her thesis on Athenian democracy (since published as a book) and now works as a tour manager for a variety of travel companies all over the world. She has published two historical novels, *Julia Stone* and *Far From Home,* both available from Piatkus. She is married and lives in Surrey.

*Also by Charlotte Hardy*

Julia Stone
Far From Home

# The Last Days of Innocence

## Charlotte Hardy

PIATKUS

First published in Great Britain in 1998 by
Judy Piatkus (Publishers) Ltd of
5 Windmill Street, London W1

This edition published 1998

**The moral right of the author has been asserted**

*A catalogue record for this book is available from the British Library.*

ISBN 0 7499 3075 6

Set in Times by Action Typesetting Limited, Gloucester

Printed and bound in Great Britain by
Mackays of Chatham PLC, Chatham, Kent

# Chapter One

If Leary hadn't been late, things might have turned our differently.

As it was, Anne was not in the best of moods. She was hot, dusty and thirsty; her cotton frock stuck to her back; the ferry from Fishguard to Cork had been delayed, so it was now nearly twenty-four hours since she had left Devon; and this eternal country bus from Cork was slow, noisy, rattly and airless. But at last, after what now felt like a lifetime, it pulled up the long narrow street of Macroom on the afternoon of Friday June 25 1920, and shuddered to a halt in the town square opposite the castle. As the conductor helped her down with her suitcase, all she could think of was the relief that Leary would be waiting with the trap and that she was nearly home. It was only ten more miles to Lisheen; in an hour she would be peeling off her clothes and sinking into a blissful bath.

But Leary was not waiting. As the bus pulled out of the square, and silence descended, she straightened her wide-brimmed hat and looked about her with annoyance. The striped awnings of shop fronts hung still, and the little houses stared at each other across the deserted square. The only sign of life was in front of the castle, which faced on to one side of the square, where three army lorries waited, and a British soldier stood on guard in the afternoon heat, uncomfortable in battlefield khaki, with steel helmet, puttees and a long rifle.

She bit her finger and consulted her watch. At last she took up the heavy suitcase with both hands and dragged it across

1

the square towards the Victoria Hotel. In the shade of a shop awning, she sat down on it to wait.

As she sat glumly, elbows on her knees, chin resting on her hands, her gaze focussed gradually on the car standing outside the hotel. It was the only car in the square, and the biggest she had ever seen. To say that it was out of place in a small market town in Ireland was hardly the point; it would have turned heads in Piccadilly or the Champs Elysées. It was the sort of car one saw in posters on railway stations for Deauville or Biarritz in which impossibly glamorous people arrived at the *plage* or a polo match, or were seen departing from the gates of a country house. The deep gleam of its brilliant scarlet bodywork, the giant polished chrome headlamps, long sleek black mudguards and running board, the spacious leather seats in pale cream (its hood was folded back) ... there could not be another car like it in Ireland.

She looked at her watch again. There was still no sign of Leary.

At that moment a man came out of the hotel and across to the car. He opened the door and was about to get in when he noticed her. He hesitated; he seemed to think for a moment and then he looked at her again.

'Can I offer you a lift anywhere?'

Anne was not accustomed to receiving – or answering – questions from strange men. She looked up from beneath the wide brim of her hat, her eyes gleaming in the shade, gave him a cool stare, and said 'No, thank you' in a colourless tone.

He was English as far as she could make out, and expensively dressed in a tailor-made Prince of Wales check suit and the sort of shoes that will last a lifetime if a manservant takes good care of them.

'You sure? I don't like to think of you lugging that great case about. You could hardly lift it.'

'You were watching?'

'My dear girl, the entire clientele of this hotel has been watching you.'

She glanced round but from where she was sitting could see no one. She turned to him, intrigued.

'Hadn't you anything better to do?'

2

'We were all riveted. In fact, I have to confess that when I saw you dragging your case over towards the car, I rashly ventured money on the outcome of our meeting.'

She took a moment to digest this.

'What are you talking about?'

'Look, I'll put you in the picture.' He leant against the side of the car. He seemed perfectly at ease. 'Knowing you Irish are devils for a bet, and feeling that as a stranger here I ought to do as the Romans do and all that, I foolishly made a small wager.' He rubbed his chin. 'Well, not so small actually –'

'What wager?'

'– and I'm rather depending on you to save the day. Tell you what, I'll split the proceeds with you.'

'Unless you tell me what this wager is, I don't see how I can decide.'

He looked back towards the hotel as if the 'entire clientele' must be craning their heads to watch, then leant towards her confidentially.

'They bet me I couldn't talk you into going for a drive with me.'

At that time of day, the 'entire clientele' of the Victoria Hotel would most likely be sleeping off their lunch. This was clearly a hoax. The hotel stared out across the square, its windows deserted in the bright sunshine. Anne drew herself up with the haughty composure some men found wildly attractive.

'And you accepted the bet?' she said coolly.

'So it would seem'. He raised his eyebrows mildly as if in expectation of a favourable response.

'Don't you think it rather foolish to let me in on the secret?'

'I'll go halves. Are you sure there's nowhere I can drive you?'

He looked at her appealingly and glanced back again at the hotel. 'Mmm? I'll look a terrible fool if you say no.'

She hesitated, appearing to give her answer serious thought. 'There is one difficulty.'

'What's that?'

She opened her eyes wide. 'You see, my father always told me never to accept lifts from strange men. And, looking at you, I'd say you were a very strange man. In fact, I'd say you were the strangest man I'd ever met.'

3

She preserved her cool exterior and innocent look. He seemed slightly put out.

'I don't know about that. My friends speak very highly of me. Some of them.'

'Oh, you have friends? Well, I suppose a few must take pity on you. And your mother, perhaps.'

'I say, steady on.'

Anne appeared to have an idea. 'Perhaps that's why she gave you such a big toy to play with?'

'Toy?' He looked round, mystified. 'I don't – you're not referring to *this*?' He touched the car.

'What else would you call it? Oh, as for the bet, I don't believe a word of it – so far. Do you want to have another try? A new tack? Do go on. I haven't anything else to do for the moment.'

Before he could go on, however, Leary appeared at the other side of the square in the trap. Anne stood up and went to meet him.

He saw her and turning the mare's head, swept in a wide circle round the square to pull up beside her.

'So you finally got here?'

Leary was an elderly man and did nothing in a hurry. He helped himself down from the trap.

'What happened? Did you get lost?' She looked down at the bent shoulders and comfortable shape of the old groom.

'Welcome back, Miss Anne,' he said as he came to pick up her suitcase. 'With all the coming and going at the house, 'tis a wonder I'm here at all.'

The strange man was before him, however, and taking up the case as if it weighed nothing at all, placed it on one of seats of the trap. The springs creaked. She was conscious, almost without realising it, of his easy strength, his shoulders and strong neck, He might well be a rugby player ... but she turned away quickly as she caught his eye.

'*Bon voyage*!'

As they crossed the square she looked back towards the man and his car and gave him a small ironic wave. She thought she had probably never met such a conceited man in her life, and felt a small glow of satisfaction that she had put him in his place. As for his bet – well, perhaps he had made some sort of

4

wager. He was probably the sort of man who went in for that sort of thing. As if all girls were there for the angling, just waiting to be charmed off their feet with a few witty phrases. She settled herself more comfortably on the old padded seats of the trap.

It was not until they had left the town and were trotting along the lane between hedges thick with wild fuchsia and hawthorn blossom that she could turn her mind away from the subject.

'And how is everyone, Leary? Are preparations well in hand?'

'Ye've been well out of it. I've near broke me back with that marquee on the west lawn.'

'Marquee?'

'Ach, there's no expense spared. Your father's bankrupting himself, is the truth of it. There's a band to play at the reception after, coming from Cork; there's them two Maloney girls from the village, running round like headless cocks; and the weight of flowers brought in, and if the colonel hasn't emptied his cellars it's a marvel – ten dozen of champagne cooling. Ten dozen!'

He lapsed into silence, and they both thought of the extravagance ahead. Her elder sister was getting married. Pippa, Father's favourite, thought Anne, as she stared away towards the mountains, hearing the monotonous sound of Maisie's hoofs and the iron rim of the wheels on the hard earth of the lane.

'I've been in to Macroom once today already. Potted shrimps!' He mumbled something else she couldn't make out and then said again, 'Ye've been well out of it.'

Leary was right, Anne had postponed her return as late as possible to avoid all this. She had not even tried on her bridesmaid's gown yet. She could not bear to be sucked into Pippa's self-importance. Since the date of the wedding had been fixed her sister had, for all practical purposes, taken over the running of the house.

At twenty-one, she was three years older than Anne. She'd only ever wanted to get married, and now she had her man, Tony Napier, an English officer stationed in Dublin Castle. They had met at a music hall, Pippa said. She went up to

5

Dublin whenever she could. She loved theatres, shopping, fun of any kind.

'What time is the ceremony?'

'Half-past eleven.'

There was a grey stone Victorian Protestant church in the village where the Hunters worshipped, together with other Protestant families; the local gentry in other words, landowners, a solicitor or two, a number of retired military men and an old admiral. They would all be at the wedding, together with colleagues of her father, fellow magistrates, even the Lord Lieutenant of the county, and no doubt many soldier friends of Tony's.

Anne was not looking forward to it. She was never quite easy at parties or dances, which was why young men found her difficult to get on with. It was all the more puzzling because at first sight she was so attractive. There was a quality about her of sunshine, an open glowing quality – something about her straw-coloured hair which was strong and cut short in a bob so that it swung easily round her head; or her slim body and long legs, brown now in summer; or her regular features, her straight thin nose, even eyebrows above cornflower blue eyes, and strong chin.

When young men first saw her they could not believe their luck and congratulated themselves on finding this pretty, wide-eyed girl. Looking at her across a dance floor, watching her dancing or in conversation, seeing her laughing, seeing the hair swing round her head as she turned to talk to someone, and the fierce, animated expression in her eyes as she talked, she was bewitching.

It came as a shock therefore to find that as they got into conversation with her, it was as if she were metaphorically kicking them in the shins or treading on their toes. Girls were supposed to look up at them with interest and attention, to laugh at their jokes, to listen patiently to their anecdotes. Anne did not listen to their anecdotes – or not for long – neither did she laugh at their jokes much. As they arrived at the carefully prepared climax of the story she would turn to someone else and change the subject, leaving them with the painful feeling of being blanked out of her attention. There was something cool and sarcastic in

6

her manner which held them at a distance and rebuked them for presuming on an intimacy with her.

One disappointed man called her a 'professional virgin' (others used a grosser term), but Cathal, her oldest friend and more perceptive, compared her with Diana the ancient goddess of hunting, and truly Anne was never happier than when she was roaming the mountainside behind the house with her dogs.

Beneath her the wheels rattled on the hard earth road. It was an exquisite afternoon and they were alone in the narrow country lane. She took a deep breath as she looked about her.

Beyond the abundant hedges, the wild flowers and rampant green of the early-summer foliage, beyond the little fields, and the brilliant yellow of the furze on a patch of bog, rose the mountains in the distance, hazy, blue-grey, mauve or lavender, always changing as the clouds moved over them, forming and reforming as the day passed, and in the wonderful openness, the great wide solitude, peace descended upon her. The mare trotted contentedly before them, Leary hunched forward in his little seat staring at nothing, and she felt herself expanding, relaxing; there was no doubt of it, Ireland was the best place on earth.

And she was nearly home. She felt generous; she was even prepared to undergo the events of the following day. She would dress up, be an obedient bridesmaid, smile at inane men, listen to their foolish chatter. After all, even if they had grown apart in the last two years, Pippa was still her sister.

Then, quite unexpectedly, she heard the sound of a motor car behind them. It was going very fast because almost before she knew it or Leary had time to pull the mare to one side, the great red car, the embodiment of ostentatious power and assurance, roared past in a cloud of suffocating, choking dust, and as she coughed, the dust in her eyes and throat, and Leary was pulling hard at the reins, the driver sounded a loud 'Poop-poop!' and waved his hand before thundering away round the bend in the lane. Ahead of them she could see the dust rising between the hedgerows as the great machine rushed on and the sound died away in the distance.

Wiping her eyes and coughing into her handkerchief, Anne was incoherent with rage. He had done it deliberately, she was certain; but he didn't know who he had been tangling with; her father was a magistrate. That conceited smirk would be wiped off his face when he found himself up on a charge of reckless conduct in possession of a dangerous vehicle ... Leary, a man inured through the years to everything, muttered soothing words to the mare.

Fifteen minutes later, as they came into Lisheen, Anne saw the car standing outside Shanahan's Bar. Springing down, she walked quickly inside. In the dim light after the brightness of the day, in the dingy smoky atmosphere where half a dozen men sat shabbily behind pints of porter, she looked around. They glanced up, startled. There was no sign of the man.

'Have you seen – the man – that car outside –' She was still angry. The men stared at the tall girl in the summer frock and broad-brimmed hat. No woman ever went into Shanahan's Bar. 'The man – in that car –'

Shanahan himself came out from behind the bar.

'What car, Miss Hunter?'

'There's only one.'

Shanahan came with her to the door and looked out. Two or three other drinkers crowded behind him.

'Where's the driver!'

'Does anyone know the owner of this vehicle?' Shanahan turned to the others like a magistrate addressing a witness, but they shook their head solemnly.

'Oh, for heaven's sake, it doesn't matter!'

She went quickly out again into the empty village street. The car stood open-topped, proud, contemptuous of this shabby village, a symbol of the great wide world, disdaining to be locked up, as if the owner could leave it like this while he went away on business, confident none of the villagers would even dare to touch it. Of the man himself there was no sign. Anne looked up and down the street, then climbed back on to the side car.

'Drive on.'

8

# Chapter Two

Nearly a mile above the village stood Lisheen House, a substantial, square Victorian house in a vaguely Tudor style, ugly but strong and serviceable, its stucco weathered to a grey. This was partly disguised by wisteria growing abundantly across the front of the house which was further sheltered on three sides by oaks and rhododendrons, now out in massed banks of white and purple. As the trap came at last through the rhododendrons to the gravelled sweep before the house which Costello had raked that morning, there was a butcher's delivery van and a motor car Anne did not recognise standing at the door. Through the mullioned windows she heard people calling to each other and from somewhere at the back the sound of hammering.

The drawing room was blissfully cool, and she found her mother stretched out there on a chaise longue. Claire was dressed in exotic, flowing clothes, chiffons and silks in strong oriental colours; her hair was bound up with a thin gauzy scarf, and a tiny slipper swung from her toe. A slender volume of poetry hung from her fingers as she languidly stretched an arm towards Anne.

'Hullo, darling. Got back safely?'

Anne bent over and brushed her cheek with a kiss.

'Uncle Gerald sends his love. Where's Father?'

Mor and Og, her two big Irish setters had risen immediately she came into the room, and Anne squatted between them nuzzling her face against theirs, crooning to them, and running her hand along their backs.

'There are a couple of military men with him at the

9

moment. That dreadful business over at Dunmanway ... '

Anne threw herself into an armchair.

'What business was that?'

She looked round the room, thinking how nice it was to be home. The drawing room was decorated with all Claire's skill and was easily the most attractive of any of her friends'. Her mother had the instinctive taste which can take things – furniture, china, paintings – and match them to create a harmonious composition, a feeling of relaxation and comfort evident as soon as you came into a room. There was nothing overtly 'arty', nothing intended to shock or impress. Traditional chintz curtains, furniture which was old and comfortable, a leather armchair or two, a sofa in a heavy, faded gold brocade, some shelves of blue and white china and a cabinet of rather more expensive Sèvres and Dresden. A number of paintings in heavy gilt frames hung on the walls, some family portaits and some traditional landscapes. The fireplace, neatly polished, was now filled with a spray of leaves, rushes and flowers in a polished brass jug; elsewhere flowers in vases stood on an old oak chest and in the centre of the polished table. A rich but unforced texture of colour and shape, all blending together to create an atmosphere of quiet contentment, a happy home.

'Oh, you won't have heard. The most terrible business – the police barracks was attacked last night and two constables were killed.'

The two women sat for a moment, thinking, then Claire went on, 'Heaven knows, one is all in favour of Irish independence. And Ireland owes England nothing at all. Quite the reverse. Still, one can't approve of murder.' She sighed. 'They're only ignorant boys.'

Anne roused herself. She did not want to get into a discussion on that subject at this moment. The clandestine war against England which erupted fitfully in the lanes and villages around them had been going on for over a year.

'I'm going to have a bath. Is there any hot water, do you know?'

'I'm sure there is. Pippa's upstairs.'

Anne was about to leave the room when they heard from somewhere above them a burst of music and then voices raised in a silly jaunty song. Anne stopped and listened to the words:

> *'Horsey, put your tail up,*
> *Keep the sun out of my eyes ...'*

'Vere's got a new record?'

'Mmm. I should think that's the twenty-fifth time I've heard it today.'

As Anne climbed the wide open staircase which rose through two floors, lit by stained glass mullioned windows, the song wound on its inane way.

It came to an end as she entered Pippa's bedroom. Pippa, clad in a dressing gown, glanced round, but as sisters they did no more than grunt familiarly to each other.

She was shorter than Anne, and everything Anne was not. She was pretty, had a more rounded figure, and hair which reached to her waist and was at this moment woven into a thick plait which hung over one shoulder. She liked men, and she liked men to like her. She knew how to work on them and, within limits, to make them do what she wanted. She would look up into their eyes helplessly, and appeal to their chivalrous instincts. She was a sociable creature and her demands were light: she wanted a home of her own, a dependable, undemanding husband who would give her no unpleasant surprises, and lots of friends who would call and keep her occupied. Tony Napier appeared to fit the bill.

'How was Devon?'

'All right. Have you got everything ready?'

'Almost, I think.'

The room was filled with clothes; thrown over the bed, over every chair, hanging from the picture rail, the edge of the wardrobe, and the mantelpiece. The wedding dress stood on a dressmaker's dummy.

'It's a dream, isn't it? I'm going to be a wow, you watch me.'

Pippa had no nerves.

'Your dress is on your bed – you'd better go and try it on.'

'I haven't put on any weight. It should fit.'

The music started again abruptly. Though Vere's room was

11

some distance away, and faced towards the back of the house, the idiotic words came through clearly.

> '*Horsey, put your tail up,*
> *Keep the sun out of my eyes …*'

'For goodness' sake, have you been listening to that all day?'

'Tiresome, isn't it? Try telling him to put a sock in it. He won't listen to me.'

Anne went quickly down the corridor and threw open Vere's door. He was lying on his bed, one leg cocked up over his knee. A prominent hole was displayed in the sole of his sock.

Vere was fourteen, and at a very inconvenient stage of development, not quite a boy any longer, nor yet a man; nothing you could quite define, in fact. He was an attractive, high-spirited lad, popular, but apt to be a nuisance where his sisters were concerned. It had been easy for them to bully him in the past, but he was no longer prepared to tolerate it and lived in a state of perpetual war with them, grudging fiercely the slightest infringement of his liberty and constantly demanding to be treated as their equal.

Anne leant against the door post and looked down at him.

'Would it be too much to ask you to turn off that row?'

'Don't you like it?' He looked up at her, quite composed.

'How could anyone *like* it? It's utterly banal.'

'Ooh!' His eyes opened wide. 'What a very *clever* and *learned* word. Did you eat a dictionary for breakfast?'

'Take it off.'

'No.'

'Vere, you little reptile, take it off this instant!'

'How much will you pay me?'

The music cantered on as she marched over to the gramophone. Vere leapt up before her.

'Don't touch it!'

'Take it off then.'

He turned to the gramophone and carefully lifted the needle off the record.

'The whole house can see that *you're* back. It was so nice while you were away.'

'Too bad. I'm going to have a bath and I want to have it in peace.'

The bath had been installed when such things first came into use. It was very large, thick vitreous enamel gleaming dead white with rusty brown marks beneath the taps, a thick mahogany surround and four lions' paws for support. It stood in the middle of the bathroom. Anne peeled off her dusty, sticky clothes and lowered herself into the great steaming tub as if her whole journey had been leading at last to this; lowering her limbs gradually into the water and stretching out; admiring her own long leg in spite of herself as she reached it up towards the big brass taps; idly wiping the steam from the cold tap with her big toe.

As she relaxed in the heat, letting her mind float free, running through her preoccupations as they gradually rose to the surface, she began to ask herself a simple basic question. Why hadn't she accepted that man's offer of a ride? Nothing could have been easier. It was a situation straight out of one of her Dornford Yates novels – and just the sort of car his heroes rode in as they sped through Europe on their secret and dangerous missions. It would have been so easy – and so nice. What perverse streak in her had made her refuse the thing she had in fact desired? She had been furious with that man as he'd roared past her in the lane – but how wonderful if she had been sitting beside him!

It was very confusing. There was something in her which spited herself. It was as if she hated herself – how else to explain it? He was a good-looking man now she came to remember him, with that strong neck, rather thick dark eyebrows and crinkly lines about his eyes, as if he had been used to squinting in bright sunlight. In fact he'd had a swarthy or sunburnt complexion altogether though he was obviously a gentleman. Nothing could have been simpler than to accept.

Instead of which she had found herself becoming cool, sarcastic, off-hand. She did it all the time. Why? She squirmed in the bath, twisting one leg over the other as she struggled to understand her own perverse character. She was afraid to let anyone come too near her – but why? How anyone could like her – let alone love her – she could not imagine.

If only she were like Pippa, she thought. Father's favourite. Pippa was popular with men; they flocked round her. She had no difficult side, she was fun, she was affectionate. Why was it so easy for Pippa, and so difficult for her? Anne twisted again in the water, running her hand over her belly, splashing water up over her breasts which were small, but high and firm. What was wrong with her?

But as she waited, no answer came. It was one of life's mysteries.

Later, wrapped in a dressing gown and glowing hot, she sat on the floor of Pippa's bedroom as her sister slowly assembled the contents of her suitcases for going away the following afternoon. She pottered about among her clothes, picking up an item here, then another, rearranging things, taking them out of one suitcase and putting them into another, in no hurry.

She turned suddenly to Anne.

'Oh, I say, I meant to tell you. You know that raid yesterday on the police barracks at Dunmanway? Apparently Cathal Donnelly was involved.'

Anne stared at her.

'Just think of it! He's gone into hiding. He was definitely identified, and there's a warrant out for his arrest. I mean – two policemen were killed. Can you *imagine*? If he were *caught* –'

They stared at each other.

'Cathal?' Anne whispered. 'But he's not like that. I mean, he wouldn't get mixed up in anything like that. Murder? Cathal Donnelly? I can't believe it.'

'It's definite. Apparently he's become the most terrible firebrand – all red hot for Irish independence.'

'Good lord!' Anne tried to picture the Cathal she knew with a gun. She had known him since they were children; probably there was no one alive she knew better or who knew her better. He was a Catholic, a medical student, the son of a local doctor. As children they had roamed together over the mountains behind the house, the dogs about them. Cathal, whom she had danced with at the Hunt Ball and Christmas parties, the only man impervious to her off-hand manner; the first boy ever to kiss her, when she was thirteen, in a broom cupboard during a game of Postman's Knock. Cathal, her other self.

In fact for a long time Anne had believed that Cathal admired her, and was quite happy for him to do so, though she had given him no overt encouragement whatsoever. However, over the last eighteen months, since he had gone away to medical school, she had scarcely seen him, and he had become noticeably cool towards her on his brief trips home.

'You used to be sweet on him at one time, didn't you?'

'I did not!'

Pippa raised one eyebrow slightly and turned again to her things.

'Still, it's not quite so odd when you come to think of it,' she went on as she opened a shopping bag and took out some things wrapped in tissue. 'Remember when he used to be called Charles? Why did he change his name to Cathal if he wasn't converted to the rebel cause? It was after the Dublin Post Office rising, remember?'

Anne remembered. That was four years earlier when the rebels made their stand at the Post Office in Sackville Street, 1916, at the height of the war. Nobody had thought much of them until it was over and the leaders were shot. Then the mood had changed. Everywhere a new spirit was in the air. More had been at stake than people had realised, and Charles became Cathal as a mark of sympathy and solidarity.

Pippa had unwrapped some things from their tissue paper.

'What do you think of these?'

She grinned at Anne as she held up a pair of French knickers in pink silk.

'Tony bought them for me in Switzer's.'

Anne knelt up and took them from Pippa. As her sister opened other packages, Anne ran the silk through her fingers. So light, so dainty, so beautiful – she had never seen anything like them. It was difficult to find words.

'Tony bought them?' She tried to sound off-hand.

Pippa had unwrapped the other things and passed them over: a delicate camisole top with lace panels over the bosom, silk stockings, a night gown in superfine jade green silk, long but so flimsy; things just running and slipping through her fingers as she held them and devoured them with her eyes.

Pippa was watching her with a wicked gleam in her eye.

'Good, eh? Tony's a bit like that. Picked up a few ideas

15

when he was in France, I shouldn't be surprised. Do you know what he said?' She lowered her voice. 'He said he wants me to be a lady in the drawing room and a tart in bed!' She erupted into giggles as Anne passed the things back to her.

Anne did not giggle. These things spoke to her of an intimacy she could not even guess at. To think that Tony, that a man, had actually gone into a shop and actually asked for these things, actually named them – how could he even look the shop assistant in the eye? Or had they bought them together? Had Pippa chosen them and Tony paid? Had they stood together in the shop, turning things over and discussing them while a shop assistant watched? She could not imagine it.

'Wish you had some?' Pippa was looking at her mockingly. 'Make a change from blue serge knickers and woolly vests, eh?'

Anne pulled herself together.

'If you like that sort of thing, I suppose,' she said coolly.

'And you don't? Go on admit it, Anne. You wouldn't mind.'

'I've never thought about it.'

She tried to sound off-hand, but the fact was she was more likely to land on the moon than ever to dress herself in these flimsy silk things which weighed nothing and seemed to caress the skin, which draped themselves across a woman's breasts, across her thighs, her bottom, which veiled the body rather than covered it, hinting at what was beneath and were nothing less than an invitation to a man, a hint, a challenge. Take me. Anne felt her heart beating rapidly. Such things were not for her. No, not by a million miles.

# Chapter Three

Anne looked at herself in the mirror nervously. The dress was conventional, sprigged muslin draped low over the hips and falling straight to mid-calf, worn with white stockings and shoes. Pretty enough without threatening to overshadow the bride. For some incomprensible reason Anne was afraid of looking too attractive; afraid of the attention it might draw.

She turned, looking at her side view. Well, there was little chance of that! What a long thing she was: a bean pole with a blonde mop of hair sheared off below the ears, emphasising her long neck.

Outside the window the garden was still, the thick foliage of the oaks and the clusters of vivid pinks and blues in the borders already, before nine in the morning, waiting breathlessly for another cloudless day. It was typical of Pippa to get perfect weather for her wedding.

Somewhere below the window she could hear Costello whistling as he polished the car. He was the chauffeur-cum-gardener; a tousle-headed young man, thoughtless, forgetful, but warm-hearted. To Leary's disgust it was Costello who would drive the bridegroom and her father in the car. Leary could not drive a car but nevertheless there had been warm words between them on the subject.

Downstairs there was a clatter of preparation, voices calling and the sound of furniture being moved.

She took up the wreath of flowers and set it on her hair.

The door opened suddenly, and a girl dressed in the same ensemble burst in.

'Oh, Anne, have you got a safety pin? Bunty's broken her suspender belt. I say, you do look pretty.'

'Mmm? Thanks, Pru, so do you.' Anne began rifling through a dish on the dressing table. The rest of the bridesmaids were preparing themselves in another bedroom.

Pru hiccupped, adjusting her flower wreath in the long pier glass. 'Your pa sent up a tray of champagne. The girls are squiffy already.' She giggled.

'Thoughtful of him. Ah, here we are. Is there any left, by the way? I think I could do with a glass myself.'

'Well, come on, then, there's loads.'

As they went out of the door, Pru went on, 'Can you imagine, Pippa looking radiant on her pa's arm, and behind her – us, all tripping over each other, and collapsing in giggles?'

'She'll have our scalps if we do.'

Outside the front door on the gravel, upright, black, stood the car with its white streamers running from windscreen to bonnet. Costello gave it a last flick with the duster.

The bridesmaids, Anne, Pru, Ethel, friends of Pippa's and the rest, would travel by waggonette, and Anne came out into the sunshine just as Leary was bringing it round to the door. He was in his black Sunday suit worn with a bowler hat and a stiff white collar. He had no tie but had been given a white rosette which was pinned to his lapel. The girls emerged in high spirits.

When they arrived at the church there was already a long line of open traps, jaunting cars, side cars, governess and dog carts along the street, two open carriages and half a dozen large cars. Grooms, jarveys and coachmen stood chatting together, leaning against their carriages as horses fed from nose bags.

Dominating this scene, dominating the entire street, was a large army lorry and an armed platoon of British soldiers standing near the church door in full uniform. They were smoking cigarettes and talking together. Anne realised they had come with Tony, they were his bodyguard, but they gave the morning a surreal air, as if they could have nothing to do with this placid scene.

The six girls clambered out of the waggonette – difficult in their hobble skirts and high-heeled shoes – and stood together, pulling and pushing at their dresses, adjusting their flower wreaths and checking each other's appearance. The church door stood open and Anne could hear the buzz of excitement inside.

A moment later the car drew up, and the soldiers quickly stamped out their cigarettes and formed up to salute.

Father, a retired colonel, was in his old dress uniform, black, with a high collar and tight trousers, and he assisted Pippa out as Costello opened the door. Vere, who was a steward, diminutive in his tail coat, was at the door. He signalled inside and a moment later the organ sounded, a loud and jolly peal of notes.

As she heard the festive noise, Anne thought how pretty the other girls looked with flowers in their hair, and what a vision Pippa was. The bride let fall her veil, took her father's arm and they entered the church as music thundered out. Anne was immediately behind her with Ethel. The guests on either side, men in morning suits, ladies in flowery hats and summery frocks, turned to watch the procession enter.

Ahead of them waited Canon Blenkinsop, the elderly Church of Ireland vicar of the parish, and nearby sat Claire, in a tailored Worth dress. At the other side stood the bridegroom and his best man. Even from the back, Tony was unmistakably a British officer in his red uniform and long polished boots. An officer and a gentleman. But even as this hackneyed phrase came into Anne's mind, her eyes had riveted themselves on the back of the man beside him. There was something about that neck and those shoulders. Even in a morning suit, even with his back to her, Anne knew instantly who he was. But what was he doing here? And what would he say when he saw her? What fresh practical joke would he have prepared?

She found her way into her pew without taking her eyes from his back. He was bound to turn round in a minute and see her. She must decide how to respond, in case he said anything to her.

Even as she pondered these thoughts, even as she scarcely bothered to wonder why Tony should be acquainted with such an odd, not to say peculiar, sort of man, let alone ask him to be his best man, or what an extraordinary coincidence it was – and yet not such a coincidence when you came to think of it, for why else should a man with a car like that be in a tiny place like Lisheen? – she realised she had been very unkind to him. Yes, she had been most unkind, not to say cutting. Instead of dreading the meeting it was up to her to be nice to him, and she now had an opportunity to thank him for his kindness in offering her a lift. It had been a perfectly proper and gentlemanly thing to do, and there had been no excuse for the high-handed way in which she had rebuffed him. As soon as she had a chance she decided to take the initiative: not apologise exactly, but let him know she appreciated his gesture.

The service droned on. It was hot now, even here inside the church. Behind her people fidgeted and somewhere a baby grew fractious, squirming in its mother's arms and making awkward and distracting noises.

Tony's voice was loud and firm. 'I, Anthony, take thee, Philippa, to my wedded wife . . . '

And Pippa's voice, high and clear, never faltered. This was her moment and she was living up to it.

A new thought came into Anne's mind. Had he known all along who she was? He'd said the clientele of the Victoria Hotel had known her. If that were the case, why hadn't he introduced himself? She rejected this line of thought, however. It looked more likely that he had been perfectly genuine, and that she by contrast had been stand-offish and unfriendly.

She would start afresh and extend the hand of friendship.

'Have you the ring?'

Poor Canon Blenkinsop. Elderly wasn't quite the word for him – senile was closer, she thought, and then rebuked herself again. No, she would look charitably on the world on this day of celebration.

The best man passed the ring to Tony and then glanced round. He saw Anne. Without seeming in the slightest surprised, he winked at her and turned again to where the ceremony of the ring was being acted out.

'With this ring I thee wed . . . '

She took a grip on herself again. Never mind the wink. Of course he was a bit odd, she knew that already. Still, he was kind-hearted. One should not judge by superficial things; his heart was in the right place which was what mattered.

Now the register had to be signed. She rose and followed Tony and Pippa into the vestry. The man followed her. He wouldn't look at her now. As Tony and then Pippa bent to sign their names, and she watched, standing behind them, the musty smell of damp plaster and old hymn books in her nostrils, the man stood at her side and refused to notice her.

First he winked at her, then he ignored her. It was most confusing and annoying. She didn't dare look at *him*.

Still, soon, at the reception, someone would introduce them, then she could take the opportunity to thank him graciously for his kind offer of a lift, and deplore the little misunderstanding that had arisen between them.

The organ started up again, the doors were opened, a square of dazzling light appeared, and as Tony and Pippa proceeded up the aisle, music ringing in the air around them, Anne took the best man's arm and followed behind them. The best man, whoever he was, certainly seemed extremely relaxed.

At the door the Tommies stood in a guard of honour, their rifles upraised as the happy pair passed beneath them. Tony's car, a smart Graham-Paige roadster, stood ready. He was to drive Pippa to the house. This was considered rather daring and modern – but then Tony and Pippa liked to think of themselves as up to the minute.

As they came out into the sunshine, the guests began to spill out over the churchyard, standing about on the path or among the gravestones.

A photographer had been engaged from Cork and the wedding groups formed themselves before the old church porch as he popped his head beneath the black cloth of his heavy tripod camera and shouted instructions: 'Bride's family!'; 'Groom's family!'; 'Bridesmaids next!'; 'Bride and groom only, please!' bobbing out from under his black cape and whipping out the heavy glass plates in their metal cases to slide them into the back of his camera.

Eventually it was time to set off for the house. Pippa was settled into the car, the train set carefully about her feet as Leary closed the door. By rights it should have been his privilege to drive them in an open landau, but there, since the war things had all changed and nobody had any idea how to do things *properly* any more, he thought. The groom driving the car! Where was the dignity in it?

Before Tony had time to put the car into gear, however, Vere darted forward, opened the dicky seat and clambered in behind them, and the car roared away down the street in a burst of laughter and applause.

Everyone now made for carriages and traps, horses were being gee'd up, there was a jingling of bridles and Leary had brought up the waggonette. The best man unaccountably was still there – in fact Anne now saw him helping the bridesmaids up into the waggonette. She held back, but at last had to allow him to help her into the back row. Leary clambered up at the front, and then to Anne's surprise the best man pulled himself up nimbly and sat beside her.

She looked away, but they had barely set off down the street when Ethel turned from the seat in front to exclaim about Tony's smart car, and Anne was relieved to be able to talk to her.

'Are they driving up to Dublin tonight, d'you know?' Ethel asked.

'I believe so,' said the best man, 'then crossing to England by the night boat and going to the South of France.'

'Fancy spending your wedding night on the Holyhead ferry! Wouldn't be quite the same.'

'The same as what?' Pru, another of Pippa's friends, leaned back and giggled.

'Let's hope they have a quiet crossing anyway,' said Ethel.

'Not too quiet, I hope.' Pru giggled again.

'Oh Pru, hush!'

Anne looked at her hands. She hated this kind of talk.

The soldiers had clambered aboard their big lorry and were bumping along at a walking pace behind the waggonette. They stood on the flat back and held on to a metal frame which was fixed over it, swaying as the lorry jolted over the uneven road. They looked very uncomfortable.

The man noticed her looking at them. He smiled.

'Make you feel safer, don't they?'

To Anne they looked pale, undersized and anaemic.

'Frankly, no.'

'Tony says Dublin Castle wouldn't let him come without them,' Pru butted in.

'Oh, he's a very big cheese in the Castle is Tony, isn't that right?' Ethel smiled engagingly at the best man. 'The groom with a bodyguard, imagine!'

It was all wrong. There was no one to introduce them properly and now, with the other girls chattering round them and flirting with him, it was impossible for Anne to say what was on her mind.

At that moment she caught his eye, and the memory of their meeting in Macroom came back in a rush.

'I wanted to say –' She didn't quite know how to continue, and her gaze fell from his.

'It's difficult for you, I see that,' he said kindly. 'Let me help you. You wanted to apologise? You've repented of your harsh words?'

Ethel's eyes opened wide. Anne felt herself becoming tense as the conversation began to take an unwelcome turn. The man noticed nothing, and went on calmly, 'I must admit when you referred so slightingly to my car, you did touch me on a tender spot. "A big toy". Hmm. Those were words not lightly to be forgotten; a man's sleep could be disturbed.' He looked at her seriously, then drew a deep breath. 'Still, on reflection, I accept your apology.'

She could feel the heat rise in her face.

'That's not exactly what I meant –'

'Oh?'

'No. – That is –'

'Well, I don't know.' He was grave now. 'One puts up with a lot nowadays. One does one's best to assist a lady – one extends a helping hand, out of pure charity as it were, and then to have one's dearest posession, the pride and joy of one's heart, ridiculed to one's face – it's very hard.'

He had kept an absolutely straight face. Anne looked down, thinking hard. Pru had also turned round to listen and she and Ethel were both smirking.

Ethel turned to Pru and whispered, 'I think they know each other.'

'I should most certainly say we do,' the man said as Anne tried to stop him. 'Though to say that I was snubbed would hardly do justice to our meeting. I was crushed lower than a beetle beneath her sandal. Reduced to utter insignificance, not to say cast into outer darkness.'

'There was a slight misunderstanding.' Anne blushed.

'Ooh, you'd best beware of Anne. She has a tongue on her.'

'Ethel, do you mind!'

All the other girls turned round now. Anne felt the blood hot in her cheeks. She turned to the man in her loftiest manner, all good intentions flown.

'If I did snub you, it was no less than you deserved. I wonder you have the assurance to sit there with a straight face. Frankly, I thought you got off rather lightly. It was the most bare-faced impertinence.'

'Anne sounds so Victorian when she's angry,' Ethel said placidly.

'Ethel, shut up and stay out of it!' She turned to him again. 'You could see how hot I was and how heavy my case.'

'I did. That's why I offered –'

'I don't think so. No, it was more an attempt –'

'It wasn't an *attempt* at anything. Just the simple offer of a lift. No strings attached.'

'And then to go flying past us! You nearly made the mare bolt, and we were covered in dust.'

'There's nothing I can do about the dust, I'm afraid,' he said quietly. 'I came upon you so suddenly I didn't have time to slow down.'

He seemed quite composed. Obviously he wasn't giving anything away. Anne turned to Ethel and changed the subject.

She had an idea, though, that a little smile of amusement was hovering about his lips.

When they arrived at the house she went indoors with the other girls without looking at him again.

Many of the guests were there before them. Pippa and Tony were at the door to welcome them, Pippa looking as if she had been wearing a wedding dress all her life. How easily it came to her, Anne thought, how graciously and pleasantly she accepted the congratulations and good wishes of the guests and how proud Tony was of his new bride. She watched him shaking hands with elderly men who mumbled through their moustaches that he was a damned lucky fellow and Pippa was a girl in a million; Tony modestly accepted their congratulations as his due.

Why was it so easy for them, and so hard for Anne? She had seen her father wipe away a tear during the wedding service. Would he have wept at her wedding?

Pippa had always been his favourite. As far back as Anne could remember, Pippa had sat on Father's knee and he had hugged her and stroked her hair and called her his little Pippin, his Pipkin, his Pipsy-wipsy. Anne had been nauseated by these familiarities. Her own name was never transformed like that, and she was glad of it. Even as a child she detested such childishness and especially hated to see her father, whom in spite of herself she worshipped, diminish his own dignity by descending to this level.

Of course she was included in these pleasant moments of childish familiarity. With Pippa still on his knee, Father would turn to Anne and say, 'But we mustn't forget little Anne ...' and take her up on the other side. She wasn't fooled, she could tell the difference, and the bitterness in her heart was translated into pride and disdain. Father preferred Pippa, but no one should see that she, Anne, cared – not now, not ever.

The guests as they came in were moving through the drawing room and out by the French windows on to the lawn where stood the marquee erected the day before by the men from Cork with help from Leary and Costello. Bridget and Mary circulated with trays of champagne; the Maloney girls and Mrs Deasey were at the buffet ready to serve lunch. The talk was loud. Over there was the Chief Constable of Cork, here was General Smeaton; those larky young men in morning suits with sponge bag trousers and gleaming plastered-down hair, laughing loudly to one another, must be friends of Tony's. Her father was in conversation with an august gentleman in uniform – the Lord Lieutenant. Father had known him in Africa, twenty years before, in Boer War days. Ethel and Pru were talking to the loud young men. My God, thought Anne, it didn't take *them* long!

At the far end of the marquee the band was setting up its instruments. They had managed to get the piano out here somehow too. The trombonist gave forth a preparatory raspberry. Somebody dropped a cymbal with a loud crash.

But that man – Tony's best man – occupied Anne's thoughts. His assurance had annoyed her more than she had expected. Amid all the animation, the chat, the high spirits, she could not unbend, forget herself and enter into the swing of things. Instead she turned away down one of the paths, between rose beds, flourishing in white and pink, pale watery delicate colours, wandering disconsolately beneath the oaks and down towards the old stone wall at the bottom of the garden.

# Chapter Four

'Hullo, Anne.'

She started and turned as a man stepped out from behind a tree.

'Cathal! What on earth –'

Cathal was not in a morning suit nor did he have on a top hat. He was in a tweed jacket and gaiters; he was freckled, flushed with the sun, hair unruly and a grin on his face.

'What are you doing here?'

'Oh.' He grinned again. 'I came to kiss the bride.'

'Kiss the bride? Cathal, they said you're wanted by the police.'

'Ah, fame!' The grin faltered beneath her anxious expression.

'That raid – is it true?'

He said nothing.

'Two policemen were killed? And you got away with all those guns?'

He was now looking at her seriously. Still he said nothing. For a moment they stared one another in the eye, then Anne drew in a slow breath.

'I had no idea that *you* – whyever didn't you tell me? That's why we haven't seen you.' She went on quickly in a low voice: 'How long have you been with the Volunteers?'

He shrugged. 'Nine months or so.'

He was embarrassed, and clearly didn't want to talk about it.

'But, Cathal, surely you could have told *me*?'

'It's top secret, Anne. The fewer who know the better.'

She glanced round and saw a group of revellers coming towards them.

'Oh, God – not here.'

She pulled him in another direction, and then noticed the best man near the marquee.

'You mustn't stay here – you're in the most frightful danger.'

She was painfully conscious of the party guests around them. Then Ethel was calling to her, coming down the path.

'Anne, come on – the speeches are starting. Gracious, Cathal Donnelly –'

She stopped dead.

'Ethel, buzz off – do you mind?'

She gave them both an odd look, and turned away. Anne glanced quickly back at Cathal.

'You must go immediately.'

'I thought I'd just say hullo to Pippa and slip away.'

'Cathal, you must go *instantly* – there's a lorry load of British troops outside, and half the constabulary of the county.'

Cathal laughed. 'Oh, I saw your father already. He gave me a funny look then said it was grand to see me.'

She pulled at his sleeve. 'What? Oh – he would! But you must get out of here now. If you are caught ... For God's sake, whyever did you come? You're mad.'

An announcement was made. Speeches were to begin.

She turned to him again. '*Cathal – go now!*'

She could see Ethel watching her. 'Coming!' she called.

Cathal turned away down the path towards the kitchen garden, and with a last look at him Anne returned to where the speeches were to be given on the lawn outside the marquee. She was aware of Ethel giving her strange looks but ignored her and concentrated instead on the best man who, it appeared, was about to speak.

But she couldn't think about that.

It was impossible. She couldn't grasp it even yet. Cathal Donnelly, the larky, lively boy she had known forever, whom she knew better than anyone alive – and who probably knew her better than anyone. Cathal, with whom she had raced across the mountain sides as a child, the dogs running before them; with whom she had trekked through the heather, picking off grouse with an old shot-gun; Cathal whom she had dared to impossible feats, who was afraid of nothing, with whom she had been caught out so many times on the mountains in the ever-changing weather, to arrive home at last, soaked to the skin but feeling blissfully happy ... Cathal Donnelly with a gun, shooting policemen? It was simply incredible.

And what madness had brought him here today? Was it as if on this day there was a sort of cease-fire – as there had been on Christmas Day 1914? It was just like her father to think so.

The speech began. As she forced herself to listen, her heart sank. This was the traditional moment for suggestive remarks, some lewd innuendo about weddings, brides and first nights. 'Anything like that', as she put it to herself, made Anne uncomfortable. The fact was, she was a prude; her school days had been passed at a boarding school in England, where among the girls gossip and speculation has been rampant, but hard facts in very short supply.

To her relief there was to be 'nothing like that'. In fact the best man's speech was surprisingly modest. He talked of his war days with Tony, how Tony always seemed to collect the medals and he himself got none, though he could not understand why. It just seemed that Tony had a gift for collecting prizes and now, today, he had collected the loveliest prize of all; the most beautiful girl he, the Best Man, had ever seen ... and so the speech went on, and finished with a toast.

The guests had barely had time to raise their glasses however, when they were interrupted by the roaring of heavy lorry engines and the sound of gunfire.

It was as if lightning had struck. Everyone looked round for cover, running in all directions at once, bumping into one another, shouting, confused. A sixth sense kept everyone permanently on the lookout for trouble, made everyone jumpy. If a car backfired in the street, people ran for cover. There had been too many random murders, too many raids at night.

In the confusion, however, a few men did not run for cover. Colonel Hunter and two of his constabulary colleagues ran into the house, just as Bridget appeared at the drawing room French windows, breathless.

'Oh Colonel Hunter – if you could come at once!'

He hurried through the house to the front door. The others crowded behind them. As they came into the hall they were confronted by a group of men in a motley selection of military uniforms, tunics of differing cuts and shades, breeches and puttees or gaiters, and wearing black tam o'shanter berets. In particular all of them were brandishing rifles and had large pistols in holsters conspicuous at their waists. Their demeanour was at once aggressive, buccaneering and exuberant. They obviously had no idea where they were.

The Tommies who had been stationed at the door were watching in helpless amazement. Outside in the summer sunshine stood three large army lorries, their engines still running.

'Is this your house?'

The man seemed to be their leader. Hugh Hunter took an instant dislike to him – an arrogant, boorish little man, looking ridiculous in a flying helmet and goggles pushed up on his forehead; a fat greasy face, a pencil-thin moustache, and a cigarette in his hand.

'May I ask –'

'I'll do the asking, if you don't mind. Is this your house?' The man was English.

'It is,' replied the Colonel.

'Name?'

'What is this?'

'What's your name? How many times do I have to ask?'

'I certainly have no intention of giving my name or anything else until I learn the nature of this disgraceful intrusion. How dare –'

The colonel was red in the face.

'You are aware that this area is under martial law?'

Now one of Colonel Hunter's constabulary friends intervened.

'Colonel, this is Captain Steptoe, of the Auxiliary Division of the RIC. They were installed in Macroom Castle last week. Captain, allow me to introduce Colonel Hunter. What is the nature of your business?'

'Friend of yours, is he? Keep still all of you! No one's to move until I say. Now then, sir, perhaps you wouldn't mind answering a few questions?'

'I certainly have no intention of answering any questions here, Captain. You have intruded on my daughter's wedding. If you would be good enough to step this way –'

'Don't move! No tricks, if you please! We have reason to believe the IRA have been using this house as a store for weapons. We shall make an immediate search.'

'*What?*' Colonel Hunter exploded.

It was clear by now that this was not an IRA attack, and wedding guests, glasses in hand, crowded in to watch, staring in astonishment at this scene.

'I am a magistrate, sir, and I must ask, by what right you have entered my house –'

'Captain Steptoe, have you a warrant –'

'Get back there, all of you! Information has been laid, and we have reason to believe arms may have been hidden in this house by members of an illegal organisation. We intend to make a search. I must ask you to remain where you are and not to hinder my men.'

Before any of Captain Steptoe's men could do anything, however, Tony pushed his way through the guests crowded into the doorway. He was purple with rage.

'You brainless ass! How dare you intrude into a gentleman's house!'

The sight of the uniform dashed Captain Steptoe's assurance a little.

'I am here on official business.'

But Tony was not to be stopped.

'Who's your commanding officer? I'll have you court-martialled for this.'

'I beg your pardon, sir. The RIC barracks at Dunmanway was attacked the night before last; two constables were murdered and a quantity of arms and explosives stolen. We have information that leads us to suspect they may have been brought to this house.'

'You suspect Colonel Hunter of being a member of the IRA?'

'You can't be too sure. This is Ireland, you know.'

'How long have you been stationed here, Captain?'

'What?' Captain Steptoe's assurance was beginning to desert him. 'Six weeks.'

31

'Well, let me tell you something,' Tony let rip. 'The Hunters have been landlords here since Elizabeth's time. They've farmed this land, and kept the peace between their tenants; they saved many of 'em from starvation in the famine; and paid passages to Canada; they've hunted, fished and shot these mountains for three hundred years. And now you – you threadbare, wretched, two-shilling, jumped-up temporary gentleman – have the impertinence to intrude on a family wedding – get out!'

Anne caught sight of Pippa's face, glowing with pride at Tony's hurricane outburst.

Captain Steptoe was conscious of his men watching him, and waiting for orders. He coughed, embarrassed.

'I see. Clearly there has been some kind of misunderstanding.'

'*Misunderstanding?*'

'Colonel Hunter, sir, if you can give an assurance –'

'Get out!'

'I shall have to make a report –'

'Out!'

'I see.' Captain Steptoe was beetroot with embarrassment. 'Well, under the circumstances, Colonel Hunter, I must, er – perhaps it would be better – I must apologise for this intrusion.'

The rifle-men, one or two of them grinning to themselves, turned and shuffled out to where their lorries waited in the sunshine. The guests burst into excited conversation. Colonel Hunter turned to Tony, and Pippa took him by the arm.

'Sorry to have waded in like that, sir,' said Tony. ''Fraid I got carried away.'

'You were absolutely right, Tony. An absolutely loathsome, common little man.' Pippa was glowing with pride.

Colonel Hunter coughed. 'Extraordinary. What on earth could have made him imagine I would be hiding arms for the IRA?'

'Malicious gossip, sir. Rebel sympathisers deliberately trying to confuse the police. Their idea of a joke.'

Anne was moving back towards the garden with the other guests when she found that man – Tony's best man – beside her.

32

'Your friend has left.'

She looked at him sharply. He didn't seem to notice but went on, in a casual manner, 'Yes. The moment we heard those gun shots, and the others went rushing indoors, he, uhm – well, actually, he climbed over the wall of your rose garden.'

The wall was eight feet high, but there were pear trees espaliered along it. It would have been easy enough.

'A pressing engagement, no doubt,' he went on.

'No doubt.'

'And what was all the fuss about?'

'Didn't you hear?'

'Er, no. To tell the truth, I find all that military swagger rather tiresome. Had enough of it in the war. And it's such a lovely day – I was able to enjoy your gardens undisturbed for a few minutes.'

'A pity. You missed a splendid example of the British authorities behaving in their usual high-handed manner.'

'And what did they do?'

'Nothing, thanks to Tony. But they wanted to turn this house upside down looking for the IRA.'

'A mistake, clearly. The last place you'd find them.'

'Clearly,' she said sarcastically.

He looked at her for a moment with interest.

'Don't tell me you're a secret sympathiser?'

'What if I were?'

He raised an eyebrow and looked about him at some of the uniforms on the guests beginning to re-emerge into the garden.

'Think they'd lock me up?' she said mockingly.

'It would depend on whether they took you seriously or not.'

The other guests were now beginning to circulate around them. For a moment Anne's wit deserted her.

'Oh dear me, you are so droll.'

'You needn't worry, I shan't give your secret away. Fortunately I'm a civilian now. I'm here solely for the fishing.'

'It's no secret. Anyway, I thought you came down to be Tony's best man?'

'I did.' He smiled. 'But your father has very kindly invited

33

me to say on for a few days. And I had, by some prescient foresight, thought to pack my rods.'

'Yes, Father's very generous. People are always imposing on him. We get all sorts staying here.'

'And now that I'm your father's guest, I think it is your duty to be a little more polite to me.'

The guests had by now all returned to the garden, and were excitedly discussing the intrusion they had witnessed.

'They're new, you know.'

'Only moved into Macroom Castle last week.'

'They get more than the RIC, I was told. A pound a day. And officers only.'

'Some officers!'

'Yes, what a toad, wasn't he? Are they all like that?'

'Don't ask me. Who's in charge of them?'

'They're not under anybody – that's the point. They do whatever they like.'

'Well, they're welcome if they put a stop to these murderers and fanatics. I mean, after the war, I was looking forward to everything getting back to normal, and now anarchy and murder – it's dreadful. Really, there's no living in this country any more.'

Anne looked round and saw Vere by her side. He was looking up at her with an open face and merry eyes.

'Oof! Did you see that, Anne? What a nasty piece of work – what are the Government thinking of, sending over a squirt like that? Did you see him, Lewis?'

So that was his name.

'Thank you, Vere, I've had my fill of the military as I was telling your sister. Incidentally, why don't you introduce me – though I feel we know each other pretty well already.'

'Haven't you been introduced? That's typical of my sister. Anne, meet Lewis Crawford. You'll have to stand up for yourself, Lewis, or she'll walk all over you. She's the terror of the district.'

'Vere – shut up!'

He giggled and ducked out from beneath her arm as she made a lunge at him.

Hugh Hunter was clapping his hands for attention.

'Ladies and gentlemen! Tony and Pippa are leaving for Dublin, so let's all go out and see them off!'

'Can't wait to get away,' Vere laughed. 'Trust Pippa.'

'No, actually Tony wants to get as far as he can while it's light. Doesn't want to run into any pot-holes.'

Anne looked sharply at Lewis; he seemed quite serious.

'Well, my dear Anne, with respect, what with blowing up bridges, chopping down trees, and digging trenches across the road, your friends have made it quite difficult to drive anywhere in Ireland these days. I don't know why Tony doesn't go by train. I would.'

'You brought your own car.'

'True. But, you see, I am very attached to the old beast. She has served me well. Besides, I haven't just got married.'

Anne felt a cold hand on her heart. What he said was true. Sympathetic as she was to the Republican cause, she was suddenly fearful for Pippa and Tony if they did indeed run into a trap. Driving into a trench – she didn't like to think of it.

Out at the front of the house, the guests were crowded round Tony's open tourer. Pippa's large suitcases were strapped on the back, and she was now dressed in a smart travelling suit. Nearby the Tommies were settling themselves in their army lorry.

Lewis shook Tony's hand.

'*Bon voyage*, old bean, and drive carefully. Have you got protection?'

'If you mean have I got my Webley in the glove compartment, the answer's yes. What's the matter, don't you trust our friends over there?'

Lewis looked at them without expression.

'Not a great deal.'

Anne kissed Pippa.

'Goodbye, darling, come up and see us soon.'

Anne was more upset than she wanted to admit. Pippa was already somebody new, a married woman, Mrs Napier no less; a door had opened to her that was still closed to Anne. Tonight she and Tony ... Anne found herself squeezing her sister harder than she intended.

'Careful, darling, you'll smudge my make-up!'

35

Tony revved up the engine, and with a roar the sleek car disappeared round the corner of the drive and through the rhododendrons. The lorry followed, rattling and bumping after them.

Anne wandered back into the house.

'Come on, Anne, cheer up. You've got a face a yard long. The band's about to start up!' Vere pulled her by the hand.

'Let go! Vere, stop fooling about. Honestly, when are you going to grow up!'

'It's a wedding – you're supposed to be rejoicing instead of looking so jolly lugubriubrious!'

'What?'

'So lugubriubriubrious!' Vere burst into laughter, and Anne couldn't help laughing too. This was the sort of childish joking they still indulged in from time to time. But she didn't want to laugh just then. She disentangled herself from Vere and turned to Lewis again.

'Did you really mean that?'

'Mean what?'

'About Tony and Pippa?'

'Why ask me? You know more about the state of the country than I do. You live here.'

'Yes, I know I do. Still –'

The fact was that what Lewis had said sounded horribly probable. She knew about trench digging to stop army lorries but like a fool it had never crossed her mind that her own sister might fall into such a trap. She bit her lip.

'If you're worried about Tony, you needn't be. You don't imagine he would take risks with Pippa, do you? He's well able to take care of both himself and her.'

Lewis's voice never rose above a mild conversational tone, casual, measured, as if he had already considered all the possibilities, weighed all the risks, and settled everything in his mind to his own satisfaction.

In the marquee the band started up; it was late in the afternoon, and couples began to dance. A delicious summer evening was stealing over the garden, the air was warm and thickly scented from the flowerbeds around them; everything was at its loveliest.

Anne was vaguely wondering whether Lewis might have

anything else to say, when Matthew Archer, a young neighbour, invited her to dance. There was nothing she could do to evade it and she was soon swept into the medley of swirling couples, moving round the lawn as the band sizzled and fizzled along in a snappy upbeat rhythm which seemed obstinately at odds with Anne's mood. Her partner's shallow remarks left her cold too, and she answered almost at random.

The band stopped at ten, thanks to the curfew. All around guests were making their farewells, hands were being shaken, and traps were being brought to the door. A car started up, and groups of people stood about on the gravel waiting for theirs.

Anne had said goodnight to Ethel, and was crossing the drawing room when she met Vere, a chocolate eclair in his hand.

'Still eating?'

'What are weddings for? Anyway don't pretend you don't like eclairs because I know you do.'

He looked into her eyes for a moment then a conspiratorial grin crossed his face. His eyes were alight with devilment.

Anne stared at him as guests passed by them.

'What are you grinning at?'

'I say – what a toad that Captain Steptoe was.'

'I'll say.'

'And didn't Tony give him a roasting.' He paused, still smirking and staring at Anne, then came closer. 'And to think he was right all along.'

He took another mouthful of the eclair.

'What?'

'Poor Captain Steptoe – if only he knew.'

'What are you getting at, you little worm?'

'Shh! Anne, that's the best part about it – he was right all along.'

'Vere, what are you talking about?'

'Listen, Anne – that raid at Dunmanway the other night . . . You'll never guess where Cathal's put the stuff. Here!'

'Here? Where?'

'Not in the house, of course, but outside – in the old cold store.'

'Are you serious?'

'You bet.'

'I don't believe it.'

'It's true, I just found it this afternoon.'

'But why?'

'Don't ask me.'

'He wants his head examining. Supposing the stuff had been found? What would have happened to Mother and Father?'

'They didn't know – they would have been in the clear. I say, where are you going?'

'Where do you think? Get a candle.'

As she stepped out through the French windows balmy warm air greeted her and seemed to cling round her, caressing her skin. She knew the way even in the dark. Vere was close behind her.

The cold store was little used. It stood in the kitchen garden two hundred yards from the house and was constructed over a stream which ran through the garden. The stones of the little building soaked up the water and by a process of continuous evaporation kept it cold. It had been in use over a hundred years. It had an old wooden door with no lock. Vere went before her and pushed the door inwards. Inside they lit a candle and Anne looked about. There were a number of old deck chairs, and two or three card tables, and behind them what looked like a heap of old sacks.

Vere pulled them out, turned over the pile and half unwrapped it. In a moment she saw the muzzles of rifles.

'Not bad, eh?' he whispered. 'Eight army issue Lee-Enfields, five pistols, four hundred rounds of 303 ammo, and twenty Mills bombs.'

'They can't stay here. Cathal will have to get them out.'

'I suppose he's going to eventually,' Vere said, 'but it's such a wizard place. The last one old Captain Steptoe would think of, eh?'

'Except that he *did* think of it. How could Cathal have been so stupid? And who tipped off Macroom Castle?' She thought for a moment. 'I'll have to try and get a message to him. God, if this were found! I'll try to get in contact with him first thing tomorrow. And listen to me, Vere – not a word of this to anyone.'

'I hear and obey, o great white mistress.'

'I'm serious!'

'So am I! You don't need to treat me like a child, thank you!'

'Never mind that. Come on, let's get back.'

She blew out the candle, and they made their way carefully to the house.

# Chapter Five

Hugh Hunter went to bed sad that night. Pippa had been everything a daughter ought to be, he thought, pretty, soft and cuddly, a bit helpless, but with a strong practical streak as well – contradictory, perhaps, but convenient too. She had always worshipped him and they had understood each other effortlessly, didn't even need to say things to each other half the time. And now she was gone. Of course Tony was a splendid young man and Hugh couldn't have asked for a finer husband for Pippa, and of course daughters always grew up in the end and got married, one had to accept that – churlish, unnatural, not to. Still, he was sad. Life would never be the same. A part of him had gone with her forever.

Anne was different. There was something awkward and spiky about her, as if she were afraid of closeness. She never cuddled up to him, as Pippa had done. She held herself aloof, was proud, had a stiff-backed, standoffish way with her, walked alone, rambled across the mountains alone, and was snappish where Pippa had been understanding and humoured her old dad. And Anne had politics on the brain, always arguing with him, contradicting him.

Good God, he did his best, served the local community to the best of his ability – and it was very difficult just now, with the troubles going on all round them. He sat on the bench, but how was he to dispense justice any more? No one would give evidence. A house was burnt down, a policeman shot in the middle of the night, and no one helped in any way. They must have known something, probably who was responsible, but no one ever said a word.

The strange thing was that he had lived here all his life – been born in the house, knew everyone in the village, and up till the war had been on the best of terms with them all. He knew about their lives, and had often adjudicated in awkward little quarrels in a private capacity – no need to make a public issue of it; the ordinary people had trusted him to give a reasonable and impartial judgement, and had abided by it too. He had fulfilled a real and useful function – or so he had thought.

Well, it was different now. No one would speak to him or his family any more. The Hunters were lepers in the village. Oh, of course, people were polite to their faces – but there was no trust, no warmth or confidence any more. He had seen crude notices nailed to trees warning people against 'fraternising with the enemy'. The enemy! A family which had been there since Elizabeth's time, on good terms with all, conscientious in its duties and so forth.

And now to have his own daughter against him too! All this talk of being an Irishwoman – it was wrong. What of her loyalty to her family? She seemed to feel none; she did not seem to *feel* at all. She was all head, that was Anne's problem, and no heart.

His wife Claire was no help. She was artistic. Years ago it had made her very attractive to him, as if she beckoned to him from some nebulous world of fairies and magical sprites. Now she just seemed vague. She would lie on the chaise longue draped in flowing chiffons and silks, embroidered slippers on her feet, and read poetry: Yeats usually, whom she had met once or twice at soirees in Dublin. She imagined herself part of an exclusive coterie, intellectual and artistic. It was she who had filled Anne's head with all that Gaelic nonsense. For any practical day-to-day purposes Claire fulfilled no function at all. Hugh did not complain, he had married for love, and still loved his wife in a deep unreflective way, but from time to time it crossed his mind that a country gentleman, a magistrate and landlord, could have enjoyed a little more support from his wife. Friends in the county seemed to have more useful spouses – one, for instance, was a trained nurse and was the unofficial local pharmacist, forever dosing the villagers and giving advice on their ailments, handing out pots of syrup and bottles of cordials which she brewed herself. Others were competent cooks who gave advice and help to some of the improvident women in the village about managing their household economy. They would bustle into the little cabins, firing off orders left and right. They were well-meaning, of course, and were tolerated for the gifts of food they brought. Claire did none of this. Her mind was far away with the heroes of old Ireland, their endless battles and love affairs, with poetry and the higher drama.

He turned over in the darkness, looking at the faint square of the window, light even at this hour, and listened to Claire's regular breathing, feeling curiously alone.

Anne slept late and cursed herself when she awoke. As soon as her eyes opened she thought of the guns in the cold store. She was angry with Cathal; he had been incredibly stupid to bring them here.

She washed herself quickly, dressed and ran down, meaning to go out straight away and bicycle over to Cathal's house.

Already the men from Cork were busy dismantling the marquee, and in the house the maids and Mrs Deasey were clearing away the debris of the wedding festivities.

Anne called the dogs, but then, as she was going out to get her bicycle, she ran into Lewis Crawford, who was unpacking some bags and fishing tackle from his car. She couldn't help looking at the car again and noticed now that it had the steering wheel on the wrong side.

The man himself seemed wide awake, alert after the late night.

'Good morning,' he said, smiling his slightly crooked smile.

'Good morning.' She was moving into the stable where her bicycle was standing.

'Did you sleep well?'

'Yes, fine, thanks.' She stopped, as if she ought to say something more. 'That's a lovely car.'

'It's a Lancia. Not very practical. Drinks petrol. Still, I'm very attached to her.'

'Lancia – is that Italian?'

'Yes. I got her from an Italian officer I met in Cairo. Won

42

'Listen, Anne, it was on the spur of the moment. I wouldn't get your father into trouble for anything, you know that. But after we got away from Dunmanway, we trekked over towards Lisheen, pretty much the whole night. It was already getting light and even before we got as far as the village it was obvious the military was out in force. We could see the whole place crawling with them. And there we were, stuck with all this stuff. We had to unload it quick, and there was nowhere except your place. Of course I knew your garden and the old cold store – honestly, Anne, it was the only place I could think of. We were in a tearing hurry.'

'When are you going to take it away?'

'As soon as possible.'

'Tonight?'

'I don't know. I've got to get the lads together, and I can't be seen myself just now. It might be a day or two. Does anyone know apart from you and Vere?'

'Well, somebody told Macroom Castle.'

'What?'

'The visit from the Auxies, remember?'

'Jesus! What happened?'

'My brother-in-law threw them out. But they could be back.'

Cathal was thinking. 'Listen, Anne, on my word of honour, the moment we can, we'll come for the stuff.'

'The sooner the better. And you'd better let me know before you come. Then I can make sure the coast's clear.'

'Right.'

He stood up and smiled. 'Will you come in for a cup of tea?'

'Thanks.' Anne went with him towards the house. She hadn't had any breakfast and was beginning to notice. Somewhere above them a lark was chirruping in the clear sky. It was going to be another heavenly summer day. The setters were lurking at a safe distance, watching the mastiff.

'Perhaps it is the safest place,' she said after a moment. 'Now we've had that visit from Captain Steptoe and his friends. Anyway, Cathal, what about your medical studies?'

'They'll have to wait. I expect the professors will still be there when this is all over.'

45

'Will you still be here?'

He glanced at her, and grinned. 'We'll just have to chance it.' He wanted to change the subject. 'I say, Anne, I didn't have time to tell you yesterday but you looked really nice in that dress. I could see all the other fellows thought so too.'

'Thank you.'

She had no talent for accepting compliments. Whatever she might think, her answer invariably came out brusque and abrupt.

'What does your mother say now you're a wanted man?'

The grin was wiped off his face. 'She's not too pleased. Better not mention it. You know, it's a pity we didn't have a chance to have a dance yesterday. It's a long time since you and I danced, Anne.'

'Whose fault's that?'

'That's true too. And I shall be persona non grata at the Hunt Ball this year, I'm afraid.'

She laughed, then checked herself. 'What possessed you to come over yesterday? Was it the wedding – or to check up on your stuff?'

'Oh, it was the wedding right enough. It's not every day Pippa gets married.'

'You're crazy.'

'Thank you.'

She was suddenly anxious. 'Anyway, should you be hanging round here? They're bound to come looking for you again.'

'Well, maybe not for a day or two. Like I said, the military was here recently. But I'll have to disappear. Mam's not pleased – especially since my Da's been laid up.'

'Laid up? Since when?'

'A month or so. He's not well, Anne.'

'I'm sorry about that. Do you know what's the matter?'

'Heart. Acute angina.'

They entered the house; in the kitchen Mrs Donnelly was preparing vegetables with Katie the maid.

'Mam, here's a visitor.'

Anne was not very welcome in a Republican household, whatever views she might hold. As far as the Donnellys were concerned she was Colonel Hunter's daughter, and her

46

protestations of Republican zeal were looked on as youthful effusions, likely to blow away the moment things grew serious. Cathal's mother was polite all the same, and made them a cup of tea, and set some slices of barmbrack thickly spread with butter on the wide table. They made conversation awkwardly while Anne ate her breakfast.

As he came to see her off, she reminded him, 'Mind, Cathal, let me know when you want to come for the stuff and I'll tell you the best time.'

# Chapter Six

As she was riding back through the village there were three army lorries outside Shanahan's Bar, and British soldiers standing in the road smoking cigarettes. They were in full battle dress but did not appear to be doing anything. Anne stopped and waited for a while to see if anything was going to happen; eventually she asked an old man also standing in the road with his hands in his pockets what was going on.

'Oh, Miss Hunter, good day to you. They're searching for weapons – I think 'tis on account of that raid the other day over in Dunmanway. They're Essexes from Cork.'

An officer came out of the bar and looked round at the small crowd, the old men and the mothers with small children, standing about in the sunshine watching the soldiers.

'Okay turn 'em out.'

A sergeant barked orders. 'Look lively now! Get 'em all out!'

He led the way and a dozen soldiers followed him inside. A few seconds later the inmates of the bar, many of them still with glasses in their hands and complaining loudly, were driven at bayonet point into the road. They stood about in sheer disbelief, complaining loudly.

The officer reappeared.

'I want this place boarded up and locked,' he said to the three RIC constables beside him.

'Now listen to me, all of you! This public house is closed down until further notice. This district is under martial law.' He was a young Englishman, and his voice sounded thin and tight compared with the warm rich brogue of the County

48

Cork. 'It is quite clear that it has been used as a meeting place for seditious elements, and this will serve as a lesson to you all!' His voice rose. 'You have been warned before, but I'll say it one more time. Anarchy will not be tolerated. We know that murderers live hereabouts, and we shall not rest until they're brought to justice. It is in your own interests to co-operate with the authorities in maintaining law and order. If anyone here has any information it will be treated in the strictest confidence, as you know. But remember this: the penalty for harbouring or sheltering a wanted criminal is a high one. You have been warned.'

He turned to his men and ordered them back on to the lorries. Their engines roared into life, shattering the tranquil-lity of the village street. For one terrified moment Anne thought they were heading for the Donnellys', but to her relief they took the road north to Macroom.

Calling the dogs, she set off for home. The drinkers stood about in the village street, their glasses still in their hands, not quite believing it had happened.

As she leaned in to her pedals and made her way up the long winding lane home, Anne was thinking of what she had just seen – about the absurdity of that young officer shutting down the village bar, and hoping thereby to defeat the IRA.

She got home and put the bicycle away in the stables, then wandered round through the kitchen garden to the cold store. No one was about and she pushed open the door and went in. In the half-light she knelt and pulled at the sacking to reveal the rifles again. She stared at them; no one ever came in here, and even if they did, they were unlikely to remark on a heap of old sacks.

There were the eight rifles. She looked at the Mills bombs, and then the pistols. She picked one up. It was heavy in her hands. In the half-light she turned it over. She gripped it, held it up and aimed. As she held it in her hand the thought came to her: this could kill a man. It could kill a policeman. It could kill Cathal. There was something horribly cold and inhuman about the idea that someone had designed and made it, all the time planning how to kill someone most efficiently.

Claire was stretched out as usual on the chaise longue.

49

'Hullo, darling, have a good ride?'

'Yes, thanks.' There was a bowl of cherries on the table and Anne absent-mindedly took one. It was typical of Claire not to ask her where she had been.

'I wonder how Pippa and Tony are getting on? They'll be in France by now.'

'Hot, I expect.'

The house seemed empty.

'Where's Father?'

'Gone into Macroom.'

'To give that horrid little man a piece of his mind, I hope.'

Claire put down her book and looked at Anne for a moment.

'Darling, are you bored here?'

'No, whatever gave you that idea?'

'I don't know. There doesn't seem very much for you to do. Perhaps when Pippa and Tony settle down in Merrion Square, you could go and stay with them for a bit. They've plenty of room, I believe.'

'Mother, I'm perfectly happy here, I've told you. Have you ever heard me complain?'

'No, darling. Still, at your age I feel you ought to get out more, meet people.'

'I get out as much as I like. And as for meeting people, I find most of them so jolly insipid.'

'Still I worry about you. I feel somehow you ought to – well, mix more. See more of life, and so on.'

'In other words, find a husband? You honestly don't have to worry. There's nothing further from my thoughts at this moment. As for moving out, I'm quite happy here, so long as you and Father don't mind.'

'Gracious, we don't mind. Of course, I understand, the last thing you want to do is go to Dublin and live in some squalid flat and learn shorthand.'

Anne looked out of the window.

'Where's Mr Crawford?'

'Fishing. He had a long discussion with your father over breakfast, and so far as I know he's down by the willows. He said he wouldn't be in for lunch so Mrs Deasey made him up a sandwich.'

After lunch, and having lounged in her room for half an hour, on impulse Anne thought she would walk down and talk to Lewis Crawford.

The river wound through the valley, slow and shallow, widening into Lough Allua. She followed the path down through two fields and came out in the river meadows, at this time of year waist-high with wild grasses and flowers, flecked with gold and pale blue, caressing her bare legs.

As she picked her way through the field she could see him among the willows with his rod. The sky was without a blemish, unbroken blue from mountaintop to mountaintop. She wore a wide straw hat, but could feel the sun hot on her arms; the air was thick with scents and the humming of insects, and the dogs raced here and there through the long grass after butterflies.

He saw her coming a long way off and watched as she came slowly across the field. He wound in his line.

They stood regarding one another for a moment without speaking.

'"Lighter was her tread than thistledown, and the glance in her eye like the sun on the lake at dawn."'

There was something simple yet affecting in the way he looked into her eyes and spoke those words. Anne was taken aback.

'What was that?' she said at last.

'A line from a book I found by my bed last night. Happened to stick in my mind. Don't you recognise it?'

'No.'

He shook his head with a slight smile on his lips.

'You and your Celtic Twilight, and not to know that. It was from an old poem.'

She should have known. Claire had put the book there. But he could not have taken her more by surprise. She tried to regain her ground.

'How's the fishing?'

He looked down into the water.

'Well, at this time of day I think the trout are asleep. They'll come up to feed when the sun is a little lower. But I'm not in any hurry. In fact, I was just thinking of taking a nap myself.'

'Oh, don't let me stop you. I just happened to be out walking.' She looked away down the river.

'Don't go just yet. Sit down – I brought a blanket – there, you see.'

He had spread a blanket under the shade of a willow. She hesitated, but he motioned her to it.

'I would offer you some refreshment, but I'm afraid I've eaten it all.'

'It doesn't matter. I had lunch.'

'Sit down, I beg you.'

She had been standing rather awkwardly, but now she sat on the blanket, tucking her legs under her skirt and took off her hat. He sat beside her.

It gave her an odd feeling, something she could not easily understand, to have a man who was actually a complete stranger beside her on the deserted river bank. At her feet, the river moved slowly, evenly, with long streamers of green weed eddying and waving in the flow, and a faint cool brackish smell. She thought how nice it would be to dip her feet in the coolness, but was awkward in Lewis's presence. He might find it funny, and make some amusing comment.

'Was your errand successful?'

'I beg your pardon?'

'You rushed off this morning without waiting for breakfast. I assume it was for something urgent.'

She looked down into the moving water.

'Yes, quite successful, thank you. That is – it wasn't very urgent, no. No –' she was becoming confused, '– just a message I wanted to send.'

She wanted to get off this subject quickly.

'You said this morning you had won your car in a bet. How did you do that?'

He noticed her change of tack and smiled, looking at her from beneath his thick eyebrows, as if in some inner recess of himself he was laughing at her. She noticed there was a slight cleft or dimple in his chin.

'It was in Cairo at the end of the war. I was out there with Allenby's lot and Colonel Lawrence. Perhaps you've heard of him – Lawrence of Arabia?'

She certainly had heard of Lawrence of Arabia.

'Strange man. Original, though. And that's what counts, isn't it?'

'Is it?'

'In this life, I should say it is. Anyway there was this Italian officer attached to the legation – he was an original too. He'd knocked about all over the Middle East, like me, so we had a lot to talk about.'

'I thought you served with Tony?'

'I did, for about eighteen months. Then I got sent out to the Middle Eastern show. Made a change from the mud of Flanders, I can tell you.'

He looked down into the river, thoughtfully. She waited.

'What about the car?'

'What? Oh, yes. Do you really want to know?'

'For heaven's sake, I wouldn't have asked otherwise.'

He raised his eyebrows at this, but then went on.

'Not the sort of thing one talks about very much, as you can imagine. Well,' he drew a breath, 'it actually took place before the war was quite over – when the Turks were in Jerusalem. We had been having a conversation which finally got round to the subject of coffee pots.'

'Coffee pots?'

'Yes. And this officer was telling me that rumour had it they had a particularly elegant type of coffee pot in the Turkish officers' mess, Pasha's crest on it – very distinctive – and he was keen to have one for his collection. Nothing simpler, I said, go in and steal one. He wasn't keen on that; too many guards, and he didn't speak Turkish. Anyway, he said, if I thought it was so easy, he'd just like to see me do it. In fact, he bet me his car I wouldn't. Well, Anne, you can understand: I'd let myself in for it, and no mistake – all the chaps sitting round, waiting to hear what I was going to say. It didn't leave me much option.'

'What did you do?'

'You've seen the car, haven't you?'

'So you got him his coffee pot?'

'Obviously.' He leant over, took up his fishing rod, and began to wind it in, concentrating on the line. Anne waited for him to continue. When he was clearly not going to, she said, 'Well, how?'

He looked round, faintly surprised, as if he hadn't expected the question.

'Oh, it wasn't difficult. The Turks were frightfully disorganised. A bit of dirt smeared on my face, I knew a couple of words of Arabic. I just passed myself off as a servant in the infantry compound.'

Anne couldn't decide whether he was making this up. Lewis was still concentrating on his line.

'The only difficult part was the British guard patrol I ran into on the way back.'

'Really?'

'Well, first of all they wouldn't believe my story. Thought I was a spy, you see, a traitor working for the Turks. Put me in a very tight spot.'

'It seems an awful lot of trouble to go to just for a coffee pot.'

'Or even a Lancia.'

'How did you get out of it?'

'Well, I had to send a runner for my commanding officer to come and get me out of jail. He gave me the most monumental wigging. The whole thing had been strictly against orders, as you can imagine. Worst of all, he wanted to confiscate the coffee pot.'

'Are you telling the truth?'

He had a maddeningly quizzical expression in his eyes; she just couldn't tell whether he was teasing her.

'Ask Tony.'

'He's in Nice by now.'

'Yes, lucky fellow. Delightful girl, your sister. Not my type, mind you, but delightful all the same.'

'And what is your type?'

'Oh, I don't know ...' He looked away. 'I suppose it's more the romantic ones I like, not that I meet many of them. Your sister is very nice – but I could see straight away she was the practical type.'

'Really?'

'Am I wrong? You're her sister, you should know.'

'I suppose she is. She always plays up to men, goes all helpless on them, but underneath that she is pretty capable.'

'That's what I thought.'

'And that wouldn't do for you?'

'Not really. I'm drawn to the sort of girl who wants the stars. I can take care of the practical side.' He looked away and they sat in silence for a couple of minutes as he seemed lost in thought, and she studied the line of his jaw and the small hairs on the back of his neck. At last, rousing herself, she said, 'Didn't you say you knew Lawrence of Arabia?'

'Yes. Interesting chap in his way. It was through him I got mixed up in the business of the Coptic monks – isn't that your brother?'

Behind them Vere was coming along the river bank. He too held a fishing rod. The dogs, who had flopped down by Anne's side in the shade, now leapt up to meet him.

'Caught anything, Lewis?'

'Not yet, old bean.'

'Wrong time of day. Wait another couple of hours. Anyway, there's a pool further down I prefer to here. Let's see your rod. Oh, good one. Did you get it in London?'

'Yes.'

'I say, do you know the Essexes raided Lisheen this morning?'

'Yes.' Anne looked away, annoyed. 'I saw them.'

'Isn't it the end? You can't even take a walk through the village these days without being stuck up by some beastly Tommy.'

'Ah – so you're a Republican too?' Lewis stretched out on the blanket, leaning on one elbow, and squinted up at Vere who was standing over them. Og had just thrown herself down panting, and Anne ran her hand over the dog's head.

'Rather.'

'I suppose if I were Irish I would be too,' Lewis said slowly.

'Would you?'

'The main thing is to know which side you're on, and then to fight as hard as you can. Have it out, that's the best way, till one fellow or the other has had enough. It clears the air. I never could stand compromisers and pacifists, moaning minnies.'

'Hear, hear!' Vere said enthusiastically.

Anne was more annoyed than she expected. There was

something very strange and interesting about Lewis which she could not quite understand, something provoking, which needled her and would not leave her in peace, and she wanted more time alone with him to try and unravel the mystery. Now Vere had broken in, and the conversation had run off on another tack.

However, later, when they had returned to the house and were just going up to change for dinner Lewis invited her to go out with him for a drive in his car, and she was slightly surprised to hear the pleased note in her voice as she accepted.

# Chapter Seven

The engine started with an ear-shattering roar in the enclosed space of the stable as Lewis cranked it. He pulled out the handle, climbed in, put the car into gear and backed carefully out into the morning sunlight.

'Jump in.'

The big car had an awesome feeling of strength and power, but Lewis was relaxed as always as he adjusted the gears and they moved away across the gravel, past the house and down the drive.

Anne had never driven in anything as big as this. She rested her arm on the side and could feel the rush of air on it. The car scarcely seemed to feel the uneven surface of the track as they drove down across the hillside towards Lisheen, and they covered the ground at what seemed an unearthly speed. Familiar landmarks which she counted mentally with such difficulty as she pulled up the lane on her bicycle, now flashed past in a dizzy succession, so that they were approaching the village almost before it seemed they had left the gates.

'You'd better tell me where you want to go.'

'It doesn't matter, except I promised Mother to get her a magazine in Macroom.'

As they came down into the village he pulled the car's long head round and took the road north. On the straighter wider road he put his foot down and she felt the force thrusting into her back as they accelerated away. It was intoxicating, a wonderful sensation of rushing along and a delicious feeling of irresponsibility, quite unlike anything she was used to; a sudden sense of holiday, as if the pressures and concerns which hung over her were miraculously lifted. She felt swept along by a power she didn't quite understand, but which she trusted implicitly.

He could see she was enjoying it.

'Lovely country you've got here,' he shouted, over the roar of the engine and the rushing noise of the air about them.

She just nodded, holding down her hat as the wind tossed it about, and smiling at him, unable to stop herself.

'You know, that's the first time I've seen you smile?'

'Am I as bad as that?'

'I wouldn't say that. But you always seem to be so preoccupied. You look as if you have weighty matters to consider.'

She said nothing.

'Why don't you take that hat off, before it gets blown away?'

Macroom was a small town. Coming in from Lisheen the road ran along near a lake and then turned and pulled up into the town at the lower end. Shops were strung along the narrow street which opened out at the far end in a market square. Facing on to this square was the large bulk of the castle, a square solid building which since time immemorial had been a barracks of the British Army and was at this moment occupied by an auxiliary unit of the Royal Irish Constabulary – the 'Auxies'. In years gone by the townsfolk had enjoyed friendly relations with the military, who apart from anything else were a source of trade and prosperity to many of the shopkeepers, tavern keepers, and hotel proprietors.

Beyond the castle and down a narrow street lay the river, a picturesque spot, where fishermen sat and young mothers walked with their babies.

The big Lancia roared up the street and into the square in front of the castle.

'You can leave the car here,' Anne said.

They walked over to the newsagent and found the magazine Claire had asked for then strolled casually down the street, looking into one of two of the little shop windows. They came to the saddler's whom Anne knew. The proprietor was standing in the doorway smoking his pipe.

'Good morning, Miss Hunter.'

'Good morning, Mr Shaunessy. And how are things?'

'Well, I don't know, Miss Hunter.' He took his pipe out of his mouth, and stared reflectively into it for a moment. 'I really don't know what's to become of us all. Since these "Auxies" arrived now, there's been nothing but trouble. And we that was always on such good terms with the military. Do you remember the band concerts on Sunday afternoon, and the sports day? And me, Miss Hunter, I don't where I'd have been without their patronage, to be sure. But now, I don't know how to tell you. They're all gentlemen, I'm sure, but there was a gang of them in the street last night and it after midnight, shouting and firing their pistols. There was a window shot out over in Flynn's yonder...'

He lapsed into silence.

'Will he claim for compensation?'

'I don't know.'

'He must – he's entitled to it.'

'Ah.'

Mr Shaunessy sucked at his pipe, and shook his head reflectively.

They strolled back in the direction of the square, and then Anne saw Cathal on the other side of the road about two hundred yards ahead of them. She was about to go across and speak to him about his folly in showing himself in the town when two "Black and Tans" – the new military police – came out of a bar immediately in front of Cathal, and nearly ran into him. One lurched up, and pushed him against the wall.

'Fuckin' Shinner.'

Cathal said nothing, just waited for them to pass, but the man turned again and looked at him closely, weaving slightly on his feet.

'Sarge! Look at this.'

He unbuttoned his breast pocket and pulled out a greasy folded copy of the wanted notice for Cathal. Cathal was staring at them impassively.

'Fuckin' wanted, ain't he? Look – it's 'im.'

The sergeant had taken the filthy piece of paper and studied it.

Cathal's face was white.

Anne and Lewis had come up now and were on the opposite

side of the road, watching carefully. Anne's heart was beating violently. Without thinking she grasped Lewis's arm. He noticed and put his hand over hers.

'It's him, Sarge – fuckin' Shinner – bastard did that Dunmanway job –'

Cathal was silent, watching the drunken policeman who had wrenched his pistol from its holster and was waving it in his face.

'Know what this is, don't you, you swine? It's yours, see? Got your name on, get it? You're coming in –'

He lurched unsteadily, as the sergeant studied the notice, and looked into Cathal's face. As he turned briefly, Anne could see the man's white face, the blue shadow on his chin, his sunken eyes, and their manic stare; he was a man on the edge of an explosion, his nerves taut to breaking point.

She was frozen.

Lewis released Anne's arm, and strolled across, as if he had just that moment come up the street. Neither of the men had noticed him.

'What's the matter, Cavanagh? Got a problem? Got a problem, Sergeant? This man is my groom. Has he been making a nuisance of himself? Come along man, haven't got all morning.'

Anne watched in stunned amazement. Lewis's voice had changed, had somehow found a "silly ass" braying tone. The policemen swung round. Lewis stood right in front of them, close up, looking into their faces.

'Fuckin' Shinner –'

Lewis was conspicuously well dressed, in a three piece tweed suit and regimental tie – obviously a gentleman – and the unkempt and disshevelled condition of the two police officers contrasted sharply with his dapper appearance and clipped tones.

'Who, Cavanagh? Don't be ridiculous, Hasn't the wit. He's my groom. I wouldn't stand for any of that nonsense. What's he been up to?'

He took the sheet from the sergeant, and looked at it for a moment.

'You're not taking him in on the strength of *this?*'

'That's him.'

'Are you mad? It's not remotely like him. Anyway it isn't him. You're searching for Cathal Donnelly, and this useless creature is Cavanagh my groom – who's kept me waiting this last half hour. Come on, look lively can't you? Incidentally, I'm surprised at you, Constable, using foul language in public. I shall report you to your officer. That's all, Sergeant. At ease.'

He took Cathal by the elbow and dragged him away up the street in the direction of the square. The two policemen watched him blearily.

Anne followed a few yards behind them, and heard Lewis mutter, 'Take your time, old bean. No hurry.'

In agonising slow motion the three of them proceeded up the street to the square. Anne burned to turn and see what the Tans were doing, but did not dare.

There was a crowd of admirers gathered round the car. Lewis courteously shooed them away, and the three of them got in. The car roared into life and in a moment they were driving back down the street; they passed the two policemen who watched them go.

Once they were clear of the town Anne looked round. Cathal was sitting back against the seat, his eyes closed, his face white. She restrained the words on her tongue, the sarcastic rebuke ready to lacerate him, and looked for a moment at his poor young face, the strain etched across his brow, the dead white cheeks, and fast breathing. Then, feeling that she was intruding, as if it were indecent to see anyone in the grip of such strong feeling, she turned to the front and looked across at Lewis. His eyes on the road, he appeared as relaxed as ever. They drove in silence almost all the way to Lisheen. As they were coming towards the village, he slowed down.

'I'm putting you out here. Won't do any good to be seen driving through the village.' He was quite expressionless.

Cathal roused himself, and got out of the car. He walked round to where Lewis was sitting and offered him his hand, almost mechanically, his face still drained of colour.

'I don't know the correct form of address for a fellow who's just saved your life, but whatever it is, please accept it. I never saw anything like that before. Those fellows are devils. I thought I'd had it.'

61

'Might be wise to keep your head down from now on, old chap.'

Cathal looked at Anne.

'Cathal – what on earth were you doing in Macroom?'

He looked down, embarrassed.

'Sounds a bit stupid. The old man's been poorly, as you know. There was a bit of a panic, and I went in to get him some medicine.'

He patted a package in his pocket.

'Couldn't Katie or your mother have done that?'

'Well,' he shrugged, 'it was rather urgent.'

He seemed in a hurry to get away.

'Good day, Anne.'

He turned and climbed into a field and began making his way up the long slope of the hill to where his home stood, a mile above.

Anne watched him as Lewis set the car in motion. Something about Cathal exasperated her. He just didn't take enough care, didn't think enough. It wouldn't have done his father much good if Cathal had wound up in Macroom castle.

And as for Lewis, at that moment she didn't know what to think. As Cathal had said, she had never seen anything like it.

They came to Lisheen, and then instead of taking the narrow lane up to the house, Lewis accelerated and they headed through the village and out on the road to the coast.

She watched the road for a long time, but in the end said softly, 'Why did you do it?'

'I expect he would have done the same.'

'Lewis, this may sound awkward – I don't always say quite what I want to say, or in the way I would like to – but I must thank you for this. Cathal is an old friend, and I've never realised the risks he runs until now. Those men were ready to kill him.'

'Fraid so.'

'Anything, the slightest movement – and they would have shot him on the spot.'

'Yes. Nerves.'

'But why did you go over? You don't even know him.'

He stared ahead for a long time without speaking. Anne thought he wasn't going to reply and was beginning to think

62

she had been tactless, when he said meditatively, 'I'd have to think about that.'

And then after another pause, 'You see, in the war, there were times like that when I thought I'd had it – several times when I was looking down the barrel of a gun, or, I don't know ... there'd be a gang of drunken soldiers with shredded nerves just looking for an excuse. And every time I walked away and found I was still alive, I made a sort of vow –'

He paused. He still hadn't looked at her. She waited.

'And then again, you see, I've killed a few men myself, not always under orthodox circumstances.'

He changed hands on the steering wheel, pulling the long bonnet of the car sharply round and over a narrow stone bridge. Beneath them, in a deep cleft in the rocks, the river dashed and sprayed, darting over rocks and cascading beneath ferns and clumps of heather.

The road was passing through country that became ever harsher, mountains rising ever steeper on either side, wild and barren, the rocks pushing through the thin soil like the bones of a starving man, and here and there clumps of brilliant gorse. For a while the crags closed right in, rising perpendicularly above them, as if the mountain had cracked in two, and the road, sunk in this ravine, found its way with difficulty round seemingly insurmountable barriers. Wild ivy clung to the rock face, and occasionally a stunted yew or arbutus grew from some cleft in the huge masses above them, while from far above, mountain streams tumbled headlong.

Anne was silent as they took in the stupendous scenery about them. After some time, Lewis went on, 'I've done things that frankly, I'm not very proud of.'

He needed time to bring together the memories.

'There was one time in Southern Lebanon. I was a company commander and we had taken a Turkish outpost on a mountaintop. It was bitterly cold, snowing, these fellows were dug in, and didn't expect any activity on our part – thought we'd be huddled round the fire like they were. So we had no difficulty in surprising them. And I found myself with a dozen prisoners, nothing to feed them, and the chance of a rescue team coming up. They were young men, younger than your friend, farm lads, ignorant, untrained, and I was in a hurry, had to get the company mobilised pretty sharp. This kind of skirmishing is all constant movement. So –' he drew a breath '– I told the men to herd them back into the command dug-out, and we tossed a couple of Mills bombs in after them.'

He still had not looked at her.

'Not a pretty story. You're the first person I've told, as a matter of fact.'

'I knew.'

'Did you?' He seemed to be genuinely surprised, and at last looked at her. 'How?'

'I don't know, I could just tell.'

They were silent for a moment, then Lewis went on, 'So there are times when I feel I owe something – I still think of those young men sometimes. At night if I can't sleep. I can still see their faces, you know, every one of them.' He took a grip on himself. 'So please don't make me out to be any kind of saint, I beg you.'

'You have implicated yourself, you know. They will remember this car.'

'I'll be gone in a few days. Shouldn't worry.'

Anne felt suddenly hurt. She didn't want him to go, not yet. There was something so – it was as if – she couldn't find the words to explain it to herself, but there was something so *interesting* about him. At every moment he was likely to say something unexpected, something that would take her by surprise. It was all new; he appealed to a side of herself that she was not familiar with, he opened up possibilities and she needed time to explore them, to get to know them. She could have bitten her lip with vexation. She had plenty of self-control, however, at all times.

'Back to England, I suppose?'

'Hmm? Not sure. Dublin for a bit. I promised I'd look in on the newly-weds.'

'Do you have a job to get back to?'

'Eventually. There's no great pressure.'

She had no way of imagining what his life might be when he got home. What kind of a job could he possibly have? She had not the faintest idea.

'And you?' He smiled.

'Me? I haven't a job, if that's what you mean. It doesn't seem very important at the moment, with the war on.'

'War?'

'The war against England.'

'Of course. Your friend Cathal.'

'You may smile, and I know it was incredibly stupid of him to walk through Macroom in broad daylight, but he's as brave as – he'd die for Ireland.'

'And you?'

'Yes.'

'Seriously?'

'What's life worth anyway, if you're not free?'

'But you are free.'

'No.'

'My dear Anne, with respect, you are as free as the air. In what way aren't you free? I'm serious. Tell me one thing you would be able to do, if Ireland won her independence, that you can't do now.'

Anne was silent. Ideas flooded into her mind, but all of them vague, nebulous; none of them touched her directly.

'You wouldn't have the King's head on the stamps, it is true; perhaps that will be a source of satisfaction. But is it worth killing for?'

Again she was taken by surprise. Until this moment she had taken it as axiomatic that the war was just and right. People would get killed; they did in wars, you had to accept that, but it was right, it was justified, because in the end, Ireland would be free, and ... and what? She realised she had never thought any further. Then she remembered Cathal that morning.

'And the soldiers in Macroom? It's all right for me, because my father's a Unionist and a magistrate. It's a different story for the poor people, the Catholics. They understand the difference between freedom and oppression.'

The sea came into view, and they swung round the coast and came into the little town of Bantry. Lewis announced that it was time for lunch so they went into Vickery's Hotel, the largest in the town, to see what was on offer, and on being told that the salmon was very good just now, looked no further but sat down to lunch.

The restaurant was nearly empty and they sat at a window

overlooking the harbour. Anne was curiously quiet and relaxed. Then suddenly she remembered something.

'What about the Coptic monks?'

'Eh?'

'You were going to tell me about the Coptic monks yesterday when Vere came up.'

'Was I? Oh, yes. My goodness, it seems a long time ago now. Wonder what made me think of that? Well, it was when Lawrence was driving for Akaba – it's a port on the Red Sea, and we – I say we, I mean myself and a miscellaneous parcel of brigands and desperadoes we'd recruited among the Druse to fight the Turks. Anyway, we were making our way across the Sinai peninsula to meet up with him. Tricky sort of place – have to be on your guard – some of the Druse don't actually know which side they're on, and there's always the risk of running into an area which was pro-Turk. Well, anyway, towards nightfall we came up to a shabby old collection of buildings which turned out to be a Coptic monastery. Pretty rare, as you can imagine – most of the Copts live in Upper Egypt – but they seemed to be friendly and there was nowhere else to go anyway, unless we just pitched camp in the middle of the desert, so we accepted their hospitality.

'Then that night the prior of the monastery, a moth-eaten old fellow with a beard to his waist, invited me to look round his library. I didn't like to refuse so in we went to a couple of rooms, thick with sand and dust and with a few dog-eared books on the shelves and, would you believe, papyrus rolls. Could have been a thousand years old. They were all in the Coptic script until I picked one book off the shelf, a big heavy thing, needed both my hands to lift, blew off the dust and opened it. It was in Greek, hand-written on vellum, beautiful script, perfectly preserved. Of course in that climate things never decay.'

He leant forward now and looked seriously into her eyes. 'Anne, I don't know much about these things, but as far as I could tell it was a copy of the Four Gospels. And as I stood there in that dusty little room, with the candlelight flickering on the shelf and the old father watching me, turning this book over in my hands, I realised that it could be one of the oldest copies of the Gospels in existence, possibly even the oldest.

Probably been there since soon after the time of Christ. Gave me a pretty odd feeling, I can tell you.'

The waiter arrived with the soup and a bottle of white wine.

'Can't imagine what the wine'll be like in a place like this, eh? Still, judging by the size of the boats out there, there must be some money washing round the town. We'll just have to chance it.'

He poured out the wine and lifted his glass.

'Here's to you, Anne. I'm grateful to you for bringing me to such a delightful place.' He sipped, and a small frown crossed his brow. 'As I thought, it's stood too long in the bar.'

Anne hadn't noticed anything about the wine but Lewis called the waiter back and told him to take it away and bring them another bottle.

The waiter stared at him. 'Is there anything wrong with it, sir?'

'It's corked,' Lewis said mildly.

'Corked?'

'Yes, corked – and we'd like one that isn't corked.'

Anne watched as the waiter shrugged and took the bottle away. In the meantime Lewis started on the soup.

'Still, they do a decent bowl of soup, it must be said. Fresh ingredients and plenty of butter, that's the secret of a good soup. Your sister now, she and Tony should be enjoying some good soup at this very moment.'

'How?'

'Well, down on the Riviera. You know yourself, the fish soups they make down there – you'd walk across France for a bowl of the stuff.'

'Would you? I wouldn't cross the road for it. I know nothing about food. It seems to me pretty insignificant compared with the important matters in life.'

'Important matters in life? My dear Anne, what could be more important than food?'

'Anyway, you're changing the subject – what about those Gospels?'

'Wait a minute, we've got to get this straightened out. I can't have you going about thinking that food is unimportant. My dear girl, you're only here once, you know. If you don't enjoy good food now, when will you? Would you pass the pepper – I must confess I do like my soup peppery. French fish soup now – that's very peppery.'

She passed over the pepper pot, and he laced his soup liberally with it.

'Ah, that's better.' He took another mouthful.

'Lewis, you really can't do this to me.'

'What?'

'You've left me hanging on in a Coptic monastery with the oldest copy of the Gospels in your hands.'

At this moment the waiter reappeared with another bottle of wine.

'Ah, let's hope we have better luck this time.' Lewis sipped the wine, looked thoughtful for a moment, then put down his glass. 'Well, it's probably the best we can hope for.' He nodded to the waiter.

'Lewis –'

'What? Oh, yes. Well, bad news, I'm afraid. My gallant companions got into an argument with some of the monks, Muslim against Christian, you see. A brawl broke out, and a lantern got knocked over . . .'

He gave her a very significant look.

'You mean . . . ?'

He nodded. 'A fire started. Of course, everything is tinder dry in the desert, and before we knew it the place was a raging furnace. I thought I'd better rescue the book and was carrying it out; it was pretty heavy. Well, the fire was roaring up on all sides, and the roof started crashing in, and in the confusion the old prior tripped and fell, and what with the roof falling in it was getting pretty dangerous, and if I hadn't looked sharp the old fellow would have roasted. And as unfortunately I've only two arms, it was either the old man or the book.'

He looked out of the window and took a meditative sip of wine. Anne could hardly speak.

'You mean,' she breathed, 'Lewis, are you telling me the book was burnt?'

He nodded, and let out a deep sigh. 'Pity, eh? Probably one of the greatest treasures in the world. Irreplaceable. There's one like it in the Vatican, only not so old. Still, out there they'd say it was fate. The will of Allah. And that's the end of it.'

The fish now arrived and put a stop to conversation for the time being.

Afterwards they strolled round the harbour, and Lewis said he thought it very picturesque; across the little bay the wooded hills rose, and behind them the grey outline of mountains; there were one or two expensive yachts at anchor, and houses clustered round the harbour, making a charming composition.

'Father has a cottage near here, a bit further along the coast, round the head there. He brings us down for the fishing sometimes. We swim in the sea in the summer.'

Lewis drew a breath.

'Lucky you. It's a wonderful country. So peaceful. And the sea air – you'd live to be a hundred here.'

He stared out across the bay thinking, and after a while said in a thoughtful way, 'You know, I could settle down in a place like this. It wouldn't cost much, and one could sit in a boat out there all day with a rod and line, watching the clouds over the mountaintop, the changing weather, and haul in the odd fish or two ... all one needs is a little place, like one of those villas' – he gestured towards the few houses which dotted the mountainside behind the town '–so long as one has enough to live on. We could drop into Murphy's Bar of an evening to listen to the locals and drink a pint of stout and smoke a pipe. Put the world – put all that – behind one; turn one's back on the whole bloody show.'

For one astonished moment Anne thought he was including her in this day-dream and was thrown into confusion. Lewis was silent. He turned and looked at her, and their eyes met, and then Anne became very confused because their eyes simply could not unlock. They just stared at one another and she was reading volumes of meaning, as if he were offering his whole soul to her, if she wanted it; only she didn't know what it consisted of and on what terms he was offering it. At last, as she was beginning to panic, he looked away and again there was a silence between them as she tried to understand what had just happened. Fighting the panic in herself, she erected her usual defence of sarcasm, and said, 'But why? I mean, why do you want to put the world behind you – why call it a bloody show?'

'My dear Anne, I couldn't begin to explain. And what's more I am becoming maudlin, a thing I abhor. Keep it simple, fight the fight, and have done with it. That's the motto of the Crawfords. Let us get back. Your mother will be pining for the *Illustrated London News.*'

The car had gathered a crowd of admirers, barefoot children, shabby loafers, and Lewis courteously shooed them away before he and Anne got in and turned for home.

# Chapter Eight

As they came through the shrubbery and within sight of the house, Anne saw three army lorries again ranged in front of the house. Her heart nearly stopped, and her mind was racing ahead, covering the possibilities, preparing a story, as Lewis pulled up at the door.

'Go on in. I'll put the Old Beast away.'

She took the magazine and went indoors. There was a roar of laughter from the drawing room, a chatter of men's voices, animated, lively, as if they had already had several drinks. She was going up to her room to wash her face but one of the men had seen her and had said something because before she had crossed the hall to the stairs her father was at the door.

'Anne! Come in – we've had a social visit. Some of the Auxie fellows from Macroom.'

'In a moment, Father, I'd just like to wash my hands first.'

Feeling relieved, she went to her room, threw off her summer dress and washed her face and shoulders. It had been dusty driving through the wild country lanes in an open car. She ran a comb through her strong abundant hair. She liked the springy feel the bob cut had given it. It had a life of its own now, instead of hanging down her back in a dead weight as it had before.

She put on a pair of stockings, and changed her dress, and was looking in the mirror to comb her hair again when Lewis's words came back to her. What a strange thing he had said: put the whole bloody show behind him. It did not tally with anything else he had said, and had instead a weird kind of fatalism which seemed out of character for him.

71

As she went downstairs she was still puzzling it out. The Auxie officers welcomed her boisterously, and she felt herself bridling, holding in, as they pressed forward to be introduced. Worst of all there was that unspeakable, greasy-faced little Captain Steptoe. Her father introduced him.

'So sorry about the misunderstanding, Miss Hunter,' he breathed at her. 'Your sister's wedding ... most unfortunate.' His breath smelled of cigarettes and whisky. 'You understand, I'm sure. At a time of national emergency, occasionally the niceties are likely to be neglected.'

She was non-committal, vague, hoping to be relieved of his company quickly.

But then it occurred to Anne that she might be able to pick their brains, ferret out useful information about future troop movements or plans, things the Volunteers could use. She became excited at the thought of what she knew and these men didn't, and despised them for their arrogance; to think they could walk into another country and give orders and throw their weight around.

'And did you find them?'

'Beg pardon?'

'During my sister's wedding when you so unexpectedly paid us a visit, you said you were searching for weapons.'

'Unpardonable. New to the country, you see. Can't imagine what you must have thought. How can you forgive me?'

'I'm sure my father already has.'

'Most obliging, your father. A real pillar of the community, Miss Hunter.'

'Yes.' She paused. 'And did you find them?'

He drew a breath, and sighed.

'Alas, not so far. In a country like this it's very difficult; the people are very difficult, untrustworthy, clannish – they'll die rather than betray their own, Miss Hunter. Only now beginning to get the measure of the task.'

He drew in another sharp breath, deeply conscious of the trust bestowed on him.

'Still, it's good to be back in harness. When the war finished, I was at a terrible loose end, kicking around, didn't know what to do. Then this show blew up, and I was in like a shot.'

He was starting to reminisce, and Anne didn't think she could stand it.

'And you're still looking?'

'Hmm?'

'The guns that were taken. You were very upset the first time you came.'

'Were we? Oh, well, we are making our searches, but you can imagine. That fellow now, Cathal Donnelly, he's a slippery one. Oh, yes, we have our eyes on him. Dangerous character, Miss Hunter.'

In the corner of her eye, Anne noticed Lewis had just come into the room, and was talking to Claire. She was torn between watching him and a desire to hear about Cathal.

'Cathal Donnelly? I don't –'

'The ringleader. A vicious terrorist.'

'You've caught him?' She sounded innocently interested.

'Not yet. But we will. But I'm sure you must find all this very tiresome?'

He had noticed her eyes flick away from him.

'Oh, no, I assure you. Do go on.'

'A pretty young lady like yourself can't be interested in this business.'

'Why not? I'm sure we're all very grateful to you for keeping the peace.'

For a mad moment she thought she would tell him she knew Cathal, and then give him some misleading information – Cathal Donelly was seven foot tall, had green eyes and a large strawberry mark under his left ear, also a cast in one eye and a limp ... But she didn't think she could go on much longer being polite to this reptilian gentleman.

'Still we don't altogether give up hope,' Captain Steptoe continued. 'There are always ways to get information. We have our spies out, Miss Hunter, unobtrusive, quiet fellows, moving through the towns and villages. A quiet drink in a bar, a chat leaning over a gate – surprising the things we pick up.'

'Good. So you're expecting to make an arrest?'

'We will catch them.' He gave her a straight look. 'I'm not here for the good of my health, Miss Hunter. We'll catch them. And when we do, we'll make it hot for them, believe me. They'll wish they had never been born.'

Anne believed him. But now he was getting into his stride.

'The trouble with these people, Miss Hunter, is they don't understand reasonable civilised methods; it's a waste of time trying to be nice to them. Brute force is what they understand. And if that's the way they want it, that's how they're going to get it. They murder a policeman, Miss Hunter – in cold blood, mark you, no warning, a cowardly murder – very well, they can expect no mercy from me. We'll use any means – *any means* – to bring them to justice. Matter of fact, Lisheen now, you'd think, a quiet enough sort of place, anglers' paradise, out of the way, lovely countryside ... a hotbed of terrorism, Miss Hunter.'

'No!'

'Right under your very nose – you'd never believe it. Old Pat Murphy that you've known for ever? A terrorist, capable of cold-blooded murder. Shamus O'Toole, amusing old character you'd think? A ruthless killer. Pretty little Biddy McCann the milkmaid? Working day and night for the Cumann na mBan.'

'I beg your pardon?'

'The women's arm of the IRA, Miss Hunter. Oh, yes, They've got girls working for them too. So you see, there, in that peaceful village, under that harmless exterior, a nest of subversion, Shinners to a man. But they've got a shock coming.'

'Have they?'

'We're perfecting a new method. Taking the villages one by one, and going through them from end to end, turning 'em over, Miss Hunter, shaking 'em out. They won't know what's hit 'em.'

'But how will you identify the IRA men?'

'Terror.'

'I beg your pardon?'

'Terrorise 'em. Give 'em a bit of their own medicine.'

'I thought you said they never betrayed each other?'

'By the time I've finished with 'em they'll be begging to tell me. Begging.'

'So you're going to raid Lisheen? Let's hope you find something.'

He pulled a silver cigarette case from his breast pocket.

'Cigarette?'

'No, thanks. I don't smoke.'

'Quite right, Miss Hunter. I wasn't thinking. Only nowadays, since the war, girls have got into all sorts of bad habits.'

'I beg your pardon?'

'I mean, smoking, wearing make-up, that sort of thing.'

He was getting away from the point.

'When are you planning to raid the village?'

'Week Monday. I can tell you, Miss Hunter, in confidence, naturally. I've warned your father. It's actually hush-hush. Highest priority.'

'I should hope so.'

Across the room Anne heard her mother's voice raised.

'My dear man, you don't know the faintest thing about it.'

She looked across the room to where Claire was talking to a young officer. Her mother was dressed in an elegant, loose tea-gown.

'The Irish were a cultured people before the English were heard of, when the Ancient Britons were running about in woad! We have the finest myths and legends in Europe; during the dark ages we saved Christianity for the rest of Europe. Do you *know*, in the eighth century Irish monks were travelling through Europe bringing learning and literature when the Goths had reduced the continent to a heap of rubble? Without the Irish, Europe would have been unspeakable, soulless, devoid of culture – like America.'

'Heaven forbid,' the young officer mumbled.

'Amusing lady, your mother,' Captain Steptoe murmured in an attempt at intimacy. Anne had had enough.

'Excuse me.'

She went across to where her mother had now attracted a circle round her. Claire was in full flow.

'And as for *English* culture – my dear man, you got it all from us! Are you aware,' she said in her most sarcastic voice, 'are you *aware* that every *English* playwright of any consequence since Shakespeare has been an Irishman?'

'Really?' the young officer said in a husky voice. 'GBS, you mean?'

'Among others,' Claire crushed him. 'Ireland has been exporting her talent to England for three centuries. We have been *bleeding*! And so long as this country remains tied to England it will continue.'

'Darling,' Hugh Hunter murmured.

'Mrs Hunter has made her own small contribution to Ireland's culture, haven't you?'

This was Lewis, preserving his cool manner at a moment when voices were just beginning to rise. Claire swung round.

'She doesn't like to boast of it herself, but I hope she won't mind if I tell you that she has appeared at the Abbey Theatre in one or two of Lady Gregory's productions.'

This unloosed a volley of comment and enthusiasm.

'An actress? No, really, you don't say! How splendid!'

Claire's vanity was soothed.

'Oh, years ago, when you young men were in your cradles.'

'Nonsense! Impossible!'

'Many years ago – and Lewis, shame on you for dragging up such an old story – well, *years* ago, since you ask, a few of us, Yeats, Lady Gregory and a few others, were very keen to revive the Irish drama ...'

She was off on a tide of reminiscence, and the young men gathered round to hear. Anne wondered how on earth Lewis knew about her mother's brief foray into the theatre – on a strictly amateur basis, of course. And she saw too the tactful way he had defused the tension which had been threatening to break up the bland atmosphere of the party. In fact, she now saw Hugh Hunter talking to him.

There was only one thought in Anne's mind. She had to get a message to Cathal tonight. She would have to go herself. This evening? Wouldn't it be rather ... she dithered in her mind. People would see her – Lewis would wonder – strange she hadn't cared what he might think before now – well, she must go tonight.

The Auxie officers had only come for a social drink and within an hour had departed, roaring off again in their army lorries with the machine-guns mounted at the front, a grotesque reminder of the state of the country.

The weather was still holding, incredibly, and it was a soft late-summer evening, the windows standing open and the scent of honeysuckle wafting into the drawing room as they came in after dinner. Bridget brought in the coffee as Claire

76

sat down at the piano to play for them. Anne stood uncertainly in the doorway and then said, 'I think I might go out for a while.'

The others made brief remarks, but only Lewis's eyes followed her as she went out to the stable for her bicycle. It would be light for an hour and a half yet, plenty of time, and there would be no one around much at this hour.

She set off down the hill towards Lisheen, and as she arrived at the Donnelly's and leant her bicycle against the wall, she was breathing hard. She pushed the hair back from her face and knocked on the door.

It was opened by the little maid.

'Katie. I have to get a message to Cathal.'

'Oh,' she was flustered as ever, 'I don't know, Miss Hunter. That is –'

'Who is it, Katie?' A voice from within.

She jumped nervously and looked over her shoulder.

'Miss Hunter, ma'am.'

A pause.

'Show her in.'

The Donnellys were gentry, on visiting terms with the Hunters. The house was not as pleasant or as tasteful as Anne's home, though, and that was due to Claire's taste. Anne was shown into the drawing room. It was a dim room, the window closed and swagged with heavy Victorian drapes, the walls hung with faded prints of Highland scenes, sideboards with artificial fruit or stuffed birds under glass covers; a cluttered feeling, an accumulation of things, none of which bore any relation to any other.

Mrs Donnelly was in an armchair, knitting by the light of a paraffin lamp.

'Good evening, Anne.'

She stood in the doorway, a picture of good health and youthful innocence, long-legged in a summer frock, her hair swinging round her face.

'Mrs Donnelly, good evening. Dr Donnelly ... is he any better?'

'I am afraid not.'

'I saw Cathal in Macroom this morning. He mentioned –'

'Yes.'

77

There was silence then Anne said quickly, 'Mrs Donnelly, I need to speak to Cathal.'

The older woman looked at her for a moment without speaking, as if unsure how to address her.

'Did you expect to find him here?'

Anne was at a loss.

'Well, this morning – I don't know – that is, I don't know where else I could look.'

'Since the wanted notice went up, he has been in hiding.' Mrs Donnelly was not pleased to say this.

'Yes, I understand. Only, you see, I have to speak to him. I have a message for him, which is very urgent.'

'Oh.'

'Are you likely to see him? Are you in contact with him?'

Anne sensed that she was meeting resistance from the other woman; there was hostility in the air, though in her anxiety to convey her message she was not fully aware of it.

'He may call here in a day or two. He never tells me, but it is possible.'

'A day or two. I see.' It didn't seem definite enough. There had to be some way of getting to him more certain – and quicker – than that.

'Mrs Donnelly, it really is very important for me to see him. Truly. I wouldn't bother you otherwise.'

'If you wish to leave the message with me, I will see he gets it when he calls.'

Mrs Donnelly stared at her without expression. Anne was thinking. Could his mother be sure of seeing Cathal within the next ten days?

'I have found out that there is to be a raid on Lisheen a week on Monday. Cathal must be told. There must be many of his comrades in the village –'

'How did you find out?'

'Oh – well, there were some Auxie officers at home today.'

Silence. Mrs Donnelly watched her. Anne began to feel guilty.

'It's true! I heard this afternoon.'

'And if it weren't true? If it were a trap?'

'What?'

'Why should you bicycle over here at this hour of the night?

78

What if you were lying and Cathal were to be killed?'

'What?' Anne felt stunned by disbelief.

'How can I trust you, Anne? The British officers told you their plans? Why should they? Or why should you tell me what they told you?'

Anne felt an intense heat in her face, was almost dizzy. She didn't believe what she had heard. Mrs Donnelly retained her impassive look, unmoving. Finally Anne found her voice. She sounded hoarse.

'Mrs Donnelly, are you saying I'm lying?'

'Why should I believe you?'

'What? But you've known me all my life – I've known you – Mrs Donnelly we've always – surely – you can't imagine –'

Still Mrs Donnelly did not move. 'In the old days, Anne, it was different. We were friends. But now Cathal has a price on his head. If he were taken he would come before your father, the magistrate, and your father would commit him for trial. And afterwards he would go to the gallows.' She paused. 'How can we be friends?'

Anne's head was hot.

'Mrs Donnelly, I am on the Republican side, you know that. I am fighting for Ireland –'

'Fighting?'

'I support the Republican cause. I believe in it.'

'How can you? Your father is a magistrate, a Protestant and a landowner.'

'That has got nothing to do with it.'

'It has everything to do with it!' She was implacable. 'Now you are full of noble idealism. But what about when the fighting begins in earnest? What if your house is burnt down by the Volunteers? What if your father were killed? This is a fight to the finish, and there will be no quarter. Will you see your house burned and not curse the men who did it? Will you weep over your father's body and not wish vengeance on the men who killed him?'

Anne listened in silence. The women stared at each other and the silence went on and on. At last Anne said, in a strange hollow voice, 'You won't pass on the message?'

'Oh, yes. I'll tell Cathal that you called, and what you said.'

Another long pause. Then Mrs Donnelly said in a matter-of-fact tone, 'You won't call again. Perhaps in the future, when the trouble is over, we can be friends. But not now.'

Still with a slight buzzing in her ears, Anne went out into the evening, now darkening about her.

She felt quite bewildered; no one had ever talked to her like that before. She could still feel the heat in her face. It was quite simply so insulting: to tell her to her face that she wasn't believed when they had known each other all their lives ... Anne mounted her bicycle and rode off down the lane, feeling quite shaky in her legs.

# Chapter Nine

All the way home her head was buzzing, her thoughts whirling about in confusion. She simply could not absorb what she had just heard. It had been utterly unexpected, a slap in the face. Mrs Donnelly, whom she had known for ever ... the thoughts went round and round. She pressed down on the pedals, concentrated on the physical movement in an effort to drive the thoughts away, and by the time she arrived home was feeling more steady. It was dark by now.

It didn't alter the problem. Would Cathal get the message? There were two other friends of his that she knew of who lived in the village, she knew them distantly, by name only. She had never visited them, and it would look most odd calling on them ...

As she was crossing the gravel space in front of the house, a figure emerged from the door, silhouetted against the light within.

'Anne?'

'Yes?'

She dismounted as Lewis came towards her, and then was pushing the bicycle round towards the stables.

'Your father was wondering where you had got to.'

'He needn't. I just went out for a ride. I'm quite capable of looking after myself.'

'That's what I told him. Only I thought it, well, rather odd.'

'Odd?'

'Well, there you were having a cosy tête-à-tête with Captain Steptoe, and then after dinner you disappeared on your bicycle in a furious rush.'

'What furious rush? I simply went out for a ride.'

'I see.'

'I think I'll have a bath and go to bed. Thank you for a lovely day out.'

She went quickly to her room.

Later, as she lay in bed, the evening still had not quite lost all its light; there was a faint glimmer at the window, a last vestige of the day. Her skin was glowing from the effect of the wind and air and the bath she had taken, and she was wide awake and could not sleep. Thoughts rushed through her mind. Confused, one moment she was with him at Bantry, looking across the bay; then Captain Steptoe, and his loathsome way of leaning in towards her in that intimate way when he had no right; and then remembering Bantry again and the look Lewis had given her in which he seemed to lay himself bare before her and implied so much that she didn't understand; and afterwards Mrs Donnelly, and her implacable look, as if Anne might be responsible for Cathal's death, which was absurd.

Above all she was filled with anxiety that Cathal would not get the message, and could think of no way she could find him. No doubt he wasn't very far away, staying with a friend probably, moving about from farm to farm, keeping a step ahead of the British.

Then she thought of Lewis waiting for her at the door. She had been so brusque with him, and all because she was still thinking of Mrs Donnelly and Cathal. She must have offended him; he probably thought she had gone to see a young man. It occurred to her that he must think Cathal was her young man. She turned over, wondering why that should concern her.

The following morning, when she came down, she found Lewis had already gone out and taken Vere with him. Apparently, her father had recommended another fishing spot, Mrs Deasey had packed them up sandwiches and they had gone.

The day seemed empty. It was extraordinary that in such a short time Lewis had assumed such importance to her. She wandered out into the garden. The dew was on the grass, and trees hung still, heavy with the fullness of summer leaf.

Everywhere was a ripeness, the borders and flowerbeds crowded with colour, and an exquisite richness of perfume in the air. The light of the morning sun fell as yet at a low angle but promised heat to come.

In the midst of this glory and freshness, she wandered down the gravelled path and felt ill at ease, out of tune with the loveliness of the morning.

Coming round to the stables, she saw Costello washing Lewis's car. 'The Old Beast.' She watched him for a while. It certainly was a car in a thousand; she had never noticed cars much before, but there was no denying the expansive elegance of its lines, and the largeness of it disdaining petty economy – the wider view of things it implied, the exuberance with which it took things in its stride. Looking at it and thinking of its owner, her first thought was: Did he really win it in a bet? And remembering that, she realised she did not actually know one thing about Lewis. He was an enigma. His family, his background, his profession if he had one, what he did if he had not ... she had not the faintest idea. Quite simply he could be anything.

She wandered back through the garden, full of these confused thoughts. Later she was in her room, trying to read a magazine but not following the words, then staring out of the window, unable to fix on anything, irritated with herself and the monotonous vacuum of her life at this moment. Men had jobs, had a purpose in life. Her father, Cathal, even Lewis, she imagined ... they had something to aim at. Whereas she was expected to hang around the house, ride a bit, go shopping and arrange flowers, until she was snapped up by some young man. It didn't amount to much.

Later in the day it became very hot, and it occurred to her to go for a swim in the bathing pool up on the mountain behind the house. She took her towel and bathing costume and, calling the dogs, walked up the hillside. Far, far above her a lark sang in the clear sky, and as she came higher and higher out on the bare mountainside, and the valley stretched away beneath her, her spirits cleared and she felt freer, and at last stopped and turned to take in the wide scene. Beneath her she could see the house nestling among the trees and rhododendrons, and further away down in the valley the river winding slowly between the fields, glinting and shining like beaten metal. Far away across the valley, the mountains were a powder grey against the sheer blue of the sky. She stood alone, as the breeze caressed her skin, and let her eyes move slowly across the great sweep of the view, thinking nothing, only feeling a great freedom, feeling herself expanding into the wide emptiness of it, and a peace descending upon her.

She came to the bathing pool. Silent, mysterious, you came upon it quite suddenly, hidden among ferns and gorse bushes, with great white rocks to one side, where she and Pippa had often sat after a swim, drying themselves in the sun. In the air was a continuous quiet gurgling and splashing, as two streams, low now in summer, tumbled down the mountain-side; a magic pool, deep, clear, and cold.

The dogs, after sniffing their way through the gorse bushes, came back and settled down near her to sleep.

She threw down her towel and bathing costume on to a white rock, kicked off her sandals and undid her belt. And then it occurred to her that she was quite quite alone, alone in the wide space of the great mountainside, and with a wonderful feeling of freedom she peeled off her clothes carefully, letting them drop to the rock until she was perfectly naked.

She sat at the edge of the pool, and let one foot slip into the water. Her leg slid down and down quivering in the clean cold-ness, until at last and quite suddenly she let herself slide right under the water and came up with a gasp, throwing back her head and sucking in air. But the charge of blood invigorated her. She reacted to the cold, and alive now, struck out for the other side of the pool a few strokes away only: turning, thrashing out, diving and kicking, enjoying the combative, invigorating alive-ness of it, and the wonderful freedom of her nakedness.

After she had swum ten minutes or so, she pulled herself up on the rock and rubbed her towel across her face and through her hair, pulling up one leg to dry it, enjoying the tingling of the blood, the stimulation and feeling of well-being, a refresh-ment after her muddle and lassitude of the morning.

But then her vigour and alertness ebbed and melted beneath the rays of the sun, and in the early-afternoon heat she lay back, looking up into the empty vault of the blazing sky through her fingers and letting thoughts wander through her mind at random, all the thoughts that had been bottled up in her now wandering lazily through her. Lewis at Macroom, and even Mrs Donnelly, now seemed somehow farther away, less important, and all the time there was a feeling of wonderful warmth and relaxation, and at last she fell asleep.

She was aware of the brightness against her eyelids as she slowly returned to consciousness and the heat against her body. She lay conscious for a few minutes but with her eyes still closed. Then, fluttering her eyelids for a moment, and screwing them up against the glare as her mind cleared, she opened her eyes. She noticed the sky, vast above her, and the sound of the gentle breeze among the gorse, and the chuckling of the water as it ran down into the pool, taking in these things as her mind assembled itself again. And then, opening her eyes wider and turning her head slightly, she saw Lewis sitting on the turf on the opposite side of the pool, his hand on Mor's head as the dog sat by him, wagging its tail.

For a long second she thought she was dreaming and in her dream this was a wonderful moment, herself lying naked and near her the face of Lewis. But in another second she sat up with a snap and pulled her towel across her.

Lewis didn't move, and for a moment neither spoke.

'What–'

'I'm sorry you had to wake up. I thought you were asleep.'

'I was. How long have you been there?'

He did not move.

'Don't worry. I'll leave you in peace to get dressed. I didn't intend you to see me.'

'Did you follow me?'

'No. As a matter of fact, I bumped into Mor a couple of minutes ago and she led me up here. The fish weren't biting at this time of day so I had rambled up for a stroll.'

She felt she ought to remonstrate in some way. He seemed so very unconcerned, as if it were perfectly natural she should lie here stark naked and he should sit and look at her.

'You should not have looked.' It sounded lame.

'There's no need to get indignant; you should be pleased. You're very beautiful. I feel I'm very lucky to have seen you. Privileged. You shouldn't be upset –'

'Upset!'

'Yes.' He leant back on one elbow. 'I think it's very lovely. Very lovely.' He gestured vaguely about him. 'You here, and all round you the great rolling mountains, the cloudscapes and so on.' He sighed. 'I suppose I should have done the gentlemanly thing and looked the other way, but the world is filled with ugliness and stupidity and it's not often one finds something really simple and beautiful. You with no clothes on – we ought to celebrate it, if you ask me.'

He ran his hand over the dog's back and looked at her thoughtfully. She stared at him, not understanding a word he was saying.

'It's a lovely spot, isn't it?'

He did not seem to be conscious of her embarrassment. She did not know what to say. He was still looking at her, would not take his eyes off her. She was unable to move, conscious of the tension in her hand as she clutched the towel across her.

'I wish you hadn't woken up.' He sighed again. 'Oh, dear, I see you're offended.' He stood up. 'I'll leave you in peace. See you at the house.'

He rubbed the dog's head again, then turned and made his way down the hill, not hurrying, his jacket slung over his shoulder.

Anne sat still, shocked, not knowing what to think or how she should have reacted – if she should have reacted – or whether she had said the right thing. Should she have shouted at him? He was remarkably calm. Did he want to seduce her? Was he one of those irresponsible men who led girls astray? She bit her lip; this was one more of those occasions where he had surprised her – and in what a way. How could she face him this evening, now that he had seen her like this?

She threw down the towel and began to dress hurriedly, then after a moment slowed down. What was the hurry? Better to let him get ahead. He had ruined the afternoon – and yet had he? She remembered that moment when she had very first opened her eyes, before she had had time to react, when she had thought it was a dream. What a wonderful dream that had been; what might come of it – she wasn't quite sure what might have come of it, but suspected it would have been new and different, strange and exciting.

When she got home Lewis was nowhere to be seen, and

Bridget the maid brought tea into the drawing room. Hugh was in his study working on his *History of the Hunter Family* and she sat with her mother and drank tea, in the cool room, while outside the window the afternoon was still bright.

'How was your swim, darling?'

'Lovely.'

'You're looking well.'

'Am I?'

'Glowing. I don't know when I've seen you looking so well. You seem more cheerful too.'

Anne said nothing, pondering this.

'Where's Lewis? Still out fishing?'

'Yes, he and Vere went out first thing.'

'Oh, Vere went with him?'

'Mmm.'

She was looking out of the window.

'Mother, what do you know about Lewis?'

'Gracious – why do you want to know?'

'I don't know anything about him. I mean, who his people are – you know. What he does, that sort of thing.'

'Well, he told me he worked for his father – they're a firm of wine importers in London. Been there for centuries, I believe.'

'What is his age? Do you know?'

'No idea. Thirty? Thirty-two? Why don't you ask him?'

'I don't like to. He'd probably make some amusing remark; he's rather a private sort of person isn't he?'

'I'm sure he'd tell you anything you cared to ask. He never seems stand-offish to me. Very well spoken, courteous; a perfect gentleman.'

'Yes, I know. Still, that's just a – well, a surface. It's what's going on underneath that puzzles me.'

'Why?'

'Why's he here?'

'I thought he came for the wedding.'

'I suppose so.' Anne lapsed into silence. She was no nearer the truth. The thing was, she couldn't actually ask him straight out. She couldn't have before; now it would be impossibly forward. She would simply have to wait for him to reveal himself, if he was ever going to.

\*

87

He and Vere came in an hour later and presented five large trout, which were duly consigned to Mrs Deasey and reappeared that evening at dinner. Lewis gave no indication, no signs of what had happened at the pool, Vere said nothing, and Anne was left again at a loss, and wondering in what way their guest would surprise her next.

That encounter at the pool had changed their relationship; she could no longer be spontaneous with him. Every moment, everything they said to each other over dinner, was coloured for her by the memory. She heard herself being distant with him, evasive and cool. It didn't alter his manner, of course; he remained reasonable, courteous and amusing as always.

After dinner they came into the drawing room and Claire sat at the piano and played Chopin for them. As the evening grew steadily more dim, Anne looked across at Lewis in his armchair, listening to the music. Then he looked at her, and she couldn't make out his face properly in the half light, but she could sense the intensity of his eyes, and because of the haunting plangency, the unfulfilled longing in the music, the inexpressible sadness of it, she was conscious all through her of a deep wave of feeling that might swell up at any moment and heard herself, almost as if she had spoken it aloud, say, 'I love him.'

As she heard it, she was afraid. It was a feeling of inexpressible joy, a flow of feeling through her that could capsize her. But she had too many things to do, too many things to worry about and busy herself with, and besides she didn't know his feelings.

After the music finished the lamps were lit, and as coffee cups were handed back and forth she looked at him again, quickly, covertly, and wondered whether she saw the same expression, or whether it had all been an illusion, an effect of the music.

That night as she prepared for bed the atmosphere in the room remained with her; she kept seeing Lewis's face in the gloom, with that glint of light in his eyes, the concentration on her as if she were the only woman in the world, just as he had looked at her by the pool. And she kept trying to hold on to herself, pretending it wasn't quite like that, he had't looked at her like that, trying to rub out the indelible impression he had made on her.

Had she really sat in the drawing room, looking at him, and heard herself say she loved him?

Could she trust the feeling she had had? A moment charged with such significance, full of meaning, if only she knew what it was. Could she trust herself to fall in love with him, a man of whom she knew nothing? Did she dare? Or was it only the loveliness of the evening, and her mother playing the Chopin? And was that what love was? That rushing surging joy that welled up within her, threatening some catastrophic change in her condition for ever? Was this the moment, and should she surrender to it?

On an impulse she threw off her pyjamas and stood naked in front of her mirror, staring at her body.

He had said she was beautiful. But what did that consist of? She moved her hands across her breasts, pushing them up; she wished they were bigger. How long and thin she was, long-legged. Her hips were too narrow. She ran her hand over her bush. He had seen it. Did he want her? Want to do *that* to her? What would it be like?

As she ran her hands across her body she couldn't help herself from trying to imagine them together. Supposing he had come across to her as she lay on the white rock? If he had kissed her, how could she have resisted him? They would surely have made love there and then. She didn't see how they could have avoided it. Looking back, now, there seemed something so enormous, so inevitable about it. He had only to touch her and she would be quite helpless before him.

Fortunately he had said nothing more about going to Dublin.

# Chapter Ten

There was a faint scratching sound. She was awake at once. She heard it again. A scratching, like mice. But it couldn't be. Then the handle of her door was opening, very slowly, a slow grating of metal.

'Anne.' It was Vere, whispering.

She sat up with a jerk.

'Anne.'

'Yes, I'm awake. What do you want?'

In the darkness, he crept into the room, until he was close to her.

'Come with me.'

'What?'

Vere whispered close to her face in the darkness: 'To my room. It's Cathal.'

She was alert.

'Where is he?'

'He's in the garden. He wants to speak to you.'

'What time is it?'

'No idea. Come now. He's outside waiting.'

'What does he want?'

Anne was out of bed and pulling a dressing gown over her pyjamas.

'He didn't say. But he wants to talk to you. I think it's urgent.'

'Are you sure the parents didn't hear anything?'

'Positive.'

In a house as old as the Hunters' it was not easy to move about without a certain number of creaking floorboards, and it was agony as they crossed the wide landing and went down the short corridor to Vere's room which looked out over the garden behind the house. Anne and he craned out of the window in the darkness.

'Cathal?'

There was a movement behind a box hedge. She could barely make out the shape of a man.

'Anne?'

'Yes.'

'I must speak to you. Can you come down? It's a bit public here.'

'All right.'

She was making her way downstairs, and then realised Vere was behind her.

'Go back to your room.'

'No.'

'Vere – go back to your room.'

'No, I'm coming.'

In the darkness they stood on the stairs. Vere wouldn't budge.

Anne turned and continued down, across the hall, through the kitchen, reaching in the darkness for the key, and in a moment was outside the kitchen door. Vere was behind her.

Cathal was waiting.

'Let's go up to the cold store, we won't be overheard.'

They made their way along the path, into the kitchen garden until they stood by the little building. Anne relaxed.

'Did you get my message?'

'The raid on Lisheen on Monday? Yes, thanks you're a pal. How did you hear?'

'Some Auxie officers came round for drinks, and one of them told me.'

'Good news for us, though. I think we'll be able to give them a warm welcome.'

'I'm glad you came. I had no way of contacting you. Where are you staying?'

'You know Martin's farm? Four miles from here, over by Clonmoyle. But I keep on the move. Never stay more than a couple of nights.'

'How can I contact you again?'

'You can't, I'm afraid. Too risky if anyone noticed you. But I'll come and see you now and then.'

'I don't like it. Suppose there was something urgent?' Cathal thought.

'Maybe send Vere down to Tom Moore in the village.'

'Rather.' Vere was there with them.

'Cathal, he is to be kept out of it. Absolutely.'

'Oh, Anne!' That was her brother.

'I understand how you feel but he's more inconspicuous, don't you see? No one would suspect if they saw him in the village.'

'Absolutely not.'

Silence.

'Well, anyway, listen, we've got to fix a time to come for the stuff in your cold store.'

'You could take it now.'

'No – it'll need half a dozen of us. And I need a couple of days to round up the lads. That's why I was hoping Vere ...'

'I told you!'

'Oh, Anne ...'

'It'd be all right just to run a message, Anne,' Cathal said coaxingly.

'Cathal! I've said it once, and I'm not repeating it.'

'Well, yourself then. You could get a message to Mickey Flynn in the village. And – can you remember this – Danny Mount at Derryvane; Pat Twomey over at Kilmichael –'

'Who?'

'I know him, Cathal,' Vere whispered.

'Will you shut up!' Anne whispered back vehemently.

'Sean McEvoy at Lee's farm down by Toone bridge. That'll do for now. Let 'em know we'll pick up the stuff the day after tomorrow, Thursday morning. Rendezvous at Castle Masters two a.m.'

'Very well. You can leave it to me.'

After Cathal had disappeared into the darkness, and Vere was turning away towards the house, Anne clutched his shoulder.

'Now listen to me, Vere. I'll tell you this for the last time: you're to have nothing to do with this, now or ever. I don't care what Cathal says, you're to stay out of it.'

'Oh, for goodness' sake, what does it matter? As a matter of fact, he came to see me last night.'

Danny grunted. Anne could see the thoughts turning in his mind – what business had Cathal creeping round to see Anne Hunter in the middle of the night? Why bring her into it? She felt irritated already, and there were others to contact, other Danny Mounts waiting. She turned to go.

'I've got to get on. Good morning.'

'Good morning.' Danny turned again to forking the hay as Anne made her way back across the hay lying in the field.

In the middle of the field, with a distant skylark far above her, the smell of the hay in her nostrils and a heavenly blue sky overhead, she could feel nothing but irritation. Danny Mount had not scrupled to hide his contempt, his superiority, his suspicion of her. A woman – why bring them into it? Women were nothing but trouble, they weren't dependable, they were hysterical; they could be cajoled, flattered, worked upon; they broke down under questioning, they were unsafe. Better to have nothing to do with them! Anne knew all the arguments.

She retrieved her bicycle and pedalled hard down the *bohreen* in a effort to restore her good humour.

Early on Thursday morning she was down again in the garden to quieten the dogs. It was a cloudy night, and pitch dark. She stood waiting by the cold house some time. The Volunteers had made their rendezvous at Castle Masters at two a.m. and it would take about forty-five minutes to get up to the house.

There was a movement in the darkness, the tap of a boot against stone, and she was alert.

'Cathal?'

'Anne? It's me.' He was there in the darkness near her. 'I've left the lads over the wall for the moment.'

'It'd be best to leave them there,' she said. 'We can pass the stuff over to them. Economise on the noise.'

'Good girl. I've got a closed lantern.'

They went into the cold store, and Cathal opened his lamp. It made a faint spluttering sound as the water dripped on to the acetylene. He was looking pale. He wore a tweed jacket and had leather gaiters round his legs. Anne had dressed.

They unwrapped the old sacks. The guns were still there.

'Phew! I was terrified someone was going to find them. Where's Vere? We could do with another pair of hands.'

'I've left him with the dogs.'

They were kneeling together side by side, unwrapping the rifles. The metal gleamed in the uneven light of the bicycle lamp.

There was a movement behind them in the darkness. Anne's head whipped round.

'Who's there?' she said in a fierce whisper.

'It's me.'

It was Vere.

'I thought I told you to stay with the dogs!'

'The dogs are fine,' he said in a loud whisper. 'But you're bound to need some help.'

'Go back this instant!'

'No, it's all right, Anne.' Cathal put his hand on her arm. 'He can help us.'

She turned to Cathal again, the three of them squatting over the pile of weapons in the uneven light of the acetylene lamp.

'Well, anyway, we've got to decide where to hold the ambush, haven't we? Have you made up your mind yet?'

'No.'

'I thought not. I was down on the Macroom road yesterday and I think the best place would be just at that bend in the road below Sheehey's farm. You could dig a trench ...'

'Grand.'

'They'll come at dawn, I expect. How many men can you get?'

'Fifteen at least.' Cathal thought for a moment. 'Could you get a message to Sean Deasey in Macroom – you know, at the Victoria Hotel? He's a groom there. Great lad – one of the best.'

'I know him. He's our cook's son.'

'Good. Anyway, come on, let's get the stuff out.'

They picked up two rifles each and carried them down the path through the vegetable garden to the far wall.

'Tom?' Cathal whispered.

'I'm here.'

'They're coming over.'

96

Cathal reached the guns over the wall and the three of them went for more.

For half an hour they went back and forth, ferrying the weapons. As they were in the cold store, picking up the last of the Mills bombs, Anne turned to Vere.

'Nip back and check the dogs are happy, then get in.'

'Oh Anne –'

'*Go on*. We've nearly finished here.'

Vere disappeared into the darkness, and Anne followed Cathal down to the wall for the last time. But then, as he was about to climb back over, she realised she wouldn't see him again until after the ambush. On impulse she said, 'Cathal, you will take care, won't you?'

Halfway up the wall, he turned back and grinned.

She reached up and touched his arm. 'Be careful, whatever you do. Remember your mother.'

He reached down, took her hand and squeezed it. 'Thanks, Anne. I know you mean well, but there's a war on. Mam understands that.'

He winked at her and was gone.

There was something very vulnerable, very precious about him at that moment.

She returned to the stables where Vere was with the dogs.

'It's okay. They've all gone. I thought I told you to stay with the dogs?'

'Yes, it was typical – leave me there while you and Cathal carried the guns.'

'I'm bigger than you,' she said impatiently.

'I'm as strong as you, I bet.'

'You're not.'

'Want to bet? We'll have a contest.'

'Tomorrow. Come on, we must get back indoors.'

She was wondering how to get that message to Sean Deasey in Macroom. Perhaps she could get Lewis to give her a lift in – or would that be too risky? How could she lose him in the town? Unless they took Vere with them: he could pretend to show Lewis some good fishing spots along the river while she ran in to the hotel. That seemed the best idea. She could easily think of an excuse.

\*

The following morning she want to her brother's room early.

'Now listen, Vere. I've got to get a message to someone in Macroom.'

She ran over the plan with him. Vere sat on his bed in his pyjamas, his eyes alert, wriggling with excitement.

'Just make it look natural, all right?'

'It's about the ambush on Monday, isn't it?'

'Yes.'

'Won't old Steptoe get a surprise! I should like to see his face when the Volunteers open up! He won't know what hit him! What a hoot!'

'It is not a hoot! When are you going to understand? This is deadly serious. People will be killed.'

'Of course they will. I'm not stupid. You think I don't know anything, don't you? Honestly, Anne, I'm sick of you. I'm grown up now, you know, and yet you always treat me like a child.'

'That's because you *are* a child.'

'I'm not – and I'll prove it. I bet I'm stronger than you!'

Vere threw himself upon her on the bed and they wrestled for a moment until he had her on her back with her arms pinned back among the disordered bedclothes.

'Let me go!'

'See – I *am* stronger than you!'

'Let me *go*!'

'Admit I'm stronger than you.'

'Vere, will you get *off*!'

'Not until you admit I'm stronger than you.'

She struggled but he was too much for her.

'All right, you're stronger than me. Now get off.'

He whooped with laughter and leapt off her and across the room in his pyjamas.

'Serves you right for being so bossy.'

'I'm bossy because I'm older and cleverer than you.'

As she was rolling off the bed, a hard pointed object beneath the blanket jabbed into her right hip. She fished among the blankets, and in a moment had brought out a Webley pistol.

'What's this?'

Vere made a lunge for it. 'Give it to me!'

Anne turned from him and climbed off the bed, examining the pistol. It was like her father's, a standard military model.

'Where did you get this?'

'Give it to me!'

'Vere! Where –' Then she understood. 'Did you take this from the cold store?'

He stopped shouting, looking at her uncomfortably.

She felt cold. 'God, you utter, utter fool! What were you thinking of?'

Vere was silent, watching her closely. Anne looked at the pistol, then at her brother, trying to decide what to do.

'Can you imagine what Father would say if he found this?'

'He wouldn't. Give it to me. It'll be all right, Anne, I promise. I was keeping it in Kaiser Bill's box. Look.'

Vere fished out an old cardboard box from beneath the bed, once the home of a white rat. She didn't hear him. Her whole body felt cold, numb, as the consequences of discovery unfolded themselves. She bit her lip.

'I'll have to get this to Cathal as soon as possible.'

'Oh, Anne!'

'Vere!' she hissed angrily. 'Are you completely stupid? Just try and think what would have happened if Father had found this, and thank your lucky stars it was me instead. Now go down to breakfast.'

She was leaving the room.

'What are you going to do with it?'

'Never you mind.'

'Oh, Anne!'

'Go down to breakfast!'

In her own room she pondered for some time the safest place to store the pistol, and eventually wrapped it in a blanket, unused in summer and lying at the bottom of her wardrobe. It would not be touched for months, and long before that she would have contrived a means of returning the pistol to Cathal.

# Chapter Eleven

Lewis was perfectly amenable to a trip into Macroom, and went out to 'wind up the Old Beast', as he put it.

As Anne was in her room, running a comb through her hair, she stopped and looked at herself in the mirror, still thinking about the pistol.

Then quite different thoughts ran through her head. She felt a surge of joy and remembered she loved Lewis. This morning the feeling was certain in her. He said she was beautiful, and must mean it, she was sure. After all, he had seen her – she reminded herself – he had seen her naked.

Now was going out with him in his car. She must look her best for him. She was suddenly flustered, and wrenching open a drawer, pulled out a bright vermilion scarf and tied it round her hair. Did it make her more pretty? She straightened her dress. She wished her breasts were bigger. Was she too tall? If only she were somehow more voluptuous. How could Lewis, how could any man, possibly find her attractive? Father preferred Pippa. Why couldn't she have been soft and cuddly like her sister? Oh, damn, there wasn't time to think of that now. She took a last look in the mirror, adjusted the bright scarf round her hair and ran downstairs.

Lewis was sitting in the car outside the front door. He seemed lost in thought, and didn't notice her immediately as she emerged into the bright sunlight. Then, with what seemed a slight effort, he smiled. Vere was sitting in the back.

'That's a pretty scarf,' Lewis said, as Anne got in beside him.

'Thank you.'

There was something slightly preoccupied about him this

100

morning, she noticed immediately. She was so accustomed to Lewis's being attentive that it came as a shock to find him distracted. She could feel herself colouring up straightaway. She trembled now to think how dependent she was on his mood. And how she had come to take his attention for granted. She had thought about him constantly over the last few days, allowed day-dreams of them together by the bathing pool to linger in her thoughts. The sense of a cloud passing over the sun, even for a moment, made her nervous.

But as Lewis slipped the car into gear, and she felt again that divine feeling of force in her back, thrusting her along; as they drove down the lane, through the village and then out on to the road to Macroom, the thick hedges, the wild fuchsia, and the brilliant yellow gorse flying by in an intoxicating blur, she relaxed and couldn't help smiling.

'Wizard car, Lewis,' Vere said, leaning forward between them.

'Glad you approve, old bean.'

'Must have cost a packet.'

'Not a penny, as a matter of fact. Your sister will tell you sometime.'

Vere dug her in the shoulder. 'What does he mean?'

'As Lewis said, another time.'

Lewis didn't seem talkative and they drove for some time in silence, until Vere leant forward again.

'Oh, I say, Lewis, you know what you were saying about the Bolsheviks on the Caspian Sea? You never finished telling me –'

'What? Oh, yes.' Lewis appeared to relax at last. 'Well, it was a very tricky problem, Vere, as you can imagine. One false move and they would have sent the whole rig sky high, and done God knows what damage to the others. Of course it was absolutely essential to keep the whole thing intact until after the conference had ended.'

'Why?'

'Obvious, my dear chap. British interests. We have a treaty with Persia to exploit their oil. The rig stood out in disputed waters, you see, and the Bolshies had laid claim to it and festooned the whole thing with dynamite. Needed very careful handling, as you can imagine.'

101

'So what did you do?'

'Well, they had left a gang of men out on the rig, with instructions to blow it up if they saw us approaching –'

He paused. After a moment, Vere interrupted impatiently.

'Go on.'

'What – where was I?'

'About the Bolsheviks!'

But by now they were driving into Macroom.

'Looks like we'll have to finish the story later, old chap.'

'Oh, Lewis! It's not fair! You must tell me – what happened?'

They came to a halt opposite the castle. Anne became tense, and her voice sounded to her harsh and unconvincing.

'Mother has asked me to get a couple of things for her – boring women's things. Why don't you go down to the river with Vere, Lewis? He'll show you where the best fishing is. I'll come and find you when I've finished.'

It sounded wooden, but Vere was swiftly beside them, his eyes bright.

'Yes, come on, Lewis.' He tugged at the man's sleeve. 'You can go on with the story. What happened to the Bolshies on the oil rig?'

Lewis appeared mildly surprised, but turned amiably away with Vere, and she heard him take up the story again. 'It needed careful planning, old chap. I decided to pick my very best men –'

She watched them set off across the little square and down the short street beside the castle towards the river. Then she turned quickly across the square towards the Victoria Hotel. It was a large square building in dingy stucco with a carriage entrance to the left-hand side. Sean Deasey was a groom – he should be in there somewhere.

As she walked under the arch there was a strong smell of horses and stables, the unmistakable smell of urine. There was no one about, though she could hear horses stamping and shifting in the stables.

She looked about. There was a man at a window. He looked out.

'Can I help you?'

'I'm looking for Sean Deasey.'

'He's having his dinner.'

'I want to speak to him.'

Her tone was brisk and authoritative, but he nodded amiably.

'Hold on then.'

He disappeared, and after a minute in which she stood staring idly up at the windows of the hotel, a slovenly youth in filthy old riding breeches came out, wiping one hand across his mouth.

'Oh, it's you, Miss Hunter.'

'Hullo, Sean. And for goodness sake, don't call me Miss Hunter. My name is Anne.'

He grinned sheepishly.

'I've a message from Cathal. It's to be on Monday morning early. You're to rendezvous at Castle Masters at midnight on Sunday and bring a spade.'

'Good work.'

As Anne left she wondered about the whole business. Was the future of Ireland to be entrusted to the likes of Sean Deasey, an awkward country boy, good with horses, but ill educated and provincial, a pious Catholic boy in the grip of his mother and his priest? Yet Sean was as brave as a hawk, and would lay down his life for his country without a second's hesitation.

What would Ireland be like when she was free? There would be no room for herself, Anne suddenly realised. No room for Protestants, no room for English-educated young ladies. She was redundant even now. The Volunteers didn't want her. Cathal only confided in her because they had known each other all their lives. It would be a land fit for Sean Deasey and Danny Mount and the others. The thought sobered her as she made her way into the newsagent's to buy a magazine, and then down to the river.

At first she couldn't see Lewis and Vere, then she made out Lewis further down on the other side talking to someone. As she walked down towards them there was no sign of Vere, but she realised Lewis was talking to Captain Steptoe.

He and Steptoe were looking up into a tall beech tree, pointing and calling out something. Captain Steptoe saw her and said something to Lewis who looked round and waved. Anne did not change her pace. She would not hurry for Captain Steptoe. At last, in the late-morning sunshine, she came up with them.

'Your brother has just won a bet, Miss Hunter,' Steptoe said with his greasy grin, cigarette in hand as usual. He pointed upwards.

Anne looked up and as she did so heard Vere's voice from far above.

'Anne! Here, look! They bet me half a crown I couldn't climb to the top. Look! Oo-er, nearly fell!' He laughed, a childish gleeful laugh, weaving about in the slender branches at the very top. 'Only joking!'

'Oh, for heaven's sake, Vere, come down at once!'

'No cause for alarm, Miss Hunter. Boys will be boys, you know.'

'And trees will be climbed, I'm afraid,' Lewis said.

Anne was always instinctively careful for Vere when they were out together. Although he was now fourteen and had outgrown her control, the habit did not desert her.

'Vere, will you come down!'

'Come and fetch me!' He swayed back and forth at the very summit of the tree.

She bit her lip. She could not rebuke two grown men much older than herself but she would dearly have liked to. What business did they have sending him up such a high tree?

'Vere, come down this second!'

'I'm the King of the castle!' her brother sang, swaying back and forth, ever more dangerously.

Captain Steptoe laughed, and Anne's patience snapped.

'Honestly, how stupid can you get? Lewis, what possessed you to send him up there? Have you no sense?'

He looked carefully into her eyes for a moment and saw the anxiety there.

'Sorry, old girl,' he said softly, then looked up. 'Vere you can come down now. You've won the bet.'

Captain Steptoe, impervious to anyone else's mood, was smirking still.

At last Vere reached the lowest branch and dropped lightly on to the grass. Anne went quickly to him and smacked his ear.

'Don't ever do that again!'

'Ow!' he dodged away out of range. 'Stop it, Anne. It was all right, Lewis said it was –'

'Anne, stop! It really was my fault, he's right.'

She stopped, exasperated and suddenly deflated. But now Vere reacted.

'Yes, see? And anyway, I've climbed thousands of trees, so you don't need to be so crusty about it – Cristabel!'

Anne swung quickly round on him.

'What?'

Vere danced away from her.

'Cristabel, dear Cristabel – I know how much you like your favourite name.'

'Vere, I've warned you –'

'What are you doing to do, then? Have me arrested?'

Lewis was watching Anne with interest and she could feel his attention. At this moment she could have died from shame and embarrassment. It was as if she were condemned to be forever humiliated and ridiculed in front of Lewis by Vere. He was like some malevolent medieval imp who would not stop tormenting her. The presence of the two men constrained her; otherwise she would have run after Vere, as she had done so often throughout their childhood, and seized him by the ear until his eyes watered and he begged for mercy.

As it was she turned abruptly back up the river bank towards the bridge.

'I'll see you back at the car.'

But Lewis had already signalled to Vere who immediately fell silent, and after a second she felt Lewis's hand on her arm.

'Anne, it was all my fault. Don't go so fast. It's all right really.'

She could not bring herself to look at him, could only feel her heart beating violently.

'I ought to get back,' she said quietly, still not looking at him.

'All right.' He turned to the others. 'Come on, Vere. Cheerio, Steptoe.'

Steptoe waved and turned away, and they made their way up towards the bridge.

'Anyway, what were you talking to that reptile for?' she said crossly, not looking at Lewis.

'Nothing – we just happened to bump into him on the bank there.' He paused. 'Did you get your errands done?'

'What? Oh – yes. Thank you.' She still seethed with irritation. She had been thinking of Lewis before they left that morning, wondering what he was thinking about her. She had put on the vermilion scarf. It has been as if she were looking forward to some – what? – some event, or development in their relationship; there was anticipation and nervousness. Instead of which all the time there had been Vere, that anarchic spirit of disorder, to torment her and muddle everything. She was churned up inside, irritated that Lewis, instead of seeing a poised and confident young woman, had seen only an anxious and shrewish scold.

He showed no sign of it, however. Unlike hers, his voice had never risen above a measured conversational tone. Whatever was happening or being said, whoever he was talking to, Lewis never altered his manner; he was always at ease, rooted in himself. Through her irritation and confusion she was dimly aware of this.

They returned to the car and drove home in a subdued mood. Little or nothing was said. Vere was aware that he had gone too far, had offended Anne more than he should, and could have said sorry, except that he didn't know how. He felt himself again the junior, the child among adults, and realised that his sister, with whom he had played and quarrelled through the years of childhood, had explored the mountainsides, had fished and swum, had now, by the mysterious process of adulthood, grown away from him, and his fooling and horseplay, his teasing, was actually a last attempt to hold her back in the world of childhood they had shared but which she had already left, and which he was on the brink of leaving too.

Which was why that evening after dinner, as the shadows of the summer evening lengthened, and Lewis suggested a stroll down to the river, he felt constrained, and remained silent while Anne looked up from a magazine she had been reading and casually said she'd come. Her parents made no sign of moving, so she and Lewis went out, across the gravelled space

106

in front of the house, past the rhododendrons, and took the path down through the fields towards the river.

The sky was still bright, but the shadow of the mountains was already creeping down across the valley towards the river. Somewhere a blackbird sang, and there was a warm musky smell from the grasses and wild flowers after the long hot day.

Neither spoke. Anne walked ahead, a straw hat in one hand, the other brushing idly across the top of the long grass. She felt it too, caressing her bare legs. It was the very highest point, the peak of summer when days seemed endless, with evenings that went on till nearly midnight as if darkness had been almost banished from the world for a brief spell.

They came to the river bank and walked along it, still silent, neither wishing to break the magical atmosphere. Beside them the river glided, silent and mysterious, only interrupted sometimes by little gurgles and eddies in the steady even flow. There would be a 'plop' and a fish would break the surface to snatch a fly that had skimmed too close. On the opposite side she noticed the expanding V-shaped waves, the little shiny nose and bright eyes of a water rat making his way sedately along in the lee of the bank. The warm air caressed her skin, but there would be an unexpected sour breath from the river sometimes.

Neither spoke. At first she didn't notice, only conscious of the summer evening in its magical loveliness, her attention caught by a clump of rowans, their red berries and fluttering leaves golden in the evening light, or the flick of a breeze across the water's surface, the sense of deep silence which seemed only accentuated by these small and irregular interruptions.

But then she did begin to notice it; notice that Lewis wasn't speaking, and it began to be significant, and she wondered why he didn't speak, and then she began to panic. Why didn't he speak? And she did not dare to look at him now, beside her on the river bank. Was he looking at her? She didn't know and couldn't look to find out. The air between them was filled with meaning; something very significant was all around them, binding them together in unspoken intimacy, but she didn't

107

know what it was or how to control it.

They stopped, still without speaking, without looking at one another but together staring down the river where the setting sun, now nearly on the rim of the mountains, was reflected like a path of golden flame in the water.

'Why did he call you Cristabel?' Lewis said softly.

'Why do you suppose?' Her voice seemed quick and harsh. Oh God, the words came out of her mouth quite differently from the way she intended. But she had always hated the name.

'Why?' he said mildly. 'Well, there is one obvious reason –'

'That it's my name?' Her voice was heavy with sarcasm. Oh damn Vere, he should never –

'It's a lovely name.'

'It's a stupid name.' She still had not looked at him. 'It's the stupidest name I ever heard and I hate it. No one ever uses it.'

'They must.'

'What?'

'They must use it. You must insist on people using it. It's a beautiful name – and it suits you much better than Anne. There's something about Anne, something abrupt and dismissive. But Cristabel is full of romance and mystery. It has overtones; it has echoes and memories. It implies more than it actually says. It's a much better name. You must make everyone call you Cristabel.'

His words confused and muddled her again. She hated that name – and for all the reasons he had just stated, because it was vague and imprecise, whereas Anne was just what she wanted to be: clear and sharp. She turned quickly, annoyed.

'Oh, you're so –'

But then she was taken very much by surprise for when she turned Lewis was right behind her, and the golden light of the setting sun was on his face, and there was a look in his eyes that was extraordinary, not like anything she had ever seen before, strong, utterly compelling, and she knew straightaway that she was helpless before him, and he came just a step towards her, as she gazed into the deep mystery of his eyes, and he took her quite deliberately, not quickly or clumsily, but with a certain inevitable power, took her by her shoulders, bare in her summer frock so that she felt a shock right through her as his strong hands took her, and then he kissed her, carefully, slowly and meditatively, never leaving her eyes, and there was nothing, nothing in the whole world she could do about it.

Why did she always feel so naked before him, as if he saw her in her entirety, saw her as he had seen her at the bathing pool, all of her, and she could not hide from him? Her heart was hammering, her chest was tight, and she wanted to gasp for air.

He was still holding her firmly, firmly but not too tight, so that deep through her she felt an unspoken sense of security, as if so long as he continued to hold her everything would be all right, and it didn't matter that she felt heady and confused because he was there.

'You must tell them. I insist.'

'All right.' She almost gulped, hypnotised by the nearness of him. He was still looking into her eyes.

'It's strange, you know,' he said after a moment, 'I feel as if I've come to the end of a long, long journey. As if for years and years I'd been wandering over the face of the earth, till I'd got dusty and stained and worn with travel, and was no good for anything anymore and had completely lost sight of what I was looking for. Then I saw you and I just knew what I had been looking for all this time. There you were, as if you had been waiting for me.'

She could not take her eyes from him.

'I have been waiting for you,' she said in a husky voice, though she didn't know she was going to say it till that moment. As he had spoken she had felt a rush of joy – that surging liberating feeling she had had the evening her mother played the Chopin, as if her heart were loosed of a great burden.

She reached up and took his face in her hands, and kissed him gently. There was about their movements a great delicacy, a reverence, each knowing the infinite preciousness of the other and that each had come home to their true self where there was no need for pretence, no need to defend themselves or give a performance or hide in any way but they could be utterly open with one another.

'You're crying.'

'No, I'm not. Not really, it's nothing. Only I'm very glad.'

They were still staring into each other's eyes.

'Cristabel,' he said softly.

'No one but you will ever call me that.'

She would have given herself to him then, thrown off her summer clothes so easily and lain with him on the river bank, but she knew instinctively that that was not what he wanted. Rather everything would take its course, in its appointed time, and they would come to that moment in the proper order.

So they wandered together, hand in hand, not speaking, or if they did, saying unimportant things, or joking, not needing to say anything important because they each knew the important thing now and were secure in it. So they were free as it were like children, free to wander as the long evening shadows closed around them, to speak only as the mood took them, either to speak or be silent.

As they came up towards the house and were about to go through the rhododendrons, he turned to her again and they kissed.

'I'll speak to your father.'

'Yes.'

# Chapter Twelve

As they went in Anne felt curiously constrained, unreal. An enormous thing had just happened, everything was changed for ever, and yet here they were, apparently the same two people walking through a door, walking into the drawing room saying things, random trival things, how warm it was, what a wonderful summer it was, how they hadn't had a summer like it in years, how Lewis must have a quite unreal impression of Ireland, it usually rained all the time – the casual chat with her mother in the dim drawing room where a paraffin lamp burned on a low table and she had been reading.

And all the time Anne was filled with an inexpressible joy, filled with significance, yet no one noticed and it was just like any other evening when she had come in from a walk.

On Sunday they went to church, a small congregation of Protestants in the Church of Ireland church, sitting in the cool dimness and listening as old Canon Blenkinsop preached a sermon on reconciliation and forgiveness, and how they should all pray that Ireland might yet be saved from a civil war, and preserved within the British Empire. How valuable to the Empire were its Irish subjects, Canon Blenkinsop told them, and what a tragedy it was that through the terrible crimes of a few fanatics and hot-heads the country was being plunged into chaos, destruction and murder. Those who lived by the gun would die by the gun, he said, and the British Government had too strong a sense of responsibility to its Irish subjects to abandon them to the mercy of gangs of criminals and murderers. But they must pray that reconciliation and

111

mercy would prevail and a way be found in which all might live together in harmony.

It was a bleak sermon and Canon Blenkinsop himself did not believe it. Anne was inwardly scornful. Not a word had been said about the rights of oppressed peoples, about self-determination. The Irish were to go on as before: 'subjects', so far as Canon Blenkinsop was concerned. Hope and pray was the sum total of his contribution to this great debate, this great struggle for the future of a nation.

Yet sharp as her thoughts were, Anne said nothing afterwards as they went home to Sunday dinner in the morning sunshine. There was now in her a gentleness, a softening, as if she had a great new purpose before her, and her other purpose, although still true and important, was yet somehow less urgent. She was quieter, more tranquil. Her mother noticed it and guessed the reason, though she said nothing.

Vere too was curiously muted, unlike his usual self. Anne noticed it only vaguely, and thought he might be still ashamed of his antics, or else that Lewis had told him to tone down his exuberance.

The day passed away in trivial domestic routine. They drank a glass of sherry, sat down to roast beef, and afterwards idled about in the garden, reading or chatting. Lewis opened the bonnet of the Old Beast so Vere could see the great gleaming engine, and Anne pretended to read a magazine.

She found it increasingly difficult to concentrate. All afternoon the thought grew in her: tonight the Volunteers would be down by Sheehey's farm, digging their trench. Tomorrow early they would be lying in wait for the Auxies from Macroom Castle. Would she hear the shots from here? She couldn't be sure. If she were out of doors she might. Her own room did not face that way. In any case she had no idea what time the Auxies would be coming. They might come at dawn, or they might not. They might have some reason for changing the date. They might not come till the evening. She just didn't know.

So the day wore away and when she went to bed she felt in a curious state of limbo – waiting. For Lewis; for the inevitable development of their lives together; and for tomorrow when the news would come of the ambush. She thought:

what of Cathal? Was it possible he might be killed? A shiver of cold fear passed through her. But it still seemed unreal. She couldn't imagine him dead. Everything seemed so tranquil here, so boring and domestic, yet tomorrow messengers would come for her father. Colonel Hunter the magistrate would be sent for and would have to go, perhaps if things had gone wrong and Cathal and the others had been captured, to sit in judgement on them, and commit them for trial on a charge of high treason. It all seemed still unreal, yet she was tense with uncertainty and fears for Cathal's safety.

So many thoughts ran through her mind that she feared she wouldn't sleep. Yet she did fall asleep as she normally did, and slept quite soundly, and woke in the morning. And her first thought as her eyes opened was of a joyful feeling of love for Lewis, and a wonderful warmth of certainty that they were to be together. So she sprang out of bed, light with energy, and washed herself and towelled her body vigorously, feeling clean and alive and tingling. And she chose her frock carefully, wanting to look pretty for him, and put a ribbon in her hair.

As the family assembled for breakfast, were all seated round the table and Bridget was setting the teapot and toast on the table, only Vere was late down. They went on eating, Bridget brought in bacon and eggs, but still Vere did not appear. At last, when they were nearly finished, Hugh, who normally expected all his family to breakfast together, told Anne to go and kick her brother out of bed.

But his bed was empty. She was puzzled. It had been slept in, but was quite cold. His pyjamas were there. She couldn't think where he could be. He didn't usually get up before the others – in fact, she had often had to turn him out before. She went downstairs.

'He's not there.'

Hugh was puzzled.

'Have you any idea where he is?'

'None.'

'Well, if he chooses to miss breakfast that's his affair. But I can't have the table laid all morning for him to come in at his own convenience. You can clear away now, Bridget.'

Hugh seemed to give it no more thought, but as she walked

out of the room the thought struck Anne like a violent blow on the head. Was it possible? Was Vere down at Sheehey's farm? An agitation seized her, a horrid dread, as if her veins were full of writhing snakes. It couldn't be possible. But it could just be. The moment she thought of it, she knew that was what had happened. She went quickly out of the front door into the warm sunshine and round towards the stables.

Lewis touched her arm.

'Anne,' his voice was calm, authoritative, 'we'll go together. We'll take the car.'

She could not think. There was only a blank white fog where her mind should be. They must just get there, and see that Vere was all right.

Lewis drove the great car down the rutted lane, driving it as if by force of will, regardless of bumps and turns, as if he knew exactly what was on her mind and was driven by the same blind urgency.

They swung into the village. It was full of people. Army lorries were parked everywhere, unevenly, at awkward angles, here and there, as if they had raced into the village and jerked to a halt anywhere. There were soldiers everywhere, in full battle-dress, their long rifles with the bayonet fixed on, and officers walking quickly back and forth, shouting orders. The villagers were standing among them, watching in a dim confusion.

Lewis was about to force the car through the village but a soldier immediately waved him to one side. Lewis pulled the car over and stopped just in front of Shanahan's Bar, now boarded up.

'What's the matter, Private?' he said calmly as the man came up.

'Road's closed, sir.'

'What's happened?'

'Not allowed to say, sir.'

'I see. Where's your commanding officer?'

The soldier looked around uncertainly. 'He should be here –'

'Anne, this is an emergency. You wait here and I'll be back as quick as I can.'

'I'm coming too.'

'No, really my dear. Better not.' He laid a hand on her arm, a strong hand that told her straightaway to do as he said. She sat in the car but could not speak. Lewis got out quickly and walked up through the village and she saw him after a moment talking to an officer. She did not dare confront her own feelings; did not dare ask herself what was up there at the other end of the village by Sheehey's farm. She sat in a frozen, atrophied state, emotionless, frightened to think for what might come, frightened to ask herself all the questions. Where Cathal was; where Vere was. Whether he was safe.

Lewis had left the officer and was running up through the village away from her. Oh God, what had happened? Lewis never ran, he was always so calm and orderly. Why was he running? She sat in the car feeling useless, forced to wait.

She waited. Time passed. The soldiers passed and repassed. Someone started up a lorry in a great roar and manoeuvred it round in the village street, and soldiers got in the back. There was a wooden frame with chicken wire fixed up over the back, so bombs or hand grenades could not be thrown in. Soldiers scrambled in, and the lorry roared off down the road behind her.

An ambulance arrived, and disappeared up through the village. Anne could not wait any longer. She got down from the car and crossed to a group of villagers. She knew them all.

'Mr Kelleher, what's happened?'

'Oh, good morning to you, Miss Hunter.' He touched his greasy old hat. 'Well, by all accounts there's been a great battle up there at Sheehey's farm beyond. There's been the military coming and going through the village now these two hours.'

'Gracious.' She tried to sound calm. 'And who were they fighting?'

'Well, no one seems to know. Some say 'twas a Volunteer ambush but I don't see how that could very well be, seeing the weight of soldiers here now.' He shook his head. ''Tis a bad business, Miss Hunter. Please God no one has been killed.'

'It'll be a miracle if they weren't.'

If Cathal had tried to take on this force he would have been annihilated. She had never seen so many troops.

'Two hours, you said?' It was a little after half-past eight now. That would make it half-past six this morning. 'Did you hear anything?'

'Oh, yes. There was a deal of gun-fire around ... what time would it have been, Sean?'

''Twas before seven this morning, and there was a great convoy came through from the south, and the next thing we heard was gun-fire – on the road there beyond.'

Anne was mystified. Why would they come from the south? They were coming from Macroom – from the north. Something had gone very wrong. With this number of troops, the Volunteers would have been massively outnumbered. But if they were outnumbered, policy was clear: they would retreat. The Volunteers could not afford to lose any men or weapons. If they weren't sure of winning they would retreat and await another opportunity. But if there had been gun-fire then there had been a battle.

'And did it sound much of a fight, Mr Kelleher? There seem to be an awful lot of soldiers here this morning.'

How did she manage to sound so calm?

Mr Kelleher sucked in his breath.

'Well now, I'd say it *was* quite a battle, wouldn't you, Sean?'

The other people nodded, standing here in the sunshine, hands in their pockets, staring glumly at the ground.

'Quite a battle I'd say. They were firing a good twenty minutes.'

'Twenty minutes sure. Maybe longer.'

'And all the time there were tenders rattling up through the village.'

Anne went cold. She couldn't keep this up much longer.

''Twas as if every lorry in the County Cork was in it this morning. And ambulances – there's six come through now, to my knowledge.'

'Oh God.' She couldn't help herself. And if Vere – where was Lewis?

But now she saw him walking down through the village with a British officer. He wasn't hurrying and his hands were by his sides. She knew something had happened and ran up to meet him.

He took her hand and held it tight.

116

'Anne, this is Major Brownlow, second battalion the Essex Regiment from Cork.' He turned to the soldier who touched his cap to her.

'Anne, get in the car and I'll explain.' He nodded to the major and they got into the car. The officer signalled to a soldier; Lewis put the car into gear and began driving slowly through the village. He was staring ahead.

'Anne,' he said softly, not looking at her. He was silent for a moment. She said nothing. She knew now what he was going to say.

'Anne, think of the worst thing that could happen. The very worst.'

'Oh God.' Her throat was tight, husky. 'He's not dead?'

Lewis nodded very slightly, still looking ahead.

'Where is he?'

'Just up here. Outside the village. One of the villagers identified his body.'

Oh God, that word. His body.

More lorries, standing about in the road all at odd angles, chaos, soldiers everywhere. Ambulances too, their doors open. She saw soldiers sitting by the side of the road while nurses in blue and white with red crosses on the breast of their uniforms were bandaging them. Men with fresh white bandages round their heads, men stripped to the waist and bandages round their shoulders and chests.

Lewis slowed the car. Ahead of them along the side of the road were what for a stupid moment she thought were old blankets thrown down; but with a sickening jolt she understood they were dead bodies covered by army blankets.

There was a kind of dizziness in her. She was afraid that when she got out she might stumble or fall.

Lewis had stopped the car.

'Show me,' she said hoarsely.

He looked at her for a moment and then walked ahead of her. A soldier was standing guard over the blanket-shrouded figures. Lewis said something to him. She didn't hear. She followed Lewis, sleep-walking; this wasn't real.

He knelt by one of the bodies. Anne knew it already. He drew back the blanket. Vere, asleep. Incredible, he was asleep. She just had to touch him, shake his shoulder, and his eyes would open, he would see her, there would be a grin of devilment on his face.

Lewis was kneeling by the body, looking down. He wouldn't look up, wouldn't face her. She was staring at Vere. Why didn't he wake up?

'They said it would have been instantaneous. Shattered the spine.'

A shudder ran through her.

'I can't find anyone who actually saw him fall. They found the body after the others had got away.'

'Got away.' Her voice was hollow, empty.

'Apparently they retreated when they saw the reinforcements coming.'

Reinforcements. It meant nothing to her.

'They said we can take Vere home now.'

How comforting that sounded. Take him home now, her little brother. Take him home. Why couldn't she weep? Why not cry aloud, why not shriek, curse, groan? Why couldn't she throw herself on his body and pour out her grief? Why did she just stand here stiff, unspeaking, stunned with disbelief?

Lewis stood up and summoned two soldiers. They came forward, alert, precise, stiff with military discipline. It occurred to her that they must have practised this. Had lessons in lifting dead bodies. They lifted Vere and the blanket half fell off him. It was awkward, the awkwardness of reality, the reality of death.

Vere was laid carefully along the back seat of the car. Lewis went away, crossed to another officer who held a clip board. She didn't believe it: Lewis was signing his name. Signing for the body.

He climbed in beside her. He still had not looked at her. He put the engine into gear and swung the long bonnet of the car round in the road and drove back into Lisheen. Neither could look at the other; neither could speak. She made herself look back, look at Vere on the back seat, covered with the blanket. She reached over and pulled back the blanket to see his face again. The head was lolling at an awkward angle. Unnatural. He couldn't have lain like that. He would have woken up. That thing on the back seat, that wasn't Vere any more; it was

118

a thing that looked like Vere, but wasn't him. Vere had gone. She pulled the blanket over his face.

'Anne,' Lewis said quietly, not looking at her, 'when we get back, better let me go in first and speak to your father.'

Her mind was blank. Tell Father? What should she tell Father? Tell him the truth: that she had allowed Vere to become involved in the Volunteers; she who had been so enthusiastic, so excited, had allowed it. And now he was dead. Tell him that.

'It's my fault,' she said, not looking at him. 'I'll tell him.'

'No. Let me go in first. To prepare him. Then he can break the news to your mother.'

They were driving up the *bohreen*, slowly, carefully; they didn't want to disturb Vere. It was all unreal.

# Chapter Thirteen

Lewis pulled the car to a standstill in front of the house. In the morning sunshine there was a stillness, a tranquillity. Another morning like all the others, sunny, wisteria hanging in abundant clusters against the front of the house. Upstairs Bridget was singing as she made the beds.

But not like any other morning. Everything was changed for ever. Lewis went in and Anne sat still, frozen, unable to think or feel.

She waited. The sun was warm on her neck. She couldn't move, only noted it by a curious detached observation, as if she were really somewhere else, watching herself sitting here in this car with the sun on her neck, and Vere lying behind her, dead.

Hugh came out followed by Lewis. He did not notice her but looked over the side of the car, saw the body, and reached in to move the blanket from his son's face. He showed no expression. He stared at it a long time then looked up, distracted, and said, 'We'd better have him brought inside.'

Anne was watching him; when at last he looked at her she saw a grey bleakness in his face. She could not move. They looked at one another, neither speaking, neither expressing any emotion, bereft of the means of expressing it.

'I'd better tell your mother,' he whispered and went into the house. For the first time she looked at Lewis. He would not meet her eyes and continued to stare towards the door, implacable, rigid, as if he were ashamed of her, as if there were nothing between them. She got out of the car, moved round it and tentatively towards him. He did not move, still did not acknowledge her. It was as if they were strangers.

Now her mother hurried out.

'Anne – where?'

She gestured into the car. As Claire looked in her hand went to her mouth. 'Vere!' She wrenched open the car door and was pulling at the body, turning it over, taking it awkwardly in her arms as it lolled across the seat. She shrieked: 'Vere! Anne – how? Oh my God . . .'

Hugh was behind her. He took her shoulders.

'Later, my dear.'

She squirmed in his arms as he drew her gently back. He looked at Anne, and she hurriedly came round to the other side of her mother. Claire would not let go of the body, hanging now at an unseemly angle over the car seat, but they gradually got her away.

'Later, my dear,' Hugh said quietly. 'We'll hear all about it. Now we'll take him upstairs.'

How comforting that sounded. As if they could just put Vere to bed and then in a little while he would wake up and everything would go on. But when would she start to feel? When would she cry out? When would she weep?

As Anne held Claire in her arms, sobbing uncontrollably, Lewis helped Hugh carefully to lift the body out of the car, then Hugh carried Vere into the house and upstairs. The others followed him into Vere's room and the bed was stripped, a cover put over it, and the body laid there. The room had never been so full and they all stood round and no one said anything. Claire still sobbed as Anne held her, but the others were silent.

As they laid out the body Anne saw the jagged mark on the side of the chest, the bloody marks on the pullover and shirt; the clean simplicity, the aesthetic unity of his body broken and disfigured.

'Mrs Deasey, will you see about preparing the body and dressing it?' said Hugh. She nodded.

'I'll do it myself,' said Claire, 'my boy –' and she made a gesture towards the body, but Hugh restrained her, and they all filed out of the room.

'Anne, come downstairs,' he said. 'Crawford, excuse us.'

In his study he confronted her. There was nowhere for her

to hide. Nothing she wanted to hide. She accepted the blame. She stood in front of her father, the morning sunlight glinting on the glass-fronted bookcases and old oak settle. She stood upright and open and took upon herself all the blame, told him everything: how she had helped Cathal, how it was through her that Vere had been involved; if she hadn't helped Cathal none of this would have happened and Vere would be alive. It was all her fault.

Hugh listened in disbelief. All this, in his own house, here, his own children. There was no room for anger, justice or punishment. His son's death swamped everything. But his bewilderment was total. He didn't know how to begin to confront what had happened. What to do next, he had no idea. He had never been able to understand the fighting anyway; the violence and destruction reported in the newspapers, the cases that came before him as a magistrate, the randomness of it, as if lives had ceased to have any value.

There had been the case of Constable O'Flaherty six weeks ago, shot dead while riding his bicycle down a country road. Why? Constable O'Flaherty, thirty years in the force, a father of six, liked by everyone, fond of a pint, an easy, kindly man you could trust with your life, murdered in a pointless, futile act of violence. What good could it serve, what good could it do to *anyone*? The villagers had been devastated, the priest had denounced the murderers from the pulpit. Hugh had watched it all in despair, unable to see any way he could help.

Now it had struck his own family and he was numb. Perhaps soon he would be able to feel. But not yet.

And Anne – of course she had always been outspoken but it had just been words, the idealism of a hot-headed youngster. He had never imagined this, that it would come to deeds, to tangible acts with consequences.

Anne kept waiting for him to react. He had to say something, do something. She was responsible, guilty. It was her fault Vere was dead. Father must do something, punish her, anything, so she could be corrected and set straight again. He couldn't just leave her to carry it all alone, all the whole weight of disaster.

Hugh heard her out then sat down slowly, like an old man. Without a word he waved her away. She was dismissed.

As she came out of the room Lewis was standing in the hall looking out of the front door, which was still standing open since Vere had been brought in. He did not turn, did not move, as she passed him and went upstairs.

Mrs Deasey was in Vere's room with Bridget. They were dressing him. There was a bowl of water on the wash-stand with a sponge in it. The water was red. The two women worked calmly and methodically. Mrs Deasey was well used to washing and dressing children.

As they finished, she took the bowl of water and two towels, both blood-stained, and went out, leaving Anne alone.

She sat by her brother in the still room. It was sunny and a warm breeze wafted through the window. A glorious day. She sat still, silent, waiting for something to come, a thought, a feeling. In the long silence only the curtain moved gently, swaying in the breeze. After a while she reached forward to brush away the hair from his forehead, where it had fallen after Mrs Deasey had combed it. But, as she touched his face, she became aware with a shock of the inert, dead weight of his head, and withdrew her hand. Vere was separated from her now.

Oh, the pity of it. If only he would wake up! It would be so easy. He would just open his eyes, glance slyly at her with his wicked grin, ready to tease her. She remembered the many times he had teased her, the many times they had played and squabbled together, the times they had climbed the mountain-side together, fished together, swum together, Vere ... and as the thoughts and memories began crowding back into her mind, the tears were released at last, the doors were opened and everything rushed out at once, her huge grief released in a hot liquid flow like a great flood bursting through. Her mind was empty and her whole body filled with the intense heat of her grief as she wept helplessly and muttered, 'Vere, oh Vere, oh dear, it's me, if only –', half-words and phrases, but really only a great feeling of devastation and loss.

At last the flood subsided and she could see again, wiping her eyes, able again to focus her thoughts, but weak as a rush, good for nothing any more, only empty as if nothing could start again ever, but her life was over for any good she could ever do.

Weak, empty and deflated, she rose from the chair, looked down again at Vere and went out and downstairs. She must go to her mother and comfort her. It would be worse for Claire. She must comfort her now.

She was going downstairs. Lewis, who was still looking out of the door, turned as he heard her on the stairs. She came down into the hall. For a moment they looked at each other.

'I'm leaving now.'

In a low croak, she said, 'Yes.'

'There's nothing I can say or do to help. Only in the way.'

She waited but still felt nothing, only empty and useless. He was looking at her, then stepped forward about to offer his hand. He held it out, and then dropped it again.

'Goodbye then.'

'Goodbye.' She nodded like a sleepwalker.

He went past her, upstairs to his room. She did not look up but went into the drawing room. Claire was alone.

'Where's Father?'

'A car came for him while you were upstairs. He's gone down to the village.'

The two women sat side by side on the sofa. Anne felt as if she were starting her life again from scratch, as it were from a new year one. She had to begin again completely, all new. She would start now. She reached out her hand towards Claire, and the two women held hands, then with a little groan her mother took Anne in her arms and they swayed gently together without speaking.

A little while later they heard the roar of the Old Beast, the crunching of gravel as it drove past the house, and then the sound of the engine dying away down the hillside.

The day passed. Hugh returned. He had had to preside at committal proceedings for the two prisoners who had been taken. Anne did not dare to ask who they were but wondered to herself for the first time whether Cathal were safe.

The day passed. Dinner was served. Claire had gone to bed and Anne sat with her father as the evening light dimmed outside the room. Neither spoke. Dishes were brought in, dishes were carried out, all was hushed. Bridget asked in a whisper whether the colonel would take his coffee in the drawing room, and Anne looked across at Hugh, who looked down at his uneaten dinner and silently shook his head.

She went to her room. She could not sleep. She could not think. She sat on the edge of her bed; she had taken off one sandal and was holding it in her hand, staring out of the window, numb and empty.

There was a faint knock at the door, and Bridget looked in.

'Miss Anne?'

Anne looked slowly round.

'Miss Anne – could you come?' Bridget whispered. ''Tis Mr Donnelly there in the stables below asking could he speak with you?'

She was alert.

'Is he there now?'

'Yes, Miss.'

'I'll come. If anyone asks where I am, say I've gone for a walk.'

'Yes, miss.'

She put on her sandal and went quickly down and out to the stable. It was nearly dark and there was no one about. Inside it was darker still and there was the smell of hay, and the sound of Emperor, her father's hunter, in his stall.

'Anne?' It was Cathal speaking in a whisper. She looked round. He was kneeling with his arm round Mor, stroking the dog.

'Thank God you came.' He looked up at her. He was gaunt in the dim light, his eyes sunken yet glowing with a feverish light. He stroked Mor's neck, and the dog wagged its tail.

'Cathal, tell me what happened.'

She was calm now, seeing his agitation.

'Oh Anne, will you ever speak to me again?'

'Tell me how it happened.'

Cathal stroked the dog's neck, holding his arm round the animal.

'I just had to come and see you, to explain. I can't tell you, when I saw Vere there –'

'Tell me everything, Cathal.'

He was still holding the dog and stroking her in a hypnotic rhythm.

'We had it all planned out. Seventeen of us, everything was ready. We met at Castle Masters at midnight, we all had spades and we dug for four hours, a good big trench across the road, just as we'd planned. It was all ready. Then all the lads deployed in the fields on both sides, everyone found a good place, and I posted Sean Deasey on the road north to give the signal. Every man was armed, ten rounds per man. We'd practised it, I'd drilled them, everything was prepared. Then we waited. It got cold. Five o'clock, six o'clock. We were frozen when the sun came up, just the first rays to warm us. We were stiff sitting there, waiting behind the hedge. Then Sean gave the signal. I passed it on. I couldn't see everybody, some were in the field beyond. My arm was aching with the long wait and my heavy pistol. Then they were there, two Crossley tenders bucketing down the road, and in a moment we opened fire and they slammed to a halt, and we were pumping fire into them.

'But then I saw something was wrong. There was no one in the back. They were empty, but already Pat Twomey and Mickey Flynn were running down towards them and firing away fit to burst. Then there was another big tender coming up, and then – oh, Anne, there was another, and another. By Jesus, there was half a dozen of them. Only they didn't come up with us but stopped up the road and there were troops spilling out and climbing up into the fields, both sides. Jesus, I thought, what's going on? Then Liam Flanaghan away to the right gives a shout and I can hear something, and then there was a tender coming up from the south through the village and another behind that. "By Jesus," says I, "where did they come from?" And there was more still and Tommies all spilling out into the fields.

'I could see if we didn't get out they would nab us all, and I was shouting to the lads to retreat, because, by Jesus Anne, they were coming through the fields towards us, and we were outnumbered, we hadn't a dog's chance. So I gave the word to retreat and we were all coming up the field as fast as we could, and the Tommies were firing and we firing as we retreated. And then – I looked round and there was Vere, right by me. "What in heaven's name?" says I. But he just grinned, Anne, and said he wanted to join the fun and couldn't I give him a gun? "Get to hell out of it," says I, "and that's an order." Honest, Anne, it was chaos. There were Tommies everywhere firing, and I'm firing too, as well as I can, trying to get away, and Vere there by me. And we were running for the hedge, just coming up to it, when he cried out and threw his arms in the air and fell right on his face. Jesus, will I ever forget it? He just cried out once and fell, and I knelt by him, and the Tommies there in the field beyond, and the bullets going by me. I turned him over but, oh God, he was dead. Clean dead, instantaneous. There was nothing I could do, him lying there dead, and the Tommies not two hundred yards away –'

The tears were streaming down Cathal's face now.

'And, oh God, oh Jesus, Anne, what could I do? Him lying there dead and the Tommies on me in one minute? So I had to leave him there in that field. And so help me, Anne, it was the worst thing I ever did –'

He broke down in sobs, still stroking the dog, who looked up into his face and sensed his grief, wanting in her dumb way to comfort him.

There was silence. Anne knelt before him, took his hands from Mor's back and brought him to his feet. He took her in his arms and they clung to each other, weeping together.

'I had to tell you, Anne. I never told him to come; I told him it was strictly against orders. But I had to tell you. I couldn't bear you to think I'd let him come.'

It was an enormous comfort to her to be held in Cathal's arms, and for them to weep together.

Slowly he gathered his composure and they stepped back. They looked into each other's tear-stained faces. He sniffed.

'You don't blame me?'

'You're not to blame, Cathal.' Her voice was filled with tears. 'It was me all the time. I told him and told him, but still he wouldn't listen. It's my fault.'

Cathal drew a long shuddering breath and seemed to take hold of himself. He pulled out his handkerchief, and wiped his eyes and blew his nose.

'Thanks, Anne. You're a real pal. My truest friend.' He drew another deep breath. 'Yes.' He paused again, still trying to get back his strength after the weeping. 'I'll have to move on. They're all after me now.'

'Where will you go?'

'Tipperary, Limerick maybe. There's a good network set up. There'll be plenty of places I can hide out for a bit. What about you?'

'I can't leave my mother and father. I've got to make it up to them. Do what I can to help them.'

'Yes.'

Soon Cathal took his leave, disappearing into the gloom of the garden. After he had gone Anne turned slowly for the house. She felt hollow and inert, as if she would never feel again, yet also enormously comforted that Cathal had come to her and had told her everything, so fully and clearly. He had given her strength, and the memory of it, the memory of him holding her, would help her face what was to come.

# Part Two

# Chapter Fourteen

It was almost dark. She turned at the end of the path, looking back towards the house which was now a large black shape against the last of the light, the oak a looming mass above her. Emotionally drained by her weeping, she was unconscious of the beauty and the stillness of the night, unaware of the warmth of the air, the musky scents of the flowers.

A bat flitted from the tree above her. She turned back up the path, walking slowly as the vast bowl of the heavens above her darkened into night and the stars began to come out.

She stopped and looking up into the darkening sky, drew a long deep breath, hoping, hoping that all might yet be well, and vowing that out of this disaster she would try to pluck some little good, however small and insignificant it might seem to others. Though how she was ever to redeem herself, she had no idea.

Unconscious of time, she walked back and forth on the path, down to the old wall beneath the great oak tree then back up towards the house, arms crossed, breathing slowly, trying to still herself.

As she went inside at last the house was silent and in darkness. Her parents must have gone to bed. She climbed the staircase, listening to her own footsteps, in a state of heightened consciousness. It was as if she were the only inhabitant.

On the landing, on an impulse, she made for Vere's room and opened the door, turning the handle carefully to avoid making any sound. In the dim room the body beneath the sheet was outlined against the last light from the window beyond. Anne stood in the doorway, her hand on the handle, staring at it.

She looked about her: the books above the bed on a shelf, the football boots hanging behind the door, and then as she turned her head, Vere's gramophone standing in the corner, the horn a dark shape, weird in the almost darkness.

It was too much. She closed the door and went to her own room.

She was suddenly awake; gripped as if by freezing iron bands clutching her body. It was true. Vere was dead. And she had done it. She and no one else was responsible.

An irrational desire seized her, making her heart beat fast, to wind back time, to wind it back to the moment when her brother had got out of bed, dressed and gone out of the house. Why had she not heard him? If she had only been awake, if she had gone out and stopped him, if only ...

The house was silent. In the darkness she lay still, tense, her heart still beating rapidly, staring up and wishing, praying, vowing to do anything if only everything could go back to the previous night and she could lie awake listening for Vere, ready to go out and stop him.

Why had it never occurred to her what her brother would do? It was so obvious, anyone could have predicted it, she had seen his enthusiasm, she should have known, have been ready to stop him.

She fell into a light doze, was gradually and intermittently aware of the light beginning to filter into her room. A feeling of helplessness came over her. She had caused this but what could she do to heal the hurt she had caused? How could *she* heal her father's and mother's pain? But, she vowed, if it took the rest of her life, she would stay with them, be with them, help and comfort them.

At last, when it was broad daylight and she heard sounds from the kitchen below, she pulled herself out of bed, sitting on the edge with her face in her hands, utterly drained and despairing as she forced herself to face the new day.

She went to her parents' bedroom; her father had risen but her mother was in bed, eyes closed. Hugh was dressed and fixing a collar stud in place. Anne looked from him to her mother.

'Is she –?'

He nodded. Anne went to Claire.

'Mother?' she whispered.

After a moment she turned her head slowly and opened her eyes a little.

'Hullo, dear.'

'Did you sleep at all?'

'A little.'

'Would you like me to send for Dr O'Malley?'

She shook her head very slightly, smiling faintly.

'I think I'll just stay here for the moment, darling.'

Anne stood and looked uncertainly at her father. He nodded towards the door. They sat together in silence over breakfast, but at the finish Hugh looked at her and asked her to go with him into his study.

Ever since childhood her father's study had been a mysterious and significant place. Important men would arrive in cars, the door would be shut and there would be the deep sound of their voices in grave conference. It held still, even now when she was an adult, a flavour of that masculine authority.

On either side of the fireplace stood glass-fronted bookcases, and in front of the window a desk, on which was stacked, among many other papers, a pile of hand-written sheets – her father's great *History of the Hunter Family*, something which they had all known about for years, something which was to be the definitive work and which she had stared at sometimes, wondering to think their family was so important that a book had to be written specially about them.

The desk stood in front of the window and looked out over the rhododendrons. Before it stood a leather-covered, round-backed chair on wheels which also swivelled. It had been on this chair, on special occasions, that as children they were allowed to sit on their father's knee and be swung round, back and forth.

On the mantelpiece among several framed photographs – of Claire, of Vere and Pippa, and of herself too, as well as one of her father talking to the King, taken years earlier at a review – among letters and some ivory elephants Hugh had brought home from India, stood a pipe rack. As Anne came in and closed the door her father had taken a pipe from this rack, stared at it for a moment, then had second thoughts and put it

133

back. He turned to his desk and put some papers into order, coughed, then looked through the window.

He picked up a paper from the top of a pile and read it. He still had not looked at her. Then, still holding this piece of paper, he turned to her.

'The inquest on Vere will be held tomorrow.'

She stiffened instinctively.

He looked down at the paper again, as if not quite sure how to continue.

'I shall tell the court that no one has any idea how he came to be involved and that it must have been by pure accident. No one will imagine he went down there on purpose.' He looked away. 'Though what they are to imagine, God alone knows.'

She said nothing. There was a long silence as Hugh looked out of the window and then back at her. Anne waited and waited, only wanting him to speak to her, to reassure her that she was not entirely lost, not entirely cast adrift. He turned, grey-faced, still finding it difficult to meet her eyes.

'I shall be lying.'

He paused again.

'And there is another lie I must tell, Anne. I mean, in covering up for you. You have been guilty of an act of treason. Strictly speaking, I should have handed you over to the military authorities.'

He turned away, still finding it difficult to face her, looking instead across the room at a steel engraving on the wall.

'When I first became a magistrate, more than twenty years ago, I took a solemn oath to uphold the rule of law. Do you understand what that means, Anne? The only difference between civilisation and barbarism is the rule of law. If I fail to hand you over to the military authorities, I am denying everything I have stood for. Can you imagine what would be said of me if it became known that I had betrayed my trust to shield a member of my family?'

She felt the blood drain from her face as his eyes at last met hers. Then he heaved a long sigh and looked down again. She waited in silence for him to go on. She understood how hard it was for him to say this and her heart went out to him; she so wanted to go to him, to comfort him in the terrible thing he had to do. She was ready for whatever he had to say, waiting for him to pronounce the penalty and then to absolve her, to free her from guilt, so that she could go on living as a woman, not as a ghost.

'An act of treason,' he repeated. He cleared his throat. 'But since you came to me immediately and told me everything so frankly, I –' he coughed again '– I have decided to take no further action. You will, however, make me a solemn oath that you will never again, under any circumstances, have dealings with the Volunteers.'

He opened a drawer, took out a Bible and held it out. Like a sleepwalker, she received it and held it in her right hand.

'I promise.' Her voice was little more than a croak. And now would he forgive her? Would he take her in his arms? Comfort her, ease this nightmare in which the world lurched around her as if she would never be able to stand straight and free in it again? She held out the Bible uncertainly and her father replaced it in the drawer. Without looking at her he muttered, 'You may go.'

That was it. There was to be no reconciliation, no embrace or tenderness. She was excluded forever from his love.

As she reached the door, he spoke again.

'This will of course, remain a secret between us.'

'You mean, Mother –'

'Your mother knows nothing of this.'

Later that morning the undertakers arrived with the coffin. Anne watched them. They had an unobtrusive, discreet manner, as if they were not really there. She followed them, watching with a fatalistic fascination. Eventually they left and the coffin remained lying on top of the bed, open. Her mother was still in bed.

Later, during the morning, the newspaper arrived. When Anne had a chance to look into it, she found that *The Cork Examiner* made no mention of Vere.

Later still, in the early afternoon, Tony and Pippa arrived. Claire had dressed and was waiting for them in the drawing room, looking washed out and ethereal. Pippa and Tony were already in black.

At first almost no words were spoken as the women

135

embraced. Seeing Pippa, it occurred to Anne that she had hurt her also, that Pippa too was deprived of a brother. How could she lie to her sister? Was she to lie simply to shield herself? To save her own miserable skin?

But then it came to her, that the secret was to be kept not to save her, Anne, but to preserve the family. It was the family which mattered, not one insignificant member of it. It was in the name of the family that she must lie to her own sister.

But later, when Hugh gave the brief, official version of events, Pippa caught her eye and Anne could see that she was not satisfied with what she had heard.

They had tea together, sitting round awkwardly with long pauses between remarks, still trying to digest what had happened, to make sense of it. Afterwards, Pippa cornered Anne on the landing. Taking Anne into her bedroom, she closed the door behind them.

'Now tell me what really happened.'

'It was like Father said,' Anne replied after a moment.

'All of it!'

'What do you mean?'

'Anne, I know you're not dim. You were always warm for the Volunteers, and so was Vere. I never took it very seriously and assumed you would both grow out of it, but it seems I was wrong. What actually happened?'

Anne could not look at her. There were some dresses lying on Pippa's bed, and she fingered one aimlessly.

'Anne!'

Pippa placed her own hand over Anne's to stop it fidgeting about among the dresses. They were face to face.

Anne turned away and wiped a hand over her face. She stared up for a moment. It was impossible to lie to Pippa.

'I tried to stop him,' she said at last.

'So you knew he was going?'

'No. I knew it was going to happen.'

'The ambush?'

Anne nodded.

'And you didn't tell Father?'

There was a very long silence.

Anne could not turn, could not see her sister, but at last Pippa said, 'I don't think I can ever forgive you.'

Then Anne spun round. 'Do you think I can forgive myself? I told Father everything as soon as Vere – I mean, as soon as he came home – was brought home.'

'You told Father?'

Anne nodded.

'So he was lying just now? He knows everything too?'

Anne nodded. Pippa sat on the edge of the bed thinking. 'He's done this to shield you. If it were me, I should lock you up, Anne, and throw away the key! You don't deserve it! How dare you stay alive when Vere is dead? How dare you do this to Father and Mother?'

Anne stared at her white-faced.

'Was Cathal Donnelly in this?'

Anne nodded.

'So he seduced you into it?' Pippa looked at her with unutterable scorn.

'No!'

'What do you mean?'

'Pippa, I swear – not for myself, I don't care any more, but for the truth. I did believe in it, that what they were going to do was right! The Auxiliaries were going to attack Lisheen and the Volunteers were trying to protect the village –'

'What are you talking about?'

'It's too complicated to explain.'

'No, its not complicated, not a bit. It's very simple. They were deliberately attacking the forces of law and order, treacherously, without warning. Decent men were risking their lives to do their duty, while you were encouraging that murderous scum because your head is full of a lot of airy-fairy nonsense and day-dreams.'

'Pippa, stop! That's not true! I did believe – I know – that Ireland should be free – it seemed only right – but I had no idea that Vere would become involved. In fact, I told him over and over again to keep out of it. Oh, God!' She burst into tears and knelt and then fell forward on the bed, shielding her eyes. 'I did try.'

The door opened abruptly and Tony walked in with a suitcase. He stopped.

'Oh, sorry.'

He stood in the doorway, uncertain.

'Come in and shut the door.' Pippa had not moved.

Tony came over and placed the suitcase beneath the window. He turned to where Anne was still lying across the bed among the dresses, all disarranged.

'Fearful business,' he began uncertainly.

'Do you want to tell Tony what you just told me?' Pippa looked at Anne's back. 'Don't you think he has a right to know?'

Anne lay still. Pippa looked up at her husband. 'If I tell you, Tony, it must never go beyond this room.'

He looked suitably solemn.

'Vere had joined the Volunteers. Anne knew and kept quiet about it. She knew all about the ambush.'

There was a very long pause, and at last Tony said, 'This is extremely serious. Colonel Hunter must be informed at once.'

'He knows.'

Tony appeared to digest this. But after another long silence, he said, 'He knows?'

'Yes,' Pippa replied, 'he has decided to cover up to save Anne.'

'Save Anne?'

'She knew the ambush was going to happen.'

'Good Lord, how?'

'It's a long story. Let's just say from a mutual acquaintance.'

Tony had by now grasped the situation.

'Anne knew about this attack and did nothing to prevent it? This is very serious, very serious indeed.' He ran his hand through his hair as he struggled to comprehend the enormity of what had happened. 'Two of our men were killed yesterday morning, and there are two IRA prisoners awaiting trial. They could go to the gallows for this. Under the circumstances I don't think I can let this stop here. I must speak to your father.'

Pippa did not raise her voice but she stopped Tony before he reached the door.

'Father knows everything, Tony. I told you. But he doesn't know that you know, and it's got to stay that way.'

'Good Lord, why?'

'Because Anne is my sister. She only told me because I forced it out of her. It must rest here.'

Anne was still lying with her face among the dresses on the bed. Tony stood looking down at her.

'Well, this is damn' poor show. Vere dead, your father and mother broken-hearted ...'

After a long pause, Pippa said, 'Quite.'

# Chapter Fifteen

The car drew up and as Costello came round to open the door, Claire stepped out carefully, almost as she if were not touching the earth, light, airy, tall and slender in black. The thick veil hung about her almost to her knees. She took Hugh's arm, and they entered the church.

Anne was behind Tony and Pippa; both women also in veils. Anne was staggered to see the church full, and many faces she did not recognise. As they came down the aisle she saw the coffin lying ahead of her before the altar rail. Even though she thought she had become accustomed to the sight by now she felt again the cold clutching at her heart. The atmosphere was heavy, solemn, people speaking only in hushed voices when they spoke at all.

She took her seat beside Pippa, picked up a prayer book and tried to focus her gaze on a page, opened at random. She did not want to look up, did not want to see that black box. Somehow it seemed too small. Was that all there was to it – was that all Vere was? That black box, now shut up for ever? How could he be captured and enclosed like that, that airy and free spirit?

And thinking of Vere boxed up for ever, she could feel tears smarting in the corners of her eyes. She reached up beneath her veil to wipe them. Glancing along the row, she could see her mother, upright, staring ahead. No one spoke.

Canon Blenkinsop appeared. He seemed so slow, so old, barely able to drag himself to the lectern. But now he began the service.

The gaps between his words were filled with an unnatural

silence. Anne had never heard so many people so utterly still; it was quite uncanny.

They sang a hymn. Her own voice sounded very far away. Was that her singing?

Then Canon Blenkinsop made his funeral oration. He talked about Vere as if he had been dead a hundred years, as if he were some ancient Roman general, and yet today was Friday, and only last Sunday they had all been sitting here together. She sat, sunk in a stupor of misery. The last five days had been a blur of unreality; she had felt like a man awaiting the day of his execution. Quite unreal. And now this speech. It was not fair on the old man really. How could he do justice to what had befallen? How grasp the enormity of the death of a fourteen-year-old boy? It was not possible. You could only endure it dumbly, endure the pain and hope that in the end it would become dulled. But put it into words – that was not possible.

Now the coffin was being lifted by six boys – friends of Vere's. The family rose, and followed it out into the church-yard. Around the church was a jumble of gravestones, some broken, some at crazy angles, some no more than grassy hummocks, graves so old that the stone had completely disappeared. Around the church they paraded along the narrow path. At the far side, in a quiet spot near the wall, a grave had been dug. A heap of fresh earth was visible, and the grave-diggers waiting.

Everyone walked slowly, heads bowed, silent. At last they found themselves standing about the grave. The beech trees hung above them in their most beautiful leaf, bright in the sunny afternoon. It seemed somehow inappropriate. The weather should be stormy, gloomy, dull or rainy for such an event. Instead in the trees overhead the birds were singing, and as Anne waited for Canon Blenkinsop to speak a brilliant dragon-fly flitted its erratic way across the grass past them.

Claire was standing close to Hugh. He looked grey, like a stone statue, rigid and staring at the coffin.

Canon Blenkinsop had finished the service, and the grave-digger now looked at Hugh. He leant towards Claire and whispered something to her, and in a strange, awkward way she bent down, took a handful of earth and gravel and threw it

141

down on to the coffin deep below in the bottom of the grave. But as she did so, and as the tell-tale sound of the earth and gravel hit the hollow lid of the coffin, she seemed to stumble and would have fallen but that he on one side, and Pippa on the other, took her quickly by the arms and steadied her, until after a moment she was able to stand again. Anne could see her weeping, see her shoulders shake as she turned to Hugh, and he took her in his arms. Anne felt an intense anger that her own mother was being subjected to this indignity, being confronted with the death of her son in this brutal fashion, forced to stare down at his coffin deep in the earth, forced to take up earth and throw it down on top.

The others stood like statues. After a moment Hugh released Claire, who turned towards Pippa, and himself threw earth into the grave. A moment after and it was her turn, but Anne could feel her hand shaking so violently, she was not sure she would be able to do it properly.

Eventually this rite was concluded, and they turned away. All over the graveyard people were picking their way carefully, heading towards the gate. Hugh turned to Canon Blenkinsop as Claire, leaning heavily on Pippa's arm, with Tony on the other side came slowly and haltingly away. Anne followed behind, unable to speak or help. It would have seemed such a colossal impertinence to push her way in, in some ostentatious display of shouldering her mother's grief; she followed silently behind.

As they came out into the road, people were standing about and conversation was beginning to spring up. It occurred to Anne how different a Protestant funeral was from a Catholic one. She had passed Catholic funerals once or twice at the other church, and remembered vividly the wailing, the poor women kneeling at the graveside, arms raised to heaven, calling and crying out, the disorganised jostling, the sense of keen emotion as everyone there poured out their grief, communing with death, recognising it, embracing the reality of it.

As she thought this she saw not far away, standing apart from the others, Mrs Donnelly. Lifting her veil, Anne approached her, standing in the village street in the warm afternoon sunshine.

They looked into each other's face.

'I am sorry for you, Anne Hunter,' Mrs Donnelly said gravely at last.

'Thank you.' It was almost a whisper. 'It was kind of you to come.'

Mrs Donnelly looked away, screwing up her eyes as if looking into the far distance against the brightness of the afternoon. 'He was a fine boy,' she said quietly, 'and promised well. Words will not bring him back, I know. But you did not deserve this, Anne. I could not have wished this on any family.'

She was silent for a moment then drew a deep breath. 'But it is always the women who bear the weight of sorrow. It is we who bring our sons into the world, who care for them, watch over them, and see them grow to manhood. And then to see them fall as they stand at the very threshold of life – it is very hard.'

'Anne!' It was Tony calling. She glanced round.

'Thank you again, Mrs Donnelly. It was very thoughtful of you.'

'Seeing Vere there, going down into the earth, I could only think of Cathal, don't you see? That it might have been him. You understand?'

'Yes, I think so. Mrs Donnelly, have you heard from him? Do you know where he is now?'

'I have not heard from him.' Her face was stone. 'Goodbye, Anne.'

As she climbed up into the trap behind Leary, she looked back to where Mrs Donnelly stood watching her.

In the drawing room sandwiches and port had been laid out. No one knew quite what to say. Anne had been to other funerals, a great-aunt, an uncle, and one grandfather, but they had been quite different. Everyone had been waiting for years for the deceased to die. The old people had all been, as it were, ready to go, everything tidied up and regularised before they passed on. It was expected, and there was no great display of feeling. Consequently conversation over the port wine afterwards was relatively uninhibited; people felt free to discuss the departed freely, to weigh them up or remember amusing anecdotes. It had really been quite pleasant.

But with Vere none of this was possible. The shock of his death, the mystery of it, the inappropriateness of it, the way it symbolised all the horrible violence in the country at the moment, all of this made it hard to find the right words to say, and people stared at the floor, unwilling to meet each other's eyes, searching for the correct words or preferring none at all.

One man did not seem at a loss for words. Captain Steptoe, in uniform, was beside Anne suddenly.

'Most regrettable, Miss Hunter. A tragic loss. We all feel it keenly. Difficult to find words to express one's sense of loss. Such a lively lad, so full of good humour, liked by all. He would have had a promising career, I feel sure. And to be cut short in his – so to speak, before he had a chance to – well, to grow to man's estate, so to speak.'

Captain Steptoe's breath smelled of cigarettes as he leaned close to her. She turned her head away involuntarily, but he had more to say.

'Yes, I was at the inquest, of course. A tragic accident, to be caught like that in the cross fire. Most regrettable. Astonishing coincidence when you come to think of it. Of all places. And at such an hour.' He drew a breath. 'The two prisoners who were taken wouldn't say anything, of course. Despite all our efforts.'

He gave her a significant look. 'Well, we shall never know now, of course.'

'No.'

'Astonishing coincidence,' he repeated. 'And no one had any idea how he could have been there.'

'No.'

'No. No one did. Most strange. And to think, only a week ago he was shinning up a tree in Macroom! And he won his bet, Miss Hunter. I shall always remember him shinning up that tree.'

The mention of the two prisoners had given her a severe jolt; she had forgotten completely about them. She had read their names in the newspaper – Michael Flynn and Patrick Twomey. She remembered the sunny morning when she had met Mickey Flynn in the *bohreen*. He had been perched as it were side-saddle, bare-backed on an enormous cart horse with a bit of frayed rope for a bridle and had given her a cheeky

144

grin, the two of them alone in the lane, chatted with her, a light-hearted boy with a Cork accent you could cut with a knife. And he had been handed over to Captain Steptoe for questioning, before going on to stand trial for his life.

As Steptoe spoke her mind was racing back over everything, every event, every meeting, trying to remember whether he could – of course, he had told her about the raid, that was true – was it possible it had been a trap? But how could he have known that she was going to run over to Mrs Donnelly's? She felt suddenly frightened he might ask her some awkward question, frightened she might inadvertently betray herself by an inappropriate reply. She looked round.

'Donnelly escaped, unfortunately. The ringleader. But we shan't give up. There's a thousand pounds on his head now. We'll see if his friends are as loyal as he thinks, eh?' Captain Steptoe's tone hardened, and he gave her a straight look. 'I mean to have him, one way or another –'

'Will you excuse me?'

Anne turned away and, blind for a moment, stared about her at the crowd of other guests. Then she made for the door, and seeing Pippa asked her where their mother was.

Pippa told her she had gone upstairs to lie down. As Anne went upstairs she removed her hat and veil, still thinking about what Steptoe had said. But as she relaxed, relieved to have escaped from him, it now occurred to her that the answer was really much simpler and threw no shadow of suspicion on to herself or Vere. She remembered Steptoe's first visit to the house during the wedding. No one had ever discovered who had told Macroom Castle about the weapons hidden at the Hunters' but it was probably some remark overheard in a bar or information from a paid informer; there were supposed to be spies everywhere. Doubtless it had been the same in this case.

Feeling relieved on this point, she entered her parents' bedroom. The curtains were drawn and the room was in darkness.

Claire was lying across the bed, fully clothed. Her hat and veil were thrown on a chair, but she was still wearing her shoes. Her eyes were closed.

'Mother?'

She stirred, and opened her eyes. She looked up at Anne for a moment without expression, then closed her eyes again.

'It's over now,' Anne said quietly, and knelt by the side of the bed.

'Thank you, dear,' Claire murmured. 'Do forgive me, I couldn't bear any more of it.'

'No.'

'Seeing the coffin in the grave, so deep, and the smell of the earth, the damp, thinking of Vere in the darkness, under all that earth ... I couldn't stand it.' Suddenly she turned her head slightly towards Anne and reached for her hand. 'But I could learn to bear it, if I only knew why. If I could understand it, Anne. It's not being able to understand which is so hard. It seems so unjust. Why Vere? Why not me? Why did not God let me die in his place? I would have willingly. I don't understand.' She shook her head on the pillow. 'I don't understand.'

Anne still held her hand.

Supposing she told Claire why Vere was dead? She had the words ready; it would take a few seconds only. She would explain about Cathal and the guns and Vere's enthusiasm – would that make it easier for her mother to bear?

But it was not for her to decide. If her father wanted Claire to know he would tell her. It was his place, not Anne's. She said nothing, but smoothed her mother's brow, running her fingers lightly across and back. Claire's eyes were closed, but Anne could sense her relaxing beneath the movement of her fingers, the muscles in her neck slackening and her head turning a little on the pillow. Her breathing became more regular, slowing and becoming deeper.

'Thank you, darling,' she murmured.

There was one other duty to be done.

In the evening, after the guests had gone, Anne changed from her mourning clothes. Up in her room, she took her beach bag and placed in it the pistol, which had still been lying where she had hidden it beneath the blankets in her wardrobe.

She called the dogs and made her way to the path up the mountainside. After the press of people all afternoon it was soothing to be alone. She was in no hurry and climbed carefully, her eyes on the path, not looking about her but sensing the silence, hearing the breeze in the heather, just allowing the thoughts to unravel in her, calming her.

At last she came to the bathing pool, and stopped to look about her. Across the valley the evening shadow was climbing up the mountain, covering the lower slopes in a veil of violet. The valley below her was already dulled, yet the sky was still bright as the sun now lay close to the distant mountain ridge behind her.

Not wanting to think, not wanting to remember, she reached into the bag and took out the pistol. She turned it over; it was heavy, large in her hand. She examined it. There were no bullets in it.

At last, standing on the white rock at the edge of the pool, she let the pistol fall into the water. It was quite clear and deep and she watched the pistol fall quickly through. It was lost to sight in a moment.

She looked up, and seeing the patch of grass on the opposite side, remembered how, just there, Lewis had once sat and looked at her as she lay naked.

She realised with a shock that she had scarcely thought of him since the death of her brother.

He had been wiped out of her life. But now, this evening, she did think of him, wondering where he was. He had left so suddenly, and had not come to the funeral.

Suddenly there by the pool Lewis was again real to her. He could have been there beside her. She felt she had known him so well. They had become so close. Things had become so natural between them. And when he had told her he loved her –

But now the improbability of it swept over her. How could he have loved her? He was so much older than she. A man who had been everywhere, travelled to faraway exotic places, run incredible risks, a man so at ease in the world; he must have had all sorts of women, could have any woman he wanted – why should he want her? Yet remembering them together by the pool, remembering the way he had looked at her – and just then she saw again so vividly the intense look in his eyes and heard him again telling her she was beautiful – all her calm was gone and she could feel herself becoming agitated. She did believe he had loved her, because he had said so – or not exactly said so, when she tried to remember exactly what had been said, but she had simply *known*. He had loved her – until the ambush.

Then he'd left. It was obvious. She had caused her brother's death, and Lewis had walked out. How he must have despised her for her arrogance, her certainty, her rude assertion that the Volunteers must be right. She had never made any secret of her support for them, and he would easily have guessed what she was up to. No wonder he would not look at her; that he had walked out on her with barely a word.

Feeling slightly dizzy, she sat by the side of the pool and covered her eyes with her hands. And as the dogs nosed and frisked about through the heather and gorse, Anne wept. She had had her chance of happiness, it had come and it had gone. These things do not happen twice.

# Chapter Sixteen

'I hate it!'

Claire turned restlessly from the window and looked down at the others. 'Why should we stay here? We must go to England! We can stay with Gerald till we find somewhere of our own.'

'That would be very difficult.' Hugh had been about to take his pipe out of his pocket.

'Why is it difficult? Resign! You can resign, can't you? Why shouldn't you resign? Tell them you've had enough. I've had enough. I've had all I can take.'

Anne hesitated in the doorway. Opposite her at the head of the table stood Claire; Pippa and Tony were still seated opposite Hugh at the breakfast table.

'I am not resigning,' he said quietly, 'I am not leaving. If we were to leave now it would amount to surrender. Besides, up to now the IRA has left us alone. They have no quarrel with us. We don't know how Vere came to be caught up in the ambush.'

'No quarrel with us? What are you talking about? And how can you bring his name into it? It's because of him! Oh God, I hate this country, the people, everything. It's all so barbaric!'

During this last speech Bridget had come into the room with a tray in her hand. She stopped in the doorway beside Anne. As Hugh saw her he turned towards his wife with a warning glance, and said loudly, 'You can clear away now, Bridget.'

But Claire had ignored his warning. She was gripping a chair back and it shook as she spoke. 'The people can't be trusted! How can you trust them? I bet they knew what the

Volunteers were up to! They hate us, I know it. And I for one can't wait to get out. I can't stand it any longer!'

'Mother! *Prenez garde!*' Pippa broke in.

Bridget was standing at the table about to set pieces of crockery on her tray, and watching Claire with an alarmed expression. Seeing the look on her face, Claire thrust the chair away with an angry gesture, brushed past Anne at the door and went out into the garden.

Anne followed and found her standing on the garden path, one hand over her face, weeping softly.

'Mother –' Anne came to her, and Claire embraced her and they clung together.

'I can't stand it.'

'Mother –' she said hesitantly. 'We could go down to the cottage?'

Claire broke away abruptly. 'What's got into you? You've become very considerate all of a sudden.'

'What do you mean? Of course I'm concerned! Don't you think I feel it as much as you? Only do let's go away for a while. I can't bear to see you like this.'

Claire drew a long sigh. 'Oh, what does it matter? Go away, stay here, what's the difference? I wish I were dead.'

'You mustn't say that! I can't bear it,' Anne whispered, holding her arm. 'Please Mother, we'll get over it eventually.'

'I don't want to get over it. My son is dead! What's the point of getting over it?'

She broke away and wandered off down the path. Anne watched her for a while and then turned away slowly.

A week had gone by since the funeral. Claire had once more resumed her regular hours, and Anne had thought she was beginning to recover from the utter prostration into which she had been thrown. And then this morning she had erupted over almost nothing, and it was obvious that recovery was going to take a very long time yet.

Anne tried to think of some consoling remark but what could she say, except, 'It's all my fault'?

Eventually, she went to seek her father. 'I was wondering –' He was at his desk, as she stood uncertainly in the doorway. 'Should I take Mother down to the cottage for a few days?'

\*

Tony had to return to Dublin. Before they left Pippa spoke to Anne. 'I'm glad you're taking Mother to the cottage. Getting away from here for a while should help.'

'That's what I thought.'

Pippa looked into her eyes for a moment. 'And it should keep you out of mischief. When I think of Tony, risking his life every day ... Anne, if you ever so much as look at Cathal Donnelly again, I'll kill you,' she said with quiet determination, held her look for a moment, then took her sister in her arms. 'Take care of Mother.'

'I will.'


The following day but one Hugh helped Costello strap two trunks on top of the large black car, and Anne got into the back with Claire and the dogs. They were still in mourning.

Two hours later they had driven down to the sea, through Bantry and out along the coast road. A few miles further on, through a tiny village and on another mile, the cottage stood a little above the road looking down on to the rocky sea-shore. The sea air lifted her spirits as Anne first saw the sunlight flashing on the long Atlantic rollers and she wound down the window to let the breeze flood into the car. She turned to Claire but she sat upright, staring ahead.

The cottage was built of white stones, bleached it seemed by centuries of wind and water, under a slate roof and with small windows deeply recessed into the stone. The only door faced away from the sea up the rocky mountainside, and a narrow path wound up from the road between white rocks jutting out at random between hardy grass tufts. Further up Anne saw two goats grazing on this, and it occurred to her that only a goat's stomach would be tough enough to digest it. The moment they had been let out of the car, the dogs had raced away up the hillside, mad with excitement, careering about the rocks, the smells, the sights and sounds.

The cottage had three rooms: two bedrooms and a kitchen with an ancient black iron range for cooking and a wide pine table scored with hundreds of knife cuts where for years food had been prepared, fish cut up, and nets mended. A paraffin lamp hung above the table.

Hugh had bought the house when his children were small,

and all through Anne's childhood they had looked forward to the summer here with childish glee. Claire referred to it as 'slumming', and always made a fuss about coming, as if she endured the privations solely for their sake. But Anne knew, or suspected, that she enjoyed the relaxed informality of their summer holidays as much as her children did.

As Costello carried the trunks up the narrow path on that afternoon, Anne stood with her arm linked through her mother's, gazing out at the rollers crashing among the rocks and dashing in to the little sandy bay beneath them. The light sea breeze moved her dress about her legs, and she had to hold her hand over her eyes against the glare from the flashing sea. Near her clumps of broom moved in the breeze. It was heavenly, and she drew long breaths as she allowed herself to relax and expand into the wide emptiness of it.

She squeezed Claire's arm and smiled to her, but her mother made no response, and after a moment turned away into the cottage.

'I'll call in on the Magills and tell them you're here,' Hugh said as he came into the cottage after them.

'Will we have to have that slut of a girl to cook again?' Claire said, throwing herself on a bench beneath the window over which Costello had thrown one of the car rugs.

'It's all right, Mother,' Anne added quickly, 'I'll go with Father and speak to Mrs Magill. Perhaps she could send Rosheen instead.'

She drove back into the village with Hugh, and they called on Mrs Magill, where it was agreed that Rosheen, who was sixteen now, could come to the cottage every day between eight and three and do for them, in consideration of five shillings a week.

Anne did some shopping and walked back alone to the cottage. The white dusty road, winding round the contours of the rocky mountainside, was completely deserted as she carried her shopping basket, all alone in the great space, the sea to her right crashing and foaming along the rocky shore.

That night she cooked omelettes and they ate in almost complete silence. Every so often her mother would sigh. The silence in the room seemed emphasised by the rhythmic crash of the waves below. Anne wondered whether this had been a good idea, their being alone together.

The following morning she was awake early and lit the kitchen range. One of their tasks at the cottage was to collect driftwood to feed the fire. There was still no sign of Rosheen when Anne took a cup of tea in to Claire who was still in bed.

The girl arrived at nine.

'I thought you were coming at eight?' said Anne as she opened the door to Rosheen, who seemed too small to be sixteen and was wearing boots which looked a size too big for her, and a dress a size too small.

'I was, Miss Hunter, but I had to stay to help dress Michael and Tobias.'

'Couldn't your mother do that?'

'Sure, 'tis Saturday and me mam had to do the butter for market, Miss Hunter.'

'I see. Well, now you're here you can cook us some break-fast, Rosheen, and afterwards give the place a clean. It's been closed up for months.'

'Very well, Miss Hunter.'

Eventually Claire had been got up, dressed, and they sat down to breakfast, cooked, in a manner of speaking, by Rosheen.

However, later that morning as they walked by the sea, or sat on the rocks, half mesmerised by the eternal crash and drag of the waves, and with the wind in their hair, Claire began to relax, and at last to talk. The dogs amused them-selves by barking at the waves.

'You can't imagine what it was like before the war –'

'I remember it very well,' Anne began, but Claire ignored her.

'How peaceful and pleasant. We never locked a door. And if beggars came to the kitchen, there was always something for them. And the parties! The tennis, the hunting, picnics by the river, always something going on, everyone in such tearing high spirits, the laughter. Oh, I can't tell you ... and now, I don't know any more, I don't understand, the people are simply so rude to one.' She lapsed into silence.

Then, as they walked arm in arm, she began again. 'Where have they all gone? Poor Teddy Wilkinson killed at the

Somme, Billy Hepplewhite too. Both Canon Blenkinsop's grandsons killed. And how I used to thank God – on my bended knee I thanked God – that Vere had been too young to be called up, that he had been spared. And then after all ... it'll never be the same, you know. All gone.' She drew a sigh. 'What fun he was! A ray of light in the house, his silly antics, his clever stunts – it was a wonder he didn't break his neck the things he got up to – climbing trees, wading into the river once in his shoes and socks all because my handkerchief had fallen in and been carried away. And then, do you remember that time – oh, he couldn't have been more than ten, and Teddy Wilkinson's younger brother was staying during the summer holidays, and they borrowed old Maloney's ass and painted stripes on him to pretend he was a zebra, and were charging the children a halfpenny a ride!' She broke into laughter then looked away.

'But it'll never be the same. You can't bring the past back to life. It's gone, all gone, and as for the future – God knows what'll happen. The IRA could burn the roof over our heads. And if they get their wretched republic we'll be governed by the likes of de Valera, with his cold Catholic piety, Griffith and the others – what a ghastly crew! I can't believe I used to be in favour of Irish independence. I must have needed my head examining. There won't be much fun any more, not for us, that's for sure.'

'It's a question of justice, Mother,' Anne began quietly.

'Justice! What sort of justice when they burn down the court house! They want us out, that's all. What's justice got to do with it? Your father's spent his life upholding justice and what has it got him except death threats?'

'Death threats?' Anne was alarmed.

'Notices nailed to trees, you know what I mean,' Claire was impatient. She got up and smoothed down her skirt. 'Come on, I'm getting a chill sitting here. Let's go and see if that slut has managed to cook any lunch.'

Anne called the dogs.

But when they got to the cottage there was no sign of Rosheen. Food stood about on the table, and as far as they could make out Rosheen must have been in the process of preparing lunch when she had gone off. Anne nearly tripped over the broom too which was left across a chair just inside the door.

But as they prepared themselves some ham and salad, and were eating their lunch, Rosheen appeared at the open door in a breathless rush, pouring out apologies. Claire cut her short.

'Thank you, Rosheen, no need to apologise. I understand your mother has a lot to contend with, with eight children. The question is, do you want this job or shall we look for someone else?'

'Oh, no, ma'am! Don't you worry, it won't happen again! 'Twas only on account of Billy swallerin' the wrong medicine.'

'Thank you, we don't want to know about Billy or his medicine! And please try not to leave kitchen utensils lying about the cottage. My daughter nearly broke her neck tripping over the broom.'

In the afternoon Claire retired to sleep, but later after Rosheen had gone home they took another walk along the beach.

'You should get out more! For heaven's sake, why are you moping around here in the country? When we get back, you must go and stay with Pippa. Heavens, Anne, when I was your age I had been out two years. I had been presented to the Viceroy at the Castle! And I have to tell you in all honesty, that dress – well, you won't see a dress like that again. White satin, of course, very simple, severe but elegant with the tiniest shoulder straps sewn with sequins. And, of course, the regulation three feathers in my hair. And a two-and-a-half-yard train! We practised a week with that train, my mother and I. You mustn't turn your back on the Viceroy, you see. You have to back out, never taking your eyes off him. The silly old thing had an enormous red beard, and the girls were so heavily powdered that before half of them were past him, he had to retire to have his beard dusted. It was perfectly white –'

'I don't understand.'

'For heaven's sake, he has to kiss each girl.'

'Pardon?'

'Surely you know that?'

'The Viceroy kisses every debutante?'

155

'Yes.'

'Good lord. How primitive. It sounds like something from the Balkans.'

'It was very splendid and gracious. Balkans indeed! And he was the most charming old silly, Lord Spencer. We danced twice. Indeed it would have been three times, only my card was quite full. Oh, my card was *always* full. The young men were quite demented if they couldn't dance with me.'

'Is that where you met Father?'

'I met your father in the most romantic way. He was a very young officer then – this was before even the Boer War. It was at a meet in County Galway. I was staying with the Marquis of Claremorris, at a large house party. Of course Galway is the most terrifying stone-wall country and the young men were simply devils for a hunt. I had already noticed your father. Well, the stone wall hadn't been built that would frighten him! He would go at anything – and rode the most enormous charger. During the hunt, I was riding in a governess cart with the marchioness – otherwise I would have ridden my own mare, of course, but she especially asked for me – and the chase had taken us over some particularly rough country, all rocks and boulders and steep little gullies, and my companion had got carried away following the chase till we came to this narrow bridge. Taking it too fast, one of the wheels hit the wall, and broke, and the cart fell over to one side so that the two of us were hanging above the stream – it must have been a twelve-foot drop. I can see it now. We were terrified, thought we must fall in at any moment, and the horse was terrified too, trying to free herself. But fortunately for us, your father happened along at that very moment, quieted the mare, and managed to pull the cart a little away from the edge and got us both out.

'After that you may imagine what my feelings towards him were! The marchioness was seated by the side of the road to recover from the shock, but I was as right as rain. And that night at the ball, it seemed we just couldn't keep away from each other. We danced every dance, and I managed to arrange with the marchioness that he should escort me into supper. It never does any harm, Anne, to help these things along a bit. And it just went on from there.' Her voice faded away into a dreamy reverie. Anne was silently digesting the story. It was out of a world as remote to her as the Arabian Nights.

'He has the most wonderful way with horses, with any animal,' Claire went on dreamily.

'I know.'

That night as they lay in the darkness waiting for sleep to come, her mother said, 'I'm glad we came, Anne. We needed to get away.'

Rosheen continued to behave very erratically, sometimes coming at eight but more often at nine or later, and sometimes remembering to bring a can of milk for breakfast and sometimes not.

One afternoon they were sitting on the old bench in front of the window in the sunshine, Anne reading a Jeffery Farnol novel, when she saw a gang of boys and youths walking past below them on the road. The boys looked up at the two women and waved. Anne waved back.

# Chapter Seventeen

'Oh, for heaven's sake, the girl is *useless*!'

'What's she done?'

'I don't believe it. She's stuck it together with *soap*!'

'Let me see.'

Claire was holding the handle of a small jug, which had been standing on the stone window sill. The jug itself lay on the floor, in pieces, in a puddle of water with flowers scattered about it.

'I was particularly fond of that jug.'

'It's a good thing the saucepans are made of steel!'

Anne burst into laughter and a moment later Claire joined in. The more they thought about her, the funnier Rosheen became.

'It came apart in me 'ands, mum,' Anne said in a parody of a Cork accent.

They bent over laughing. Then, as Claire was recovering, she said suddenly, 'Do you know, that's the first time I've laughed?'

Anne understood immediately. 'I'm glad,' she said after a moment, and bent to scoop up the flowers. 'I'll walk into the village and see if I can find another pot.'

'Oh, don't bother. There are thousands at home. I'll bring one down the next time we come.'

But the following afternoon Anne did walk into the little village to do some shopping. At first they had asked Rosheen to shop for them, but it had been a fiasco. Half a pound of bacon had mysteriously turned into a leg of pork, a pound of jam became Brussels sprouts. It had been impossible.

As she walked back through the village, for some reason she was reminded of the time she had come down to the coast with Lewis; couldn't help remembering the lunch they had eaten together. It seemed a very long time ago, another age, another life. She wondered where he was now. What he was doing. Whether he was even in the same country.

The memory of Lewis just then was so vivid, and so painful, that she did not notice a group of youths slouching on the opposite side of the road, cloth caps pulled down over their brows, their hands in their pockets, who had been watching her and one of whom called out something, which she did not catch. Then she did notice them, glanced briefly across the road severely, and one of them called out something which she also did not understand, and the others laughed, watching her.

She felt herself colouring up, and turned her head abruptly to ignore them. They laughed again, but soon she was out of hearing range. They did not seem to have anything to do except lounge about on a street corner, it seemed, but it took a little while before she could forget the uncomfortable feeling they had given her. 'Common boys', was how she described them to herself. But there had been a time when they would not have jeered like that.

By coincidence that evening Claire raised the subject of Lewis. They had been at the cottage over two weeks by now, and she had begun the process of recovery, had succeeded at least in climbing out of the pit of utter despair into which she been thrown. They had both been browned by the sun and wind, and were rested.

'I wonder what became of Lewis Crawford?' Claire said as they sat in the kitchen. Anne was reading a novel. Her eyes stopped following the words, but it was a moment before she could bring herself to speak.

'I've no idea,' she said faintly.

'He never wrote to you?'

'Why should he?'

'Why should he?' her mother echoed incredulously. 'My dear girl, he was very taken with you, it was obvious. And you did not appear exactly oblivious to his charms, either.'

'Obvious?' Anne asked carefully, with her eyes still on her book. 'I did not think it had been obvious.'

159

'Well, it was, I assure you. To those with eyes to see. Has he written?'

'No.'

'Pity.'

'Why?'

'Anne, you don't have to be bashful with me. He is a very attractive man. Any girl would be glad to catch him.'

'I did not set out to catch him, as you put it.'

'Have it your own way. But he liked you, didn't he?'

'Yes.'

'A lot?'

Anne drew a long breath. 'I thought he loved me.'

'Did you?' Claire raised her eyebrows. 'Good for you. Did he propose?'

Anne nodded. There was a pause.

'Then he just went off?'

She nodded again.

'No explanation?'

Anne was silent.

'Well, he may write. Of course, with Vere –'

'Yes.'

Claire was watching Anne, who finally raised her eyes from her book to meet her mother's. 'Poor girl,' she said gently. 'I hadn't realised. You must have been in love with him too.'

'I was.'

'What can I say?' Claire said at last. 'These things never work out smoothly, I'm afraid. We just have to get over them as best we can.'

That night as Anne lay in bed waiting for sleep her thoughts were filled with the memories which had been raised by Claire; things she'd never expected to remember but now were as familiar to her as her own hands: the afternoon she had sat on the riverbank as Lewis told her about his car and the story of the coffee pot, and she had studied the back of his neck as he looked up at Vere; the drives through the lanes, the fuchsias so abundant in the hedgerows, and herself beside Lewis, swept along by the strength of the great engine, as if the car were some magic carpet – because there was something about him of the Arabian Nights, all his adventures in the desert, as

160

if he himself were some character out of a fairy tale. But then the ambush had come, he had seen through her, despised her, and departed. She did not expect to see him again.

There was a cracking noise against the slates above her; at first she couldn't think what it was, but then from the kitchen they heard the sound of breaking glass. She sat bolt upright in bed, and heard Claire move too.

'What is it?' she called.

'I've no idea,' Anne said. 'Wait a moment.'

She pulled herself quickly out of bed and threw her dressing gown round her shoulders. She went into the kitchen. It was almost pitch dark, though the windows let in a vestigial moonlight. The dogs stirred in the darkness, and Anne whispered to soothe them.

Another crack against the slate above her, and the sound of something hitting the wall outside. Anne felt the clutch of fear in her stomach. Claire was behind her.

'Someone throwing stones,' Anne whispered with incredulity. 'I'll light the lantern.' She fumbled for the matches on the narrow shelf above the range, and in a moment had lit the lamp.

Now they heard men's voices outside, jeering catcalls. Anne was suddenly angry.

'I'm not putting up with this.'

'Where are you going?'

'To tell them off. It's a gang of village boys.'

'Anne! Leave them! They'll soon get tired of it.'

'They've broken a window! Why should they get away with it?'

She turned towards the door, but Claire caught her shoulder. 'No! Wait! They'll soon go away.'

The two women stood together listening. There were shouts and more singing, and Anne recognised the tune of a Republican song. After a while the song grew fainter and they understood the lads were moving away.

Her heart was beating fast. In a way she would have preferred to have gone out and confronted them, than skulk here inside. It was always better to face things, she believed.

'They've gone,' Claire said at last. 'It's all right. We can go back to bed.'

But it took a very long time before either woman could sleep. The memory of the breaking glass and the jeers left a very unpleasant taste.

The following morning, with the sun streaming in through the windows, the memory of the night seemed somehow improbable. Outside, below them, the sea crashing against the rocks, and the great sweep of the heavens seemed so beautiful, it was almost impossible to believe there had been such ugliness as they had heard. But the pieces of glass lay on the floor to remind her.

Anne walked into the village and arranged with the glazier, who was also general handyman, joiner and plumber, to come out and fit a new pane of glass.

Walking back through the village she saw three youths lounging outside a bar, and crossed to them.

They seemed defensive at first, furtive, and did not like to meet her eye, though one stared down at her with an arrogant, cocksure look. They kept their hands in their pockets.

'Somebody smashed our window last night, and it's cost me three and six to have it mended. Who's going to pay?'

They did not answer. The bold one looked at the others and smiled in a sideways fashion.

'Well, when you see the people who were outside our cottage last night at midnight, throwing stones, will you tell them to let me have the money?'

At last the bolder one said, with an impudent grin, 'If we see 'em, we'll tell 'em.'

'Thank you.'

She walked away.

Later when she got back to the cottage they discussed what to do.

'Do you want to go home?' her mother asked.

'Do you?'

'I hadn't thought of going just yet.'

'Nor I.'

'Well then, that settles it. I don't imagine they'll come again.'

The next night they lay awake apprehensively in the darkness. In the end Anne fell asleep, and woke in the morning feeling things had returned to normal, and that they were unlikely to be troubled again.

The glazier called to mend the window pane, and Anne and Claire settled down again to reading and walking along the beach.


Anne started awake. There was a loud hammering on the door.

'Anne?' Claire called in the darkness.

'Yes, I heard it.'

'Wait.'

A moment later it started again. The dogs had woken up and now began to bark.

'Oh God, do you think it's them?'

Anne scrambled out of bed. 'I'll light the lamp.' She felt her way into the kitchen and, fumbling in the darkness, found the matches and succeeded in lighting the paraffin lamp. Claire appeared at the door in her dressing gown. The dogs were very restless, barking, rushing at the door then backing away.

The hammering started again.

The two women looked at each other. Anne made up her mind. 'I'm damned if I'm going to give in to them. How dare they?'

She moved toward the door.

'Anne! Wait! You're not going to open it?' Claire's voice was shrill.

The hammering recommenced even louder, and she turned uncertainly to her mother.

They heard a voice. 'Anne! Are you there? Wake up!'

They looked at each other. It was Pippa's voice.

Anne quickly unbolted the door and her sister, in a travelling coat, clasping an armful of bags and travelling rugs, pushed past her.

'Sorry it's so late – we got held up. Anne – what on earth – are you all right?'

She drew her dressing gown round her nervously.

'Yes – we thought it was someone else.'

'Who? Hullo, Mother.' Pippa threw the things down on the table and gave her mother a hug.

'Is Tony there?'

'Yes.'

'Thank God.'

'Thank God?' Pippa was unbuttoning her coat. She looked into both their faces. 'What on earth's the matter?'

'We'll tell you later.'

'We should have been here hours ago, but the road was blocked so we didn't get to Lisheen till gone six. We had to detour through half of north Cork. Tony's coming in a mo. He's just unstrapping the cases.'

'Oh, I can't tell you how glad I am to see you!' Claire embraced her again.

'What are you doing here?' Anne said stupidly after a moment, still trying to recover from the fear she had felt.

'What do you think? A bit of sea air, if you don't mind. Holidays – you're still allowed after you're married, you know.'

'Of course, sorry. But why didn't you write?'

'It was a bit of a last-minute thing. Tony got a few days' leave so we just set off. Anyway, what's it matter? There's plenty of room.'

At this moment Tony himself appeared in the doorway with two suitcases. He was in civilian clothes.

Anne stirred the fire to life in the range, and set the kettle over it to make a cup of tea. Later, as they sat round the table sipping tea, she explained their nervousness. 'I can't tell you how reassuring it is to see you.'

'You should have had a man with you,' Tony said. 'Why didn't Hugh leave Costello?'

'It's never been necessary before.'

'Times have changed,' he said grimly. 'Anyway it isn't going to stop us getting some sea air. Blow all that smoke out of our lungs, eh, darling?'

'Hear, hear,' said Pippa.

They all woke late the following morning. Rosheen had arrived, and made some tea, and then over a late breakfast they decided what to do.

'It'll be best for you to come back with us next week,' Tony said. 'We haven't got room in the car but I'll wire your father to come and fetch you.'

164

'Are you going to leave the car there?'

It was standing on the road below the cottage.

'What? Oh, you think our friends of the IRA might want to borrow it?'

'It's no joke, darling,' said Claire. 'We had the car borrowed earlier in the year; fortunately it was found three days later in the village, a bit muddy but otherwise unharmed. But some of our friends have never seen theirs again.'

Tony smiled conspiratorially. 'Well, as it happens, Claire, I've been rather cunning. A pal of mine in the sappers made me up a very ingenious little device – a wooden brush for the distributor in the magneto. Impossible to detect but of course the car won't start – and it only takes a second to fit. Very handy.'

They packed up a picnic lunch and took it down to the beach. After they had finished eating Pippa went off with Claire to stroll along the sands, with the dogs barking and leaping in and out of the rollers.

Anne sat clasping her skirt round her legs, staring out to sea as Tony helped himself to one last sandwich. He was a heavy man and had a man's appetite.

He talked about life in Dublin between mouthfuls.

'Life goes on, y'know. We get about. There's lots to do. We went to the theatre on Saturday – *Charlie's Aunt* – laughed myself silly. And we get up a party to go dancing at the Café Cairo most weeks. We don't let the war stop us, I promise you.'

'Is there much of the war? I mean, do you see a lot of it in Dublin?'

'What? Oh, a fair amount. We're kept busy. Course, a lot of the time it's a wasted journey. We get a tip off, and go haring off to some address, but by the time we arrive the bird has flown. The city is full of informers, we're always getting tip-offs, but they're usually a step ahead of us. Take that Michael Collins. We know where he hides out, but whenever we get there, he's gone. Slipped through the net again. He's a fish swimming in his own sea.'

Tony lapsed into silence, his gaze far away for a minute. Then he wiped his fingers. 'Thanks awfully, that was top-hole. Time for forty winks, I think, while Pippa is off with your mother for a heart to heart.'

He arranged himself on the rug, and adjusted the hat over his eyes. As she saw him in danger of nodding off, Anne said hastily, 'We were talking about your wedding the other day. It was a wonderful day, Tony. There'll never be another wedding like it. But we –' she stopped and forced her voice into a slower, more casual mode '– we couldn't remember the name of your best man.'

'Lewis Crawford.'

'Oh, of course.'

Silence. After a while, Tony said sleepily, 'What about him?'

'Nothing.' She gazed out to sea. 'We were just discussing the wedding.' Her voice drifted away. And then, after another long pause, 'He was a rather odd sort of man, wasn't he?'

'Lewis?' Tony's voice was slightly muffled beneath his hat. 'I suppose he is, if you put it that way. Goes his own way, really.'

'Did you know him in the war?'

'Mmm? Known him for ever. Since school.'

'Oh?'

She was frightened Tony was about to fall asleep. But after another long silence he began: 'He was a couple of years above me, a bit of a ringleader. Crawford and Co, we were called. He taught me to smoke a pipe, I recall, in the furze on the cliffs behind school. Out of bounds, needless to say. His elder brother had been there a few years before him. He's a bore – didn't fight in the war.'

'Didn't he?'

'No. Got out of it somehow. Not much love lost between them, I fancy.' Tony paused but then chuckled and went on, 'There was this master, Stokes, a vindictive little swine, caned the daylights out of the smaller boys. Took a real pleasure in it. I could see Lewis wasn't going to stand for that. Well, Stokes was a great one for fitness, and used to swim in the sea. We all did. Of course it was a boys'-only school, no ladies around, so we swam in the buff. Stark naked. Well, one day while Stokes was out at sea, pounding up and down, Lewis went down and stole his clothes. I was in on this. Out comes Stokes, shivering, and can't find his things. I piped up and said I had seen a man creep down and take them. "Run off

166

and find him, Napier," cries Stokes, so I grabbed my things and scooted off. In the meantime it turned out the headmaster's sister was on a visit and Lewis was escorting them about the place, a beatific smile on his face. He led them right past where old Stokes was skulking in the furze bushes. "Oh, there's Mr Stokes, sir," cries Lewis. "Mr Latymer, sir, Miss Latymer, here's Mr Stokes." The beak wasn't too pleased, but his sister played right up to Lewis. "Mr Stokes, for heaven's sake, man, whatever are you doing with no clothes on?" Tony paused. 'He was rather more subdued after that. He couldn't exactly pin anything on Lewis, but he rather suspected.'

After a while Anne said, 'You were in the army with him too, weren't you?'

'Hmm? Yes. Followed him into the regiment.'

'And did you fight together? What was he like?'

'A bit of a poet, old Lewis. Never saw him open a book at school, mind, but we'd be stuck in some God-forsaken hole of a dug-out, up to our ankles in water with the rats sniffing about, and Lewis would be up on a bunk with a book of Horace or some such. In fact that reminds me – he went out on a night raid with his platoon once and brought back a couple of prisoners. One of 'em was an officer, and this chap happened to see the book in his pocket, and before you could blink he and Lewis were jawing away about Horace, as if they were the greatest pals in the world.'

'Does Lewis know German?'

'Oh, yes.' Tony lapsed once more into silence, but after another long pause said rather sleepily, 'Great one for the lingo. Picks it up in no time. Speaks all kinds of languages. Arabic, too, I shouldn't wonder.'

And that was all she was going to get out of Tony.

# Chapter Eighteen

Anne turned away from the window at last and wandered aimlessly across the room. The rain beat steadily against the window, distorting the view, so that the trees outside were reduced to dim dark outlines. There was a chill in the air, and she shivered suddenly. The house was silent, and she clutched the cardigan around her shoulders before pausing at the table before the sofa. Yesterday's newspaper lay on it, and she stood staring down at it. She didn't want to read the newspaper.

Suddenly making up her mind, she went out into the hall to the cupboard beneath the stairs where raincoats and mackintoshes were kept. It was time to take the dogs for a walk. They sensed her intention immediately and sprang to life.

Autumn had arrived quite suddenly. The long unbroken sequence of brilliant days had ceased almost overnight and the weather was back to normal: shifting, uncertain skies, the massing of clouds. Now a sudden dash of rain against the windows; then a flash of sunlight, dissolving and shifting as the clouds moved, a rainbow appearing with kingfisher brilliance for a moment.

They were back in Lisheen. Pippa and Tony had stayed at the cottage for four days, then Hugh had come down and the cottage had been locked up and they'd all returned home, Pippa and Tony to Dublin.

Anne was suddenly faced with autumn at home with her parents.

Pulling on her mackintosh, her rain hat and wellingtons, she set out up the mountainside, the dogs leaping ahead. The rain was steady, but she enjoyed the fresh feeling against her face, her hands dug deep in her pockets, glad to be out alone, feeling nothing except the vast sense of the air about her, as she climbed steadily the narrow path up the mountainside.

Away across the valley the clouds hung against the side of the mountain, covering the upper slopes, a soft hazy cotton wool that shifted and would break suddenly, to reveal a flash of sunlight on a brilliant green slope, before closing in again. Around her the ferns were brown and drooping in the steady rain, and there was a keen smell of wet earth, wet grass, of the wetness of the whole world drinking in the rain after the long dry summer.

When she got back, feeling much more cheerful, a car was standing outside the door and as she was peeling off her wet things in the hall, she could hear voices in the drawing room.

She found her parents drinking coffee with Mr Daley, her father's land agent. He was a stout middle-aged Irishman, wearing a capacious Ulster of thick tweed, thrown back over his shoulders as he spoke, gesticulating with both hands.

'He told me to my face to go to blazes!'

'Confound the fellow,' muttered Hugh.

'I said we'd sue.'

'Oh?' Hugh put down his coffee cup. 'And what did he say to that?'

'He laughed. Said he'd like to see the peeler that would enforce the order.'

'Hmm.'

Anne sat down beside them. 'What's happened, Mr Daley?'

'What's happened?' her father interrupted. 'The world's gone to the devil.'

'A tenant of your father refuses to pay his rent.' Mr Daley normally had an affable, wheedling manner, and a store of jokes that were invaluable when it came to the delicate matter of extracting money from tenant farmers.

'Who?'

'Oh, Martin, over by Clonmoyle.'

Anne knew the Martins. She had bicycled to the farm two months earlier with a message for one of the boys.

'What are you going to do?'

'What can we do, Miss Hunter? Your father's right. No

169

policeman will enforce an order at the moment. We're helpless.' The agent turned to Hugh. 'He had the impertinence to tell me the Irish people had their own Republican courts now that protect the poor.'

'I'll give him Republican courts! I'll horsewhip him first.'

Later, after Mr Daley had left, Hugh returned to where Anne was sitting with her mother. After walking up and down the room a couple of turns, he exploded in exasperation: 'First one thing, and then another! The country's going to the dogs. I can't get my rents, and in the meantime law and order have become a farce. The court house burnt out. I told 'em I'd hold court in the schoolhouse.'

'When was this?'

'While you were at the cottage. But I needn't have bothered. Can you imagine – giving judgement in a schoolroom? Anyway, Maclean – this happened while you were away – had his car stolen one night. It was found in Macroom three days later. Maclean had a pretty shrewd idea who was behind it, and as it happened a shopkeeper in Macroom had seen Matty Nolan driving it through the town late one evening. So Nolan was arrested, and Shaunessy was sent for to give evidence.' Hugh gave a wry smile. 'In the meantime, Shaunessy had developed an acute attack of amnesia – couldn't remember a thing after all – and this was after he had described the whole thing to Maclean, mark you. But never a word could I get out of him.

'"Now then, Shaunessy," I said to him, "you told Mr Maclean you saw Matty Nolan driving his car through Macroom." "I never said any such thing," he shouted at me. "It's all a mistake."'

Hugh sighed, and stuffed his hands in his pockets. 'There was nothing I could do. He wouldn't speak, and that was that. Afterwards I caught up with him outside his shop. "Look here, Shaunessy," I told him, "perjury's a very great evil." "And so's a bullet in the stomach," says he, and with that off he goes.'

Hugh was almost out of the room when he turned. 'I'm out of a job, that's what it amounts to. They do what they like, take what they want, and no one will say a word. The

170

Volunteers are a law unto themselves. It's pure terror. I might as well give up for any good I can do.'

'Are you going to give up, Father?' Anne asked.

'Never.' He grunted, and pulled a pipe out of his pocket. 'Otherwise what's it all for, eh? I've sat on the bench for twenty-two years and I'm not going to be driven off it by a gang of farm lads. I'll hold court if it's in a barn!' He went out and moments after that they heard the door of his study bang.

Later Anne knocked on his door.

Hugh was standing before the mantelpiece scraping a pipe. He nodded her in. On the desk stood his *History of the Hunter Family*. She looked at it for a moment and then said, 'Are you working on your book?'

'Hmph. Not much else I can do at the moment.'

'Father – what Mr Daley said about the Martins' rent – is it going to make a big difference?'

'It will do if it gets round. If the others catch on – which they very well may do – it could become serious.'

She stood in the doorway, her hand on the handle, uncertain how to proceed. 'Because, you know, I wouldn't want to be a burden. I mean, if things are going to get tight, I can get a job.'

Hugh grunted. 'I dare say we can make do if the worst comes to the worst. I have my pension, and your mother has a bit of money. We won't be quite broke.'

'I know, but it isn't right for me to be living off you if you are going to be hard up.'

'Oh, yes? And what do you want to do?'

'I don't know. Get a job, I suppose.'

'Get a job? Is this some kind of a joke?'

'No, it is not.' She couldn't help her voice rising. 'Girls get all sorts of jobs nowadays, you know, secretaries and so on.'

'No daughter of mine goes out to work. This is your Republican nonsense again. You haven't learnt, have you?'

'Learnt what?'

'Has your mother been at you? Does she want you to go to Dublin and live in some flat? Get into all sorts of bad ways, eh? Mix with all sorts of undesirables?'

171

'I didn't say anything about going to Dublin! I only thought I should make some contribution if you're going to have difficulties ...'

'Thank you! When I need your help, Anne, I'll inform you. In the meantime your place is here.'

Ten days later a man in a raincoat and a Homburg hat cycled up to the door, and was still pulling off his bicycle clips as Bridget greeted him.

He was shown into Hugh's study, but only a few minutes later they could hear from the dining room Hugh's voice, raised first in incredulity and then it seemed in anger. A few moments later the study door opened abruptly. Anne went out into the hall. She saw Hugh wrench open the front door, and the man raised his hat and went out.

The dogs had leapt up, barking at the sound of the raised voice, and Anne attempted to still them.

'Of all the confounded – no, no, and a thousand times no!' her father shouted after the visitor.

The front door slammed.

'What is it?'

Hugh came towards her and she retreated into the dining room where Claire was finishing her breakfast.

'Darling – do you know who that was? I still don't believe it. Damn his confounded impudence!'

'Who was it?'

'That solicitor from Macroom – Smythe. Look at this.' Hugh was still incoherent as he thrust out a paper.

Anne took it and was looking through it as he went on. 'It's a summons to appear before a Republican Arbitration Tribunal.'

'But why?'

'This is Daley's doing! Damn him, going behind my back. He's taken Martin to the Republican court.'

'What?'

'Don't ask me to explain! I'll just give it to Daley when I see him. A damn' solicitor summoning *me* to appear! What on earth does Daley think he's playing at?'

'Perhaps he thinks you can call Martin's bluff?'

'I'll call his bluff! Damn Martin and all his tribe! To think that that man – I've known Martin since he was born. Went to his father's funeral. And now I think of it, I paid the nurse who attended his wife's first lying-in.'

He stalked out of the room. Claire and Anne looked at each other.

'Typical of tenants,' Claire said after a while. 'So ungrateful. I never liked Martin.'

However, when she thought about it, Anne decided that it was her duty to support the Republican court, even if it gave judgement against her own family. British justice had always favoured the gentry, people like herself, it was well known. It was only a matter of common justice to support the Republican courts that were trying to set up a system that would be fair to the poor, the real people of Ireland.

After long thought and in some trepidation she tackled her father about it. She opened the door to his study.

'Father, I think you should go.'

'What?'

'That Republican tribunal – you know.'

'Anne ...'

'Look, I know what you're going to say.' She came a step into the room. 'But if for no other reason, you can't be any worse off, can you? Martin won't pay his rent. There's nothing you can do to force him – unless you go over there with a shotgun and demand it to his face.'

'Hmm! I might just do that!'

'No! At least the Republican Tribunal is a peaceful organisation. It can't do you any harm to go, even if you only give them a piece of your mind.'

Hugh stared at her across the study, and slowly nodded his head. 'I should have expected you to come down in their favour. Anne, have you actually thought what you're saying? If I attend this so-called tribunal, as you suggest, I am admitting to the world that the British system of justice in this country is worthless! That the rebels have won!'

She looked at him steadily. 'I think you're afraid to go,' she said quietly.

'Afraid?'

'I think you're afraid to go and face them.'

'How dare you!' He started to his feet. 'Get out of here!'

173

'Father, you don't have to recognise the court. Don't you see? You can tell them that you don't recognise the court if you want to. Tell them what you think of them. But at least go! You won't compromise yourself in any way.'

'I compromise myself simply by being there!'

'At least give it a try.'

He was staring at her in fury, but for a moment at a loss for words. She turned and ran quickly out of the house and slammed the front door behind her. The dogs began to bark.

However a week later Hugh did drive in to Macroom, and Anne went with him. The tribunal was to take place in Smythe's solicitor's office.

'Mind, I concede nothing,' her father said as they were driving into the town. 'I just want to let them know what I think of them.'

'That's all right.'

They met Martin on the steps of the office. He was in a black suit that looked as if it came out only on Sundays, and took off a flat cap as they went into a dark office that looked out on a stable yard. A desk was covered with papers, and shelves were stuffed with parchment rolls thick with dust. As she sat and looked down at the linoleum on the floor, Anne's heart sank. The whole place had a dingy, seedy air. Daley arrived soon after, bustling in looking important as he always did, and he and Hugh went into a huddle in the corridor outside the office. Hugh returned looking black. Martin was on the opposite side of the room, looking out of the window.

No one spoke.

Then Mr Smythe – he of the bicycle clips – came in followed by two other men she did not know, and they took their places behind Smythe's desk.

Her father immediately recognised one of these men, a large, complacent type in a new-looking tweed suit and hard collar.

'Hmm! O'Halloran! Now I understand,' he muttered.

Mr Smythe, who seemed very polite and mild-mannered, opened the proceedings, by introducing the two men, one a solicitor like himself. But he had scarcely got going when Hugh stood up.

'I want to say I do not recognise –'

Daley took him strongly by the elbow, and tried to press him down. However Hugh pulled his arm away and went to the door.

'I do not recognise the legitimacy of this court! I give notice, this assembly has no legal validity!' And he went out, slamming the door. The three men behind the desk stood up in consternation, but Daley was quicker and called out strongly, 'Never mind, gentlemen – let the court proceed! I undertake to speak on behalf of Colonel Hunter.'

After a moment's whispered discussion the tribunal sat again. Martin sat on the other side of the room, smiling, his arms crossed.

Anne got up and walked quickly out into the corridor. Hugh was not there, and she went into the street. Her father was halfway up the pavement on the other side, and she ran after him.

'Mr Daley says he's going to stay to represent your interests.'

'Daley can go to hell! As soon as I saw O'Halloran, I saw what was up!' Hugh would not slow down.

'I don't understand?'

'He put Martin up to this! And I'll bet he's in cahoots with Daley too. I should have known!'

'Who is he?'

'A confounded gombeen of a fellow! No family at all. His grandfather made a fortune buying up encumbered estates after the famine. He thinks he can get his hands on my land through this Republican court, confound him!'

He stalked on in silence and then swung round. 'Anne, this is your doing! I should never have listened to you. It was a mistake coming in. I've made a fool of myself. After all these years, I can't believe it. After all these years…'

They drove home in silence. After the fiasco of the court appearance, Hugh shut himself in his study for the afternoon.

Anne found Claire alone.

'Father's very upset. He walked out of the tribunal,'

'I knew he would. What can you expect? What did Daley think he was doing?'

*

175

However, late that afternoon Mr Daley appeared in his pony and trap. He looked cheerful, and asked to speak to Hugh, but Anne knocked on his door with some trepidation.

'It's Mr Daley,' she said quietly. Hugh was at his desk writing.

'Tell him to go to the devil.'

'Good news,' Daley whispered.

'He says it's good news, Father.'

'Does he?' said Hugh expressionlessly.

'Martin's agreed to pay,' Daley whispered to Anne.

'*What?*' Her voice was loud in surprise. 'Father, Martin's going to pay!'

Hugh swivelled in his chair to face the door where Daley was crowding in over Anne's shoulder.

'We got a judgement, sir. I knew we would!'

'Are you mad?'

'Not a bit of it! I knew it all along!'

'But how?'

'Didn't I tell ye?'

Hugh got up. 'What on earth...?'

'Isn't it what I said, Colonel! The *legitimacy* of the court, sir, would be *impugned* if they failed to uphold the rights of property!'

'What? Martin's a notorious Republican!'

'Indeed, sir – and that's the whole point! If you could only have seen his face when they gave judgement in your favour! I thought he was going to have an apoplexy! He simply could not believe it! But it was a Republican court, you see, so he couldn't dispute the verdict now, could he? We all know what happens to those who do!'

He raised a knowing eyebrow.

'And when is he going to pay, I wonder?' Hugh said rather cynically.

'Oh, he's paid – that's why I wasn't over earlier. The money's in the bank, Colonel!'

Hugh stood grey-faced, still struggling to come to terms with this. Later, after Daley had gone and the three of them sat over tea, he still could not take it in.

'They recognise me as a landlord, but not as a magistrate. The world's gone mad!'

*

The effect on Claire of this extraordinary verdict was quite different. She was very relieved. 'Well, darling, I really wasn't looking forward to spending my old age in poverty,' she said to Anne after Hugh had gone out.

And then, after a couple of turns about the room: 'We mustn't let them see that they have triumphed! It is our duty to carry on as normal! Anne darling, we must get out. And we ought to have people over to dinner – the Archers – we owe them a dinner.' She swung about. 'And, heavens, how dingy the place has become! We must spring clean the house –'

'Spring Clean? Mother, it's October!'

'Never mind! We'll wash the curtains!'

When this idea was put to Bridget, she could only say, 'Sure, didn't we wash the curtains back in May, Mrs Hunter? And how are we going to dry them when it's raining every day?'

Claire opened the piano again, and rattled off a movement from a Beethoven sonata. 'I am determined that Vere's death will not crush our spirits! I know he would not have wanted us to mope for ever.'

On another wet afternoon she had an idea for 'An Evening of Gaelic Song and Verse'.

'It is up to us, the educated élite, to hold aloft the beacon of Irish learning and culture. I am an Irishwoman first and foremost.'

Anne looked up. 'Are you sure, Mother?'

'What do you mean?'

'I am beginning to think we belong to a different Ireland than the others – the "mere Irish" as Grandfather used to say. I am beginning to wonder whether we belong at all.'

'How can you say such a thing? Anne, I am ashamed of you! This is your country! You were born here! The family has been here for centuries!'

She looked down and murmured, 'I suppose so.'

On another afternoon of steady rain they sat together in silence. Anne was reading, and Claire had been sewing when she looked up from her work and out of the window.

'What is it?' Anne asked.

'Oh, I was thinking of Vere.'

There was silence between them for a moment. Then Claire said dreamily, 'You know, I see now that he will always be with me. On his birthdays, I shall think, Vere would have been fifteen, or sixteen, or – and then, twenty-one, and he would have come of age, and there would have been a special party for him, and he would have received the key of the door, and then when he would have been twenty-five or -six, I shall look at young women in the street and think, Vere might have married her, or her, or her...'

Anne crossed to her mother as her voice faded into silence, and took her in her arms.

As Claire wept she looked up and whispered, 'Do you think he can see us, Anne? Do you think he's looking down and watching us?'

'I am sure he is.'

# Chapter Nineteen

Anne wiped the window with her glove again and looked out. There was little to see. Through the slanting rain in the dying light she made out a wasteland of railway lines, sidings, carriages, and a shunting engine sending up puffs of steam as it negotiated a line of filthy black coal-trucks. All the dismal debris of a railway station.

The train was slowing, bumping across tracks, coming at last under the wide canopy of the station. The two officers who had shared her compartment stood up to reach kitbags and suitcases from the rack above. One of them lifted hers down too. She yawned; it had been hot and stuffy in the compartment, but there been complaints when she had tried to open the window, and she had sunk slowly into a lethargic doze.

She was in Dublin, at the Kingsbridge station. As she walked up the platform among the other passengers there were soldiers everywhere scanning people as they passed. At the front of the station she looked out at a dreary prospect of wet cobbles, the vast industrial outline of the brewery opposite, a street light coming on, and the lamplighter descending from his ladder. There was an armoured car standing in the road, and two big army lorries opposite, and near her a group of Tommies in great coats and steel helmets smoking and talking among themselves. She could hear their English accents and how odd they sounded.

There was an old wreck of a side car standing near her, the horse's head drooping in the steady downpour, though the jarvey was nowhere to be seen; and two motor cabs, their engines idling. Looking up at the low monotonous expanse above her, she was inclined to take one. Then dismissed the thought.

In a letter Pippa had told her to take the tram along to O'Connell bridge, and then another to Merrion Square. Anne turned up the collar of her long navy blue raincoat and, pulling her felt hat down tight, took up her suitcase and raced across through the rain to where the tram stood waiting.

She knew Dublin slightly but had more often passed through it on her way to school in England than stayed to explore. Pippa knew the city better. She had often come up to go shopping before she had got married, and now she was living here.

The tram lurched into motion, rattling and bumping across lines and gathering speed as it set off along the quay. Anne stared out at the river on her left, half visible in the rain, dirty, grey, the buildings beyond it shabby and mean. She had never liked Dublin only – her attention was distracted by a furious hooting and she turned just in time to see the two army lorries come racing and bumping over the cobbles past the tram. She thought there must be some chase, some emergency, but no one else even turned their head. The man next to her did not look up from the newspaper he was reading.

As she was waiting for her tram in College Green, the elegant façade of Trinity College dark behind her and the cobbled street glinting in the light of the shops opposite, there was another blare of hooters and three large lorries with the odd-looking chicken-wire frames fitted over them went roaring by and away down the street. Somehow the war seemed more immediate here, the enemy more numerous and apparent.

When her tram finally pulled up she climbed in, soaking wet by now and dripping in her saturated raincoat, and sat in the warmth. It was filled with evening rush-hour travellers: office girls chatting to each other in the Dublin accent which sounded so harsh to her ears, after the soft brogue of Cork, and gentlemen in raincoats and Homburg hats and spats reading the evening newspaper. Looking over a man's shoulder she saw the front page of the *Dublin Evening Herald* filled with a story of a raid by government forces on the offices of an illegal Republican news-sheet.

Then she was hauling her suitcase along the broad pavement of Merrion Square, squinting up in the rain at the majestic brick façade, and trying to make out the house numbers in the distant light of a street lamp.

Number thirty-nine. She pulled at a brass handle in the wall and heard a distant jangling.

The door flew open and Pippa was there, by now visibly pregnant. She shouted back over her shoulder: 'It's all right, Mrs O'Connor, she's arrived!' then took Anne by the elbow, and pulled her in. 'Come in, you look like a drowned rat! You'd better bring your suitcase up yourself. If we leave it to Mrs O'Connor, you won't get it till midnight. Mrs O'Connor!' she shouted down over the banisters into the basement. 'Bring some hot water up for my sister!'

The hallway was paved in stone, and a staircase with a graceful wrought iron balustrade led upwards. Anne shook out her hat and followed Pippa up two floors, where she threw open the door to a small bedroom furnished simply with an old dark oak bedstead, a wardrobe and wash-stand.

'You'd better get out of those things first, and then we can have tea. Tony will be in later. Once you've changed, come downstairs. The drawing room is the next floor down.'

Left alone Anne unpacked her things. After a few minutes there was a knock at the door; a plump middle-aged woman had brought a copper hot-water can.

'Thanks. You must be Mrs O'Connor?'

'I am. Welcome to Dublin, Miss Hunter. If you'd like to give me your wet things, I'll take them down to the kitchen to dry.'

Anne washed and changed and twenty minutes after she had arrived, found her way down to the drawing room.

It was a large pleasant room with a cheerful coal fire burning. Around her on the walls hung sporting prints, pictures of race horses and fox hunts in Victorian style, and in front of the fire, in a deep, comfortable old sofa, Pippa was curled up sewing.

'I've told Mrs O'Connor to bring us some tea.'

Anne sat in an armchair to one side of the fire. It was bliss to relax in these comfortable surroundings, and for a moment she simply enjoyed the warmth and the friendly crackle from the flames. Pippa looked the picture of domestic contentment.

'Thanks for having me,' Anne said at last.

'That's all right,' Pippa said briefly without looking up. 'Mother said you needed a change.'

'Oh. Did she?'

'Yes. I hope you've been behaving yourself?'

'What you do mean?'

'You know very well what I mean. Have you?'

'Since Vere died I haven't done anything or seen anyone except the family.'

'Good. Come here and give me a kiss.'

Anne crossed and gave her a sisterly peck on the cheek.

'Anyway, how are you?' she said after a moment.

'As well as can be expected. For someone who's expecting. I saw the doctor again yesterday. It should arrive in the middle of April.'

'How wonderful!'

'It is and it isn't. You can imagine how I feel about Tony every time he goes out on some night raid. It was bad enough before ...' She bit off the end of the thread, and held up the little piece of work she had in her hands to examine it. Anne saw it was a baby's smock. 'If anything happens to him ...' Then her voice picked up. 'Anyway, I'll be able to show you round in the meanwhile.'

'Thanks. It seems a long time since I was in Dublin.'

The housekeeper brought them a cup of tea, and then a little after seven Tony came in. He was in battle uniform and had a large pistol in a holster at his belt. He looked ready for action, and seemed full of energy and resolution. With him was a friend.

'I've brought Sandy back for a bite of supper.'

'Good evening, Pippa.'

Sandy was thin and quite good-looking, with a mournful smile which Anne thought quite attractive in a man. He was quietly spoken, rather in Tony's shadow – but perhaps that was only because he was a guest.

'Make yourself at home, old man. Whiskey?'

'Very kind.'

'Can't have you skulking off to that God-forsaken room of yours.'

'What's wrong with it?' Pippa looked up.

Sandy shook his head with a wistful smile. 'Oh, it does me well enough, Pippa.'

'Bosh!' Tony was fiddling with bottles on a side table by one of the tall windows, now curtained for the night. 'It's the most dismal little garret, on the top floor. Why can't you get yourself some decent digs? And that landlady of yours is enough to curdle the milk. Say when.'

'Thanks, old man. Much obliged. Anyway, I prefer to be on the top floor. No unpleasant surprises.'

She noticed now he had a faint Scottish accent, and when he raised his glass, thought what kind eyes he had.

At one point, when Sandy was out of the room, Tony whispered, 'Be nice to him, Anne – he's had a hard time lately.' And she immediately felt drawn to him. He had a secret sorrow, she had felt it instinctively the moment they met. Perhaps he had lost a comrade in battle? It often happened. She saw that they had a bond in common.

During dinner Sandy did not have a lot to say; Tony kept things going with an account of his day: a chase out to Blackrock in the suburbs after a member of the clandestine Republican Government – a wild goose chase as it turned out. 'The bird had flown.' Then a tirade against Lloyd George: 'That perfidious little Welsh goat – pardon the expression, ladies.'

Pippa raised her eyebrows to Anne. 'In the end you get used to army talk.' But at length, over the coffee cups, Anne found herself tête-à-tête with Sandy.

It turned out he was a widower. Pippa had managed to slip this snippet of information to Anne during the evening, and she immediately felt a rush of sympathy. It gave him a certain dignity – he was a man who had suffered – and for a moment she wondered whether perhaps his wife had died in childbirth. She had a horrible vision of Pippa suffering the pangs of birth – how easily these things could go wrong. She felt doubly drawn to Sandy as he held his coffee cup, gazing into the fire with a mournful expression.

'It was the most terrible mix up, Anne. I shall never forgive myself –'

'What do you mean, Sandy?' she said softly.

183

'Well, you see, Audrey suffered from high blood pressure and the doctor had prescribed tablets for it. I myself didn't think she needed them, but the doctor knew better. And I – by the most cursed of evil coincidences – have to take pills for a weak heart. I shall never forget that night.' He drew the most painful of long breaths. 'Audrey had just gone upstairs to clean her teeth – she was most particular about cleaning her teeth – and she always took her tablets before going to bed. We kept them all in the bathroom cabinet. I heard the most terrible crash, and rushed upstairs.' He paused, looking down, unable to meet Anne's eyes. 'She was lying on the bathroom floor. Dead.'

'You don't mean –'

Sandy nodded, and caught her eye; obviously she had read his mind. 'She took the wrong tablets. The most appalling thing.'

Anne was almost speechless. 'How terrible,' she breathed at last.

'Mind you,' he continued in his intimate way, his voice low, looking deep into her eyes now, 'she wasn't herself. There's no doubt to my mind – I told the coroner this, and he agreed – the balance of the mind had been disturbed.'

'Heavens!'

'It was only two days since Jip had been run over.'

'Jip?'

'Our Yorkshire terrier,' he sighed. 'Delightful little fellow, Audrey took it very hard. He went everywhere with us, you see. Devoted to us. And then one morning – it was a Saturday, I remember – he heard the cat's meat man ringing his bell, and ran out into the road. Jip always recognised that bell, and knew there'd be some special treat for him. I blame myself, Anne. You see I'd left the garden gate open – by pure chance, as it happens – and yet, looking back, I wonder if it wasn't fated? I was trimming the privet hedge, and out ran Jip.'

He gave Anne a significant look.

'You mean ...?'

Sandy nodded again. 'Right under the hooves of the milkman's horse – old Dobbin, a lovely old fellow, pure-bred Suffolk Punch. I try to tell myself he wouldn't have felt anything.'

'Dobbin?' Anne breathed. Sandy thought for a moment.

'Jip. I should never have opened that gate. Strictly speaking, I was under orders from the MO to take no violent exercise – since my hernia operation, you see. I can't bring myself to look at that hedge now. I've never touched it since that day.'

'I should think not. Who trims it?'

'I have a man. Anyway the house is let while I'm over here. A very nice couple – he's a cripple,' Sandy added thoughtfully, 'but his wife is devoted.'

Tony showed Sandy down to the door at ten. As he came in again, he said, 'Good of you to take on old Sandy, Anne. He really appreciated it, I can tell you.'

'Oh,' she said faintly, 'it's nothing. Was he making it up?'

'Don't think so. Why?'

'He sounded like the Ancient Mariner. I couldn't believe it.'

'Anyway it makes a big difference to him, thanks again.'

That night Anne stood in her room, staring out of her window into the square. The streetlamps showed in glimmering spots beneath her in the blackness, islands of light diffused by the trees. She stared idly at lights in other windows, wondering who lived in the houses. She watched the smoke wafted from chimney pots by the wind, leaning with her chin on her hand, thinking or not thinking, only letting thoughts flow through her mind as they chose, idle thoughts, and feeling glad she had decided to come.

Then from somewhere far away she heard a repeated cracking sound, and it was a moment before she realised it was the sound of gun-shots; and a moment later the distant sound of lorries revving violently and driving over cobbles at high speed. She waited in case there should be more, tense, straining to hear, but the city settled down again and she was left apprehensive and alert, wondering what had happened, and whether anyone had been killed.

The following morning it had stopped raining, the sky was filled with racing high clouds, and the trees in the square in front of the house reached up, desolate and bare, in the cold winter air.

Anne and Pippa made their way down the wide empty street, wrapped in overcoats, woolly hats pulled down to their ears, striding along the wet shining pavement.

The centre of Dublin was busy.

'We could look round Switzer's, and then go for coffee in Bewlay's – what do you say?'

Anne nodded. They walked down Grafton Street which was busy. As they walked through the smartly dressed morning crowds – for this was after all the most fashionable shopping street in the country – elegant women would sometimes get in and out of large cars, squired by men in well-fitting overcoats and tight bowler hats or escorted inside by chauffeurs. Or it might be officers in uniform, brisk in elegant top boots, polished to a deep gleam, and snug-fitting Sam Browns, or important-looking men carrying briefcases, striding past. Shopkeepers would appear at doorways, rubbing their hands together as they wished a very good morning to each important and valued customer. Dublin looked normal, secure, safe. For a moment there was no sign of military activity, no rushing lorries.

Outside Switzer's an old beggar woman accosted them, three overcoats hanging open, every one of them a grease-encrusted, frayed, disintegrating relic, while beneath them her ancient blouse was unbuttoned at the neck to the chill February wind. A haystack of a hat, which had once had some pretensions to finery, was perched on the back on the abundant grey mass of her hair.

'For the love of God, lady, will yiz give an old woman a copper, that's lost her man fighting for his King and country, God bless yiz, and a pretty young colleen like yeself, and me with never a sixpence to pay the rent and won't I be put out in the street this very Saturday –'

Anne was already feeling in her pocket for her purse but Pippa laughed and put her own hand over her sister's. 'My treat! This "ould wan" is the notorious Meg. I'll give you sixpence, you old hypocrite, if you promise you won't spend it on spirits!'

'Lord bless you! Sperrits!' She drew herself up haughtily. 'Do I look the sort? Sperrits! Be the Blessed Virgin, have I lived this long to be lectured be a chit of a girl! Have I fallen

186

so low that I'm not allowed a drap of Christian cheer, but a child is to tell me what I may or may not do?'

'Go along with you, Meg,' Pippa said cheerfully, 'we know you of old.'

But the old woman would not let her continue. 'Let me tell yiz, young lady,' pointing a finger in Pippa's face aggressively, 'there was a time when I could hold me head up higher than some here that now lord it up and down, that should know better than to take advantage of a broken old lady that's known better times.'

'Well, really.' Passers-by turned to watch as Pippa, embarrassed, attempted to shield herself from the 'ould wan's' breath. Meg leered into her face, warming to her theme.

'Sperrits!' she went on, in a voice now broken with emotion. 'I should think I should have need of sperrits in me lowness of heart, brought down to beg from a girl that should know how to respect them that have suffered the woes of the world.'

Pippa, flustered, was about to open her purse to give her more when Anne, who had been watching with rising incredulity, stopped her and turned to the old woman.

'Hold your tongue, you old fool! Who do you think you're talking to? You should be grateful for what you have! Come on, Pippa.' She took her sister's arm and steered her into the shop.

As they came into the warm, hushed interior of the great department store, Pippa looked round at her and a grin slowly crossed her face. 'Still the same old Anne after all, I see.'

'I can't stand the hypocrisy of it. It's one thing to give a beggar money, but to be browbeaten into giving more –'

Pippa threaded her arm through Anne's and gave it a squeeze. 'Come on, what do you want to look at?'

But a moment later Anne disentangled herself and turned quickly out of the shop again, reaching her purse from her pocket as she pushed through the door. A few seconds later she returned, and took Pippa's arm.

'I'm learning,' she muttered, without looking at Pippa, 'only very slowly. Very, very slowly.'

Later, on their way up to Bewlay's Oriental Café, they passed the Café Cairo. An advertisement outside proclaimed

'Tea Dances'. Pippa looked at Anne to see if she had noticed. She hadn't. Pippa jogged her elbow.

'Tony and I go quite often – with friends. You'll have to come, you never know who you might meet.' She gave her a significant smile.

Pippa decided to give a dinner party – partly to introduce her sister to some of her friends – and Anne spent the afternoon helping her with the preparations. Mrs O'Connor was no great cook, though Pippa was quite particular about food. She would have been down in the kitchen herself if she hadn't to be in the drawing room welcoming guests. Anne limited herself to helping to set the table and tidy the drawing room. The coal fires left a permanent layer of grime over everything during the winter months, and needed continual attention.

On the night she washed her hair, and changed into a plum-coloured velvet dinner frock. Looking at herself in the wardrobe mirror in her room, she felt depressed. At this minute she had no great wish to make herself presentable. For whom, after all?

The guests began to arrive, and Anne stood awkwardly ready to make what small talk she could.

Then Sandy appeared and, seeing her, made straight for her. Anne's heart sank. A single man – it looked as if she would be stuck with him for the evening.

But even as she thought this and Sandy was telling her how much he had enjoyed their last conversation, and appreciated her sympathy, she saw over his shoulder the door open again and Lewis Crawford come in.

# Chapter Twenty

Tony was talking to him, and they were laughing. Then Tony touched his arm, and was leading him across the room, and she was making an absurd pretence of listening to Sandy, and Tony was saying, 'Lewis, do you remember Anne, Pippa's sister? Anne, this reprobate is a chum of mine, Lewis Crawford.'

He was offering her his hand and smiling, and her heart was beating so painfully she could not think of a word to say, but in any case Tony had gone on, 'Of course you know Sandy,' and Lewis had turned to him. 'Sandy, haven't seen you in ages.' And they started talking. Anne was waiting for Lewis to turn back to her but he wouldn't.

A moment later Pippa was at her elbow, 'Anne darling, keep Sandy company. Lewis! Why haven't we seen you lately? Come and tell Pippa *all* your news.'

And she had taken his arm and steered him to the sofa. There were only the five of them in the room as yet, and Tony was at a side table pouring out sherry. As Pippa and Lewis sat on the sofa, Anne was able to recover her wits and watch him. He was there in a real physical way she had not remembered. He seemed perfectly relaxed, but had greeted her as if she were a distant friend he barely remembered.

'How's the little one? Any movement?'

'Yes, Lewis, as a matter of fact. I can definitely assure you he's there. He woke me this morning, kicking.'

'Perhaps he was dreaming?'

'Dreaming? Can babies dream in the womb?'

'I say, steady on, Lewis.' Tony crossed with glasses of

sherry on a silver tray. 'Bit early in the evening for all that, isn't it? Sherry, Anne?'

'Thanks.'

Her voice sounded colourless, distant. Lewis did not notice in any case, and went on. 'The question is whether babies are awake or asleep before they're born? I'm inclined to think they're asleep. Ergo, they must have dreams.'

'But what would they dream about?'

'This is typical of you, Lewis,' Tony said as he offered him the sherry. 'Not two minutes into the room, and you've started some hare.'

It was true, thought Anne, now a little more in control of her own breathing. Whenever Lewis was there people perked up, turned round, put down their sewing or the book they were reading.

'Perhaps they have ancestral dreams,' he went on, 'falling out of trees, that sort of thing, memories passed on through the generations. And then, when you move I expect he's aware of it, or if he's asleep he senses it and it enters his dream – you know how when you're asleep, outside events get incorporated into your dream?'

'Like when you dream there's someone knocking at the door, and it turns out to be a branch knocking at the window? Well, chin-chin, everybody.'

They all raised their glasses.

'Here's to the wee one,' said Lewis.

At that moment the front doorbell rang beneath them again, and Tony went out of the room.

Two women soon entered, followed by a man talking to Tony. The man, like all the others, was in a dinner jacket, wing collar and black tie, and the women were in new evening gowns. As Anne looked at them she wondered why she was in this dowdy old velvet frock when the woman being introduced to her – Dora – was in a striking and flimsy black silk dress barely past the knee, bare shoulders with shoe-lace shoulder straps – a dress that betrayed every movement, every shudder or wriggle of the body beneath it as she moved.

Dora was the sister of the woman married to the man with the ginger moustache. They all seemed much older than Anne and to have known each other for ever.

'Lewis!' Dora saw him across the room, and moved quickly away from Anne. She wore yards and yards of jet black beads that rattled and clashed as she moved. Anne saw that Lewis knew her too, and was pleased to see her. He smiled at her in a way he had not done at Anne.

She drew a long breath, and turned again to Sandy.

The married woman, Winnie, was in an elegant brick-red dress in the medieval style with a low waistline at the hip and 'peasant' embroidery around it, a gold fillet in her hair. She started talking to Pippa about her four-year-old daughter, who had made such a fuss as they were about to come out this evening – as if they had never been out and left her before – but children were not the most considerate of beings, apparently. 'I told her I'd take her to the zoo. That shut her up. Selfish little beast! You don't know what you're in for, Pippa, believe me!'

Pippa was in the elegant maternity gown they had bought together in Switzer's – eau-de-nil washed silk, with a thick girdle round the hips, long tassles hanging down from it, and stockings to match.

Dora had now lit a cigarette, and they had been joined by the married man. Anne watched Lewis talking to this man – Pat Quinn, the one with the ginger moustache. Lewis was standing with his feet apart, one hand in his pocket, the other tapping Mr Quinn on the chest to make a point. Mr Quinn laughed, Dora laughed, and unexpectedly there arose within Anne a spirit of resistance. Lewis looked so easy and relaxed – why should she wait for him to snub her again? For the first time since Vere's death she felt a resurgence of her old spirit. He had found her wanting; dropped her in Lisheen. She did not intend to mope after him.

She realised with a start that Sandy was talking to her and dragged her attention back to him. All the guests now appeared to be present, and Pippa announced that dinner was ready. Sandy offered Anne his arm, and as they went down to dinner she was relieved to see that Lewis had Winnie, the married lady, as his partner. Once they were seated at the dinner table, however, she found herself still next to Sandy, but opposite her, although Winnie was on one side of Lewis, Dora was on the other, the further side. Anne could see her face as she leaned in to Lewis, but not his.

'Audrey gave me many happy moments, Anne, which I shall always treasure.' Sandy leaned closer with his wistful, confidential, button-holing manner. But she was straining to hear what that Dora was saying. 'A paragon of a woman – I shall never forget her. You know, I can remember our wedding day as if it were yesterday. Audrey looked ravishing in her bridal gown. And her father was a charming old chap – one of the real old school – deaf as a post, but you know, I thought his deafness rather suited him. So, of course, it was perfectly natural he should get the two churches muddled up.'

Anne wrenched her attention away from Lewis. 'Pardon?'

'I told him St Botolph's, Aldgate – it's an old church in the City of London – and he thought I'd said St Botolph's, Aldersgate. Another church altogether. Perfectly reasonable mistake.'

He shook his head slightly still with that mournful smile.

'Perfectly understandable mistake, no fault of his, Anne,' he went on hastily. 'But of course we were waiting in St Botolph's, Aldgate, all the guests, guard of honour, the vicar, everything ready, and there was no sign of Audrey.'

Now she distinctly made out the words, 'You were positively invited –' and Dora was leaning in towards Lewis, tapping him on the arm, and Anne was straining to catch his reply, but Sandy went on.

'I don't mind admitting for one moment – one disloyal moment, Anne – I thought she had funked it.'

'You had your usual luck, Dora,' Lewis was saying.

'Absolutely! The filly romped home! Told you she would, by half a furlong. At three to one too. Your loss. Lovely animal – I was offered a hundred and twenty for her right after the race.'

'Not my loss, as a matter of fact, Dora. I had a little arrrangement with a chap here in Dublin –'

'Lewis told us about your win, Dora!' Pippa called across. 'Congratulations. And he told us to have a fiver on Scarlet Lightning. Lucky you.'

'Luck had nothing to do with it. It's breeding.'

The soup was being served now, and Anne realised with a jolt Sandy was still talking. 'You know what the City's like, Anne – a church on every corner – so even when the chauffeur had found out the mistake, he was still hopelessly lost, asking everywhere. Still, all's well that ends well.'

He picked up his soup spoon with relish.

'Audrey turned up all right, bright as a button.' He took a mouthful of soup. 'And it was hardly her fault if, in the rush, poor dear, she should have tripped on the steps –'

'Oh no! Really?' Anne didn't know how long she was going to be able to keep this up.

''Course, anyone else would have said, a hundred years of bad luck, tripping on the church steps. But you didn't know Audrey – that wasn't her way –'

'Lewis!' Tony called across the table. 'Tell us that story you told me – about the old fellow down in Ennistymon.'

A slight frown passed across Lewis's face as he was distracted from Dora, but now Winnie added her appeal. 'Oh yes, go on, Lewis. I've been dying to hear it too.'

He looked round as if slightly surprised and also annoyed.

'Oh, I don't know ...'

'Yes, come on, Lewis.'

It was now impossible for him to get out of it, whatever it was, so he began. By this time the whole table was silent, waiting for him.

'Well, it was towards the end of the last year – I told you, Tony, you remember, after I got back from Clare. I'd been down to Ennistymon to visit an old couple, the Farrells. Didn't relish going, to tell the truth, he was a vile old curmudgeon, and gave his wife a hell of a time. But he was a client and duty was duty, so I duly arrived one evening last November. Got delayed through having to make a detour, and didn't get there till after dark. It's happened before and I expected they'd put me up. Nice big house they've got – or rather, had – but as soon as I arrived I realised something was up. The old butler was very gloomy, shaking his head and muttering as he showed me into the big old drawing room. I asked him what the matter was: "The missis is gone," he muttered. Well, to tell you the truth, I wasn't a bit surprised. In fact I was surprised she hadn't gone years ago – because they were both getting on a bit, and I should say the old boy must have been nearly eighty. "He drove her out," the old fellow repeated, "drove her out of her own house."' Lewis looked round. 'I should explain, she had been an heiress. When they married, he didn't have a penny and took her name as part of the deal. He'd given her a rotten life, by all accounts, and they had never had children. The butler fetched me a drink. "The master will be along directly," he said, "he'll tell you himself." Finally the old man shuffled in, looking terrible, and already well drunk, I'd say, and I was beginning to wish I'd put up in a hotel in Ennis. The place had the most horrible atmosphere.

'He starts on at me, railing against his wife for leaving him. She could die under a hedge for all he cared, and so on, terrible things. I said I was only here to take an order for wine, and I was sure they would sort things out amicably. He laughed in a most horrible way. Oh, yes! He'd sorted her out! And he only wished he'd done it years ago. In the meantime he'd been helping himself to the drink. He was going it pretty strong, and I was tipping half of mine into the aspidistra, as the saying goes.

'At last the butler announced dinner, which was just as well, as I was about to start chewing the carpet. But there was a very strange thing because when we sat down there were three places set. Couldn't make it out. Anyway the old fellow said nothing and the butler brought in the soup and started serving it and later brought in a bit of beef. But just as I finished lapping up my soup, I happened to look up.' He paused, and looked solemnly round the table. Everyone was hanging on his words. 'There was an elderly woman sitting in the empty place opposite – and I swear I had never noticed her come in. She looked very grey, I thought, as if she were ill, and just sat there very silent and still. Strange as it sounds, it didn't strike me as odd at the time. But the old fellow had just stood up to carve the joint when he raised his head and saw her too. He gave the most God awful shriek, dropped the carving knife, and fell under the table. It was pandemonium.

'I shouted for help and knelt by the old man under the table, trying to loosen his collar and calling all the time for the butler. He came in eventually and we managed to drag the old fellow free and stretch him out on the carpet. He was dead, of course; a stroke. And when I looked up, the lady had gone. A bit stupidly, I said, "Where's the lady gone?" "What lady?"

said the butler. I told him about her, and showed him where she had sat.' Lewis's voice had sunk. 'The butler looked at me very oddly, and after a while he said, "She came for him, you see. I knew she would." "Who?" I asked. "Mrs Farrell. He thought he'd got rid of her. He was wrong."'

His voice sank into silence. The table, even Sandy, had sat riveted by this tale. As Lewis finished there were murmurs, 'Extraordinary!', 'Reminds me of a story –', 'Amazing –'

At last Lewis drew a long breath and picked up his glass. He looked into it meditatively for a moment, and then went on, 'The worst thing was we'd opened a very fine bottle of Château Margaux, laid down in '05, just ready to drink. I couldn't bear to let it go to waste, so the butler and I finished it off.'

'Oh, Lewis!' Pippa screamed. 'You've done it again!'

The table exploded into laughter.

Later the ladies withdrew and went upstairs as the men were lighting their cigars.

Mrs O'Connor brought in a tray of coffee, and Anne made up the fire which had burnt low. It was easier to occupy herself with trifling duties than try to hold her own with the other women who were all older than herself. She knelt and poked at the fire as Pippa was pouring coffee.

'I can never quite imagine him selling wine, can you, Pippa?' she heard Winnie saying. 'Has he ever sold you any?'

'Why not? I imagine he could sell anything. But, no, he hadn't sold us any. Given us the odd bottle, mind you.'

'He went to work for his brother, didn't he?' Winnie went on. 'I don't blame him. After the war jobs were hard to find. And I don't think he has any money of his own. Not to my knowledge, anyway.'

Dora lit a cigarette as Anne stood dusting her hands, and took a coffee cup from Pippa.

'Who's he with these days?' Dora asked casually.

Pippa looked at Winnie and they both shrugged. 'No idea. Didn't he have a fling with Molly Byrne?'

'I don't think there was anything in that. If you ask me, I think she put that story about because she was keen on him and he wasn't obliging.'

'He's certainly very discreet,' said Pippa. 'Whoever it was, you'd never know.'

There was silence for a moment as they all thought about Lewis and women, and then Winnie said carelessly, 'With all that travelling, he's probably got a girl in every port.'

'A girl in every castle!' Pippa and Winnie looked into each other's eyes and burst into giggles.

'A barmaid in every pub!'

'A laundrymaid in every hotel!'

'A stablegirl in every hayloft!' They were helpless with giggles.

'I don't think he's that sort,' Anne said very unexpectedly. Her voice sounded loud and harsh, and the other heads turned.

'Ooh!' Winnie's eyebrows rose as she sobered herself. 'Do you know him, Anne? Are you the dark horse? Don't say –'

'No, of course not.' She was confused. 'I only meant – he doesn't give that impression, that's all.'

'Don't go by impressions, my dear.' Dora leant over to put down her coffee cup, breathing out cigarette smoke.

'What do you mean?'

'Anne, don't be such a prig,' Pippa interrupted. 'I bet you're only annoyed because you weren't sitting next to him yourself.'

'Rubbish –'

'No, she had to listen to Sandy instead!' Winnie giggled again. 'Pippa – how could you do it to her?'

'Someone had to.' She turned to Anne. 'What's the matter? I thought you two were hitting it off so well?'

'Are you serious?'

A little later Winnie and Pippa were head to head on the sofa in discussion about small children, and Anne found herself by the fire with Dora.

'I think I'd pity the girl who had Lewis Crawford,' she said casually as she lit another cigarette.

Anne said nothing. When it was clear that she was not willing to enter into a juicy gossip, Dora continued, looking at her: 'He's too much of a rolling stone. When would you ever see him?'

'I really have no idea,' she said distantly.

The older woman looked down into the fire, with her head on one side.

'Well, be warned. He's a heart-breaker, that one.'

Anne said nothing and after a moment, looking up into her eyes, Dora went on, 'And one day he'll get his comeuppance.'

'What do you mean?' Anne couldn't resist saying.

'He'll find a woman who'll break his heart instead. It always happens. He'll end up married to some woman who'll lead him an absolute dog's life. I've seen it before.'

# Chapter Twenty-One

A little later there was a sound of feet on the stairs and the men came in, talking loudly among themselves.

'Any of that coffee left?' Tony was slightly flushed and rather boisterous.

'I'm surprised you've got room for it. You look full of port.'

'I say, that was uncalled for! Lewis, Sandy, Pat – am I full of port? I call you to witness, I've had as much as a man's entitled to – a married man, mark you.'

'Ah, but once you're married everything changes.'

'I'll lend you my red pencil, darling,' said Winnie, 'then you can mark the bottles. Anyway, come on, Lewis – coffee?'

He had been by the window. He had pulled back the curtain and was staring out at the night.

'Stopped raining anyway,' he said as he came back and threw himself into an armchair opposite Anne, looking at her calmly and steadily. 'There was a bit of sunshine this morning, thank God. Sometimes I think I'll go mad if the sun doesn't come out.'

'You've come to the wrong place for sunshine,' Pippa said, handing him his cup. 'I should have thought you would have realised that by now.'

'Hmm. I should have stayed in Egypt.' He was looking into Anne's eyes. 'I could get used to the Arab way of life. A lot of sitting about and drinking coffee. It would suit me perfectly.'

He was still looking at her while he talked to Pippa; looking at her in a calm meditative way, as if he were weighing up in his mind what to do with her, and whatever he decided she would have no choice but to obey.

But now, after hearing him discussed by the women, and after hearing the things Dora had said about him, Anne felt a stiffening of her resolve. Everything about him, his casual assurance, his ease, his worldly cosmopolitan way, all looked hollow, like a mask, a performance. And underneath, beneath the mask, was – what was the word that woman had used? – a heart-breaker.

Dora could not have had any idea of the effect that word had had on Anne, that word she had dropped so casually; Anne instinctively distrusted the woman but what she said made immediate sense of everything.

Dora perched herself on the arm of the chair in which Lewis was sitting, with her back to Anne, just as Sandy was leaning over to take Anne's coffee cup. In the most barefaced way Dora leant over him, her yards of jet beads clashing and swaying as she flicked them, talking to him in a low voice as if they were alone in the room.

'It's my birthday next month, you know,' Anne heard her say softly.

'Really?' He looked up, interested.

'I'm getting up a little party to go to the Café Cairo. Shall I send you an invitation? You're such a good dancer, Lewis. Will you come and dance with me?'

She dangled her beads back and forth in front of his face as if trying to bewitch him. Lewis smiled up at her. 'How can I resist?'

Then she leant over and whispered something, and he laughed. With a cat-like smile she rose, her mission accomplished.

Anne could feel her heart beating. There was something so shameless about it. Yet Dora did not seem to have been aware of her watching them.

Once she had taken herself off to talk to someone else, Anne found Lewis's eyes on her again. He leant forward.

'You don't seem to have much to say for yourself,' he said in an easygoing but familiar way, as if she were his sister.

'There doesn't seem any need. Everyone else has so much to say.'

Lewis looked round at the others, all talking loudly to each other, and smiled slightly. 'No doubt a lot to catch up on.'

'No doubt.'

After a moment he rose, came across to stand over her with his back to the others, and said more quietly, 'How are you?'

'As well as can be expected. How are you?'

'Me?' He shrugged. 'Much as usual. The same old round, you know.'

She said nothing. After a pause he went on, 'How long are you in Dublin?'

'No idea.'

'Pleasure or business?'

'Business? What business have I got, Lewis?'

He smiled archly. 'I don't know – but girls seem to get up to all sorts of things nowadays.'

She did not answer, and there was another long pause.

'Your parents – are they well?'

'What do you think?'

He nodded as if he understood what she was hinting at. Then after a very long silence, during which he looked away as if deep in thought, he went on, 'I wanted so say –' He seemed curiously hesitant now, unlike his normal self. He leant over her, but she did not move, sitting back in her chair, suddenly quite relaxed, her arms stretched out on either arm of the chair. She felt like a judge.

After a long silence, he picked up the conversation again with an effort.

'You know, I never wrote to thank you. You gave me a very pleasant time, you and your family. Lovely part of the world, Lisheen. Little corner of paradise.'

She looked up at him steadily. She couldn't understand what he was getting at. It was as if he were talking to the wrong girl. He appeared to have no memory of what had passed between them the previous summer, no memory that he had once asked her to marry him.

'You're very lucky. And your parents – will you remember me to them? Decent sort your father, pity there aren't more like him.'

She stood up abruptly. 'Hasn't it got hot in here all of a sudden? I think I'll go out for a breath of air.'

As she stood on the doorstep, it was all she could do to keep from crying. She could feel the tears smarting in the corners of her eyes. She stood taking in long gulping drafts of the cold night air, dragging the oxygen into herself as if to reflate her empty body, to pump herself up again to normal humanity after being utterly wrung out.

Then her eyes focused on the car parked outside the door. 'The Old Beast' in all its glory. The car summed up all that was so unjust, so cruel about it; the dream she had held so long, that bright memory, now tarnished and shabby. What was he? A philanderer, a 'heart-breaker'. That woman, who knew so much, and had such an easy worldly way, she knew him, it was obvious. She and Lewis were a match for each other. She had made Anne feel an utter amateur. And Lewis had noticed Anne watching them; that was why he was so awkward with her, it was obvious. The hypocrite. How tawdry, as if she were some ignorant girl for him to dazzle, an easy conquest, and something for him to boast about in the saloon bar.

She stood staring across at the wintry outline of the trees in the dark square, it seemed for ever. Then there was the sound of voices above her, and she collected her scattered wits to return to the drawing room where everyone was making their adieux, hands were being shaken and cheeks kissed, and Pippa was being congratulated on a magnificent dinner – as always – 'And wasn't it wonderful – we didn't mention the war once all evening!'

'Can I offer anyone a lift?'

There was a clattering of feet on the stairs, the door was closed and she returned to the drawing room, alone for a moment, and began absent-mindedly collecting glasses on to a tray.

The door opened again. She turned; it was Lewis.

They faced each other in silence for a moment across the room.

'I left my gloves.'

He looked vaguely about, and then at her again.

Voices outside the door. Lewis turned a last time.

'Sorry. Well, perhaps we might meet sometime?'

The door opened and Tony and Pippa came in. Lewis wished them goodnight again and went out.

Tony gave Pippa a peck on the cheek. 'Congratulations, darling. Another triumph.' They threw themselves into the armchairs on either side of the fireplace, almost as if Anne were not there.

She did not sleep well that night. Seeing Lewis had brought everything back: Vere, the ambush, the days with Lewis himself, the horrible disappointment. In a night which seemed to go on forever, she found herself condemned to go over and over events, emotionally churned, forcing herself to face the fact that Lewis had never loved her; he was merely a seducer, had played with her.

Anne woke feeling heavy and useless. However, she pulled herself out of bed, and went down to breakfast. Tony had already gone out. Pippa was having hers in bed, and later Anne went to see her. Heavy with pregnancy, she was propped up on pillows, a breakfast tray across her lap.

'How do you feel, darling?' Pippa might seem made of steel sometimes, but she also knew how to take care of herself. She was sitting up buttering toast.

'Fine, thanks. Did you sleep all right?'

'So-so. The lump gets very energetic early in the morning, but he's settled down for the moment. I shall stay here for the morning, I think. Are you doing anything?'

'I've arranged to go and see Aunt Ju.'

Pippa nodded. 'I thought you would.'

'What does that mean?'

'You couldn't keep away for long, could you?'

'I like her! Besides she's always been very good to me.'

'Hmph.'

'You're such a snob, Pippa! Just because she doesn't fit in with your ideas of respectability.'

'Or politics!' Pippa said with a sneer. 'You'll want to discuss the latest doings of your Republican friends, I suppose?'

Anne went cold. 'As a matter of fact, no. I gave Father my promise, as you know, and I shall keep it. But I like Aunt Ju very much, she's very interesting. And I may say, Pippa since you are being so free with your opinions, I have always hated the way you and Mother gang up on her.'

202

'Pooh! She lives like a tramp–'

'She does not! How can you say that!'

'She fills her house with all sorts of undesirables –'

'It's not her fault if she hasn't got much money.'

'And I suppose it wasn't her fault for running off to France and marrying some Bohemian so-called painter, who proceeded to spend all her money and then leave her in the lurch?'

Anne was silent. She turned in the doorway and said, 'Well, there is obviously no point in our discussing Aunt Ju. We will just have to agree to disagree. See you later.'

'Ta-ta.'

Aunt Julia lived a walk from Merrion Square in a less respectable area of the city, a Georgian house like Pippa's, but in a sadly run-down condition, weeds growing between the steps leading down into the area in front, and the old fan light over the front door in want of a clean. The door itself could do with a coat of paint too.

As Anne pulled at the antiquated brass bell-pull she heard within a ferocious barking, and as the door was opened Aunt Ju was shouting, 'Down, Mungo! Down, Jerry! Down, I say! Will you get down!' as two Highland terriers pranced round her in paroxysms of barking.

Anne was admitted by Mrs McEvoy, who had been with Aunt Ju ever since Anne could remember, a woman who did not suffer fools gladly and had taken over the running of the house to a large extent, leaving Ju to attend to her many interests.

The dogs were pacified and Anne was led up into Aunt Ju's drawing room. A room less like Pippa's could not be imagined. It had a shabby but comfortable feel to it, an old-fashioned, cluttered feel, and as always when she came to visit, Anne felt at home, as if with this woman she would not need to put on an act or pretend, and that there was no hurry.

Aunt Ju was in an overcoat and returned to a large table covered with papers, newspapers, journals, books, as Anne knelt to pacify the terriers.

'Come in, Anne, it's lovely to see you.'

'Oh, sorry – are you about to go out?'

'Eh? Lord, no! McEvoy, light us a fire!'

Mrs McEvoy leant against the door and said in a sarcastic

voice, 'Before you talk of fires, have you paid the coalman yet?'

'Hasn't he been paid?'

'*Hasn't he been paid?*' Mrs McEvoy mimicked her. 'You know very well he hasn't.'

'For heaven's sake,' Anne cried out, 'I beg you – don't light a fire on my account!'

'Nonsense. You are my favourite niece and I don't see you as often as I'd like. Go on, McEvoy. The coalman can wait a few more days. Has Mr Hannigan paid his rent?'

'He has not.'

'Well, catch him before he goes out tonight. I know him of old.'

In fact, the room was not warm, and it was easy to see that Ju was economising on coal. Beneath her overcoat, she wore what had once been a very elegant day gown, rather long by the standards of the day, in a design of gold and brown. Her hair was put up in a haphazard fashion, as if she'd had other things on her mind at the time and had thrust pins into it at random. She might not be able to pay the coalman but she wore a gold brooch at her neck. Anne was always conscious of a contradiction – or indeed many contradictions – in her aunt. In many ways she was like Hugh. She was an intelligent woman who wrote with a neat quick hand. A pen had been in her hand at the moment Anne came through the door, and the pince-nez she wore gave her a bookish intellectual aspect. Otherwise she lived in a chaotic disorderly house, full of lodgers and the numerous friends and acquaintances who were to be seen passing through at all hours of the day and night.

'And bring us some coffee.'

'You must be busy.' Anne watched as Ju shuffled through some letters on the table, among the great heap of papers. Mrs McEvoy was now busy assembling a fire. Ju held up a letter she had been writing.

'The White Cross, Anne; help from America for prisoners' wives and families. While you are in Dublin you might like to help?'

'I'd love to. I'd like to do something useful.'

'Good. We'll go down together later. The Americans have been true friends. They have been sending over boxes and boxes of food, clothing, blankets, tools – an amazing variety of things. I can't tell you how invaluable it has been. Some families have suffered very badly since their men went to prison.'

A thought occurred to Anne.

'I'd love to,' she repeated. 'You can't imagine how useless I feel sometimes, living at home. Only it might be rather awkward. You see, I made a promise –'

'What promise?'

'It's not easy to explain.' She glanced over at Mrs McEvoy on her knees in front of the fire, then lowered her voice. 'Father made me swear an oath to have no further dealings with the Volunteers.'

'I don't understand.'

Anne was very uncomfortable. 'It wasn't something I could tell you about before. I shouldn't really tell you now ...' But at last she gave her aunt an outline of what had happened.

'And what if you had refused the oath?'

'That isn't the point, Aunt Ju! How could I refuse after what happened to Vere? I don't think Father will ever forgive me.'

'I see. It is more complicated than I had realised.' Mrs McEvoy had got the fire started and went out of the room. Aunt Ju crossed to the fireplace and sat in an old armchair. Anne followed her and sat in the chair opposite.

'Your father means a lot to you, doesn't he?'

'After what happened, sometimes I think he must hate me. I could understand it if he did,' Anne said in a low voice.

'Anne –'

'Anyway, it's not just what happened to Vere. He's always preferred Pippa to me.'

'Are you quite sure?'

Anne nodded. Aunt Ju was thoughtful. 'That's not what he tells me,' she said at last.

'What do you mean?'

'Your father has a very loving nature, Anne. He doesn't show it very well – or very often, perhaps. But he wants to love you if you'll let him.'

'If I'll let him? Aunt Ju, I'm not stupid! I can remember, time after time, all through my childhood, Father preferring my sister, giving her first choice, picking her up first. I know what I saw. And I don't mind! If that is how he prefers it, so be it, I'm not complaining. In any case, it's in the past now; we're grown up and can take responsibility for our own lives. It would be childish to go on bearing a grudge.'

Anne found herself more agitated than she had anticipated. The thoughts had rushed out without her expecting it. After a very long pause, Ju said carefully, 'Anne, you are his daughter. It is impossible for him not to love you. He held you in his arms when you were a few minutes old. He sat through the night with you when you had the measles. He saw you in your white dress the day you were confirmed. It is no more possible for him not to love you than for the sun not to rise.'

Anne had no answer to what her aunt said. Fortunately Mrs McEvoy reappeared with a tray of coffee, and as Aunt Ju poured it, Anne looked round the room, trying to digest what Ju had said, to reach out to that larger view of things.

The windows were partly obscured by dusty swagged old curtains; the bookcase behind Aunt Ju's head looked as if it was in constant use, the books jammed in unevenly and many more pushed in on top, as if she had just been reading one and had thrust it in hurriedly when her attention was distracted; the mantelpiece was cluttered with Meissen figures, an ormolu clock, letters, invitations, a stuffed bird; the floor strewn with oriental rugs, now faded and worn; there was a substantial Victorian brass fender before the fire; and on the table beside Ju's chair, magazines, and a large magnifying glass. In the opposite corner stood a Chinese screen with an exotic shawl thrown across it. Anne's eye came to rest on an oil painting hanging opposite, an Impressionist landscape, and then not far away, a portrait of the young Ju, also Impressionist.

Ju, who was her father's elder sister – and therefore, as a Hunter, warranted an entry in the *History* – had gone to Paris in her youth to study art and there married a French painter who had come back with her briefly to live in Ireland before declaring, apparently, that the rain would drive him into the lunatic asylum, and disappearing back to France. It had been put down politely to a 'difference of temperament', though Claire had once announced that she had 'no idea how any man could live with your sister'! There had been a son from the

206

marriage who lived in France and came over occasionally to visit his mother. Ju now lived with her dogs, her lodgers, and Mrs McEvoy.

As Anne took her cup she said, 'Aunt Ju, I must apologise for that outburst. You're so busy, and have so many things to think about. Please ignore what I said just now.'

Aunt Ju took no notice of this but said, in her low even voice, in that thoughtful manner which had such a reassuring quality, 'You know, Anne, you take after your mother – I've often noticed the resemblance. Much more than your sister.' Aunt Ju's face lit up. 'You should have seen her when she was your age! Claire Edgeworth was a catch, let me tell you. You have inherited her looks.'

'Really? I don't think –'

'Oh, yes, dear – surely you can see the resemblance?'

'I've never thought about it.'

Aunt Ju looked carefully into her eyes. 'She was the belle of the ball. Your father was besotted with her when they married. I remember the first time he brought her home to meet our parents – the pride in his eyes as he introduced her. And I think in a way he looks on you as a continuance – an extension – of your mother. Can you understand that?'

Anne had an odd feeling she was being asked to look at her parents as a fellow adult, not a child; she was flattered and felt grateful. Ju, in a subtle way, was inviting her to grow up.

'And my sister takes after him, if I think about it.'

It was still difficult for her to grasp the idea of her mother and father behaving just like people of her own age; yet it was for this kind of frank open exchange, in which nothing was forbidden, that she so valued her aunt.

The conversation shifted, and soon got round to Lewis. Anne outlined the meeting with him at the dinner party. Aunt Ju listened patiently.

'Are you sure you weren't rather hard on him?' she said carefully.

'Was I?'

Her aunt thought for a moment. 'Perhaps he was trying to patch things up? It sounds like it.'

'I don't think so. And neither would you if you had see this woman. They were like that.' Anne twined her fingers together. 'As if they had known each other all their lives. I hated her. But I could see how well they were getting on together. Anyway, why should he want to patch things up? He walked out on me in Lisheen after Vere had been killed.'

'Obviously I wasn't there, so I can't really tell. But from what you've said, he may simply have left because he felt in the way. And anyway, why should he think Vere's death was your fault? You never told him about the ambush, did you?'

'No.'

'Well then, dear, I think you've got hold of the wrong end of the stick. Of course he would leave at such a moment. Anyone would.'

'Do you think so?'

'Of course.'

'I never made any secret of my sympathies for the Volunteers.'

'But you never mentioned the ambush?'

'No, I'm sure I didn't.'

'In that case, he can't have left for the reason you think. I am certain you are exaggerating. Why on earth should he despise you? He'd asked you to marry him, hadn't he?' Ju placed her hand over Anne's. 'It was a terrible moment for the family, and he took himself off out of consideration for your feelings.'

Anne felt hugely relieved at this interpretation. Not only did it lessen the weight of her own guilt, but it also put Lewis in a better light. Of course, it was the gentlemanly tactful thing to do, to take himself out of the way.

'You think I should have been more friendly the other night?'

Ju shook her head with a world-weary smile. 'Anne, I know you of old. You put people off, you're so brusque and off-hand. You don't realise you're doing it. He was trying to re-establish a friendship, and you snubbed him to death.'

Anne frowned. 'Do you think so?'

'Let me see your hand. Your right hand.'

Anne held it out. Aunt Ju took it in her own, held it in a way Anne felt she had done many times before, a professional sort of way, turning it slightly, folding it to show up the lines better, looking at the fingers, the finger nails, and then reaching the large magnifying glass from her side table, and examining the lines methodically.

'You must be careful, Anne,' she said slowly, after a long examination, 'It seems sometimes you can be your own worst enemy.'

'What do you mean?'

'You hold people at a distance. Yet you crave intimacy. You are afraid of something.'

'I don't know –'

'People often are. It can take years before we are ready to know and to accept our true selves.' She continued with her examination. 'You have a profound capacity for love, Anne. Yet you are afraid of it. You should not be. It is capable of sustaining you and carrying you through difficulties.'

Ju put down her magnifying glass, and turned to pour out another cup of coffee. 'Nothing is impossible,' she said carefully, as she put down the coffee pot. 'You have a generous spirit but you have been too hard on yourself. You have always cared for others. You must learn also to care for yourself.'

'What do you mean? I'm the most unbearably selfish person I know.'

'No, my dear.'

'Aunt Ju, if I had really cared for others, if I had cared for my brother and my parents, none of this would have happened! That's the whole point!'

'Of course you owe your family a duty,' the other went on, ignoring her words, 'but you have a duty also to yourself.' She paused, and Anne looked up to catch her meaning. 'Do you understand me? You have rights too.'

Later, as Anne was about to leave and they were standing together in the doorway. She embraced her aunt, kissed her cheek. Ju said out of nowhere, 'Buy yourself some clothes, dear.'

Anne turned back.

'Be kind to yourself, do. You're entitled to a treat.'

Although Aunt Ju's words had an enormously cheering effect on Anne, much later that day when she had got back to Merrion Square and tried to think things out, she still came back to the moment when Dora Keene had sat on the arm of Lewis's chair and invited him to the dance. That moment would not go away. It had been so brazen, and Lewis had obviously been so happy to accept.

It would obviously be better for Anne's peace of mind to put him out of her thoughts for good. Let him go to his dance with Dora Keene, and good riddance! The philanderer and the flirt; they deserved each other.

# Chapter Twenty-Two

It was several weeks later on a blustery March morning, while Anne was eating breakfast with Tony and Pippa, that Dora's name came up again.

'I saw your friend Dora yesterday afternoon,' Pippa said archly, looking across at Tony.

He looked up sharply. 'Dora Keene?'

'Mmm.' Pippa smiled knowingly.

'My friend? How do you make that out?'

'Oh – one has eyes, you know, one notices things.'

Tony put down his newspaper. 'Pippa, what exactly are you insinuating?'

'Are you sure you don't know?' she went on lightly.

'You said Dora was my friend. In what way exactly is she my friend – any more than she is yours?'

Anne, her eyes on her plate, continued to butter her toast, slowly and carefully. Tony and Pippa seemed oblivious to her presence.

'Oh, I got the impression she had bestowed the light of her countenance on you.'

'*Meaning?*' Tony was growing irate.

'Meaning that you are not exactly indifferent to her charms.'

He brought down the level of his voice. 'Pippa, you are my wife whom I have sworn to love and cherish till death us do part, in sickness and in health, so I will overlook the malicious intent in those words. Otherwise I might get very angry indeed. If that woman cornered me for ten minutes in the refreshment tent at Leopardstown races, I can assure you it

211

was ten minutes too many. I cannot abide her; she is a scheming, malicious trollop, as all the world knows, and desperate besides. She's the wrong side of thirty, and if you think I would waste one single breath on her, far less listen to her brazen propositions, you are off your charming little head.'

There was a lightening of the atmosphere after this, the newspaper was picked up, and Anne went on with her toast. But after another minute Tony said, 'In any case, it was my distinct impression it was Lewis she was angling after. Didn't you see the way she was at him the other night?'

'What other night?'

'Darling – you may remember giving a very successful little dinner party not so long ago, in which Dora was very obviously out to entrap Lewis.'

'Oh, that,' Pippa said airily. 'She'll have no luck there. I know Lewis too well. She's not in his class. He has too much taste.' She giggled. 'What a slut!'

'You invited her.'

'Darling, what could I do? I wanted to invite Winnie and Pat, so Dora had to come too. She's been living with them since her divorce. Winnie's my oldest friend. I can't help it if she's got an evil witch for a sister.'

'Hmm.' Tony turned a page. 'One feels for Tommy Keene. Lucky to get out alive, eh?'

'Telling me.'

Anne had an indistinct feeling, something she could not well analyse, that Pippa and Tony had just enacted some little ceremony, some rite that took place only between married couples, and which had the effect of cementing them more snugly together.

She could hardly wait to get out of the house, and as she walked quickly along the pavement of Merrion Square on that blustery March day, it was as if the strong invigorating wind might carry her off at any moment. She wanted to cry from happiness.

How could she have doubted him? How could she have been so stupid as to imagine he would be taken in by that insinuating, manipulating woman?

Lewis had been innocent all the time.

She bounced along the pavement. How beautiful Dublin was

this morning, how elegant Leinster House, she thought standing before it, her mind still ablaze with the wonder of Lewis, his shining image untainted by any contact with that woman. As if he would have been taken in by her! How could Anne have thought it for an instant?

A coldness came over her. Lewis had spoken warmly to her, Anne, at the dinner party. Obviously he had forgiven her for what had happened in Lisheen, and wanted to renew their friendship. But what had she said? She had spurned his offer with cold words. He made a gesture of friendship, and instead of accepting it in the spirit in which it was made, she rebuffed him.

Dora Keene had not rebuffed him. She had invited him to her birthday dance. The thought of them dancing together made Anne quite cold. What had he said? 'How can I refuse?'

She chewed her lip as she walked on. However, as she thought it over, she began to see that his reply had in fact been ambiguous. It was not a glad acceptance; those were the words of a man in an awkward situation – just like Tony in the refreshment tent – a man cornered by a powerful and scheming woman. Lewis had been playing for time. As if he would be eager to go dancing with a woman like her!

However, a moment later, as she thought carefully over that scene, she cooled again. His reply had been ambiguous, but on the other hand he had not said no. Anne had no idea whether Lewis had in fact been to Dora's birthday party; whether they had or had not danced together.

Had Dora spent the evening drifting round in his arms? Could even he have held out a whole evening against her charms? A woman like that would use every weapon available to her.

She had turned the corner into St Stephen's Green and was passing the Shelbourne Hotel when she saw the Old Beast standing outside. She stopped and then looked up at the imposing façade above her, the top-hatted doorman, the carpeted entrance, the life-sized Egyptian figures holding lamps along the front. The most elegant, respectable hotel in the city, and just the sort of place one associated Lewis with.

As she looked at the car again, something else came back.

What had Dora said? 'One day he will get his comeuppance. He will end up married to a woman who will lead him a dog's life.' Like a thunderclap, the truth revealed itself – it was Dora herself she meant! Dora, who intended to entrap and marry Lewis. And wouldn't she give him a dog's life!

For a moment Anne felt quite dizzy at this appalling prospect, but as she stared at the car there arose in her a monumental resolve. Not while there was breath in her body! The very idea of Lewis married to Dora was grotesque; she, Anne, was honour bound to do everything, strain every nerve in her body to prevent it.

She must rescue him from Dora. It was clear.

She was still staring at the car as these thoughts raced through her mind. But then she started round. Suppose he came out and found her there? What would he say?

After their last conversation she must not be found here. She hastened on.

She would write him a letter, explain everything, apologise for her brusque rebuff and intimate that it would be very pleasant to meet up again.

She stopped on the pavement. No. Not a letter. That would give him the chance to rebuff her in return. How could she be sure of conveying everything she wanted to say in a letter? This matter was too important. It had to be face to face. Only then could she be sure.

She was walking slowly down Grafton Street, through the morning shoppers.

She stopped again. She must not underestimate Dora Keene who was a formidable woman. It was one thing for Tony and Pippa to laugh about her over the breakfast table, but they were not up against her.

This was going to require a more sophisticated approach. It was no good just blurting things out to a man like Lewis. Especially since she had obviously put him off by the way she had spoken.

She cast her mind back to the dinner. The other women, older, more experienced than herself, had worn elegant, sophisticated clothes. Clothes that proclaimed they were women – not overgrown schoolgirls. That was what her aunt had said too.

She took out her cheque book; she still had over fifty pounds. It was enough.

She spent the whole afternoon in Switzer's going through racks of clothes, looking them over, trying some on and dithering hugely. The things didn't suit her – or did they? They certainly made her look different. Sometimes they made her look middle-aged; sometimes they made her look frumpish; sometimes they made her look even taller than she was – oh, it was impossible. She would throw the stuff down, aware of the assistant, a poor little Dublin girl, waiting patiently for her to make up her mind. In the end, she apologised to the girl for keeping her hanging around so long, and wandered off through the other departments, looking vaguely at handbags, and then at household linen, and suitcases and furniture – it became ridiculous, she couldn't concentrate – until she found herself in Ladies' Underwear, turning over the fine French lingerie that Pippa had been given for her wedding. And again the fascination and the fear that was mixed with it took possession of Anne, and she lingered, more and more fascinated, and finally she said to herself that, well, it might come to that – it was difficult to know – and perhaps she ought to be prepared for all contingencies. So not quite knowing what she did, and feeling embarrassed to point the things out to the sales girl, she started choosing: fine fancy frilly light silk things, silk knickers and camisole tops, and then silk stockings. Feeling quite light headed, she got carried away and took no notice of the prices which were ridiculous, picked all kinds of things ... it all seemed unreal, quite unlike her normal self.

Once she had this bag in her hand, however; and it was comforting to think that no one could know what was in it, it just looked like any other shop bag – once she had broken the ice as it were, she felt emboldened and marched back up to the dresses and coats and skirts, and feeling deliciously free and much more confident, began to make decisions. Thinking of the silk underwear in the bag, she began to ask herself what was appropriate to wear over it, what was stylish and confident and modern and adult, and amazed herself by this sudden liberation. Things which earlier had seemed somehow too, well, cosmopolitan or whatever, she suddenly liked on herself. It was time to grow up. So she made her purchases, and waited while the girl screwed up the money into the little shuttle and popped it into the air tube, and heard the whoosh as it was sucked down.

She waited, sitting staring across the shop, the bags – big ones now – standing on the floor at her feet, not thinking of the large hole she had just made in her bank account, but sensing a strange exalted feeling as if she had made some irreversible decision; she was committed to her task, and this was an earnest of it. A bank account, or the lack of it, seemed irrelevant. What else was she saving for?

With a sudden whoosh, the shuttle reappeared, and the sales girl gave Anne her receipt. She picked up her bags and made her way out into the street.

It was just getting dark as she emerged into Grafton Street, and mingled with the crowds surging up and down in the bright lights from shop windows. How strange it was, all these people going about their business – here was another woman with Switzer's bags just like hers, and over there was a British officer with a lady on his arm, and a gentleman in a bowler hat, looking as if he had come from a solicitor's office. In the most elegant street in Ireland it was a joke to think there was a war on, impossible to believe.

As she passed the Shelbourne she saw the Old Beast again, and instinctively drew back, then crossed the street. Suppose Lewis came out and saw her? He could ask her what she was doing, perhaps he would want to see her shopping, see her new underwear – already her heart was beating fast at the very thought of it. Besides she had not yet thought out how she was to engineer an encounter. It was essential that she arranged it – that he should not take her unawares. He had taken her unawares so many times in the past, she remembered. She must be careful.

Back in her room she opened her bags. First she looked at the two dresses she had bought. One of them was very expensive indeed, an afternoon tea-gown in French *crêpe de chine*, very fine sheer silk. Fortunately she could wear it, because she was thin; a dress like that showed every bulge. It was a restrained brown and beige stripe cut on the bias; she wondered if he would know it was expensive. She thought he probably would. Perhaps he would ask why she had suddenly bought herself such an expensive dress? What would she say?

The other was an evening dress in emerald green and mauve, with a sash round the hips, tied off at the back in a sort of bow. A heavy silk satin which caught the light as she moved in it.

And then the underwear. She took out the things, and held them in her hands, turning them over, holding them up to the light. Well, she must see the effect of this ensemble. Now. In the cold empty room, she threw off her own clothes and put on the underwear. The silk was cold on her skin, so light, weightless. She forced herself to look in the mirror on her wardrobe door. She stared at her body in these strange exotic things. How was the effect? Better than blue serge knickers and a woolly vest?

She reserved judgement while she slipped on her afternoon tea gown, the *crêpe de chine*. It fitted her well. It ran sheer over her flanks and bottom. It was easy to move in; she hardly knew she was wearing it. She turned quickly. The dress swung round her thighs in a most becoming way. She was feeling better and better. She rolled on the silk stockings and clipped them up. Again she turned in front of the mirror. There was no disguising the effect: she looked good. She looked very good. In these clothes she could stroll into the lounge of the Shelbourne and feel herself the equal of anyone. As she took the dress off, shivering slightly in the cold room and slipped into the other, the evening dress, she was already asking herself: Yes, but he's bound to notice. He might like it, but he's bound to notice. He's bound to ask himself, why?

Turning again in front of the mirror, it was as if there was a new Anne. A more confident, more adult her, who could take a man like Lewis Crawford in her stride. Unexpectedly she smiled at her own reflection. Let him wonder.

# Chapter Twenty-Three

It was 1 April, April Fool's day. Tea time. Around Anne other well-dressed men and women were having tea. Waiters were bringing silver trays, plates of sandwiches and little cakes; the Shelbourne was the most exclusive place for tea in the city. The old paintings looked down from the walls, windows were shrouded with heavy swagged curtains, and a fire burned merrily in the elegant Georgian fireplace. It was very discreet and refined. She sat alone by the window so she could see who came in and also be visible from the hotel foyer. She didn't want to miss him if he came in.

It was very difficult. She had to allow herself to be seen yet he must never think she had come on purpose to find him. It was going to need all her concentration.

This had taken a week to plan. She had scouted the place three times. Sometimes the Old Beast was there; sometimes it wasn't. Today it wasn't. So he must be out somewhere. It was a gamble she was taking that he might just come in while she sat there and just by chance see her.

The waiter was bending over her.

'Can I get you anything, madam?'

'No, I'll wait a little. I'm expecting a friend.'

'Very good, madam.'

She looked out of the window. Winter was coming to an end. St Stephen's Green looked bedraggled and forlorn, but there was the smell of incipient spring. It was not yet here but it might soon be. It had been raining but had stopped; the streets were still wet, and the stormy clouds moved threateningly across the sky. It was still cold.

Her dress was thin. She should have had more sense. It was all very well to put on a super-fine silk dress, all very well to know you were looking good, but if you were shivering and blue with cold it somehow diminished the effect.

She was still huddled in her overcoat. Although it was warm enough in here she couldn't quite bring herself to take it off. The dress was extremely elegant. Once she had taken off her overcoat everyone would see it. Lewis would see it, eventually. He would be impressed. Everybody would be impressed. But that meant she would have to live up to the dress; she would have to be elegant and sophisticated to match. She had doubts as to whether she would be able to carry this off.

She had doubts as to whether she shouldn't just have worn her usual clothes, her dark blue skirt, her cardigan and blouse, normal clothes that no one took any notice of.

Sitting here, still with her overcoat around her, she could watch the door and see out of the window when the Old Beast should draw up. But she mustn't let him know that she had seen him arrive. This was most important. It must seem as if he'd found her, and when he did she would look up in a vague off-hand manner and say something like, 'Oh, hullo, I'm just waiting for a friend.'

Wait a minute ... if she said that he might take himself off again. It was the sort of tactful thing he would do. He was never pushy; quite the reverse. It was going to have to be handled very carefully. Anne frowned. This was getting very difficult. She couldn't tell him she was waiting for him; she couldn't say she was waiting for a friend in case he withdrew too quickly. She couldn't seem too forward; but she mustn't seem too distant either.

There was more to seduction than she had imagined. She had always had an image of temptresses as women in slinky dresses and make-up, who smoked cigarettes and wound men in the toils of their cunning arts until they were helpless slaves. Of course she had always despised such women, looked down on them from a very great height indeed. But the one thing she had never asked was how they did it. It had somehow seemed automatic, yet now that she found herself about to begin, nothing about it seemed easy. She hadn't the faintest idea what to do.

She was nervous and bored. She would have got up and gone for a walk or to the lavatory, anything to break the monotony. But she didn't want to give up her seat. This was the only one from which she could see both the door and through the window. If she were away two minutes he might have come in and gone upstairs, and she would have to go through the whole performance again the next day.

'Hullo, Anne.'

She looked up sharply. It was Lewis.

'I thought it was you. How are you?'

He turned to pull a chair across from the next table, asking an old lady whether it was taken. In astonishment she wrenched her head round but could not see any other door. Where had he come from?

'May I join you?'

'Oh, yes. I – er, that is, I am expecting a friend.'

She was confused. Where was the car, if he had come from inside the hotel? And she had mentioned her friend too quickly. He might take the hint and go away.

He pulled his chair up to the table and sat back in it, comfortable and relaxed. He was in a tweed suit and wore a regimental tie. 'I was sitting over there reading the paper, then looked up and saw the back of your head. I just knew it was you.'

She nodded faintly. She couldn't think of a thing to say. This was ridiculous. What would one of those women have said? What would Dora Keene have done? She huddled her overcoat round her, covering her silk dress.

'Cold? It is rather, isn't it? When's your friend coming?'

She could see the clock over his head. It was just after four.

'Half-past four.'

'Good. We have a little time.'

'Yes, I got here early; rather cold out – as you said – so I came in to warm up.'

'Very wise. What have you been doing?'

'Nothing in particular. I'm going back to Cork soon, so I'm just clearing up before I go – that sort of thing.'

Suddenly her nerve stiffened. She must try and take control of the situation.

'And what about you, Lewis? Are you keeping busy? What was it you do – the wine trade, wasn't it?'

'Extremely boring, I'm afraid. Usually try to keep it a secret. I'm in the wine trade, as you say. Old family firm, in the City. City of London, that is. My elder brother is due to take over when the old man retires, which rather leaves me on the side lines. When the war stopped I was at a loose end so they took pity on me, and gave me a job peddling the family wares. To tell the truth, I'm more of a hand at drinking it than selling it.'

She couldn't remember ever seeing him drink much. But the main thing was to keep him talking. That was what men liked most of all, someone had once told her; to hear themselves talking to an attentive woman.

'Why don't you take that coat off? You must be hot in here by now.'

This was it. Without saying anything, she stood up and slipped it off her shoulders, and over the back of the chair.

She was acutely conscious of Lewis's eyes as he examined her dress. For a moment he said nothing as she sat and tried to arrange herself, crossing her legs and pretending this was something she did all the time, sit in expensive hotels wearing thin silk dresses in winter.

Lewis looked into her eyes with a faint amused smile. He looked and looked and still didn't say anything, and she began to feel flustered.

'Four-thirty, you said?'

'Yes.'

'Well, we have a few minutes in hand.'

What did he mean by that? He was hinting at something. Clearly he had noticed the dress, taken it in, as she'd known he would, appraised it, knew what it cost and knew it was not the sort of thing she wore normally. She was more agitated than ever; all her control gone again. Men were supposed to be impressed. It was all part of the business of seduction.

He took up his narrative where he had left off. 'I can't say there's a great market for fine wines over here, compared with the Home Counties. Still, it's got me introductions to some of the most eccentric old types I've ever met. We have a number of personal clients, ancient Irish families out in the country-side, you know, who cultivate a taste in claret – as I was saying the other night. It's the traditional drink of the hunting classes, they like the stuff and they know it. The firm has been supplying them for generations. So for want of anything better to do, I've come over to keep up the connection – take a few orders, and be entertained in some of the draughtiest castles you're likely to find. That's a beautiful dress.'

'Thank you,' she blushed.

'It's difficult to concentrate with you in that dress. Is it new?'

'What? Oh, yes.' Should she have admitted that? Still it was better now that he was beginning to show some interest. It was much easier this way.

'I'm glad you bought it. I like you in that sort of dress. It brings out – well, how shall I put it? – I feel it brings out the real you, in a manner of speaking. Did you buy it recently?'

'Oh – er, fairly recently, you know.'

Again she saw the faint smile playing round his lips. He knew something. Damn him.

'And don't you find the war getting in the way of your business?' she asked conversationally. 'Don't you find it difficult getting round the country?'

'All the booby-traps, you mean? Trenches dug in the road, trees chopped down, that sort of thing? Well, I have to exercise a little ingenuity, I agree. I usually stop in a town, go into a pub and chat up the locals, find out the state of the country, or bribe a man to ride with me to the next town, to make sure we avoid any traps. Touch wood, it's been all right so far. Anyway, I don't expect the war to go on much longer.'

'Don't you? Why?'

'The people are getting tired of it. So's the Government. They aren't getting any joy out of it. They're getting a rotten press abroad. America, France, they're all dead against us – the British, I mean.'

'So they should be.'

'Well, I wouldn't know. I try to take as little notice of it as possible.'

The waiter was at his elbow.

'Can I get you anything, sir?'

Lewis looked up, and then at her.

'You've got your friend coming, haven't you? Pity, I could do with a cup of tea. Tell you what, why don't we order something – and then I'll take myself off the moment your friend shows up?'

He smiled at her and she thought, Does he know? He seems to look right through me and see everything I'm thinking. Well, he won't know everything I'm thinking. She took yet another grip on herself.

'We can't have you dying of thirst, Lewis. Let's have some tea, anyway.'

The waiter went off with the order.

Outside the afternoon was bright, the sky high with clouds racing through it. Lewis looked out.

'Spring can't be far away. You can feel it, can't you? Everything about to burst through. It's all there, just out of sight. You know it, but you can't see it. You go out and the wind chills you and you realise it's still winter. That dress can't be very warm ... Still, you've got your overcoat. I've always thought it's very hard on women. Look at me; here I am in a tweed suit, waistcoat and all, thick shoes and socks, and there you are looking extremely lovely, in a dress that must weigh nothing at all. It's a wonder you don't catch pneumonia.'

Again, she felt the heat in her face. This trick of throwing compliments into the middle of the conversation without pausing in his flow confused her and made her forget what she was going to say.

The waiter arrived with the tea tray and set it down on the table between them.

'Will you be mother?' Lewis smiled humorously up at her from beneath his strong brows.

Over his head she saw it was four-thirty already. Lewis couldn't see the clock and was unlikely to be pulling his watch out every five minutes to check the time. He appeared completely at ease.

'Thanks,' he said as she handed him a cup. 'The national drink of Ireland, as they say. Hot and strong, just how I like it.'

He took a sip.

'So, when are you off to Cork?'

She shook her head vaguely and looked away from him as she tried to think of the right answer.

'I'm not sure. In a day or two, I expect.'

He nodded without saying anything, and sipped his tea.

223

'I must consult my diary and see if I have any clients in that part of the world so I can look you up.'

'Do.'

This was no good. She was putting him off. He was bound to go soon and wasn't showing the slightest inclination to invite her out anywhere with him. He was being very affable and polite, but obviously must believe she had warned him off the night of the dinner party. Snubbed him to death. Well, she had only herself to blame.

Annoyed with herself, she shifted in her chair and recrossed her long legs. The silk made a faint hissing noise as her legs crossed. Lewis leaned forward confidentially.

'You know, that's a sound a man might die to hear.'

He was looking into her eyes.

'What?'

'That sound of your legs crossing in silk stockings. You will have to be very careful when your friend arrives. It might have an unpredictable effect on him.'

'It's a girl.'

'Oh. Then there's no problem. Could I trouble you for another cup of tea?'

Flustered, she took his cup and poured out the tea. Her hand was almost shaking. There was something, improper, almost indecent, in that remark. Surely gentlemen didn't make remarks about such things to a lady's face?

'Still, a pardonable mistake.' He took his cup and sat back in his chair. But he looked into her eyes. 'With you in a dress like that, I'm afraid I could draw only one conclusion.'

She was stuttering, her head whirling with confused thoughts, 'Oh, I didn't put it on for her – no, I, er, well, if you want to know, I went for an interview this afternoon.'

'Really?'

'Yes, a job – that is, well, I have been thinking whether I shouldn't settle here in Dublin and get a job, so I went for this interview.'

'I imagine they were very impressed. I would have been. Did you get the job?'

'I don't know. They said they'd let me know.'

She didn't believe a word of it, and she didn't think he did either.

'You know, since you've told me it's a girl friend you're meeting, Anne, I confess you've set my heart at rest. I really was fearing the worst, to be honest. And it emboldens me to make a request: whether we might have dinner together one evening? Or go to the theatre, perhaps?'

He sipped his tea, looking at her over the rim of his cup.

Very carefully, with studied movements, she picked up her handbag and took out her diary.

'Oh, but I was forgetting. You're going back to Cork.'

She opened her diary. 'I have a couple of days yet. We could perhaps do something together. What did you have in mind?'

'The Gaiety? Do you like musical comedy? Perhaps not. Rather superficial for you? I was forgetting you have your mission in life.'

'Thank you,' she said hurriedly. 'It would be nice to go to the theatre.'

'Excellent. I'll get tickets.' He took out his diary in turn. 'Would Saturday be convenient?'

'Saturday?' She glanced into her diary, full of blank pages. 'That seems all right. I'll look forward to it.' She said this as coolly as if she had made an appointment to meet a stockbroker.

'Let's assume I get the tickets, I'll pick you up at your place at half-past six, shall we say?'

He smiled, and she couldn't help smiling back. Why had she ever doubted him? Obviously he must still love her – or at least have forgiven her for her coldness towards him.

The conversation turned to other matters; she didn't afterwards remember what, and in any case it didn't matter. Five o'clock came and went, Lewis drank another cup of tea. He didn't appear to notice the time; and as she sat in a haze of contentment, an idiotic smile kept creeping over her face. He didn't seem to have noticed her friend had never turned up, and she didn't care. Nothing could go wrong now, she was sure of it. Sure of herself and Lewis; there was something just so natural and right about them together.

At that moment Sandy walked into the foyer, looking round vaguely, and spotted her.

'Anne!' He came towards her, and then recognised her companion. 'Lewis too, what a bit of luck!'

225

# Chapter Twenty-Four

Lewis looked up at Sandy, and then at Anne.

'Hullo, Sandy, nice to see you again. How are you?'

Sandy seemed delighted to see Lewis. 'I've been dining out on your ghost story ever since, old man.'

'Very kind,' murmured Lewis. He pulled his watch from his waistcoat pocket. 'My goodness – is that the time? I'll be late.' He stood up. 'Sorry, you two, I've got to go and change. Will you excuse me? Got an appointment.'

He turned away, giving Anne a wry smile as he went.

Sandy turned after him. 'So soon? Won't you stay –'

Anne wanted to call, 'See you on Saturday –', but Sandy was beside her, and then Lewis had disappeared up the stairs.

'What a stroke of luck meeting you here!' Sandy turned back to her, rubbing his hands together. 'But you've had tea, I see.'

She was staring blindly at the stairs.

'Yes.' She stood up abruptly and picked up her overcoat. 'I must be getting back.'

He was quick to help her on with it, like an experienced valet. He had that same slightly obsequious, ingratiating manner. 'Tell you what, I'll walk with you – I'm going that way.'

Anne said nothing as they crossed the lounge and passed out into the street. And what was Lewis thinking at this minute? That she had been waiting for Sandy? That she had lied, saying she was waiting for a woman friend? That she was stringing two men along at once?'

She felt like death, but Sandy did not seem to notice and

was chatting cheerfully as they walked round to Merrion Square. Tony welcomed them in his usual expansive manner.

'Sandy! Just in time for a drink! What'll it be – whiskey?'

Anne excused herself with half a syllable and went upstairs, just catching the words 'You'll never guess who –' as the door closed behind her. It wouldn't take Pippa long to work out what had happened.

By the time she had washed her face, changed her clothes and combed her hair, she felt a little calmer and was able to return to the drawing room. Tony and Sandy were deep in conversation by the fire, and she picked up a newspaper and carelessly threw herself on to the sofa.

The page was a blur while conversations were continually running through her head: 'Oh, no, I wasn't waiting for Sandy. That was pure coincidence.' And: 'Oh – my friend Margaret? I can't imagine what happened to her...' Whatever she said, it sounded utterly lame. Lewis was an observant man – he would have seen well enough how attentive Sandy had been to her over dinner that night. And he had remarked on her new dress. He was quite capable of drawing conclusions.

She turned a page, without having read a word.

Tony's voice rolled over her.

'We're being asked to do a policeman's job, Sandy. It puts us in a very difficult position. A soldier is not a policeman.'

'Quite right, old man,' Sandy muttered.

'We're not officially at war!' Tony leant forward in his armchair. 'They don't seem to understand that! If only we were, it would be different. If L-G would only give us the green light to go ahead and declare all-out war, we'd clear this problem up in ten days. A week!'

'As it is, look at the mess we're landed with,' Sandy chimed in. 'They've handed over to these Black and Tan fellows, a rabble of drunken scum. A disgrace to the uniform, some of them. How can we ever win a war like this?'

'It's not soldiering as I was taught it,' Tony said lugubriously. 'Another, old chap?'

He crossed to the drinks table and started opening bottles. Anne was staring at a blur of print. Dora Keene would never have made such a blunder. Dora would have used Sandy as a weapon to tempt Lewis; she would have played one off against the other.

'Tony heaved a sigh.

'Well, drunken rabble or not, we have to fight fire with fire. Ever since last November, when the Cairo Group was practically wiped out, what option have we had?'

Sandy shook his head gravely, and then after a pause, 'Cairo Group? I don't recall –'

'Detectives – our chaps – trying to run down the IRA. Dangerous job, Sandy, cloak and dagger stuff.'

'I remember now – and all shot in their beds. Makes you wonder what the world's coming to.' Sandy stared at the carpet. 'No wonder some of our fellows ran amok.'

'Shooting unarmed civilians in Croke Park? No excuse, Sandy. The IRA may shoot men in their beds; doesn't give us the right to go shooting civilians.'

Anne turned another page, without having read a word. She wondered whether she shouldn't put the problem to her sister. Pippa knew so much more about men than she did.

'Trouble with you, Tony, is you're too much of a gentleman,' said Sandy after a pause.

'I'll be glad to be back in England, I don't mind telling you. We can't win this one. The longer we stay, the worse it's going to get. Say when.'

He squirted soda into the glasses.

'Why were they called the Cairo Group?' Sandy asked as Tony handed him his glass.

'No idea. Code name, I suppose. Or else maybe they used to meet in the Café Cairo. Anyway they weren't all killed, fortunately. Or our job would be even more difficult than it is already.'

She would talk to Pippa. Pippa would know best.

After dinner, Anne managed to get her sister alone in her bedroom.

'I like your new dress, by the way – meant to tell you,' Pippa remarked casually as she brushed her hair.

'Oh, thanks.'

'I thought it was about time you bought yourself some new clothes. You were always so snooty about it before.'

'Was I?'

'You jolly well know you were. Whenever I brought anything new, you used to look down your nose at me, as if I were some sort of shallow butterfly, flitting from flower to flower. I'm glad you've woken up to a few home truths at last.'

'What home truths?'

Pippa put down her brush and turned to look at Anne who was leaning disconsolately in the doorway.

'You're not really that naïve, so I'm not to going to spell it out – not at this time of day.'

There was a pause. Anne said at last with difficulty, 'This may sound a bit stupid, but there is something I wanted to ask you about.'

'Oh, yes?'

'It's about the dress, as a matter of fact.'

'It's a very nice one. You've got better taste than I gave you credit for.'

'I bought it for Lewis.'

Pippa looked up at her.

'Pardon?'

'I waited for him in the Shelbourne, and he invited me out to the theatre on Saturday.'

'*Did he?*' Pippa stared up at her. 'Anne, good for you. But I never knew you were sweet on him.'

'We got to know each other last summer when he came to stay. But then – after Vere got killed, he – well, he left.'

'Why?'

'Why do you think?'

'Well, I never. Lewis Crawford.' Pippa turned back to the mirror. 'You certainly kept very dark about it.'

'But you see, Pippa, I've got myself into a bit of a jam. Lewis didn't know I was waiting for him.'

'Didn't he?'

'No. Er – I told him, well, to make it sound more natural, I told him I was waiting for an old school friend.'

'So? He wouldn't care about that.'

'I know. But just then Sandy walked in.'

For a moment Pippa stared up at Anne who was standing over her, then she burst into laughter.

'What's funny?'

'I don't believe it. *Sandy!* Oh, no! What did Lewis do?'

Anne was desperate. 'What do you think? Obviously he thought I had been waiting for Sandy. I don't know what do.'

'*Sandy!*' Pippa was still laughing.

'And we had just arranged to go to the theatre on Saturday. Lewis said he'd get tickets.'

'You're seeing him on Saturday?' Pippa sobered up a little. 'Well then, what's the problem?'

'Can't you see?'

'Darling, I can't see there's any problem at all. In fact, if you ask me, it adds piquancy to the situation. Lewis will be biting his finger nails worrying that you're seeing Sandy.'

'But I'm not!'

'He doesn't know that.'

Anne turned away and wandered about the bedroom, clasping and unclasping her hands.

'I couldn't bear to let him think I was seeing Sandy. Do you think I should write him a letter?'

'What's the matter with you? Let him sweat a little. It never does any harm.'

Anne could not imagine Lewis sweating. 'I don't like it. Pippa, I can't bear the idea of Lewis going round thinking I am seeing Sandy. I can't bear it! And suppose he didn't turn up on Saturday – all because of a misunderstanding? I think I'd die!'

'Because of Sandy? Are you serious? You know Lewis, don't you?'

'I thought I did.'

'Well then, trust him. Anyway, there's no law says you can't have tea in the Shelbourne if you want to. Lewis hadn't asked you out by then, had he?'

'No,' Anne said dubiously.

'Well then! You weren't deceiving him.'

'But still, he'll think –'

'It never does a woman any harm to preserve a little mystery. Why can't you get that into your head? You don't have to go spilling all the beans into his lap. Hold yourself aloof. Wait till he comes to you.'

'Like I did in the Shelbourne?'

'Exactly. And make sure you're looking good. Like you were in that dress – you were definitely on the right lines there. You've got to make him grateful that you've even noticed him, let alone consented to grace him with your presence at the theatre.'

Anne wandered about the bedroom while Pippa tidied her dressing table. It didn't sound right; and she could scarcely imagine Lewis feeling grateful to her for going out with him. It was she who was grateful.

That night in her room she decided to write to him. There was something in her that could not bear a falsehood, however innocent or oblique.

The letter she wrote was very short. She said how much she had enjoyed their little chat in the Shelbourne, and how much she was looking forward to going to the theatre with him. And in a postscript she remarked on the extraordinary coincidence that Sandy should have walked in at that very moment.

This seemed to hit the right note; she wasn't grovelling to him. And Lewis would easily pick up the casual reference to Sandy.

The next morning without saying anything she went out intending to leave the letter at the hotel. But as she was crossing the foyer, and before she had had time to leave the letter with the reception desk, she heard her name and, turning, saw Lewis himself coming out of the breakfast room. She thrust the letter hurriedly into her pocket.

'Good morning.' He smiled down at her.

Her mind was a blank.

Then, without quite knowing how, the pair of them were strolling along the pavement together, bound for the post office. The letter was still in her overcoat pocket. They talked about various unimportant things, Anne didn't mind what they talked about; there was a special closeness about them which was all she could ask for, and she knew that everything could be ironed out between them as time went by. She didn't feel in any hurry. So she was quite relaxed when he said, 'I was very sorry, you know, about Vere. I often think of him.'

'I do too,' she said quietly.

'Of course it was worse for you.'

'It was worst of all for my parents.' She thought for a

while. 'For months afterwards, I couldn't bear to think of you.'

'Why?'

'Because of what had happened. You see, I was responsible for his death.'

'What on earth do you mean?'

'And in a way – because of you. Because of us.'

'Why should you think that?'

'Because of the time we spent together, I was somehow neglecting him. Allowing him to slip by me. Do you see?'

Lewis was listening thoughtfully, looking down at the pavement as they walked. At last he turned to her, a serious expression in his eyes.

'Anne, that's absurd. If your brother chose to get up at five o'clock in the morning – or whatever he did do – you can't be held responsible for that. Your only responsibility is for your own actions. Vere was old enough to know what he was doing.'

'He was still a boy.'

'He was fourteen, and should have known better. You shouldn't be so hard on yourself. You have a right to your own life too.'

'Thank you,' she said softly. It was as if he had lifted a weight from her shoulders, and without thinking she slipped her arm through his.

Later that morning they were crossing the O'Connell bridge, on their way back from Clery's department store in Sackville Street. Two army lorries stood across the bridge at right angles, and traffic was only allowed through the middle, one vehicle at a time. Auxies in their tam o'shanter berets were stopping passengers and questioning them, demanding identification papers. They had rifles slung across their shoulders and carried pistols.

Anne showed her passport, and Lewis pulled a small buff card from his pocket. She thought it was an army pay book. The Auxie studied it.

'What's this?'

'Eh?' Lewis looked up. 'Oh, sorry. Wrong one. Here.' He fished into an inner pocket of his overcoat, and as he did so she caught a glimpse of the handle of a pistol. A momentary glimpse and then it was gone.

The Auxies was studying this other, small white notebook form of identification – if that was what it was. Anne had never seen it before.

In any case she wasn't thinking about that – or any other kind of identification. She could still see the handle of the pistol. It had burnt itself on to her retina, as if she had been staring at the sun. Surely Lewis, of all people, must know the penalty for carrying a weapon? He could go to prison.

Another Auxie had come across to them, and Lewis turned to Anne. 'Excuse me, some kind of mix-up here. Soon sort it out.'

He walked away, and she watched him talking to this officer. Lewis must have said something funny because the other man laughed, and a moment later they shook hands. He came back to where she was standing among the morning crowd, waiting to get over the bridge.

'Sorry about that, Anne. Wrong pass book. Don't know why I still carry it about with me. Left over from the old desert days. Serves me right.' He drew a breath. 'Now, what about a spot of lunch? What do you say? Is there anywhere you'd like specially?'

She couldn't think what to say, whether to mention the pistol or not. If that Auxie had seen it Lewis would have been hauled in without a second's delay. And surely, she thought, he must know the penalty? There was something foolhardy about it, but in a way it fitted in with the other things she knew about him, the 'stunts' he had got up to in the desert and so forth.

But it was not easy to mention it to his face.

'Would you believe it, Anne, that was a chap I was at school with. Small world, eh? Don't envy his job, though. A fellow in his position – he could get a bullet in the ribs at any moment. Any time of the night or day. You'd never know who was going to pull out a gun. Could be anyone. Anyone at all.' He shook his head. 'A bit too risky for me. Had my fill of all that out East. Still, with any luck it'll be over soon, and they'll all be able to go home.'

'Yes.'

Later that afternoon he took her back to Merrion Square.

'Are you still game for Saturday?'

'The theatre? I'm looking forward to it.'

'Good girl. I got some tickets. I'll call for you at six-thirty.'
He strolled off along the pavement.

Anne found Tony in the drawing room, and tackled him right away.

He appeared to be mystified about Lewis and his pistol. He raised his eyebrows, studied the carpet, and gave it some deep thought. Finally, he drew a long breath, and addressing a picture on the wall, delivered his verdict.

'Well, Anne, you know yourself the state of the country. What can you expect? He's driving round the country all on his own; never knows what to expect.'

'But, Tony you know it's strictly illegal for civilians to carry a gun! He could go to prison for it! I couldn't believe it when I saw it.'

He shrugged his shoulders. 'Well, I don't know.' He seemed at a loss for words, shook his head and stared at the carpet again. 'That's the state of the country for you. Poor old Lewis obviously feels safer with a gun in his pocket. Can't say I blame him.'

This picture of Lewis, alone in a country lane in his car, now filled her with fear. What a fool she had been! She had always thought of him as invulnerable, as if he led a charmed life. But when one read of the murders, the ambushes, the kidnaps, almost daily in the newspapers; and Lewis out all alone driving down the country lanes – and in such a lovely car. He was not invulnerable; he could stop a bullet in some chance encounter as well as anyone else.

The idea of his being caught in some ambush, perhaps mistaken for someone else, for a British officer; a picture of him slumped over the steering wheel of the Old Beast with blood running down his chest, was more than she could stand. She rose quickly, went up to her room, and had to walk backwards and forwards for some time, window to door, door to window, before she could calm the agitation she felt.

234

# Chapter Twenty-Five

'Oh, golly that's him!'

'Don't worry, darling, Tony'll keep him entertained. Now turn round again, and let's get your seams straight.'

She could hear Lewis's voice, and Tony's, on the stairs as she lifted her skirt to adjust her stockings.

'Not too tight, darling, or they'll ladder.'

'I know, I know! I wasn't brought up in a convent!'

'You act like it sometimes.'

Anne was all fingers and thumbs as she adjusted her suspenders for the third time. 'Are they straight now?'

'Nearly.'

'Oh, sugar! What do you think of this scarf? It matches, doesn't it?'

'It looks fine.'

'I'd better get down.'

'Don't worry! Let him wait a minute. Never does any harm.'

Anne took a deep breath, and looked herself up and down in the pier glass in Pippa's bedroom. The evening dress was elegant, a design in emerald and mauve, long and emphasising her slender figure. She had also tied an emerald green scarf round her hair, the ends of which hung down her back. Pippa had approved her taste.

'If you can learn to stop panicking, and take your time, you'll do very well. Now just relax, and wait for him. Let him make the moves, there's no hurry. And don't go all spiky if you feel nervous. I know you, you've put off more men that way ...'

'He must be waiting –'

'All right, off you go – no, don't put your overcoat on yet. Let him see the dress. Honestly!'

Lewis was in a dinner jacket and black tie beneath his overcoat and hat; he and Tony were at the fireplace, drinking whiskey.

Anne could tell in the split second before he said anything that he approved of her dress, and she relaxed at once. As they came out of the door, and turned along the pavement, she said, 'No car?'

'No, the Old Beast is in for repairs. They're having the devil's own job finding parts for her. That's the trouble with a foreign car. Can you bear to walk?'

'What are we going to see?'

'*The Naughty Wife*, with Gladys Cooper.'

'What's that?'

'Don't tell me you never heard of it? It ran in the West End for years.'

'Really?'

He laughed. 'I understand. You have been devoted to your cause. I should hardly expect you to know about such trivialities. But with me, you see, it's exactly the other way around.'

'What do you mean?'

'Oh, well, after the war I never wanted to think about anything serious again. Had enough for a lifetime, I promise you.'

'In Egypt?'

'Yes, all around there ... Mesopotamia, Palestine, you know. Still planning to go back to Cork?'

'I think so – at least, I was.'

'I dare say I'll be able to get down to see you.'

She slipped her arm through his, and squeezed in against him. He smiled and seemed to cheer up.

'Anyway, this whole show's going to be over soon.'

'Is it? How can you be sure?'

'Things one overhears in hotel bars, that sort of thing. And reading the newspapers. I don't think it can go on much longer.'

'Don't you?'

'No. I should say Lloyd George is preparing to do a deal

with the Sinn Feiners, and they'll cobble up something between them.' He thought. 'He's got to do something. Public opinion is moving against him. All the shooting – it doesn't look good. Not for the Government's reputation. They've got to do something. Let's just hope it's sooner rather than later.'

'Yes,' she said hurriedly. She didn't want to discuss politics now.

Then, out of nowhere she said, 'Did you enjoy the party?'

'What party?'

'Dora's.'

'I didn't go. What was it like?'

'Oh, I couldn't go. I – I thought she had invited you?'

'She did.'

There was a long pause as she listened to the sound of their shoes on the pavement. She couldn't think what to say next and was beginning to wish she hadn't started on this subject.

'Out of town, I suppose?' she said at last in the lightest tone she could find.

'Why do you suppose that?'

'You said – well, I mean, you said you had been invited, but didn't go.'

Lewis said nothing, and she cursed herself for her stupidity in even mentioning the woman. She had obviously annoyed him.

At last, what seemed minutes later, during which she had wished she were at home, wished Dora Keene at the bottom of the sea, and realised the whole evening was going to be a fiasco, he said in a distant way, 'Anne, do you know Dora Keene well?'

'I don't know her at all. I've only met her once.'

'So she's not a friend of yours?'

'No. Not at all.'

'Good. Nor of mine.'

'Ah,' Anne said lightly.

'In fact, since you mentioned her name, I may as well tell you – I can't stand the woman.'

She felt a deluge of relief, and a grateful desire to offer him something in return for this admission, and couldn't help blurting out, 'Lewis, since you're being so frank with me, there is something I want to tell you.'

'Yes?'

'That afternoon in the Shelbourne, when we had tea and Sandy walked in – I wasn't waiting for him.'

'I didn't think you were.'

'Oh.' She was taken aback. 'I thought –'

'You told me you were waiting for a school friend.'

'That's right.'

'What happened to her, by the way? She never showed up.'

After a pause, Anne swallowed. 'Lewis, there's something else I'd like to tell you.'

'Oh, lord this is an evening for revelations! What is it this time?'

'There was no school friend.'

'What?'

'No.'

'You mean you were sitting there having tea all by yourself?'

'Not exactly.'

He looked down into her face which happened to be illuminated at that moment by a streetlamp, saw the anxious look on it, and slowly his own face creased into a teasing, knowing smile. She couldn't resist smiling back into his eyes, and then he simply bent down and kissed her. She threaded her arms round his neck and they tightened their hold on each other.

At last they let each other go and turned along the pavement, her arm in his. Lewis said in a tone of great relief, 'Well, thank God we've cleared up that little mystery!' and they both burst into laughter.

They walked on in silence. Anne didn't think she had ever been so happy.

The theatre was full. Lewis had got them a box, and she was able to look down on the audience, comment on them and point out things. She felt quite light-headed, almost drunk; nothing, absolutely nothing, mattered. The evening was passing in a blur of happiness. The show was light, bright, silly, lovely ... everything was just such fun.

In the interval, she had an ice cream and Lewis had a whiskey.

Then they were out on the pavement again among all the other people excitedly discussing the show and how much they had enjoyed it, and there was an effervescent atmosphere of pleasure and gaiety.

'It would have been nice to have gone for a bit of supper,' Lewis said, as they set off along the dark pavement, 'but with the curfew –'

His attention was distracted.

'Excuse me.' He took her arm, and guided them both into a dark side street. When she looked up at him, he put his finger to his lips. 'Shh. I'll explain in a moment.'

She looked back, and after a few moments a group of men in raincoats and felt hats walked past towards Grafton Street. Lewis let them get on a few yards, and then took her arm again.

'Rather embarrassing, Anne, sorry about that. You wouldn't think me a gambling man to look at, would you? Here I am, giving away all my guilty secrets.' He laughed. 'Fact is, it was a fellow I owe money to. The gee-gees, I'm afraid. Don't worry, he'll get it. That's the trouble with selling things on commission – your income tends to fluctuate, up one month, down the next. And then, when I take myself off to the races once in a blue moon, it's ten to one I won't have any luck. So I need to keep out of his way till I'm in funds again.'

Although Lewis was as relaxed as ever and made charming and inconsequential conversation all the way back to Merrion Square, Anne was filled with anxiety again. He was off his pedestal. The idea of him getting into the hands of those men, some sort of semi-criminal fraternity – bookies, race-course touts, horrible men – she couldn't bear to think of it. How could he have let himself get involved with anything like that? Be in the power of men like that?

As she was about to open the door, he stopped her.

'Before we go in, when are you going down to Cork?'

'Well, I hadn't actually fixed a date ...'

'It's just that they have dinner dances at the Shelbourne, and I thought it might be rather fun to go.'

She nodded, and they kissed again, and then she couldn't help blurting out, 'Lewis, those men – you will be careful, won't you?'

'Oh, heavens, don't give it thought. I'm sorry I mentioned it. Really, Anne, its nothing. It was only that – well, with you on my arm, I didn't want to get into a row about it in the street. Don't worry, he'll get his money. He always has. He knows me of old!'

She was not very relieved to hear this, but it was the best she was going to get, so she accepted it.

'Till next Saturday, then?'

They went upstairs where Tony and Pippa were sitting by the fire waiting to hear about *The Naughty Wife*.

In bed, in the darkness waiting for sleep to come, Anne ran the events of the evening through her mind.

The memory of that moment when he had steered her into a side street would not go away. It had been a nasty shock to think he could be in any kind of danger. It had foolishly never crossed her mind before; even all his driving round the countryside, even the pistol in his pocket, none of it had actually struck her as dangerous. But that tangible sign, those real men whom he wanted to avoid ... Now his safety was hers too. How could she be well or happy while he was in danger?

It was odd that she had never before thought of Lewis as a gambling man. Yet why not? It seemed quite natural; after all, he was a man who had had adventures in the desert, and kept them all enthralled with his stories – risk-taking would be in his blood.

And the way he had steered her into the side street; it showed he cared for her – she revered him for that. At the moment it was as if her whole mental horizon was filled with Lewis. He was like a great sun in her sky. What a relief when he had told her his real feelings for Dora Keene, and how easy he had made it for her to confess about Sandy in the Shelbourne.

She squirmed with pleasure at the thought of the dinner dance on Saturday. She must buy herself a new dress; she would do him proud; she would wear a dress that would leave him in no doubt as to her feelings for him.

She fell asleep.

240

# Chapter Twenty-Six

Anne had washed her hair but did not put on any make-up. Even at this moment, some deep-rooted puritan streak rebelled against the idea.

She took yet another look at herself in the mirror on the wardrobe door. If Lewis liked her in the beige tea gown, and the emerald and mauve evening frock, what was he going to say to this? This was one she had not even showed to Pippa yet. This was her trump card; tonight she was staking everything.

The dress was the very latest fashion. It reached barely past the knee and made her legs look longer than ever. She just prayed it would be warm in the dining room of the Shelbourne.

It was one thing to carry off the tea gown and the evening dress, but this? Bare arms, bare back, and a deep V in front – pale apricot and silver, a wisp of silk muslin and gauze to her knees. If it hadn't been for the cold she could scarcely have known she was wearing it. As it was she had goose pimples.

But in the midst of her nervousness something else told her she did not merely look very, very good, but more than that, more than any question of taste or style, there was something frankly erotic about the effect. It gave her an inexplicable sense of excitement, something she could not hope to explain to herself.

She had chosen the dress in Switzer's, spent an afternoon going through racks and racks of things, in the end choosing the one that said what she wanted to say most unambiguously. It gave her an enormous confidence, knowing he wanted her, he had shown that over and over. Everything seemed to be building between them.

That other moment – that evening by the river when they had known they loved one another, before everything had gone wrong – had not been mentioned between them since she had come to Dublin. Yet this evening it seemed – she tried to visualise the scene, herself in this skimpy frock, Lewis across the table, the candles – it seemed that tonight they might be able to repair the damage done in Lisheen. Be able to heal the mistakes and blunders that had separated them since Vere's death, and restore again the magical understanding and acceptance they had found that evening on the river bank.

She heard a rumble in the street which could only be the Old Beast, and then the jangling of the bell in the kitchen far below. She picked up her scent and gave herself a little splash behind the ears. She took her overcoat down from the door, picked up the tiny vanity purse in silver she had bought with the dress, and went down into the drawing room.

Lewis was alone, in full evening dress, white tie and tails. He looked very handsome; distinguished, she thought – the word sprang to mind immediately. And she could tell he liked her dress.

He was holding a small posy of flowers and offered it to her.

She had seen *corsages* before but no man had ever offered her one. Lewis wanted to pin it on for her, and she had to hunt about for a pin, which she found, and then he was bending over her, and carefully pinning the *corsage*, the little bunch of flowers, on her dress, leaning in close and concentrating, his hands brushing against her breasts as he worked, shielded by such a thin layer of silk. She watched his eyes as he concentrated on the pinning, and felt her heart beat uncontrollably. Within a minute of coming through the door he was in this intimate position, so close to her she could smell the faint manly smell of him, and was confused beyond expression.

'There.' He stood back. 'Very nice.' It was as if he hadn't noticed the dress at all, only his own handiwork. 'Ready?'

As she turned to go she caught a last glimpse of herself in the mirror. How pretty the *corsage* looked; what a pleasant, considerate thing to think of. And how he had made her heart beat as he'd pinned it on.

They went down into the car and drove round to the Shelbourne, about a minute's drive. A lorry load of Auxies rattled up, and Lewis swerved in to let them go by. It was something she did not notice any more.

The Shelbourne was ablaze with lights, and well-dressed people were all about them in the foyer: people who spoke with educated voices in English accents, as if their Irishness were diluted simply by walking through the door.

There was a cloakroom, and she took off her coat.

Lewis suggested they should have an aperitif before going in to dine, and taking her arm, steered her to the bar.

'Two champagne cocktails.'

There were so many elegant and half-dressed women about in the hotel that Anne felt more at ease than she had thought she would. So far Lewis had not made any reference to her dress. Clearly he thought it was quite normal for her to go out wrapped in two skimpy yards of silk and gauze; as she relaxed she felt herself become excited in anticipation of the evening ahead.

The cocktails came and she saw they were in very small glasses. She said nothing, except, 'Thank you.'

He raised his glass.

'Here's to peace.'

Anne raised her glass, and sipped the drink. It had an interesting flavour, bitter-sweet. She had drunk champagne before, at Christmas and so on, but this had a more complex taste. It was nice too, she decided.

Lewis was talking about his car. 'Fortunately the mechanic was very good, knew his onions, I can tell you. There's a dealer in Manchester so he was able to get the parts he wanted with no trouble and put her back together again, better than new. He set my heart at rest, Anne. I'm very attached to the Old Beast, just wouldn't feel at home in any other car.'

They went into the dining room. The band was playing discreetly, musical comedy selections, and they waited at the door while the head waiter found their reservation in a book then took up enormous leather-bound menus and led them among the tables, where other people were sitting. They came to a table for two, with a candle on it, and he pulled back a dainty chair for Anne.

Lewis sat opposite her and they opened their menus. Lewis had two menus, she noticed. She studied him over the top of hers as he was concentrating. What was it about him? He always had that casual, easy-going manner, so effortlessly in command that she knew she could trust herself implicitly in his hands – and yet, as she studied him, she thought again how little she really knew about him. His school days with Tony, the wine firm, his adventures in the Middle East ... yet she knew nothing about his family. It didn't add up to very much. She trembled to think that her happiness now lay in his hands.

'What are you going to have?'

For what seemed the hundredth time she took a grip on her thoughts.

'Oh, let me see. I'm not very hungry.'

'Really? Well, I'm ravenous, I'll be honest. A steak, I think. Go on – you must have something.'

In the end he ordered oysters to start with, and steaks to follow.

'And let's have a bottle of your best champagne.'

'*Oui, monsieur.*'

'Did you hear that?' Lewis said as the waiter retired out of earshot. 'He's as French as I am.' He laughed, a frank open sound, and rubbed his hands together. 'Oh, I'm enjoying myself, I don't mind telling you. Sitting here in all this elegance, with the most beautiful girl in the room opposite me. I'm very grateful, Anne. You look like a goddess.' He paused, looking into her eyes. 'Like to dance?'

She stood up. They were the only couple on the little dance floor: it was early yet – everyone else was barely into their hors d'oeuvres – but Lewis was hardly the man to worry about a thing like that.

The band was playing a sentimental foxtrot. He took her in his arms and they drifted round the floor lazily following the rhythm. He seemed to be far away, staring over her shoulder – she couldn't see his face as he held her close to him, but she was acutely conscious of his hand against her bare back, and her hand in his, warm and dry, a man's hand, twice the size of hers. Being so close to him, in a strangely public intimacy, a private world in the middle of the other diners, she felt every-thing, was aware of everything and especially of him, so close, looking across her shoulder, and then once into her eyes and smiling – not saying anything, just smiling.

He hummed snatches of the tune the band was playing, and then looked into her eyes again and said softly, 'Cristabel.' He looked away again and they went on, lazily drifting around the floor, and she didn't mind if the band never stopped. It was the most divine thing she had ever done, just drifting round lazily, noting the old chandeliers overhead and the mirrors on the wall in their gilt frames and other inconsequential and unimportant things, aware all the time of Lewis holding her through the thin silk.

'I told you it was the right name for you – and now, you see, you've proved me right.'

'What do you mean?'

'Oh, before you were all ferocious with me, stand-offish, prickly and self-conscious. Now you're yourself, a beautiful woman not trying to prove anything. Cristabel. Glad you came?'

She didn't dare to speak. Only looked away and nodded faintly.

When they returned to the table, the oysters had arrived. Also the champagne. The waiter opened the bottle and poured them both a glass. Then Lewis lifted his and offered a toast.

'Here's to us, Cristabel.'

She raised her glass to him and drank. She had never espe-cially liked champagne, but here tonight, in the dim light of the room, with the band playing behind her and Lewis looking impossibly glamorous opposite, it was the appropriate, the right thing to do.

They ate the oysters, and then after a while he looked up and said, 'You see, the secret is we have a lot in common; we are very alike. What I mean is you're a second child and so am I. So we've both had an elder brother or sister who got all the attention, the first-born and all that, and we've felt a bit shut out, a bit second best. And consequently we both feel we've had to prove something. That's why you've always been so prickly. But you've learned your lesson much quicker than I have.'

'What lesson?'

'Well, here you are tonight – look at you, a poised confident young woman, in charge of her own life. It doesn't matter whether you're the second, the third, or the fifty-first, does it? You're yourself, which is what matters as far as I can make out.'

'You never struck me as being second best to anyone.'

'Oh, you should see me at home. Big brother lords it round the place, makes the decisions, runs the firm. I'm very small beer, I promise you. So I've always gone out looking for some stunt, to prove I was as good as him. Silly eh?'

'Like in Egypt, you mean? When you got your car?'

'Did I ever tell you about that?'

'Umm?' She smiled lazily at him, leaning her chin on her hand, quite ready to hear the story again.

'Extraordinary story – not a particularly glamorous one, I must admit, but that's war for you. It was a present actually, from the King of Egypt.'

Dimly, through a haze of champagne, she registered something. Lewis went on, in his usual style, 'A number of us had been seconded to military security – very tricky situations used to erupt – and there had been a plot to assassinate him. The King of Egypt doesn't actually have any power, Anne, frankly he's just a stooge we put up, but we all had to pretend he was the real thing. Anyway, there were a number of dissident chaps who wanted a republic and to be free of Britain – just like your pals, actually – and we had to keep tabs on them. Not very difficult frankly. They gave themselves away everywhere they went and we had plenty of money to splash around so we had all the information we could use, then when we were ready we set the trap, they walked into it, and that was that. Afterwards a grateful king made me a present. Not supposed to accept gifts, actually, Anne – it's against the rules – but I thought, "What the hell? It's a lovely car."'

'Lewis!' she exploded into astonished laughter. Did he know what he was saying? She set down her glass and went on, in a tone somewhere between teasing and laughter, 'I heard somewhere you had won it in a bet.'

'Really? What bet? Oh, you mean the one with the Greek millionaire in Alexandria?'

246

She couldn't believe it, and still laughing she managed to say, 'Lewis – are you serious? What Greek millionaire? You told me you had dressed up as an Arab servant and stolen a coffee pot from the Turkish officers' mess.'

'Did I? Whatever possessed me to say a thing like that?'

But ever so slightly the bubble began to deflate, and a realisation was slowly percolating into her consciousness. There was a pause, as they continued to look at each other. The laughter stopped. Then she tried to smile again, but failed, and at last said, 'So it's not true?'

''Fraid not.' He shrugged and smiled.

'Well, is there anything else you've told me that isn't true? What about the family wine firm – does that really exist?'

'On my oath, I swear – in fact, I'll introduce you to the family. Once this show's over.'

She was silent but at last was able to say, 'So that was what you meant by being yourself, was it?'

'Anne,' he reached over and took her hand, 'trust me, I beg you. Once the show's over, I'll explain everything. It's very complicated.'

She was sitting bolt upright now, trying to understand but feeling dizzy. Everything was beginning to make sense. 'So you were in military security in Egypt?'

'That's right.'

And then it came to her.

'Were you one of the Cairo Group?'

'Yes.' He was very surprised. 'How did you know about that?'

'So you came over – I mean, after the war –'

'How did you find out about this? Has Tony been talking about me?'

'It was something he said – he didn't mention your name.'

Lewis leaned in and took her hand.

'I didn't want to have to tell you, not till it was over.' He was talking seriously, confidentially, in an undertone. 'This is very hush-hush, obviously. And this isn't the place to talk about it. But, well, the thing is, a group of us were recruited in Cairo, because of the work we'd been doing out there, and came over here to help clear up this mess. It's not been easy, I can tell you; very unpleasant, frankly. Still, with any luck it should be over soon.'

She couldn't hear him.

'And you're not really a wine salesman?' she was able to say.

'Oh, yes, the firm really exists – and it gives me a very useful cover.'

She pulled away her hand, repeating stupidly. 'And that story about the coffee pot, it wasn't true?'

Lewis now realised how upset she was. He tried to take her hand again, but she pulled it away.

'Sorry if it's been a shock.'

Her whole body was now gripped in a down-dragging feeling, as if she were hollow and was being filled with cold water, dragging her down, cold shrinking, filled with fear. She gripped one of the sides of the table. 'But that means – if you're a British agent – oh, God!' She had to rest her head on her hand. 'That means – I can't believe it – that morning when you and Vere went down to the river bank and met Steptoe, Vere must have told you about the ambush, and you told Steptoe – that's why you bet Vere he couldn't climb that beech tree. You had arranged to meet Steptoe. And that's why you were so ready to drive me into the village the morning Vere was killed. You knew already he was dead! And that's why you left so suddenly, without saying anything.'

She pulled herself away and stood up. Her voice was hoarse.

'Lewis, it was you who betrayed the Volunteers. You who killed Vere!'

The blood was drumming in her temples. She could hardly keep her balance. Lewis had stood up too by now. He reached for her.

'Anne —'

'No, don't touch me! How could you? I don't believe it! Oh, God, I don't believe it!'

Other people had turned to look at them, but she was conscious of none of them. She snatched up her little bag and walked quickly between the tables towards the door of the restaurant.

Lewis caught up with her in the foyer.

'Anne, calm down and listen for a minute.'

'Calm down? What are you saying? You killed my brother,

and you want me to calm down? You told me lie after lie after lie, you've told me nothing but lies ever since I've known you, and you want me to calm down? What is there to calm down for? Take away your hand!'

She attempted to make her way towards the cloakroom.

'Anne, for heaven's sake –'

She turned blindly.

'You're a fraud! You're not real, Lewis. Oh – get out of my way!'

There was no one in the cloakroom at that moment, but she couldn't bear to wait. Without saying any more, she threw off Lewis's hand and pushed her way through the door into the darkness outside.

She didn't stop running till she was in Merrion Square. Hardly knowing what she was doing, she burst into the drawing room.

Pippa was curled up sewing baby clothes. She glanced up.

'Have a nice dance?'

'I'm going home tomorrow. Please don't ask me why.'

She turned out of the drawing room again and ran up to her bedroom.

# Part Three

# Chapter Twenty-Seven

There was a knock on the door.

'Anne,' Pippa whispered. 'Anne.'

She did not stir.

The door opened a fraction and her sister was there.

'It's Lewis downstairs. He wants to talk to you.'

Anne was standing by the window looking out. She did not move, and when at last she spoke, her voice sounded muffled and low. The room was in darkness, except where the paraffin lamp Pippa was holding shed a soft light through the open doorway.

'I don't want to see him.'

'He's very upset. Says he wants to explain.'

After another long silence, Anne's voice came again: strange, detached. 'Tell him to go away.' She would not move. Pippa came towards her.

'What on earth's happened?'

'I can't explain.'

'Well, I can't just chuck him out. Can't you come and speak to him for a moment?'

Silence. Anne did not move. As Pippa closed the door at last and returned downstairs, Anne stared out into the dark square where the streetlamps were visible between the trees, their light broken and diffused. Her mind was blank. A little later she heard the front door close below her, and then footsteps on the stair.

Pippa reappeared at the door. 'He's gone. What on earth's happened between you two?'

Silence. Anne leaned against the window frame, her arms crossed.

'Anne, something's happened. What is it?'

'I can't explain.' Her voice was flat, distant.

'He was terribly upset, said he had to see you to explain. He's going to write.'

'I'm going home first thing tomorrow. If any letter from him comes for me, please return it.'

Pippa crossed the room and at last tentatively reached out a hand to touch Anne's shoulder. Instantly she moved away and leant against the wall. She would not look at Pippa.

'Anne,' she said, softly and insistently, 'you must tell me what's happened.'

'I can't.'

'Why not?'

'Please don't ask. I can't explain. And please don't mention his name again.' Her voice was a monotone.

At last Pippa rose, and went out. Anne stood against the wall, arms crossed, still in the flimsy dance dress, staring at the doorway where Pippa had gone out, but seeing only the river bank at Macroom, seeing only Lewis, his hands in his pockets, in affable conversation with Steptoe, and then pointing up at the tree where Vere was waving from the topmost branches. It wasn't possible ... but it was. Even at that moment, as he waved to Vere in the tree, he was betraying the Volunteers to that man.

She crossed to her bed, and sat, then lay in the dark room. She remembered now her first conversation with Steptoe in the drawing room at home, and the anticipation in his voice as he'd told her how he was going to take the village apart, house by house, to find the Volunteers; how he would 'terrorise' them, 'give them a taste of their own medicine'. She remembered his wet lips, and the way he would flick his tongue across them as he spoke, relishing his little joke, giving her slightly sideways glances as he drew on his cigarette as if they were in some way in league together, or as if he were about to make some lewd suggestion. And it occurred to her, something of which she had been only dimly aware at the time, but clearly now, that in his enjoyment of this, the way he was going to terrorise the village, the way he had described it, it was as if in a grotesque way he had been attempting to woo her, that this was his language of love.

This was the man in whom Lewis had confided, the man with whom he'd planned the destruction of the Volunteers.

She did not sleep. She would have gone down to Cork then and there but for the curfew. In any case as soon as the light of dawn showed, about half-past five, she pulled herself up from the bed where she had been lying, still in her dance dress, threw off the counterpane she had drawn round her some time during the night, threw off her clothes, and naked in the cold room, washed herself in cold water.

She dressed herself in a three-quarter length navy skirt, woollen vest, blouse, golfing cardigan – layers of clothes to hide her nakedness, to cover up the thoughts and memories of the previous evening which tried to intrude, to turn her back into her normal self. She pulled the suitcase out from beneath her bed and, opening it, began to pack her clothes. As she laid in the new ones she had bought, the brown and beige, the green and mauve, and at last the wisp of apricot and gauze, this nothing of a dress, this talisman or token of anticipation, this pathetic remnant of a hope destroyed, she had to stop and rest her hands on the sides of the suitcase, hang her head and wait, her mind blank, till she could control herself again and continue with the packing.

Then, her head swimming with tiredness, she went down to the kitchen and asked Mrs O'Connor for a cup of tea and some toast, and while she was waiting in the drawing room looked up the time of the trains. Pippa and Tony were still in bed. It was Sunday morning, and the house was silent.

She scribbled a short note to them, left it on the dining table, and then was on an outside car – which by good fortune she had stopped at the end of the square – for the Kingsbridge station.

British Tommies, in greatcoats and holding rifles, were on the platform, stopping people and looking in bags, but like an apparition Anne walked past the sleepy, bored soldiers, opened a carriage door and got in.

It was the longest journey of her life. She had made many train journeys; all her school days had been made up of train journeys, back and forth to Dublin and across to England. She had often returned to school depressed, hating to leave her home and her dogs and the mountains, hating the restrictive

255

cramped atmosphere of school, staring gloomily out of train windows – oh, she had made many miserable train journeys – but this was the worst. She felt annihilated in the spirit.

Tears came into her eyes as she stared out of the window and thought of Vere, seeing him suddenly so clearly as her eyes stared unseeing through the grimy glass and watched the fields flit by, the telegraph poles, in their monotonous rhythm. Her little brother – how could Lewis have done it? It was worse than shameful. She felt he had no more right to a place on this earth after what he had done. Sniffing and blowing her nose as she stared out, she did not have even the will to hide her tears from the two men who shared the compartment with her and who looked at her over the tops of their newspapers from time to time but said nothing.

It was afternoon when she arrived at Lisheen, tired and dusty, her eyes itching from the train smoke which always managed to infiltrate the compartment and left her grimy and uncomfortable.

Her father was out, but Bridget told her Claire was in the garden and Anne went in search of her. As she made her way down the path she saw her mother ahead of her, squatting in the path and attacking a flower bed with a trowel. It was a hazy, overcast afternoon, threatening rain, and Claire was wearing an old raincoat, wellingtons, and a pair of thick gardening gloves. Seeing her mother there alone in the garden, still raw and waiting for summer, prodding and digging at the rich black earth, Anne stopped with a sort of shock. Squatting bareheaded, her hair disordered, Claire looked old and slightly mad; she looked like some eccentric old woman, like Miss Forster, an elderly single lady who lived in the village, untidy, unkempt, hunched over her little spade as she jabbed at the earth.

Anne felt a spurt of anger; her mother whom she adored, reduced to this, reduced by Vere's death and the war. She had an impulse to rush forward, snatch her mother in her arms to protect and comfort her.

She stood over her.

'Hullo, Mother.' She tried to sound as normal as possible.

Claire barely looked round. 'Hullo, dear. Got back then?'

After a moment, standing with her hands in her raincoat pockets, Anne said, 'Yes. I had enough of Dublin. Rather be here.'

'How are Pippa and Tony?'

'Oh, fine. Where's Father?'

'Gone into the village to the post office.'

Claire had still not turned, and was concentrating on bedding in the plants she had in the box beside her, taking them out one by one, and setting them in the little holes she'd dug with her spade.

There was something very odd about this scene. Anne had never seen a trowel in her mother's hands in her life. Still Claire worked carefully and methodically. After looking round vaguely, Anne said, 'Why isn't Costello doing that?'

'Costello has gone missing.'

'What?'

'More important things to do, I expect. More important than bedding out plants. Still we mustn't complain. At least Leary hasn't joined the IRA. And Bridget and Mrs Deasey are still here.'

'Good Lord.'

'Oh, we're not the only ones. The Archers' chauffeur is now in Cork jail.'

'Timothy O'Malley? What did he do?'

'He was captured when a gang of men attacked a police barracks.'

Anne was silent. There didn't seem to be anything to say. Claire continued with her bedding.

'I'll have a bath.'

'Yes, dear. Then we'll have tea.'

That evening Anne went to her father's study and found him oiling and polishing his army revolver. He told her about the night they had come for the guns.

'It was about ten – we were just going to bed. There was a knock at the door and half a dozen lads standing there, two of them holding pistols. I recognised one or two of them – Danny Mount, do you remember him? And Costello, lurking at the back looking sheepish. They were very polite and wanted to know whether I had any guns. So I gave them the shotguns.

They were very grateful, I must say, and apologised for putting us to any inconvenience. It was a farce. Costello didn't know about this, fortunately. I keep it in an old cardboard box under the bed. They weren't inclined to search too thoroughly.' He drew a breath. 'Next time, perhaps I'll be ready for them.'

Hugh sipped his whiskey and soda.

'You mustn't!'

'What?'

'Father, you wouldn't stand a chance!'

He looked at her strangely. 'I suppose you'd know,' he said sarcastically. 'You've got a bit of a nerve to lecture me about guns.'

She looked away. 'Father, I know what I did can never be undone. But if anything should happen to you or Mother –'

They looked at one another for a moment in silence. Then Hugh grunted.

'Many Protestant families have gone to England.' He went on with his oiling. 'I don't know which is worse, the IRA or the so-called Black and Tans. I've fought in India, I've fought on the Afghan frontier. I've seen my share of bloodshed, but this...' He polished more vehemently. 'There was the shooting at Mallow station – it was while you were away – they shot a police inspector – and his wife too for good measure. But the Auxies were no better. When they arrived they shot three railwaymen who just happened to be on the station. Then there was the train ambush at Upton; five civilians killed including a woman – that was in February.' He frowned as he adjusted his pistol. 'Then there was the murder of Captain Compton Smith. They took him as hostage for some men awaiting execution in Cork jail, and after the sentence had been carried out, shot him in cold blood. There are six men in Cork now under sentence of death. It'll be a miracle if hostages aren't taken.'

He polished in silence for a moment, then Anne said, tentatively, 'What do you think will happen?'

'Heaven only knows.'

'I heard rumours in Dublin,' she said carefully, 'that Lloyd George might be preparing to do a deal with de Valera.'

'Oh, they keep talking about it, but nothing happens. Besides, Lloyd George has to settle with the Ulster Unionists first. They'll never accept a deal, I know them.' He thought for a moment. 'Whatever happens, things will never be as they were. Our world is finished, I do know.'

Anne could think of nothing more to say. She felt the whole thing had simply grown too big for her to comprehend. All they could do was to cling together and hope that as the whirlwind swept through the land, it would not carry them away with it.

Anne went to find her mother to talk to her. Seeing Claire shrivelled with fear, vulnerable, reduced, she felt a hot anger and yet could not for her life know whom she should direct her anger against. Her mother, after all, had always been a nationalist, all for Ireland's freedom. But now? Principles didn't seem relevant anymore. Where was right and wrong when the killing went on night and day, meaningless and random? The only thing left was to survive and hold the family together if they could.

'Seeing you again,' Claire said, 'and knowing you are safe, and Pippa, I feel better. Ever since Vere's death I have had such a terrible presentiment that another of you might be – taken. So long as you are both still safe, I think I can stand it.' She looked away as Anne sat holding her hand. 'I often think of him. Do you?'

Anne nodded.

'Often. It's – oh, I don't know – anything can start it. I hear a footstep on the stair, or in the hall, and for a mad moment I think it's Vere. And then sometimes, if I'm here in the room alone as evening is drawing in, I look up and for a moment it's as if he is sitting in that chair. He could so easily be. Sometimes he seems so close – so close, as if I could just reach out to him –'

Anne leant forward gently and they put their arms round each other, and sat in silence, rocking back and forth.

'I know I mustn't say anything. I don't want your father to know, poor dear. We never talk about it – about Vere, I mean.'

Seeing her mother and father like this, made Anne burn inwardly with a terrible anger against the man who had caused it.

*

Summer came suddenly, taking them by surprise, as if one day the trees were still bare against the sky and the next there was a lush new growth clothing them, a fresh exuberance of green everywhere, a lightness in the air, an intoxication to breathing as if she might become drunk just walking in the garden, and Anne's spirits rose. Who could be so hardened as not to feel it?

They talked of dog breeding. Hugh said Og should be bred from and they made plans to take her to Bandon to a friend who had a stud dog. So one morning, light and clear, and promising to become hot, they harnessed the trap, put a lead on Og and went over to Bandon for the day. Trotting through the narrow lanes with the blossom on the whitethorn, and the puffy clouds high about the mountains, Anne felt there was a rightness, a proper normality in the world that would always assert itself in the end, and however great their troubles might seem, the great world about them would not let them absolutely go under, but would buoy them up in the end. And on a day like this, trotting through the lanes, she felt a little of her own troubles too sliding off her, wafting away on the light summer breeze.

# Chapter Twenty-Eight

Early in May they received a telegram from Tony. Pippa had had a baby boy, and both were doing well. They would be coming down in two weeks, as soon as Pippa was out of the nursing home, for the christening.

Claire read this, and then putting the telegram down into her lap, closed her eyes and murmured, 'Thank God.'

Anne was standing in the doorway in a pair of old jodhpurs and an open-necked blouse. She had been in the stable mucking out when she had seen the telegram boy arrive.

'That makes me an aunt,' she said, raising her eyebrows, and then thought for a moment. 'And you're a grandmother.'

Her mother opened her eyes and got up from the sofa where she was sitting.

'Don't get too close.' Anne stepped back. 'I've been working in the stable.' She was about to go out, then said, 'Do you think you can get used to being called Granny?'

'I think I can get used to anything, now that Pippa has had her baby and you are both safe.' Claire straightened her back and took a deep breath. 'Though I must say, I don't feel old enough.'

'I'll tell Father.'

Anne found Hugh in his study. The room was a fug of tobacco smoke and he was bent over the pile of papers which comprised the *History of the Hunter Family*.

'There'll be a new chapter to your book. Pippa's had her baby.' She showed him the telegram. 'And they'll be down in two weeks.'

As she was standing by his shoulder looking down at the

mass of papers before him, not wanting to leave yet, she said, 'And how is the book?'

Hugh tamped down the tobacco in his pipe and swivelled back and forth in his chair for a moment. 'Coming along,' he said at last.

'You've been working hard on it lately,' she said brightly.

'Of course I have.' He looked up at her with a sardonic look. 'What else have I got to do? Thanks to your friends I no longer have any function in this county, Anne.'

Rebuffed, she said quietly, 'They only want justice, Father.'

'And I didn't give them justice, I suppose?'

She drew a breath. 'You know that is not the point,' she said at last, then made another effort. 'Where have you got to?'

He raised his eyebrows, then picked up the sheet in front of him, stared at it for a moment, then said, 'To tell the truth, I'm slightly stuck at the moment. I've written to the Blennerhassetts in Limerick but haven't heard from them yet.'

'Who are they?'

'According to the parish records here a Prudence Hunter married into the Blennerhassets in 1763. I remember vaguely my grandfather talking of the Blennerhassett connection, but I haven't been able to track it down. And there were so many Prudences in the eighteenth century. The other possibility is the records office in Dublin. If I had thought of it, I would have asked you to call in while you were up. I'll write to them. A Blennerhassett sat for Limerick in Parliament through most of the last century.'

'I was rather hoping you would have turned up something more exciting.'

'Oh, there are plenty of exciting bits. Prudence Hunter is rather dry stuff, I admit – though you never know. If the Blennerhassetts come up with any letters, it could get more interesting. But there was Tobias Hunter –'

'Who was he?'

'A sea captain. The younger brother of Jeremy Hunter who inherited the estate in 1787. He went into the navy and then emigrated to America. Fought against the British in the War of 1812. There is quite a tribe of Hunters in Virginia now.

I've been corresponding with Caleb Hunter, a lawyer in Alexandria, and he's sent me a lot of interesting stuff.'

Hugh had been polite enough but she felt the distance between them still. But where she had once been ready to provoke an argument, now she was more ready to seek a compromise. She feared, though, that after what had happened there could never be true reconciliation between them. She returned to the stable and worked hard for the rest of the morning, trying to calm herself.

A few weeks later she was in the village when she saw Mrs Donnelly about to go into the village stores. It was warm and sunny and Mrs Donnelly was in a summer dress and cardigan. Anne left her bicycle against Shanahan's, still closed and boarded up, and caught her just as she was opening the door.

'Mrs Donnelly.'

The older woman turned to her in the doorway, and hesitated. She said nothing at first, looking Anne over.

Then: 'Hullo, Anne. It's a long time since we saw you.'

'I've been in Dublin.'

'Oh, yes. Staying with your sister?'

'That's right.'

Mrs Donnelly had her usual calm expectant manner, polite and measured, so that Anne had to make all the conversation. She wanted to ask about Cathal, but didn't quite know how to mention his name. At last she said, 'And Doctor Connelly – is he any better?'

'My husband died, Anne. In March when you were away.'

'Oh.' She hesitated. 'I'm very sorry to hear that.'

'It happened quite suddenly. We thought he was making progress. I had hoped he might have recovered so far as to be able to get out of bed in the warmer weather. But there was a relapse, and quite quickly one afternoon he died. Even before I had had a chance to call in O'Malley.' There was a pause while each looked away. 'And I had no chance to get word to Cathal.'

'I'm so sorry.'

'And then, at the funeral, of course the police expected Cathal to attend. Obviously the British thought it was too good an opportunity to miss. So out of respect for the dead the church was half filled with police and spies, there were plain-clothes police in the road, and in the fields round the village, I believe. No doubt they were up the trees too.' She drew a breath. 'Fortunately Cathal has many good friends in the village. He was warned in good time.'

'How terrible.'

'You may say so.'

'Have you heard from him at all?' Anne asked hesitantly.

'He came a week or so after the funeral, and we went down to see the grave during the night. We laid flowers there together, Anne, and said a prayer.'

'How is he?'

'As well as can be expected.'

'Do you see him often?'

'What do you think?'

'I mean – is he well?' Anne felt awkward and knew she wasn't expressing herself very well. 'He hasn't been caught?'

'No, he hasn't been caught – so far.' Mrs Donnelly did not enjoy discussing her son with Anne, it was clear. 'And he's quite well, thank you.'

Nevertheless there was in Anne an unexpected need which had surfaced just then, and she pressed on without heeding the woman's feelings. 'Mrs Donnelly, if you should – I mean, when you next see Cathal, would you give him my regards? Remember me to him, that's all.'

After a moment the older woman said, 'If you wish.' And then, 'Goodbye, Anne.'

She was about to turn back to the shop when she thought of something. 'I hear your sister has had a baby. Will you congratulate her for me?'

She went into the shop, closing the door behind her, leaving Anne in the sunshine.

On impulse she pedalled through the village to the Protestant church, and walked among the graves, over the grassy hummocks and lop-sided tombstones, till she came to Vere's grave by the wall, beneath the tall beech tree. Already the gleam of the new-polished stone was dulled beneath a patina of lichen, and the grave had started on its journey towards obscurity, towards the anonymity of the other graves. It came as a shocking thought to Anne, as she stood looking down and reading again the inscription, that in a few years, perhaps a very few years, as the stone became more mossy, strangers would stand here looking down at it and would have no idea who Vere had been. They might notice that he had died at fourteen, and might wonder why. And for a few moments they might look at one another and shake their heads, before moving on to look at other graves in their idle curiosity before going back out into the road, getting into their traps or cars, or mounting their bicycles and continuing on their journey.

This idea that the memory of her brother would fade, that he had merely joined the great army of the forgotten in the graveyard, was indescribably distressing to her. She determined that he would *never* be forgotten, and later that afternoon returned with some flowers she had cut in the garden and laid them on the grave.


As the door opened there was a concerted roaring of dogs, which filled the house. Aunt Ju came in, beating down her own Highland terriers, 'Down, Mungo! Down, Jerry! Down! Will you get down!'

Anne was restraining Mor, and trying to greet her aunt at the same time. 'Come in, it's lovely to see you, it's been an age....'

As the dogs were sobered up, Claire had come out from the drawing room and was saying, 'Ju! Come in, Pippa and Tony have arrived, and the baby's adorable!'

Her mother had so improved in appearance as to be unrecognisable since Anne had returned to Lisheen. This was mainly due, Anne thought, to the news of Pippa's baby; this afternoon Claire had put on one of her Worth dresses and her emeralds.

'Claire darling, you're looking *much* better!'

'Of course I am! Pippa and Tony came down last night. Come in and see my grandson.'

The drawing room was crowded. Pippa sat on the sofa in regal splendour with little Jeremy in a christening gown which was a family heirloom – 'four generations of Hunters have been christened in it, Pippa, so for heaven's sake don't spill anything on it!' – and talking to Winnie; Tony was with Hugh and Pat, Bridget was setting down the tea pot and everybody was talking at once.

Winnie and Pat had come down with Pippa and Tony to be godparents. When they had arrived, the previous evening, Winnie had been unable to resist leaning over the coffee table in the drawing room where the women were sitting round after dinner and confiding that *'Sandy sends his regards!'* in a heavy stage whisper, which of course Pippa overheard. Anne was covered in confusion, and muttered something like: 'I don't – that is – how is Sandy?' in an unconvincing tone. And then, 'I don't really...' But Winnie had gone on in the same intense tone, 'You seem to have made a tremendous impression on him. He's always talking about you.' Anne, growing red-faced, had had to state rather more firmly that she was sure that Sandy was very kind and so forth, but that there was categorically *nothing of that kind between them*, and she hoped that would be the end of it. Whereupon Pippa and Winnie had exploded into giggles, so much so that Pippa nearly spilled her coffee cup, and finally Claire, who had been listening to this with increasing mystification, asked whether she might be allowed to share the joke, and Anne said there was no joke, and that Winnie and Pippa were behaving like a couple of nine year olds.

Things got rather more serious later as they were going to bed when Pippa appeared at Anne's bedroom door, holding an envelope in her hand. Anne, sitting on the edge of her bed, looked up at the letter as Pippa tentatively held it out.

'He's very unhappy. He really begged me to talk to you.'

She was still holding out the letter.

Anne did not move. 'I can't read it. Please return it.'

'He's very upset. I've never known him like it. What on earth happened between you?'

Anne looked down and took a deep breath. 'I told you before,' she said in a low voice, 'it's not something I can talk about. I can't, so please don't ask. I said I didn't want to speak to him, and I specifically asked you to return any letters that might come for me.'

'Anne, he's a very old friend – well, of Tony's anyway – I can't. I mean, I told him I would do my best for him.'

'Please don't say anymore!' Anne stood up abruptly.

266

'Pippa, I *told* you! Now I'm going to bed. Good night.'

But it was easier to close the door behind Pippa than to eradicate the image of Lewis which had returned so vividly the second she saw the letter. All these weeks since returning she had been hoping he would somehow just go away, that his memory, and the memory of them together, would somehow gently vanish like the smoke of a summer bonfire in the garden, and would not by contrast eat into her like a corrosive liquid, biting into her, causing her sometimes in bed in the darkness to curl up and clutch herself until the pain should pass.

Aunt Ju admired the baby, accepted a cup of tea, and at last took Anne by the elbow halfway through a conversation with Winnie, saying, 'Now then, Anne, come into the garden with me. I am *gasping* for a cigarette.'

And Winnie just had to watch as Ju conducted Anne through the door. It didn't take long for the conversation to come round to the subject of Lewis.

'He told so many lies. Of course I sometimes used to wonder at the time, but it didn't seem to matter then... I just loved to listen to him.'

They were strolling in the garden. Ju had her arm through Anne's and was smoking a cigarette.

'But when I found out about Vere and Steptoe, everything suddenly seemed so tawdry. Not only that he had betrayed Vere and the Volunteers, but that he had been lying to me. I couldn't trust him. At least, I didn't know whether to trust him or not, which comes to the same thing.'

'How did you find out?'

'He admitted he was a Government agent – a spy – and it became obvious he was responsible.'

Ju was thoughtful and Anne pulled a dead rose head from its stalk, and was crushing the leaves together in her hand.

'A lot of young men found it difficult to adjust after the war,' her aunt said at last. 'It had a very destabilising effect on the personality.'

Anne turned at this.

'After all, if a man has been risking his life – if he has been involved in secret work, using subterfuge, telling lies, making up stories – he is bound to have difficulty adjusting to normal life. Some men never do adjust you know.'

'Don't they?'

'It's not something you're going to read about in the newspapers, obviously, but there are still thousands in mental hospitals recovering from the war.'

'Are there?'

'Oh, yes. We are only beginning to understand the real cost of it now.'

'That's terrible.' She looked down at the crushed rose leaves in the palm of her hand. Lewis was not only morally corrupt but mentally unstable as well. He was not a whole human being.

'Did you go to bed with him?' Ju asked casually.

'No!' Anne exclaimed.

'I just wondered. And you've no need to sound so shocked. People do, you know.'

'Do they? I mean, before –?'

'More than you think. But it's of no consequence. Not now, at any rate. I take it you're not seeing him again?'

'I couldn't.'

But neither could she stop the image intruding into her mind of herself and Lewis naked together in bed. She drew a long breath; it was no use thinking such things. It only made it more cruel.

The summer had truly arrived, and in mid-June had achieved perfection, a matchless profusion of colours and scents, a richness of foliage in the borders and the banks of rhododendrons. One evening Anne wandered through the gardens, soothed and relaxed by the balmy air and the scent of the stocks beneath the wall of the house, then idly wandered down the gravelled path that brought her to the cold house. Standing before it, she remembered the events of the previous summer. She shivered when she remembered Vere and his importunity, the way he would constantly evade her, popping up when she wanted him out of the way and.... But she didn't want to go on. It had happened. The little stone house stood silent, unknowing, untouched by tragedy. She turned and wandered back through the garden, and across the west lawn where she had stood on the afternoon of Pippa's wedding talking to Lewis, and he had pointed to the high wall with the espaliered pear trees which Cathal had scaled with such ease.

She was just about to turn into the house when the kitchen door opened and Bridget appeared.

'Miss Anne,' she whispered, and came up to her. Anne stopped as Bridget took a letter from her apron pocket.

'I was asked to give this to you. Sorry I couldn't find you sooner.'

Anne looked down at it. 'Thank you.'

A moment later she was reading it by the fading evening light, as Bridget hurried back indoors.

It was from Cathal, saying that he would be down by the willows that evening at nine if she would like to come.

She looked at her watch. It was nearly nine already and she set off immediately through the rhododendrons, taking the little path which led down through the meadows to the river.

# Chapter Twenty-Nine

As she arrived she saw him emerge from among the trees where he had been sitting on the river bank. At first he seemed to be the Cathal she had always known, but as they talked she saw there had been a change in him. There was something rough and unkempt about his clothes, for one thing; his tweed jacket was worn and crumpled, his trousers and gaiters dirty and boots dusty. The man himself seemed somehow harder, more experienced, his face browned by the sun and the light in his eyes shrewd and determined.

For a moment they looked at each other, then he held out his hand.

'Glad you could come, Anne.'

'I wondered whether your mother would tell you,' she said softly.

'Why? She tells me everything.'

'I didn't think she likes us to know each other.'

'What I do is my business. She knows that.'

There was a pause as Anne studied Cathal's face, then at last she said, with an effort, 'She told me about your father. I'm sorry.'

He looked down without speaking.

'But you,' she went on hurriedly, 'tell me what you've been up to?'

He leant against one of the trees which hung over the river, his hands in his pockets.

'It's been a long time since we saw each other, Anne. You knew about Mickey Flynn and Pat Twomey?'

She nodded.

'Brave lads. They never flinched when that dawn came.'

'In Cork barracks?'

He nodded. 'They never betrayed their comrades.' Cathal drew a breath, looking down. 'A man doesn't forget that, not in a lifetime. I led them into it, Anne. Ever since then I feel I've been carrying on the fight in their names, bearing the flag they let drop, you know?' He looked up at her. 'As if my own life no longer has any value in itself, but is just something to lay down in my turn when the time comes. Up till that night it had just been a game. You know what Mick Collins said? "Let's see which is tougher – the body or the lash." There's nothing can stop us now.'

There was something hard in his eyes as he looked at her and spoke the words. A chill ran through her as she thought of the two boys marched into the barracks yard at dawn to stare down the barrels of twelve rifles.

'What have you been doing?' She wanted to shake off that mental picture.

He shrugged. 'I've been everywhere. I don't believe I've slept in the same bed twice since I last saw you. I was in Dublin during the winter.'

'Were you?'

'Hunting G Men – government spies. The city is crawling with them. Pathetic creatures. You'd see them in a bar, looking like some Stage Irishman.' He laughed grimly. 'They only needed a bit of shamrock in their hats to complete the picture. And leaning over the bar to order a pint of porter with a "Top of the morning to ye" and a "Bejabers".' Then he grinned suddenly, and she saw the old Cathal in him. 'The ones that got away were only too glad to take the first boat to Holyhead in the morning, I tell you.'

'Cathal ...' She hesitated. 'You remember the ambush here, when Vere was killed ... I found out how they were betrayed.' She paused again. 'It was a man – you met him once – that time in Macroom when you were nearly arrested. It was him – Crawford. I would never have known it, and yet afterwards it made sense. He just looked so obviously not the sort of man you'd expect to be a spy.' She sighed. 'Oh, God, I suppose that's the whole point, isn't it?'

Even then, calling him by his surname as if somehow to

271

distance herself from him, she felt a pain inside as memories of him flashed through her mind.

Cathal had been listening to her carefully. 'I remember very well. Why shouldn't I? He saved my life.'

'That's what I don't understand. I mean, if he was a spy ...'

'And he betrayed us. How?'

'Through Vere. Vere blabbed to him and he told one of the Auxie officers.'

'How did you find out?'

She looked away. For a moment her mind was blank. 'Something I heard,' she said faintly.

Cathal was watching her. 'Well, I wouldn't be in his shoes, that's all.'

Later, as she was about to make her way back across the meadow, and was shaking hands with Cathal, he said, 'Anne – about your parents. You should warn them. The way things have got now there's always a chance they might get a visit – I mean, by way of reprisal. I can't always control things. It's got much bigger than last summer.'

'Reprisals?' She felt a shaft of fear run through her.

'It's nothing personal. But your father being an RM and living in the Big House ... some of the lads, well, it's a red rag to a bull in a manner of speaking. And he's never made a secret of his pro-British sympathies.'

'Oh God,' she breathed.

'I'd warn them, if I were you. Tell them to go to England.'

They parted and as in a dream she made her way slowly back across the meadow, holding her hat in her hand and trying to think what would be best for them all. Her father was not the type to leave – yet. Except that if he feared for her mother he might be swayed, and Claire would not leave without him, that was certain.

But, if she were to warn him, how was she to explain where she had received the information?

The next morning she spoke to Hugh in the stable where they had gone to prepare a litter for Og who was about to whelp. Hugh had such a gentle way with the pregnant bitch and as Anne watched him with her, arranging her basket in the corner of the stable, she felt a tremendous protective love for him.

'I saw Mrs Donnelly in the village,' she began, and proceeded to relate what Cathal had said. Hugh listened gravely as he arranged the old blankets in the basket. Og sniffed about him, assisting him, instinctively knowing what he was up to.

'What were you doing talking to Mrs Donnelly?' He looked up coldly.

'I saw her,' Anne stuttered. 'I mean – we've known her for ever – I could hardly cut her –'

Hugh looked down again at Og, and then after a moment said, 'There have been a number of incidents in the county – a family down in Rosscarberry in January were given twenty-four hours to leave the country, and their house was set on fire. I suppose we ought to be grateful to Mrs Donnelly for thinking of us. No doubt she is *au fait* with these things.' He grunted. 'It's just what the Volunteers would like, isn't it? To see us scuttling out to England.'

As he stood up Anne faced him. She was very serious, and wouldn't be swayed by his opposition.

'I think you and Mother should go to England. Just for the time being.'

'That's considerate of you, Anne,' he said sarcastically.

'For Mother's sake!'

He looked down at the basket where Og was turning and fussing the blankets in the basket, arranging them to her own satisfaction.

'You want us to go to Gerald in Devon?'

'Yes!'

Again he was thinking.

'And what would we be supposed to do there? Can you see us in Torquay, living in some dreary little villa in a suburb? I couldn't give the Volunteers the satisfaction. Anyway, the struggle's not over yet.'

'It is. Even if you can't see it. We have already failed, Father. We cannot win this war. The English have been here for over three hundred years and we have never succeeded in making the Irish accept us.'

He opened his mouth but she anticipated him.

'You must go to Uncle Gerald's!'

He looked about them, out of the stable door at the sunlight across the gravel and the wisteria against the wall of the house.

'You say we? What about you?'

'I'm staying here.'

'I see – you mean you have been standing here trying to persuade me to take your mother to England, and all the time you intend to remain yourself?'

She sounded uncertain. 'I hadn't thought yet –'

'Oh, I understand. I'm sure you'd be very happy to stay and watch your friends have their little tin-pot triumph. Well listen, Anne, I've stuck it this far and I think I'll just have to stick it to the end.'

Three days after that, late in the afternoon, she was in the stable checking that Og's basket was comfortable. The bitch was about to give birth, they expected it that night or the following day.

She went indoors where Claire was sitting in the drawing room and had just asked Bridget to bring them a cup of tea. Anne heard the distant rumble of a car and recognised the sound instantly. Only one car sounded like that – she would have known it anywhere. Without thinking she rose and went quickly to the window. And a second later, as in a dream, the long gleaming red bonnet of the Old Beast swung through the rhododendrons, and pulled up before the house.

'Who is it?' Claire was reading a magazine.

'It looks like Lewis Crawford,' Anne said as distantly as she could.

Claire looked up sharply. 'Really?'

There was the jangle of the bell, and the sound of Bridget's feet crossing the hall. A second later the door opened and Lewis came in, cool and relaxed as ever.

Claire went quickly to greet him.

'Lewis! What a pleasant surprise!'

'Just happened to find myself in your part of the world, so I thought I'd give you a call. See how you were. Hullo, Anne,' he added in an offhand manner.

'Hullo.' She was cold. This was something she should have foreseen. But nothing he could say would make any difference.

274

'You're just in time for tea.' Claire had come to life. Going to the door, she called: 'Bridget! Bring another cup for Mr Crawford, and make a few sandwiches too.' She turned to him. 'I expect you're peckish.'

'I wouldn't say no.' He looked at both of them. 'And how are you?'

'You missed Tony and Pippa; they were here a couple of weeks ago. Pippa's had her baby, you know. Things have been so flat since they went back.'

'Oh, I've seen Jeremy – the little tyrant. I don't think I ever saw a woman so besotted with a baby.'

Claire laughed but Anne cut in stonily, 'And how many women *have* you seen with babies, Lewis? A confirmed bachelor like you?'

'Ah –' he threw himself into an armchair '– that's the point. Being a confirmed bachelor, as you say, I get the entrée into everybody's house. I am required to admire babies all the time, Anne.'

She wished she hadn't provoked him into this conversation. It looked too like intimacy. 'No doubt you find it very tiresome.'

'Why?'

'Other people's children usually are. Or so I'm told.'

'Oh, Anne, don't be such a killjoy!' Claire exclaimed. 'Wait till you have children of your own.'

Lewis looked at Anne as Claire spoke these words. He looked at her so coolly, she felt an intense irritation and distaste that he should be so relaxed and intimate with her.

Bridget brought in tea.

'And where's the colonel?'

'He's here. I'll call him now.'

Hugh was very pleased to see their visitor, and it didn't take him long to invite Lewis first to stay for dinner and then for the night.

'Yes, do stay, Lewis. I couldn't bear to think of you in some dingy hotel, dining alone.'

'That's the life of a salesman, Mrs Hunter. I've grown used to it. Better than hanging about at home, sponging off the family.'

'Did you never think of making a career of soldiering,

275

Crawford?' Hugh asked. 'A fellow like you could have done well for yourself. Tony told me a lot about your career in the war.'

'Had enough of all that, sir. Had enough for one lifetime, I assure you. Besides, peacetime soldiering – what is it apart from paperwork, amateur theatricals and having affairs with other men's wives? Excuse me, Anne.' He nodded in her direction, then shook his head. 'Didn't fancy it.'

She was staggered at the cool way he told these lies. But then she wondered whether Tony knew about Lewis's work – obviously he had told Hugh nothing.

A little later Lewis went upstairs to stow a bag in his room, Hugh had returned to his study and Claire had a chance to whisper to Anne, as they put tea cups and plates on to the tray, 'I don't think this is just a coincidence, dear. Lewis hasn't come all the way down here to admire our roses.' And she looked at her daughter with wide eyes.

'I can't imagine why he has come then,' Anne said coldly.

Claire tapped her on the wrist playfully. 'Oh, don't play the innocent! I think we both know well enough why he's here. And I am very pleased, I admit it. He's a personable young man, and fascinating company, very original. You could do *much* worse.' And she looked rather serious.

Anne stood up abruptly. 'Mother, I'd prefer not to discuss it.'

'Anne dear.' Claire stood up too, and her manner stiffened a little. 'I don't know what happened between you last summer, but if Lewis has come down here to see you – which he obviously has – well ... How can I put it so that even you will understand?'

Anne turned at this flick of sarcasm.

'Shall we say that eligible men don't exactly grow on trees these days?' Her mother raised her eyebrows. 'You don't really want to spend the rest of your life down here in the country with two old crocks, do you?'

'I've told you before, Mother,' Anne said almost desperately, 'I like it here. I've always liked it here. I like it here more than anywhere I've ever been. I've never had any desire to leave. That may not sound very exciting to you, but it suits me fine.'

She went out of the door and was about to go up to her room, when the thought of meeting Lewis on the stairs sent her into the garden instead.

Fortunately he didn't follow.

Later he joined them for dinner, and although the conversation was light and inconsequential, she was waiting in dread for what was bound to come sooner or later.

Sure enough after dinner, when Lewis and Hugh had joined Anne and Claire in the drawing room, and the French windows were standing open, she watched with a feeling of inevitable doom as Lewis glanced across to the windows, where the garden could be seen outside beginning to shade into night, and lightly suggested a stroll.

'The scent of the stocks is just heavenly.' He stood up. Of course, as she knew they would, her parents remained somehow rooted to their chairs, in fact her father even picked up a newspaper, and like some prisoner being led forth to execution Anne found herself following Lewis out into the garden.

But even though this gloomy feeling hung over her, a deeper inner resolution was hardening.

They walked for some minutes in silence down between the flower beds to where the oak trees loomed over them, beginning to darken against the sky, which at last after the summer day was losing its brilliance and turning from its light azure towards violet. A young moon was visible above the mountain. For a while she studied the flower bed, conscious all through her of the man beside her, then she stiffened. It was time to get this over with.

'I must say, I never thought even you would have the impudence to come here.'

'Anne, I have the right to be heard. You went out in such a fearful temper it was impossible to make you listen to sense.'

'Sense?'

'Will you give me two minutes to explain exactly what happened? You leapt in to judge me before I had a chance to explain myself fully. Besides, in that hotel it was impossible.'

She was silent.

'All right, I am a British agent. I came over with a bunch of chums after the war. They recruited us in Egypt as I told you, where we'd been up to our ears in military intelligence. And more than that. It was an unreal world. We'd put a king on his throne. It was a game, Anne, a stunt. And when we came over I thought this would be just another one. What did I know about Ireland? Most Brits haven't the faintest notion about the place. Apart from some vague music-hall comic routine or a chorus of 'Danny Boy', the English know nothing of this country. That's been the whole problem.'

He paused, then took a deep breath. 'As for the tall stories ... If you knew the stories I've *had* to tell, sometimes to save my life!' He had grown more intense, and turned to her abruptly. 'And, yes, I did tell Steptoe. I didn't like it but it was my job, not to mention my duty. I had to tell someone, and it was just my bad luck to bump into him on the river bank. Of course I didn't mean to harm Vere! I had no idea he was going to be in the ambush! I felt terrible about it, destroyed. That's why I left when I did.'

All this time she had listened, looking down, unable to meet his eyes, and in fact closed her own as if wanting to shut out his words. Still looking down, she said in a low intense voice, 'You betrayed Vere. What he told you in his silly innocence, in his childish excitement, as if it were some adventure out of the *Boy's Own Paper*, you went and cold-bloodedly informed that unspeakable man – I can't even say his name – that perverted, sadistic bully. You talked to him, you joked with him, you sent Vere up that tree ... and all the time you were betraying him. How can I ever forgive you for that, Lewis? Even if I could bring myself to speak the words, I could never wipe out the memory. It happened and it can never be undone.'

He made a slight gesture and would have spoken but she went on in the same low monotone, 'But it's not just that. It's all the lies. At first I thought, "Is he telling the truth?" But I didn't care because I so enjoyed hearing you tell your stories. Now I see that it's more serious. You simply can't help it. You're a congenital liar. It's in your nature. Even if the ambush had never happened, even if Vere were still alive, how could I ever live with you? How could I ever trust you?'

They continued their walk in silence, came to the wall and the old bench, and he would have sat down but she turned back. Almost a suppliant, he had to follow her. She felt completely in control of events, utterly indifferent to the man beside her, indifferent to the outcome of this conversation, or indeed to anything at all. He was grovelling to her now and when he did speak at last there was a note of desperation in his voice.

'I didn't mean to come here today. I didn't intend to come till after the fighting stopped. Didn't mean to get involved at all, as a matter of fact. Strictly against orders, you see. But it was you. You were just so beautiful. From the moment I first saw you in the town square with your great suitcase, I just knew it was you. Girls in that situation usually look round helplessly till some man offers to carry their case. But you weren't like that. You just hauled it across the square. You looked strong, independent. I could see it all, watching you. I liked that. And when you were so rude and off-hand, and sometimes plain awkward, I didn't mind that. It made you more attractive, and, well, it made you more of a challenge. It sounds a bit old-fashioned perhaps but I wanted to get the better of you, if you like. Subdue you – wipe that arrogant look off your face, to put it bluntly. As for the stories . . .' He shrugged. 'It's just a handy way of amusing people. I can't help it, it's always been in me, and I could see the effect it was having on you. I knew you'd find out all about me in the end.' He sighed. 'I suppose I was depending on your charity to let me down lightly.'

There was a long silence. She couldn't look at him, though she was intensely conscious of his beseeching face so close to hers.

Suddenly she shivered.

'We'd better go in.' She didn't want this conversation to continue.

'Anne –'

But she had set off up the path ahead of him, and he followed her in silence.

She didn't want to think, tried not to think.

Her mother and father were about to go to bed, sitting opposite one another in the light of the paraffin lamp, sipping cocoa. Over all four of them hung a deep silence.

'I think I'll go to bed,' said Anne finally. Then: 'Good night.' Without looking round at them, she left the room.

# Chapter Thirty

The candles stood ready on the hall table, but feeling still very
agitated, she did not take one and made her way upstairs in the
gloom. But at the top of the stairs she stopped, and on an
impulse turned down the short corridor to Vere's old room.
As she put her hand to the door handle, she felt suddenly
constrained. She breathed in deeply and opened the door. The
window was still a square of light in the gloom, and she saw
the bed opposite her, made up, and on the shelves above it
Vere's things, untouched since his death, a few schoolboy
annuals, a pair of boxing gloves, a stamp album. Everything
was as it always had been. Gradually she pushed the door
open, standing in the doorway, not really knowing why she
was here but drawn by some unconscious instinct. She sat
down in the old red plush armchair, its stuffing showing and
scarred from years of juvenile battering. She stared across at
the bed and the window beyond it, not thinking, but willing
just to let her mind ramble, perhaps to allow herself to recover
from the meeting with Lewis.

Then, just at the head of the bed, it was as if Vere were
sitting there. It could be him, though it was difficult to make
out his face against the light from the window. But he was
definitely wearing Vere's clothes because she recognised the
snake buckle on his belt and the way he rolled up the sleeves
of his shirt. He was sitting cross-legged, as he used to do,
relaxed, as if he were going to ask her a riddle or tell her
some silly schoolboy joke.

It wasn't a trick of the light; it *was* him sitting there,
looking at her. She was sure it was him, even though she

couldn't exactly make out his face. And she knew he was smiling at her – not larking or grinning as she'd thought at first – he was smiling as if he were deeply happy and contented. Because of this she wasn't at all frightened to see him, and felt very relaxed too, so that they could just look at each other and be glad to see one another. He was there so palpably, she felt she could have got up, crossed over and touched him, except that she didn't need to, because he was setting her at ease. He didn't say anything, yet all the time he was communing with her; she could hear, exactly as if he had spoken, his voice in her head.

'You're not to blame for my death. I knew what I was doing, Anne, and I accept the consequences. It's not your fault – I'm not a baby. There was nothing you could have done to stop me. You were asleep when I got up and went down to Sheehey's farm. So just be patient and happy because it's going to be all right. You'll see.'

As she sensed these words in her mind a wonderful deep peace came stealing through her, and she was so grateful to Vere for telling her this. She wanted to say thank you, would have said it, but she knew he understood her because he was still smiling at her, smiling in a very benevolent way, as if he were much older than her, and knew far more than she did about everything, about people and their feelings. And because of his benevolence and his peace she knew he would not mind if she were to fall asleep here in the chair, and could feel herself falling asleep as he watched her, still smiling serenely.

When she woke it was dark, and there was a violent ache in her neck where her head had fallen back across the top of the armchair. With difficulty she pulled herself out of the chair and stood up, stretching and wondering what time it must be.

Then, in her own room, as she changed into her pyjamas, she thought about what she had seen and whether it had in fact been a dream; it was impossible to say now. Whether it had been a dream or not didn't matter ultimately because what Vere had said didn't change, and she felt a sense of deep warmth and comfort because he had not forgotten her and was still watching over her.

\*

The following morning Lewis left. They did not speak privately again, and as she watched him drive away Anne thought how shallow he was compared with Cathal. How honourable and open was Cathal, fighting honestly for his country; how shabby seemed Lewis compared with that; Lewis the betrayer, the liar, the man of straw.

Eveything about him – his glamour, his easy manner, his great car, all the things that had so impressed her – made her sick to think of them now. How could she have been so taken in? How could she have been so juvenile, so naïve? She was so angry with herself, biting her lip, as she imagined him in some hotel bar, telling his tall stories to the barmaid, seducing her with a few jokes and his smooth patter, or standing with his foot on the fender in front of the fire, his whiskey and soda in his hand as he boasted to his fellow travelling salesmen about his conquests. It was all so tawdry.

She turned back into the house.

That evening Og gave birth to her four pups, little wet blind things, crawling over each other as she licked them; tiny restless, black grubs, slithering over and round each other, making tiny squeaks as they found their way to their mother's teats and sucked lustily. Squatting over the basket where Og lay oblivious with her litter, Anne felt enormously reassured; other, better, real things went on in the world, and even if it were only a dog and her puppies, here was something real and good and it was at least one small reassurance of normality.

It was only a few days afterwards that late at night, just as they were about to go to bed, they heard the rumble of a car and the crunching of tyres on the gravel outside. The sound was familiar; in a moment Anne realised it was the Old Beast and her heart sank to think that in Lewis's conceit and arrogance he still had not given up, and had come back to try again.

She took up the paraffin lamp and went quickly to the front door in the time it took for the car to draw up before the house and the bell to ring.

Hugh and Claire looked up as she crossed the room into the

282

hall and went to answer the door. Bridget had come out of the kitchen but Anne was ahead of her.

'It's all right, Bridget, I'll answer it,' she said briskly. She was in no mood to be conciliatory.

Hugh was coming through the drawing-room door as she pulled back the bolt.

'Anne –'

'It's all right, Father, I think I know who it is,' she said briefly.

As the front door swung open and the light from the paraffin light shone out she saw a group of young lads, every one of them holding a gun, filling the doorway; saw what seemed a thicket of gun barrels, rifles, pistols, revolvers, and in their eyes the alert bright light of intense concentration. They were all in shabby working clothes, ragged bits of scarf tucked in the necks of their jackets, cloth caps on their heads. For a second no one moved.

'Hugh Hunter,' one of them said, 'we've come for ye.'

They came forward and she stepped back, and as they came into the hallway she could see them better. They were young, as young as Sean Deasey and Danny Mount, who in fact she now saw among them.

Hugh seemed perfectly calm.

'Where are you taking him?' Anne said sharply.

'Shut up or it'll be the worse for ye.'

By this time Claire was in the doorway. Some unexpected spirit of defiance, a breath of her old self, now inflated her. 'How dare you, you foolish ignorant boys! How dare you have the impertinence to intrude –'

'Shut up!' The leader, who if anything seemed even younger than the others, pressed towards her. Anne saw the keen urgent expression on his face, the bravado, the fear. He raised his revolver, pointing it at Claire. 'You – shut up!'

She was quelled, and Anne put her hand on her mother's arm as they both watched. Though they looked so young, she saw these were not green or callow youths. These were men like Cathal. Battle hardened now, they had shed their inhibitions, lost their virginity. They would not be stopped. She tightened her grip on Claire's arm.

'Come on now! And be quick about it, will ye?'

Hugh had been standing perfectly still, white in the face. He turned to Claire, and then to Anne.

'Take care of your mother.'

'Don't worry, Father. Trust me.' They embraced. He walked forward.

'You murderers!' Claire screamed, and two of the men whipped round as if a shot had gone off. Anne could say nothing. She had foreseen it, and now it was happening as she'd known it would, and she was quite powerless to prevent it.

The men hustled Hugh out of the door where Anne could still hear the engine of the car running. As she and Claire went forward, watching the group of them opening the car door and Hugh getting in and looking back one last time, Anne saw as if in a dream that the car was indeed the Old Beast.

The engine revved. They heard the inexperienced driver crashing the gears and letting in the clutch wrongly so that the engine roared horribly out of control, then the wrenching round of the wheels on the gravel, and the violent acceleration away through the rhododendrons. Anne, suddenly as cold as ice, raced to the telephone and had snatched it up even before the sound of the car had died away.

The telephone line was dead, of course.

Claire stood in the doorway watching, shrivelled, hunched, old with fear. But Anne was now the very opposite, elated with adrenaline, her mind clear, quick, weightless on her feet.

'I'm going into the village. I can phone from the post office.'

'Are you leaving me?' Claire cried, unnaturally loud in the night stillness. Bridget was still watching from the kitchen doorway.

'Mother, they won't come back tonight, will they?' As if she were a child who had asked a foolish question. 'I must go into the village this instant. Bridget, look after my mother, I beg you. I'll be back as quick as I can.'

Looking round her for a moment, and then rushing out of the still open door, she ran round the back of the house to the stables, heard the dogs greet her as she pulled open the stable door and wheeled out her bicycle. She did not stop to light the acetylene lamp, but threw herself across it and pedalled vigorously away through the rhododendrons and down the *bohreen* towards Lisheen. Though it was dark it didn't matter because she knew the way yard by yard, and there was a vestigial light from the young moon and the stars in the clear summer sky which kept her to the path.

Bumping down the *bohreen* she was possessed by a frantic urgency, a sense that a second lost could cost her father his life, even if he were to be saved at all, and she had no idea what was intended. Whether Hugh was to be shot at once or kept prisoner she could not guess, and the terrible uncertainty drove her down the lane, pedalling as hard as she could.

The village street was dark and deserted as she drove herself furiously along to the post office, threw the bicycle to the ground, and knocked violently at the door.

There was no sound. Again she pounded as hard as she could on the door.

At last there was a movement at the window above, and a casement opened.

'Who is it?'

'Oh, Miss Burke – it's me – Anne Hunter. I do apologise for disturbing you at this hour of the night, but I must make an urgent telephone call and our line has been cut off, do you see? It's a matter of life and death, I swear!'

'For Heaven's sake, at this hour of the night – a telephone call?'

'Yes, really, Miss Burke. Let me in this minute, I beg you. It's my father – he's been kidnapped! I must telephone!'

'Mercy!'

The casement closed again, and a moment later the door was opened and Anne went in. It was a strange feeling to find herself in the post office, in the middle of the night, lit by a candle. Miss Burke, a middle-aged spinster, led the way through to the switchboard, from which she controlled all telephone calls to and from the village, and sat down.

'And whom did you wish to telephone?'

'Macroom Castle.'

Miss Burke said nothing, but slipped the earphones over her head. She pulled out one of the connecting pins on its cable, inserted it into a socket in the board in front of her. After a moment she indicated a telephone hand set at the side. 'Pick it up.'

Anne heard a man's voice and quickly told him what had happened. As he replied she had the impression he was used to this kind of call. He was taking down the information in a practised manner.

She returned the telephone to its cradle.

'Thank you. I do beg your pardon for disturbing you at this hour of the night.'

Miss Burke answered civilly, and Anne let herself out into the dark roadway. For a while she stood holding her bicycle indecisively, unwilling to let anything remain undone it was in her power to do.

She thought of Cathal. There must be a possibility he could help to save her father – if he learned what had happened. She did not know where he was – he might well still be in Dublin. In an agony of indecision, she mounted the bicycle and set off towards the Donnellys' house. It was late but no matter.

Again she threw down her bicycle and hammered on the farm house door. Again there was movement at the window. Anne was brazen.

'Mrs Donnelly, it's Anne Hunter, I must speak to you, please let me in!'

And again she was facing Mrs Donnelly in the sitting room, the dim view of Highland cattle on the wall over the fireplace just as she remembered it. Mrs Donnelly had drawn a shawl over her night gown, and her hair hung down in long plaits over her shoulders.

Anne explained breathlessly. The older woman listened in silence and as Anne finished still said nothing.

'You must get a message to Cathal!'

'I have no idea where he is.'

'Mrs Donnelly, by this time tomorrow my father may be dead! He may be dead already! Cathal is my only chance!'

'I don't think he will be dead – not yet. He has been taken hostage.'

'What?'

'You know very well, there are six boys under sentence of death in Cork.'

'You know where he is?'

'No.'

'Then how –'

286

'It's obvious. It's our only chance of saving them.' As always she was calm and deliberate. 'It's one life against six, Anne.'

'They won't do it. I mean – the Government, they'll never exchange those men. They never have, never. My father will be murdered!'

'Control yourself. I told you before – this is war, Anne, and it will be fought to the finish.'

'It's not war! You don't take innocent people hostage in a real war! It's murder!'

'It's war all the same. In a war you use any means to win. Any means. The trouble with you is you believe your own propaganda, Anne. You imagine all British officers are gentlemen and play cricket. We know better. And we have only one aim: to win. Everything else comes second to that. Even your father's life, I'm afraid.'

Anne couldn't think. There was something about the way the other woman spoke that was so incredibly hard; she had never heard anything like it. As Mrs Donnelly spoke, and as this realisation filled Anne, she said, without thinking, 'If anything happens to my father, I will never forgive the men who did it. I will find them, and will make them pay.'

As if Mrs Donnelly had perceived victory there was a relaxation in her, and she said, almost meditatively, 'Yes. You understand now. At last you understand. You had better go now.'

'You won't send a message to Cathal?'

'What message? And how do you know he didn't order the capture of your father?'

'He wouldn't!'

Again Mrs Donnelly gave her that level stare.

'You still haven't learnt, have you?'

'No! Cathal wouldn't – he warned me!'

'Warned you?'

'That is,' Anne stumbled, suddenly frightened to harm Cathal, 'I mean – in a vague general way.'

'And did you heed the warning?'

'My father wouldn't leave the country.'

Mrs Donnelly gave a slight shrug. 'I'm sorry for you then,' she said softly.

287

# Chapter Thirty-One

Bumping down the lane again in the darkness, Anne felt all through her the freezing feeling of utter helplessness, a blind searching appealing feeling to anything that would help to find Hugh, heard herself swear over and over that she would do *anything* to save her father, make any sacrifice, undergo any torture, any humiliation, anything if only he might be safe. And heard herself curse the men who had taken him, hating them with an intensity she hadn't known she possessed, and then hating herself and blaspheming that if her parents had only gone to England, even a few days before – even the day before – they would have been safe, whereas now Hugh could be anywhere and she would never see him again, and it must be her fault, she must have brought this upon them through some folly or omission she had committed, if only she could think what it was – but all her thoughts were helplessly jumbled together into a horrible cold fog of fear.

She was bicycling through the village, and was about to turn up into the *bohreen* towards the house when she heard a gunshot, and then another, and in a moment the sound of lorries, and looking back she could see away beyond the village behind her searchlights sweeping across the hedges and then piercing the sky.

She quickly dismounted and pulled the bicycle back with her against the wall of a house until they should have passed – because here there was nowhere to hide anyway, looking back down the village street in the darkness.

Then, as she watched, a lorry came round the farther end, its enormous spotlight beam sweeping past her as she pressed back against the wall, and then over the line of little houses. Immediately afterwards there was another lorry, another searchlight, and then another and another behind that. They came roaring violently into the street, and guns were going off, crack, crack, and she screamed out as she heard the whine of a bullet pass right over her, and crouched back even tighter into the shallow doorway she found behind her.

She was terrified in case she were caught in one of those searchlights which were sweeping back and forth, up and down the little village street.

The lorries had screeched to a halt not fifty yards from her, and in the uneven light she saw troops – no, they weren't troops, they were Auxie officers, because they were wearing their characteristic tam o'shanter berets. They were running across the road and she heard the firing of guns. They seemed to be firing all at once, in any direction, aimlessly; the whole night air was filled with the random cracks of rifle fire, and then the smashing of glass, and confused shouts.

She could not think what was going on, except that this was an Auxie raid and, feeling her heart beating violently, pressed herself back still holding her bicycle handlebars. She watched with mesmerised fascination, feeling a horrible jelly-like sensation in her limbs, as if she were incapable of doing anything.

Windows were being smashed, and still the constant crack, crack of gun shots, and shouts, all confused at first but she began to understand them. 'Come on, out with you! At the double. Get out of there, you scum, get out of there...' And the sound of windows being opened, and then a man's voice raised in anger, and a woman's scream, and a shout, and people appearing on the street in nightclothes. Then she felt the door behind her move and made way as a man – it was Mr Murray, she knew him, of course – came out with an overcoat over his pyjamas.

'What in heaven's name –'

The firing was still going on, and then Anne jerked round as she heard an explosion, and a brilliant eruption of flame and smoke from a house further down on the right. Fire was engulfing it, lighting up the street with an eerie flickering brilliance, and in front of the light figures were running back and forth. The Auxies were shouting and firing into the air, and then there was a man's cry and she saw someone falling in the roadway. There were confused shouts, protests, cries, and lamentations, and the Auxies' violent, brutal shouting and cursing.

As people were appearing at their doorways, they were being prodded by the officers at their rifles' ends, and in a second a young man stood in front of Anne, pointing his rifle at her. 'Get in line! Are you deaf? Move your fucking arse or I'll kick it.'

As she pushed the bicycle, the soldier saw it.

'Hullo! What's this? Out after curfew! Don't move – back there against the wall. And don't try anything!'

She dropped the bicycle handlebars as if they had been red-hot, and flattened herself against the wall. The officer held his rifle almost in her face and she could make out beads of perspiration on his forehead, glinting in the uneven glare from the searchlight, and the bright light in his eye.

Around her, people were making their way into the street, and being formed into a line.

Rifle fire was still going on, a random crackling sound.

'Don't move or you'll be shot! You stay right there!'

The people, bedraggled in their nightwear, lined up in the street, and there were crashes and shouts from inside the houses, and the smashing of another window, and confused cries, and another burst of rifle fire. People looked round, staring up at one of the houses on the same side as Anne was standing against the wall – she couldn't see it from where she stood. There was a shout, and a rifle shot again, and then a man's cry. The shouting became more confused, everyone shouting at once now, and some women weeping, and a harsh burst of orders, though whether the soldiers were shouting to each other or the villagers she couldn't tell.

'Now listen to me!'

She looked to her right where an Auxie officer was addressing the line of villagers. She recognised the man – it was Captain Steptoe.

'I'm going to say this once, and I'm not going to repeat it. I've run out of patience tonight. Tonight was the straw that broke the camel's back. I'm an evil bastard at the best of times, and if you didn't already know that you're about to find out. So I'm just going to say this once. Tonight – not two hours ago – Colonel Hunter was kidnapped. A fact which many of you know very well. *Don't you!* All right, I'm giving you one chance. I want Colonel Hunter and I want him now! Don't pretend, and don't waste my time. I don't propose to leave this village alone until I get him back – unharmed – and I'm starting now. There's one house alight. How many more do I have to fire till we have him, *eh*? Think it out – and think it out quick because I'm a very impatient man, I've a short temper and it's a foul one at the best of times. You've tried it to the limit already, so *talk!*'

The searchlight was now played along the line and Anne saw the villagers shrink in its harsh glare.

There was another crash and a splintering of glass up the street, a thud, and then a muffled explosion and a burst of light into the night sky.

'Another one gone! Who's next, eh? I'm taking this village apart, house by house, just watch me! And you know something? I enjoy it! I do! I enjoy watching your miserable little hovels going up. By Christ, it's a real pleasure!'

The people stood mute in cowed silence as Steptoe screamed at them.

'What's that? I don't hear anything! I know you're pretty stupid at the best of times but are you really going to watch me destroy the whole village – are you?'

Another window smashed.

'All right!'

Three officers huddled together with him now, and they appeared to be having a discussion. At the same time another man came over to where Anne was still pressing herself against the wall, and her guard turned to him.

'Caught her, Jimmy, out after curfew. See the bike?'

The man turned to her abruptly.

'Out after curfew? The bitch. Bring her in. Okay you – over here.'

He seized her shoulder and thrust her violently forward. In her fear she wanted to cry out, but was too terrified. It was as if these men were not subject to any rules of normal behaviour at all but were a law entirely to themselves with absolute power of

291

life and death. She wanted to say 'But I'm innocent!' only the thought kept coming to her: These men are all here because I telephoned. It's my fault – someone has already been killed and it's my fault. And her will was paralysed. So as the man took her she was utterly unable to resist, felt herself shrivelled to insignificance before the strong thrust of his arm, only filled in her bowels with that horrible water-feeling of fear.

Steptoe had changed his plan now; he was walking along the line of people and pointing to some of the men. As he did so they were roughly pulled out and urged towards the lorries. Anne too was ordered to go to one. She was about to climb up when she turned her face a moment in the searchlight and Steptoe saw her.

'Miss Hunter!'

The soldier who was holding her pulled her back.

'What the devil? Jimmy – what's this?'

'She was out after curfew. Found her dressed with a bike.'

'Stop! Let her go. What's happening?'

Around her men were being forced up on to the lorry at the open tail board.

'I had to come out to telephone about my father. Our phone was cut.'

'My God! I do most awfully apologise. Come this way.'

Steptoe led her away a couple of paces.

'Miss Hunter, I'm most awfully sorry about this. Had no idea. Terrible misunderstanding.' He was grovelling. She managed to keep her head, fighting against the weakness in her. 'Wait, I'll get someone to see you home.' He looked round. 'Wilf!'

'That won't be necessary!' Her teeth were chattering with nervous tension, but she was quite decided. 'Thank you, Captain Steptoe, I am capable –'

'No, that's all right.' He was still looking about him. 'Wilf! See Miss Hunter home!'

Anne was suddenly very angry. 'Thank you, but I have no wish to be escorted by you or any of your colleagues! I am perfectly safe in this village. Or rather I was. You nearly frightened me to death, you have wrecked the village, and I would frankly die rather than be seen with you or any of your friends!'

Clutching her bicycle, she turned abruptly away from him.

Steptoe said nothing more, and in a short time the Auxies were climbing back on the lorries, the engines were revving, and they were swerving about and reversing in the street, headlights sweeping across the house fronts. Then they were roaring back up the road and away into the darkness of the night.

The people immediately began rushing about, trying to save what they could from the burning houses, shouting to each other. She heard women's cries, moaning and keening: 'Oh, Jesus, Mary and Joseph! Oh, sweet Mother of God!'

Three houses were alight; people were running in and out, bringing pieces of furniture, and Anne forced herself into action. She crossed to one of them, wanting to go in, but the house was already well alight, and there was little she could do. As she stood at the doorway helplessly she saw a man looking at her strangely, and seeing the look in his eyes wanted to scream at him, 'But it's my father they've taken!' Only the flickering light of the burning houses confused her, and then others came up bearing a man's dead body. They took him into a house, and the man turned away to follow them.

There was nothing she could do. She was quite redundant, irrelevant, as if the struggle were going on without her; as if their fears and anxieties were not hers. She wanted to scream out, 'But they *are* mine!' then she remembered her mother and ran to find her bicycle, threw herself on to it, and set off up the *bohreen*.

The moon had set by this time, but there was a little light from the stars. She had no strength; her limbs felt as if they were filled with water, and she had to dismount and walk the bicycle for half the way before she was able to get on again, and pedal slowly and with such difficulty to the house. She dropped the bicycle before the door and rapped on it.

'Bridget, it's me! Let me in!'

'Oh, Miss Anne, I'm that glad! We heard the gun shots and didn't know what to think. Are you all right? You look terrible!'

Claire was at the drawing room door and Anne went to embrace her. They went, holding each other, into the drawing room, and Bridget was saying, 'Will I make you a hot drink?'

All Anne's limbs were trembling now, she was dizzy and had an overwhelming impulse to weep. It was only seeing the pinched haggard face of her mother that stopped her, and she tried in short broken phrases to explain what she had seen.

Finally, after she had drunk a cup of cocoa, they went to bed. It was half-past two by this time.

Claire was still in bed when Anne went to find her the following morning.

'I'm going to Macroom now. To see if I can get any word of Father.'

'Darling, will that be safe? Surely they will bring us news as soon as they know anything?'

'I know, but I can't just stay here. I'm going to bicycle down to the village and get Byrne to drive me. Shall I tell Bridget to bring you something?'

'No. Thank you, darling, but I couldn't touch anything.'

'It isn't going to help Father if you starve yourself. You must keep up your strength. Sorry to use such a cliché, but it's true.'

Claire looked away, and already Anne could see tears forming in her eyes.

'I'll tell her to bring you a cup of tea.'

The village was a forlorn sight. Three houses were burnt out and still smouldering, and people were standing in the sunshine looking at them and talking quietly. Outside the burnt-out houses, various pieces of furniture stood awkwardly in the street and two men were in the act of trying to rope a sideboard on to an ass-cart. Fortunately, it was a sunny day.

Mr Byrne ran a one-car taxi service in the village. He drove Anne to Macroom. He was a bald, middle-aged, fat man, and short of breath, but talked continuously as he hunched over the steering wheel.

'What a terrible thing, Miss Hunter. A terrible thing! In all my life I never saw such a night! Savages is the only word for it, savages! Coming roaring in like that in the middle of the night, terrifying innocent people, burning their houses, shooting and killing. And poor Mr Cavanagh dead, I still can't believe it, shot dead in his own home, Miss Hunter, a man that never harmed anyone in his life! How could they do it?' He shook his head. 'And his house burnt out. Mrs Cavanagh now, what is she to do? She'll be thrown upon the parish. Unless her daughter can take her in, which is not very likely, and she with eight children of her own to think for.' He jerked his head round. 'Begging your pardon now, Miss Hunter, it is yourself must be sick with worry for your own father, wondering where he can be now the Volunteers have him. Where will it end?'

'It won't end till I have my father back,' Anne said quietly.

Mr Byrne shook his head. 'Ah, well, please God he'll be found alive.' He sighed. 'This is no way to fight a war, Miss Hunter – murder, kidnapping, burning and frightening people in their beds. What's to become of us all?'

'I don't know,' she muttered. 'But I won't give up till he's found.'

# Chapter Thirty-Two

Macroom was full of military activity; Mr Byrne had trouble getting up the street as three Crossley tenders came down towards them and he had to pull in to let them pass. Outside the castle there were yet more – five in a row. There was a soldier on duty in the gateway, and several orderlies, or whatever they were, doing things with the lorries – one of them had its bonnet up.

Anne found it frightening, this feeling of power – of potential violence. From here they could go out and reduce a village to a heap of burning debris.

She asked at the gate for Captain Steptoe. He wasn't available but she was taken inside to a shabby little room and interviewed by another officer. He was sitting at a desk, smoking a pipe, and there was a black Labrador at his feet. On the wall was a large scale map of the area, and below it stood a rack containing rifles. On another table stood a ticker-tape machine, and as they talked this would come to life from time to time and begin to chatter out a message. He would get up, cross to tear off the message and read it.

He was a young man; he seemed decent and wanted to be helpful. He was full of concern for her father, and listened carefully as she repeated her description of the kidnapping.

'Area Command is taking this very seriously, Miss Hunter, as you can understand. A full-scale search for your father started at dawn, and we have reinforcements coming from all over the country. You may rest assured that what can be done, we will do. We will take the county apart house by house if necessary until your father is found. Road blocks were set up within an hour of your message so they won't have got very far. The Essex regiment is out in force from Cork, and we have an aeroplane making an aerial search.'

As she listened to this, he made her conscious of the enormous might of the British Army – that they had the resources of the entire empire to draw on. It seemed inconceivable that the IRA could escape.

Yet a moment's thought reminded her that for two years these forces of the Crown had been rendered utterly impotent by the guerrilla tactics of the Volunteers. In the hills and narrow lanes, across the mountainsides and through the copses, the young men, who had grown up here, who knew the countryside in their sleep, had made fools of the British, had held off forces ten times their own strength. Cathal, with seventeen lads, armed with pistols, and only ten rounds per man – pathetic supplies – was ready to take on an organised and trained army that had seen service in every quarter of the globe.

'There is talk that my father has been taken hostage for six men under sentence of death in Cork jail,' Anne said quietly. The young officer was embarrassed and looked down.

'Yes. It seems probable. We haven't had a message yet, but –'

'Has a date been set – for the execution?'

The young man was uneasy; he shuffled some papers on his desk.

'I believe – the eighth.'

'Of this month?'

He nodded.

'Three days? Oh God.' She thought a moment. 'They've done this before, haven't they? And when the men weren't reprieved, they shot their hostage, didn't they?' She could hear her own voice rising.

'I'm afraid so – yes. But I assure you –'

'Three days? You'll never find him – he could be anywhere.' The wild mountainous landscape of Cork was suddenly before her eyes. 'You'll never find him. It's impossible.'

He looked at her, willing her to believe him.

'We will find him if it is humanly possible. You may be sure of that.'

Here in the midst of this show of power and strength, where everything was official and imposing, where there were uniformed men looking military and efficient, it seemed possible, and Anne was briefly reassured.

But the moment she was beyond the gates, back in the market square of Macroom, watching the little stalls and women buying food, going about with shawls over their heads and baskets on their arms, and a farmer coming by on an ass-cart, all the reality of Ireland was present to her again. She looked back and saw the castle and the men in it as what they were – an alien presence, not of the land but settled upon it by force. An immediate realisation came to her: They'll never do it. She saw her father dead, saw his face with a bullet hole in his forehead, a hole with a dribble of blood from it, his body alone, cold, thrown under a hedge, his dead body left alone there.

Shaking her head, she crossed the square quickly to the post office and sent a telegram to Tony telling him what had happened.

As she sat beside Mr Byrne on the way back to the village a settled resolution came upon her. I will do anything to find him, I will do anything, go anywhere, kill anyone to save him.

If they had set up road blocks within an hour of her call, that would mean – what – the gang could have travelled about twenty five miles? At night? Less possibly. Twenty five miles in any direction: it was an enormous area. And they could have abandoned the car and walked across the mountains. They did that all the time. Those lads were capable of walking all night across the mountains, it was nothing to them. They could be forty miles away or more.

She saw an aeroplane coming low across the fields from her left, and watched it as it swooped across and went on until it had disappeared. It was a bi-plane and so low she could easily make out the pilot in his goggles. It was comforting to know the search was continuing. Wherever Hugh was being kept, it was unlikely they would try to move him – with so much activity all around, they would lie low. A few fields away she saw a farm house – Lee's farm where Sean MacEvoy worked. Perhaps Hugh was there. She wanted to tell Mr Byrne to turn the wheel and drive there now. Just to make sure. It was madness. There were so many farms in County Cork, dozens and dozens, and her father could be in any one of them.

When Anne got home Claire was wandering round the house like a ghost, unable to concentrate on anything.

'After Vere, I could never sleep properly, afraid that one of you might be taken. If we had gone to Devon –'

'She won't touch a drop, Miss Anne,' Bridget told her and Anne took Claire and sat her at the table and told Bridget to bring some scrambled eggs on toast and a cup of tea. She made Claire sit quietly and told her more or less what she had heard in Macroom, emphasising how seriously the Army were taking the situation, and the vast forces they could wield. And slowly she began to soothe Claire, who ate her lunch.

Afterwards Anne took her to her bedroom and saw her into bed again.

Standing alone in the drawing room, and looking out across the garden she tried to organise her thoughts, to ransack her brain for any idea, any leads that might help. Danny Mount was her only clue – but it wasn't much help. Wherever he was he wouldn't be at his farm and neither would Hugh.

After two turns through the room she decided to go to the farm anyway. She didn't expect anything from it, but she must try. She wheeled out her bicycle and set off for Mount's farm, down the *bohreen*, through the village, a mile along the Macroom road, then up another narrow lane. High, high above her tiny puffy clouds scurried in the upper reaches of the sky so far above as almost to be out of sight, and she could hear somewhere a skylark singing as it rose higher and higher. She was hot under the bright afternoon sun, and could feel the summer frock sticky against her back.

Pressing into her pedals she did not look up until she came to the corner of the *bohreen* and saw a column of black smoke climbing thin and straight into the clear air. Alarmed she set forward more quickly.

The cottage had been burnt out, the thatch completely gone, and the blackened interior open to the sky. Part-burnt beams had fallen and were leaning at crazy angles against the end walls, the chimney stack standing alone. The nauseous stench of burning was strong. Near her a fence had been smashed, and lorry tyres had ground curving marks in the dusty summer earth. Silence hung over the scene. She pushed her bicycle closer and made her way round to the haggard at the back.

The lean-to and small barn were wrecked, and near her on the ground lay a dead cow, flies feeding on a stream of blood which had dried into the dusty earth.

Before she had a chance to decide anything, Mrs Mount appeared at the side of the burnt out cottage, her hair scraped back in a bun, and wearing a long apron to her ankles. She saw Anne. The two women looked at one another.

'Mrs Mount –'

Mrs Mount spoke at last, grudgingly,

'What do you want?'

'Oh Mrs Mount, what a terrible thing! Who could have done –'

The other woman looked at her.

'Somebody gave Danny's name to the Auxies.'

Anne stiffened. She was forthright. 'I gave his name, Mrs Mount. I saw your son last night. He helped to kidnap my father. I gave his name. I'm looking for him. That's why I'm here now.' She hesitated. 'But I never thought –'

'Are you pleased then? I only wish they had taken all your family, every cursed one, so this might have never have fallen on me. Where is it I am to sleep? And Danny not here to help, but only myself alone to make do. And the cow too they killed, and laughed when they did it. Oh God that ever I should have lived to see this day! What do I care for you or your father? Let him rot in hell, let you all rot, and me left alone in this house where I came as a bride four and twenty years ago, now to see it a ruin and never a man's hand to lift the roof tree above me. And Danny too gone from me. Oh God!'

Anne, still holding the bicycle, waited as the woman spoke, standing simply, her hands beside her.

'I'm sure someone in the village will take you in, Mrs Mount. Or won't you come to our house until the roof can be mended?'

'May I lie dead in my grave before ever I cross your threshold, Anne Hunter!'

Anne reacted now. She hardened.

'You may hate me if you please. I can't do anything about that. But I want my father. The Volunteers have him and I will find them, whether you help me or whether you don't.'

'Get you gone from here, Anne Hunter. What have I ever gained from you or your family but ill luck?'

Anne looked again at the roofless cottage, the thin black smoke rising still from within, the rafters fallen this way and that, and then down again at the cow, lying unnaturally in what had once been a farm yard but now could not be called anything, a meaningless space surrounded by wreckage.

As she made her way home she sought feverishly in her mind for any other possible line she might follow. She could go to the castle again, to find out whether they had any fresh news.

Later that afternoon, tired, hungry and depressed at the scale of the problem as it had been revealed to her, she was pulling up at last to the house when she saw a car and a military lorry at the door. A sentry stood at the door, and three soldiers were lounging by the lorry smoking cigarettes. She realised immediately they must have had some news of Hugh and, throwing down her bicycle, rushed inside. As she was at the drawing room door a tall British officer turned to her. It was Tony. He was frowning and impatient.

'Thank God, there you are. Come on – we haven't time to spare.'

'Where's mother?'

'Upstairs packing. You'd better, too.'

'Packing – why?'

'I'm taking you back to Dublin now.'

'What? No. I mean –'

'Anne, this is not the time for heroics – get your stuff – just enough for a few days anyway. We don't know how long –'

'You're taking mother? Oh, thank God, Tony, yes. But I'll stay here. I've got to be – in case Father –'

'You can't do your father any good here – and you may be in considerable danger yourself. I'm taking you both now. Your cook has fled –'

'Mrs Deasey?'

301

'Yes. But Bridget and Leary have agreed to stay on in the house, so hurry up – I want to get back in daylight.'

'Have you just driven all the way from Dublin?'

'Yes.'

'You must have left the moment you got my telegram. You're very, very kind, and I'll be eternally grateful for Mother's sake – but I'm staying.'

Although Tony had taken her completely by surprise this was very clear in her mind.

'Anne I haven't got time to argue. You are being a nuisance – but then you've been a nuisance ever since I've known you. I've only tolerated you for your sister's sake. You're selfish and immature, and if you stay here you'll be hindering us rather than helping. You can't do anything to help; you'll just be one more thing for us to worry about. Go and pack your stuff – and do it now.'

Listening to the brusque tone of authority in his words, she recognised just the tone she had resented ever since she had been a schoolgirl: Men Know Best, it said. She could feel her face redden as she spoke, slowly and carefully.

'I'm old enough to know what I'm doing, and I'll do as I think fit. Thank you for taking care of Mother but I'm staying here. I don't need you to look after me, and I didn't ask for your opinion of me.'

For a second they stared at one another then Tony walked quickly past her and upstairs. She was left alone, her heart beating.

She could hear Tony and Claire upstairs talking, and Claire opening and shutting cupboards and chests of drawers. Her mother never could travel without trunks of clothes; it was the actress in her. Tony can get exasperated with her instead of me, Anne thought. As she still felt her heart beating, she was thinking very quickly: If I stay here, what will I do anyway? Perhaps I will just be a nuisance? Have I always been a nuisance or was that just Tony's exasperation? He always sems to be exasperated anyway, it's habitual with him.

She heard her mother give a cry, and there was a swift clatter on the stairs. Claire appeared at the door.

'Darling, you must come! You can't stay here – it's impossible! If anything happened –'

'Mother – I'll be all right, I promise.'

'I can't leave you!'

'Yes you can. Go and finish your packing. It's very good of Tony to have come all this way. Don't let's keep him waiting.'

Now he was coming down with a suitcase and carrying it out into the sunshine. Anne stood in the doorway watching. He returned and she caught his eye briefly. Claire looked at him, then embraced Anne for a moment in silence. She whispered, 'Darling you must come! I can't leave you here. If anything should happen –'

'It's all right Mother. You're not to worry about me. I'll be able to take care of myself.'

Tony was coming down with another suitcase.

'What in Heaven's name does that mean? If a dozen armed men come as they did last night, do you propose to fight them off? Anne, you've got two minutes, then I'm going. Now then, Mother, if you please, this way.'

Claire swept Anne into her arms again.

'Darling, how can you possibly?'

'Father wouldn't leave – do you remember? And I'm not leaving either.'

She watched as Tony pulled his car round, the soldiers climbed back into the lorry, and the convoy set off through the rhododendrons and was gone. Sunshine beat down on the empty space where they had been, and utter tranquillity spread and spread across the space, in at the door and through the room, silence extending and deepening in her mind, until she could hear, somewhere far away in the kitchen, Bridget at work. As the silence spread and settled round her, Anne relaxed and began to feel better. Her mother was safe. Now she was free to concentrate on Father.

But suddenly feeling hungry and realising she had had nothing since lunch she went into the kitchen where Bridget was washing dishes.

'I'm just helping myself to a sandwich. Don't bother yourself,' she added, as Bridget put down the pot she was washing. 'Bridget you're sure you don't mind staying on in the house with me?'

Bridget was an orphan. It was difficult to think where she

could go in any case. She was a merry cheerful girl though and had been in the house for eight years.

'Sure, I'll stay, Miss Anne; and I'm glad for Mrs Hunter that she's to go to her daughter's. Won't it set her mind at rest? And I'm surprised at yourself now that you didn't go too.'

'I'm not leaving – not while there's a chance I might hear anything of my father.'

'And what might you hear, Miss Anne? The Volunteers have got him, and they could be anywhere. Anywhere at all.'

# Chapter Thirty-Three

She seemed to have been pedalling for ever. The sweat was running down her face, dripping down her body, the harsh glare of the afternoon sun unrelenting, a pressure against her eyes.

The thought of Hugh obsessed her; yet she had not thought what she would do if by some miracle she actually found him. What would she say to his captors? Please give me my father back? Suppose they took her prisoner too? It would not do him any good, but it would make her feel better. At least they could die together.

All day she had been cycling along narrow country lanes to farms, dropping the bicycle in the hedge and spying with her binoculars for some sign of the Old Beast. She assumed they would still have it though there was no certainty of that.

And now, as the evening was just beginning to draw on, and the shadows to stretch across the fields, she found herself on her way to Martin's farm, a mile off the main road down a narrow *bohreen* with its thick hedges overgrown, the dry ditch on either side now thick with grass and wild flowers. She was just crossing a little bridge over the river when she glimpsed a hundred yards away to her left a man fishing and it crossed her mind in a vague sort of way that he looked like her father. She was about to lean on her pedals again to climb the other side when she stopped and looked again, and staring through the fog of weariness and anxiety it came to her in a surreal way that the man was indeed her father. She called out.

He looked up and saw her, and a moment later she had

dropped her bicycle in the lane, run along the bank and thrown herself into his arms.

'Thank God you're safe! I don't believe it, I don't believe it!'

He held her without speaking, and at last Anne pulled herself away.

'Oh, God, Father.' She could hardly get the words out. 'You can't imagine the nightmares I've had thinking about you, where you might be, whether you were still alive or dead. Oh – you can't imagine!'

'Calm yourself, my dear,' he said patiently. 'I'm still here, as you see – for the time being, anyway.'

'What do you mean? And anyway you mustn't stay here – what are you doing fishing at a time like this? You must come home immediately!'

He chuckled. 'One thing at a time.' He stood away from her and looked her up and down. 'How is your mother?'

'Tony came down yesterday and took her to Dublin.'

'That's good. She'll be safe anyway. Why didn't you go with her?'

'Go with her? Are you mad? I've been looking for you!'

He looked at her strangely. 'You were so worried about me?'

She was brought up short by his tone. At last she said quietly, 'What do you mean? How could I stop worrying about you?'

He was still studying her, and seemed to be thinking. She did not notice, and went on hurriedly, 'Father, you must come home now!'

'Ah, you see, Anne, that's it. I can't come home – not just yet.'

'What do you mean?'

'Well, you've found me down here by the river – by permission as it were.'

'I don't understand.'

'It was rather tedious sitting in a farm house all day so they said I might go fishing if I gave my word not to try and escape.'

'And you did?'

'As you see.'

She took a moment to digest this.

'But that's madness. You must escape – now!'

'I'm afraid I can't, Anne.'

'Your life depends on it.'

'Oh, you mustn't despair. They're a decent set of fellows. I assure you we've been getting on very well together – I can say I've been treated like a gentleman by gentlemen.'

'*Gentlemen*? They're going to murder you!'

'Well, that remains to be seen.'

'What does that mean? In two days those boys are due to be shot in Cork and you know they'll never be reprieved. I don't believe this is really happening. You've got two days to live and you're talking about "decent fellows" and "gentlemen"?'

'It's war, Anne. That's what it's about, isn't it?'

She looked up at him, and her face set.

'Father, enough of this. Come now – take my bicycle. You can get a good headway. I'll wait here and take the responsibility.'

'I can't.'

'You must!'

'I can't, I've already explained.'

'Father, I am ordering you to get on that bicycle and ride as hard as you can to Macroom. You'll easily make it before they catch you. You'll be safe in the castle for the time being.'

He said nothing, and before she could do anything about it, she could feel tears smarting in her eyes. She just could not help it.

'I don't believe it. You're going to let yourself be shot for nothing. It's so unfair. You must make a run for it. You must!'

She dragged a hand harshly across her eyes. He was looking at her as if in some way he was seeing her for the first time. Then he took her in his arms. 'That's my good girl. It's not been all in vain, you know, if I have a daughter like you, is it?'

'I don't care! I just want you to escape now while you have the chance!'

'But then, you see, what would be the point? We'd have lost the battle altogether, wouldn't we?'

307

'What do you mean?'

'What would honour mean, Anne? What does a man fight for if not honour and decency?'

'That's all words! I can't stand it! Just go, for heaven's sake!'

'There, there.' He rubbed his hand across her back, still holding her. 'Don't fret. I've been in worse scrapes than this in my time. The game's not over yet you know.'

She pulled herself away. 'Very well. If you won't escape, then I'm staying with you.'

Hugh smiled. 'It wouldn't do any good, Anne.'

'I'm not leaving, I'll refuse. If they shoot you, they'll have to shoot me too.'

He looked up, and away, towards the farm. 'You'd better go now. They'll be calling me in for my dinner.'

She looked up into his face and he smiled. 'Oh, you needn't worry. They look after me very well.'

This was the last straw. His humour and relaxed manner were too much for her.

'Go now,' he said.

'I can't.'

'Anne,' he took her by the arms, 'you must go now. What will be, will be.'

'I'll go to Macroom Castle.'

'I doubt if it would help. Either the Volunteers would shoot me before the Auxies arrived, or they'd escape across the mountains to another farm. Go home, it's best. Everything will work itself out one way or the other.'

Impulsively she reached up, took his head in her hands and kissed his cheek, then turned, walked quickly to where she had thrown down her bicycle and set off up the lane without looking back.

Her thoughts were too black for words. She had decided instantly to go to Macroom. It was impossible simply to return and wait at home; she would go mad with anxiety. The lane sloped gently up from the river and she bent into her pedals, unseeing in a black hopeless rage. The world was seized by an intolerable madness, an insane destructive passion pulling it to pieces, and she was flailing in the midst of it all, like a drowning man amidst the wreckage of a ship.

With her head down she didn't see the horse until at the shout of a man's voice she jerked her head up, saw the animal right over her, swerved violently to avoid it, and in a moment had tumbled on her back in the ditch with the bicycle across her. Miraculously she was unhurt.

The man on the horse, a black shape against the evening sun, shouted harshly down, 'Will ye look where you're going! Ye've near frighted the mare!'

She looked up at him, lying in the ditch among the long lush grass and wild flowers.

'I'm sorry.' She struggled to right herself, but was unable to move. She tried again, then fell back. 'Would you mind helping me? I seem to be stuck.'

The man, who was in a ragged black overcoat and an ancient bowler hat, astride the horse without any saddle, seemed in no hurry. He pulled a bottle from his pocket and took a long swig. He replaced the bottle, wiped his mouth with the back of his hand, swayed slightly, and stared down at her.

'What are ye doing down there?'

'I fell here trying to avoid you. Didn't you see me, for heaven's sake? Will you please give me a hand!'

The man appeared to be considering this. Anne had realised by now that he was drunk. Several seconds passed as she watched him then he appeared to come to a decision because he began gently to slide down the horse's side as if he were going to dismount. But instead of bringing his other leg over in the normal way he simply continued to slide down the horse's side and then fell flat on his back in the lane with a heavy thump.

There was complete silence. Anne was in despair, he had either concussed himself or broken his neck. She tried again to move, but she was off-balance, her head lower than her legs, one of which was half out of the ditch, and the heavy bicycle lay across her chest and shoulders so that she couldn't get any leverage to lift herself.

'Oh, this is *absurd!*'

She now heard as if from far away a slurring drunken voice singing: 'As I was sittin' with me jug and spoon, one summer evening in the month of June ...'

Anne closed her eyes in exasperation as the shambling figure slowly began to right himself.

'You're drunk!' She couldn't help saying, but then more plaintively, 'Please, *please* help me!'

The man had balanced himself precariously and slowly swivelled to where she was lying helpless. He stared down at her for a moment as if considering what to do, then turned to his horse.

'I'll just tether the mare.' He took the piece of frayed rope which was all the horse had by way of bridle, led her to the opposite hedge and sought for some time for a suitable branch to tie her to.

''Tis a most elegant piece of horse flesh,' he rambled, as he fidgeted in the hedge. 'By Fiddler's Elbow out of Fairy Tread. And won the Leinster Plate at Mallow races by a length in '17, and the Longford Stakes last year...'

At long last the horse was secured and the shabby reprobate shambled back to Anne. With glazed eyes, stubbly chin, and bowler hat pulled low over his brows, he loomed over her, looking her up and down. He swayed a little and a slow smile appeared on his lips.

'Ah,' he breathed. 'A patriotic shade of green, to be sure.'

As he looked down she realised for the first time that her skirt had been thrown up over one knee as she fell, and that a glimpse of her jade green knickers must be visible. He seemed to be considering this, swaying over her, more and more fascinated by what he saw. Her exasperation turned to fear. She struggled to lift herself again, but couldn't.

'*Please!*'

At last he appeared to have decided. She screamed as, with unexpected alacrity, he plucked up the bicycle, propped it against the hedge, took her by one hand and in a single movement set her upright in the lane. They were face to face. Then she froze.

'*Lewis Crawford!* What –' They looked into each other's eyes, until she managed to control herself. She drew a long breath, relaxed, and after a moment said quietly, 'How predictable.'

'Predictable? I say, steady on.' He looked hurt.

'What on earth do you think you are doing?'

310

Lewis took off his bowler hat and ran his fingers through his hair. 'Now confess, Anne, you were fooled for a minute, weren't you?'

She was cold. 'What are you doing here?'

He reset his bowler. 'Well, you see – rather embarrassing actually – after we last spoke I went to that hotel in Macroom where we met, and got rather drunk. Then the following morning, when I finally staggered out, I found the Beast had been stolen. Foolish of me. I usually remember to disable her. But then, I wasn't thinking straight, what with – well, the way things had gone. Between us, I mean.' He drew a breath. 'Still, in a way it's turned out useful.'

'What do you mean?'

'Obvious. I only have to find the Beast and I've found your father.'

'I can save you the bother. He's here.'

'Where?'

'Just up the lane. In Martin's farm. But he doesn't want me to go to the military.'

'Hmm.' Lewis rubbed his stubbly chin.

She had taken him in now. How ridiculous he appeared, wearing what looked like some fancy dress outfit: 'Come as a tramp.' She felt depressed.

'It might be best if I took a look round first. Scouted the place a bit.'

'How do you plan to do that?' She couldn't keep the scorn from her voice.

He shrugged. 'Pretend I'm lost. Or up the wrong *bohreen*.' He put on his Cork brogue again. 'Am I in the right way for Murphy's farm?'

Her father was in deadly danger; she must get to the authorities as quick as she could, and here before her was the man to whom she would once have entrusted her life – and what was he? A buffoon. She turned away.

'Do what you like. I must get on.'

'Where are you going?'

'Where do you think?'

'Macroom?'

She took her bicycle from the hedge.

'Anne.' His voice stopped her. 'Your father's right. No use

alerting Steptoe and his Myrmidons – not yet anyway. In any case, you might be in some danger yourself. Go home. I'll come and find you when I've seen what I can, and we'll talk about the best way forward. We've got a bit of time yet at least.'

'How do you know?'

'Trust me. I do know a few things. Go home now. I'll come as soon as I can.'

She looked at him darkly. 'First thing tomorrow morning, I'm going to Macroom Castle.'

She mounted her bicycle and rode off, but at the corner of the lane she stopped and turned to look back. Lewis had untethered the horse and was standing with her in the narrow lane looking after Anne. For a moment they looked at each other, then with an impatient miserable shake of the head, she turned and pedalled round the bend in the lane.

# Chapter Thirty-Four

What she did all that evening she never could remember afterwards. Like a sleepwalker she wandered round the house, unable to fix on anything. There had been something ridiculous about Lewis in his disguise, something foolish and amateurish; it vexed her more than she had expected. He was a sort of gentleman versus the players, strolling in, in his fancy-dress, as if he refused to take the business seriously. But they were not players; they had killed men and would kill Hugh. Oh, he was such a fool! Why couldn't he take it seriously? She was reminded of what Cathal had said about the G men in Dublin, scurrying back to England when they were found out. She couldn't imagine what Lewis could do to save her father and was angry with herself for not going directly to Macroom that evening.

She went to bed at last, but could not sleep. Horrible images intruded into her thoughts. Her father standing noble and dignified in some country lane or against a wall, his hands bound. He would disdain a blindfold; that was the sort of man he was – he would never allow them to see he was afraid. And Sean Deasey and Danny Mount and the others lining up opposite and aiming their pistols... She would turn, writhe, in bed, trying to banish this picture.

But she did drift off to sleep, because some time during the night she was being shaken. She opened her eyes. Standing over her with a candle in her hand was Bridget.

'Miss Anne!' she whispered. 'There's someone at the door. Shall we open it? I've woken Leary.'

Anne started up in bed, pulled her dressing gown quickly

313

round her, and they went together downstairs by the wavering light of the candle.

The bell jangled again, unnaturally loud in the stillness of the night, just as Leary appeared tucking his shirt into his trousers. They looked at each other.

'It's possible it's Lewis Crawford,' she whispered to the others. The bell jangled again, and her heart was beating. 'It must be him. Open the door, Leary.'

The old man slid back the bolts and unlocked the door. As it opened they saw Hugh, looking dazed and pale, leaning against the door jamb.

'*Father!* What on earth –'

'Hullo, Anne.' He took a step forward. 'Bridget, Leary.' He nodded to them as he embraced Anne. She could feel him shaking. 'Sorry to wake you at this hour.'

'Father, what happened?' He looked exhausted.

'Let me get inside the door.' He chuckled for a moment.

She took his arm and was leading him into the drawing room.

They went in together, Leary bolting the door behind them and Bridget quickly lighting two paraffin lamps. As Hugh helped himself to a whiskey and soda at the sideboard, the bottle clattered against the glass; Anne took it from him and poured him a drink. She placed the glass in his hand and led him to an armchair.

'Tell us what happened?'

Hugh took a mouthful of whiskey, and was now filling his pipe. He drew a long breath, and shook his head as if he could still not believe he was home. 'To tell the truth, Anne, I don't know myself what's happened,' he said at last.

'What do you mean?'

He turned to the two servants in the doorway. 'Thank you, Bridget, and you, Leary. You can go to bed if you want to.'

'Will I make you a sandwich, Colonel?'

'No. I'll just finish this then go to bed myself. I'm completely done in.'

They left the room. Hugh fidgeted with his tobacco pouch, filling his pipe and then lighting it.

'Father –'

'It's been a damn' strange business.' He drew on his pipe

for a moment as he relaxed at last, and was able to order his thoughts. 'They'd been coming and going all day from the cottage. At one point an aeroplane came over and they were rushing about like wasps when their nest is overturned. They ran out to get the car into a barn. As it was they'd left it in the yard, and it was perfectly visible –'

'Father! Never mind about the car! How did you get out?'

He took another mouthful of whiskey, draining the glass. 'Would you mind giving me a refill, my dear?'

Anne leapt up and took his glass to the sideboard.

'Anyway, about – well, whatever the time was – about three hours ago, I suppose, some more of them arrived, and I was shut in a bedroom. They appeared to be having the most God-almighty row, shouting, and then something smashed. I had no idea what it was all about. But finally the door opened again and I was brought out. The room was crowded, and frankly I was rather confused and dazed – I had been sitting in the dark. For one moment I thought I must be going mad because one of them looked exactly like Lewis Crawford, only got up in a tramp's outfit. "Crawford?" I said. "Good evening, Colonel," he said – and it was him, Anne. They were all watching me very closely. "You know him?" one of them said. "Of course I do," I told him. Anyway, they were about to hustle me out of the room, but I managed to turn back to him. "Crawford," I said, "what are you doing here? What's going on?"'

He looked up into Anne's face as she was handing him his whiskey. He could hardly speak.

'Do you know what he said, Anne?' He stared into her eyes. 'He said, "Don't worry, sir. It's all for the best."'

'All for the best?' She mouthed the words, standing over her father.

They looked into each other's faces.

Anne sat down in the chair facing her father. 'What happened next?'

'Well, they pushed me out of the door to the car, put me in it, and blindfolded me. I tell you, Anne, I thought it was my last hour. I was certain they were going to shoot me. We drove – I don't know – it seemed to go on for ever. But then the car stopped, the blindfold was removed, and I found

315

myself in a lane. "You can thank your friend, Colonel," one of them shouted, and they drove off. I hadn't the vaguest notion where I was.'

Anne stood up again and walked a couple of paces towards the sideboard. She felt faint; and for a moment thought she might collapse.

'Anyway I started to walk, and after about an hour – I hadn't really got a very clear idea; they'd taken away my watch – I found myself in Shanacrane, and then it took me I suppose about two hours to get here.'

Hugh looked up at her.

'What the devil was Crawford playing at, Anne? Have you any idea? I couldn't make it out. And what was he all dressed up for?'

She raised her head and her voice shattered the night stillness. 'Oh, the *fool*!'

Resting her hands on the edge of the sideboard, and hanging her head, she tried to stop the tears. 'No, I didn't mean that!' She turned back to Hugh and then couldn't stop herself. 'Don't you see? He's taken your place!'

'What?'

She nodded, unable to speak as the tears flowed down her cheeks. 'Oh, God, Lewis!'

'Taken my place?' Hugh was alarmed. 'You must explain?'

'Father, Lewis Crawford is a British agent. He was looking for you, and I told him you were in the farm house, so he said he would just scout round and see how the land lay and then report back to me here. I never dreamed he would actually go in, and now he's in the most terrible danger, and I never realised, and he did it to save you.'

She knelt by her father, and he took her in his arms as she wept.

Hugh said nothing for a long time, and in the silence of the night Anne sobbed helplessly against his shoulder.

'And it's even worse than that because I told Cathal that Lewis had betrayed the Volunteers, and they will never release him now, I know it, it's impossible, and he'll be shot, and I couldn't stand it!'

Hugh stroked her back. As he looked up he saw streaks of light between the curtains.

316

'It'll soon be dawn. We must decide what to do.'

Anne looked up, wiping the back of her hand across her eyes.

Hugh got to his feet. 'The first thing we must do is to telephone Macroom Castle. Let them know what has happened.'

She pulled herself up. Her father was thinking aloud.

'He won't be at Martin's, that's obvious. They'll have moved on...'

She nodded again.

'And that puts us back where we started. They could be anywhere.'

'And on Friday they're going to execute those boys in Cork jail, and Lewis will be shot.' Her voice was remote, drained of feeling.

Hugh looked down at her. 'What?'

'Didn't they tell you? That's why you were kidnapped.'

'They never told me anything. My God. Friday?'

He strode into the hall and picked up the telephone. Anne's mind was a blank except for an image of Lewis in a narrow country lane, lying in the ditch, with flies crawling over him and a red hole in his forehead.

It seemed to take for ever before Miss Burke answered the telephone, and then Anne heard Hugh speaking to someone and detailing what he had already told her.

At last he returned. 'The Auxies are going over to Martin's now.'

'They won't be there.'

'No. Still, there may be some clue.'

'There won't be.'

Hugh took a turn about the room. 'Lewis Crawford... I'll be damned.'

'Lewis *is* damned. He has damned himself.'

'How did you find out he was a secret agent?'

'What does it matter? It's too late now. Oh God, I wish I were dead. How could he –'

Hugh stopped her. 'We'd better get some sleep. They're sending someone round at eight. Let's try to rest. You look done in.'

She turned like a sleepwalker. 'Yes, go to bed. And then wake up and everything will be all right.' The tears started

317

again. 'And when I think how rude I was to him, and all the time he loved me –'

'Go to bed.'

Hugh and Anne slowly climbed the stairs, his arm round her shoulders and the tears running down her cheeks.

She lay in bed and eventually fell into a light doze but every now and then would start awake as a memory of the farm, or of her father fishing or of Lewis looking ridiculous on his horse, jostled and pushed itself into her consciousness.

At eight she pulled herself out of bed, feeling dizzy and light-headed, and pulled on her clothes.

Hugh was there when she got downstairs, and Bridget put the teapot on the table and brought them fried eggs and bacon. They sat in silence over their plates. Anne felt as if she might be sick at any moment, but forced herself to eat slowly. After two cups of tea, however, her brain gradually began to clear and she was able to look at her father, haggard and thoughtful across the table.

They heard the sound of an engine, and a moment later Bridget came to tell them a car had arrived for the colonel from Macroom.

'Tell him to come in, Bridget.'

And a moment later a young officer entered.

'Sit down, young man, and have a cup of tea. We're nearly ready.'

'Don't wait for me, Father. There's no point in my coming. It would be better for me to wait here,' Anne insisted.

'Are you sure?'

She nodded.

While Hugh finished his breakfast the young man explained that a raiding party had gone out at six to Martin's farm. They listened in silence. The young man's enthusiasm, his self-assurance, grated.

'Every man in Southern Command has been mobilised, sir,' he said jovially. 'It's quite impossible they should escape. I should like to see how far they get! The entire Essex regiment, and all Auxiliary forces. All leave has been cancelled. I should like Mr Martin to explain what he thought they were up to.'

318

Anne listened with leaden spirits. She had heard it all before.

Eventually Hugh went off in the car, and she was left with Bridget and Leary. But what she was supposed to do now, she had no idea.

She wandered round the house like a ghost. She would have a momentary impulse to get out her bicycle and go into the village. But wherever Lewis was he was not in the village and it was certain no one there would have any idea where he might be now. Father had been put down near Shanacrane. Did that mean they had gone towards Dunmanway? Or towards Bandon? Perhaps that was just a bluff, and they had in fact headed over the Derrynasaggart mountains in the direction of Killarney, thirty miles off? Perhaps they had bypassed Macroom and headed north towards Mallow?

In a sort of sleepwalk she took the binoculars and called the dogs, and set off up the mountainside. But after a few hundred yards she returned to the house. What was she thinking of? Suppose some message came while she was out?

It was in the early afternoon that Bridget came to find her in the garden.

'Miss Anne, if you could come –'

'What?'

She turned as if a gun had gone off.

Bridget nodded back. 'In the kitchen,' she whispered.

Anne followed her quickly. As she came into the kitchen she saw Katie, Mrs Donnelly's maid, in her neat coat and little black straw hat.

'Katie?'

She squeezed her hands together nervously, licked her lips.

'Miss Anne, I was asked to give you a message.' She glanced round at Bridget, and bit her lip. 'In confidence.'

'Sorry!' Bridget jumped up, 'I'll make meself scarce.'

'A message?' Anne whispered. Katie came quickly to her, looking up with her little mousey eyes, shining, keen, into Anne's eyes.

''Tis from himself.'

'Cathal?'

Katie shook her head rapidly. 'No, the other gentleman.'

'Who?' Anne was suddenly terribly agitated. 'Lewis?' she

said loudly. Then, 'Mr Crawford?'

Katie nodded vigorously. 'Poor man. I couldn't refuse him, Miss Anne, and himself in such terrible danger.'

'What message, Katie? Where is he?'

'At the house above, Miss Anne.'

'What?'

'This very morning they came over. I was not even up, and there was a terrible hammering at the door, and when I went down there were a dozen or more, and Mr Crawford among them. Away in they came, and Mrs Donnelly there, and Mr Donnelly too –'

'Cathal?'

Katie nodded and then went on, 'And they ate breakfast and then locked Mr Crawford in the outhouse and had a long conference. An hour they were talking, and then away every man to his own home, and left only Mrs Donnelly and myself and Sean Deasey to guard Mr Crawford.'

'But why have you come, Katie? Won't Mr Donnelly be terribly angry with you when he finds out?'

'Oh, Miss Anne! You see, 'twas an hour ago when I took a bit of dinner in to Mr Crawford, and he started talking to me, and telling me he was in a fearful danger, but didn't mind for himself at all, only for you, because he was afraid you might not understand. He was only begging me to take you a message, that you was not to worry about him, and he did do it out of his –' Katie became flustered and looked down, twisting her fingers together. 'He said he would have liked to write down his message only he had no paper or pencil, so he asked me to tell you as best I could, that – well, he said, for himself he didn't mind dying, because every man has to die one time or another, but he couldn't bear to die with any misunderstanding between you and him, so he only asked me to let you know that he –' she swallowed '– he loved you, and had always loved you, and you were the only woman he had ever loved, and he hoped you would remember him, and not think too hardly of him after he was gone.'

There was a long silence. Anne stared into Katie's face.

'He said that?'

The maid nodded. 'He did, miss, as near as I can remember.'

'And he's there now?'

Katie nodded again. Anne thought for a moment, then shook her head.

'Oh, Katie.' She took the girl's hands. 'How did he seem?'

'Well enough, Miss Anne, only fearful dirty and maybe a bit tired, I think.'

'And he said that?'

Katie nodded. Anne bit her lip. 'Have you any idea what they are going to do? Are they going to move on?'

'No idea, miss.'

'Thank you, Katie, you have been a real friend and if I can ever repay you for this, I will. You have done me a true service.'

'I couldn't bear you not to get the message, Miss Anne.'

'Thank you. You must go back now, or they will ask where you've been.'

'That's all right, miss. Mrs Donnelly sent me to the village stores.'

Katie went out of the kitchen door, and Anne went through into the drawing room, running those words over and over in her mind.

321

# Chapter Thirty-Five

She knelt quickly and looked under her parents' big double bed. Sure enough there was an old shoe-box, which she quickly pulled out. In it, beneath some socks, lay her father's pistol. She snatched it out, stood up and sat on the edge of her parents' bed.

The pistol was a military model, a Webley, big and unwieldy. It glistened with oil; her father had cared for it, and it was neat, ready, in working order. She turned it round in her hands. There were bullets in the chamber. There was something frightening about it as she examined it, turning it over, studying it, briefly flexing the trigger until as she saw the hammer begin to draw back, she quickly released it. She held it out and looked along the sight. It was heavy – almost more than she could hold at arm's length.

She put it down in her lap again, staring at it and trying to order her thoughts.

Going down into the hall where the raincoats and overcoats hung beneath the stairs, she took her old beach bag, and put the pistol into it, then went out to the stables. The dogs were ready to go with her, and she had to order them back indoors vehemently.

It was now mid-afternoon and the sun was hot. She felt exposed in her summer frock, naked somehow in the face of what was to come. But she did not allow this thought to dwell in her mind as she set off down the *bohreen*. As she pedalled through the village and then up the narrow lane to the Donnelly's house, she tried to form a plan but none would come. She had no idea what she might find when she arrived;

whether Lewis would still be there; whether there would be one armed man or twenty; whether Cathal would be there, and if somehow she could persuade him to let his prisoner go. She pedalled hard.

As she threw down the bicycle outside the stone wall the house seemed quiet, deserted. She opened the gate and was making her way down the path towards the door when a window opened on the ground floor, and a young man leant out, holding a rifle. She recognised him as Sean Deasey.

'Stop there! Who are ye and what do ye want?'

She stopped.

'Sean, it's me, Anne Hunter. I have a message for Mrs Donnelly,' she said quietly.

'What message?'

'It's private. And very urgent. Is she in?'

'Don't move. Wait there.' The boy disappeared.

Anne waited. The sun was hot though beginning to decline in late afternoon. She was perspiring from her cycling and her legs trembled slightly.

The front door opened, and Mrs Donnelly looked at her.

'Anne? What brings you here?'

She was still halfway up the path. 'Oh, Mrs Donnelly, I have a very urgent message. Can I come in?'

The older woman looked at her for a moment then moved back. 'Very well.'

As Anne went into the drawing room, Sean relaxed and lowered his rifle.

'Sorry I didn't recognise ye at first.'

'That's all right.'

Mrs Donnelly faced her. 'What brings you here, Anne?' she repeated.

The three of them stood in the room as Anne, not allowing herself to think or feel, put her hand into her beach bag. 'I've got something here for you.'

She pulled out the pistol and pointed it at Sean. 'Don't move or I will certainly shoot you. Put down that gun.'

He was amazed, frozen, staring at the pistol. She could feel her hand shaking slightly. Mrs Donnelly was away to her right side. Anne felt only an intense concentration.

'Put down that gun.'

Suddenly Sean dropped to his knees, his arms stretched upwards, and screamed, 'Don't shoot, miss, please! Please don't shoot!'

She tightened her grip, holding him in her sight as he knelt before her.

'I won't if you do as you're told.'

'Please, miss, I beg you, don't shoot! Don't point that gun at me, please!' He was petrified, his voice unnaturally loud in the room. She felt embarrassed by his vehemence.

'I'm not going to shoot you, I told you, so long as you do as I say.'

'Please, Miss Anne!' he shouted. 'Please, please, don't shoot! I'll do whatever you ask, only don't point that gun at me, I beg of you!'

'Be quiet, Sean! Now listen to me –'

'Please, miss –'

'Sean, will you listen! Just show me where Lewis Crawford is, and you'll come to no harm.'

'Oh, yes, I'll show you,' shouted Sean at the top of his voice. 'I'll show you, miss, if only you won't point that gun at me!'

'Don't be so childish! Come on now, where is he?'

Sean rose, pointing in terror at her pistol. 'Only turn it away from me!'

'I'm not going to turn it away – and I certainly will shoot you if you don't show me immediately where Lewis is!'

'Okay, okay, I'll show you,' he shouted.

'And stop shouting! Go on –'

With terror written all over his body, half cringing, he pointed towards the door, and began to move towards it. Mrs Donnelly watched without speaking.

'It's this way, Miss Anne, by the front door.'

She followed him into the hall and Sean was just opening the door when she felt the cold pressure of metal against the base of her skull.

'Drop it or I'll blow your head off,' Cathal said calmly.

In a second Sean had disappeared through the door.

The gun was pressing against her neck so hard her head was forced downwards. She allowed the pistol to fall from her hand to the carpet.

'In there.'

As she turned back into the drawing room, she was aware of him kneeling and picking up her gun. As he came into the room after her, she saw he was in his shirt and trousers, and barefoot. They looked at each other for a moment.

'I was asleep above there when Sean's voice woke me.'

Sean now returned to the room. Anne looked round at the three of them watching her closely. There was a moment of silence then she said gravely, 'Cathal, you can't do this.'

She tried to gather her wits and took a deep breath.

'That man once saved your life.'

Both Mrs Donnelly and Sean turned to him at this.

'What does she mean?'

'Tell her. Last summer –' Anne began.

'Okay, I don't deny it.' He was brusque. 'But he wiped out that debt when he betrayed us.'

'Cathal, tell her! Tell your mother!'

'Okay! Last summer I was in Macroom – that time I went in to get the medicine for Da. Two drunken Tans stopped me in the street and recognised me. They would have taken me into the castle, only that man – Crawford – intervened, and told them I was his groom, and they believed him.' He looked briefly at his mother and Sean. 'It doesn't change anything. He betrayed us! Pat Twomey died, Mickey Flynn died! They died because of him. That clears the debt!'

'Cathal!' Anne screamed at him. 'Killing begets more killing! If you murder Crawford, it won't save your friends, you know that! It's got to stop!'

But he was as vehement as she. 'Tell that to General Macready! Tell that to Lloyd George! Six hundred years the English have had Irish blood on their hands, Anne, as you well know. We've talked it through, many a time. I'd be betraying the men who trusted me. I'd be betraying the men and women who have suffered over the centuries. The men and women who died in the famine. Who died in this parish, Anne, buried in the churchyard there below. It's got to be a fight to the finish. It's the only way!' His voice dropped unexpectedly, and his tone hardened. 'It's the only way. It must be. And if Crawford must lose his life, so be it. We haven't come this far to stop now. Too many men have died Anne. If I released him it would make a mockery of their sacrifice, as if they had died for nothing. It has to be. Don't say anything, Anne, it has to be.'

There was a moment as they stared into each other's eyes. At last she said quietly, 'And Vere died for nothing too? Do you remember him? My brother died too, Cathal.' She started towards him, beseeching him. 'In his name, spare Crawford. You can afford to. You're going to win this war, we both know it, Cathal. In Vere's name, spare Crawford.'

He was silent for a long time as they looked at each other. His gun had lowered a little in his grasp. At last he said, 'I'm sorry for Vere, too, Anne. I have not forgotten him, believe me.'

The other two were watching him carefully. He looked away, thinking, but at last as he glanced back at Anne she saw he had not changed his mind.

'If those lads are not reprieved, he dies.'

She flung herself at him. 'You know they won't be reprieved! I hate you!'

Sean quickly took her shoulders and pulled her away, and she was helpless in his strong grip. Cathal was looking at Sean over her shoulders. 'Put her in with him.'

He handed Sean her pistol, and glanced at his mother. She pulled a key from her pocket, on a long piece of string, and handed it to Sean. He prodded Anne and she made her way through to the front door.

'Away round to the left.'

As they came round the side of the house there was a stone lean-to shed, with a stout wooden door.

'Stand away from the door,' Sean shouted. 'Okay you, over there.' He pointed to one side, and taking the key, unlocked the heavy padlock on the door.

'In with you now.'

In the moment before the door closed behind her, she saw Lewis in his shirtsleeves, his stubble chin. She caught a glimpse of a heap of hay, and some farm implements standing against the wall. Then the door was shut and they were in darkness.

Lewis took her in his arms, and she was trembling.

'Oh Lewis –'

After a moment, he whispered, 'Anne, why did you come?'

'You sent the message,' she said simply.

'I thought you'd send the military once you knew where I was.'

'I thought I could save you. I thought if there was a siege you would never get out alive. I must have been mad. I'm so sorry, Lewis.'

He was stroking her back as he held her, her head against his shoulder.

'It doesn't matter now. It was brave of you. I certainly didn't expect it.'

'Lewis, I tried to persuade Cathal. But it didn't make any difference.'

'No. I knew it wouldn't. Even if you had been able to persuade him, the others would never have agreed. They'll all be here tomorrow morning for the grand ceremony.'

Suddenly she felt utterly limp, as if her bones were all of rubber. He sensed this and they sat in the warm hay. Lewis held her, his arm round her shoulder and for a while they were silent as she tried to calm herself.

'Lewis –'

'Hmm?'

'When my father got home last night and told me what had happened –'

'He got home safely?'

'And when he told me what you had done, it was, well, it was simply the bravest thing –'

'Ssh.'

'All my life I won't be able to thank you for that.'

She snuggled closer to him, and he stroked her hair slowly, thoughtfully, and it helped to calm her. Suddenly she started up, restless.

'Oh Lewis!'

He was awake. 'What is it?' he whispered.

'I couldn't bear it if you were to be –'

She heard him draw a long breath. 'Don't let's talk about it. I wouldn't mind so much if it weren't for you – that you would be unhappy over me. Promise me, you'll try to forget me.'

'I could never forget you. I will never forget you as long as I live. There's no chance of escaping from here?'

But he held her close again.

'Be calm.' Then after a while he said quietly, 'Anne, this isn't a very agreeable thing to have to say, but there are a few matters we must settle.' He paused. 'I don't think I'm coming out of this –' Anne moved in his arms, but he held her tight. 'So, there are two things I want you to do – afterwards.' He released her, and appeared to be rummaging in a pocket. He took her hand, and she felt him place something into it. 'This is my room key. I want you to go to the Victoria Hotel in Macroom, and ask for room five. Show this and – I don't know – say there's been an accident, and you've come to collect my things. Now, there are two things you have to do. You don't mind, do you?'

'No – of course not.'

'Thanks. One is – In a briefcase you'll find a card, from an Import/Export company with an address in Curzon Street in London. If you could take the card to them for me. They'll probably want to ask a lot of questions. About me – and how you come to know me. And they may be a bit ferocious. Sorry to do this to you, but it has to be done, if possible. Part of the contract. The other thing is – my parents. In that briefcase you'll also find an address book, and in it you'll find my parents' address; it's a place down in Surrey. You'd do me a real favour if you could go and see them, get my stuff to them, and well, tell them – I don't know – tell them anything you like, only try to make it sound honourable. Needless to say, they don't know anything about – this.'

He was silent. Anne whispered, 'Lewis, of course I will.'

'Thanks.'

And then, after a long silence she whispered hesitantly, 'Why did you do it?'

He seemed to think for a while, then, 'After your brother had been killed, I didn't think I had the right ever to speak to you again, ever to be loved again. I thought I had forfeited all right to happiness in this life. That's why I went away. Then when we met again I couldn't help hoping there might still be a chance that we could be together.' He took a breath. 'Well, you know what happened. But then, when I heard your father had been kidnapped and was very probably going to die too, I didn't think after everything that had happened between us that I could endure it – go on living knowing you had lost your brother *and* your father. So, having lost you anyway, I thought it was the least I could do to make up for the loss of Vere.'

Much later, after it seemed they had sat in silence forever, holding each other, and Lewis gently stroking her hair, she stirred a little. 'Thank you for your message – the one Katie brought. It's the nicest message I have ever received.'

'I wish it had been longer. I had to keep it simple so Katie could remember it.'

'I thought it was lovely.' She paused. 'What do you mean – longer? I mean – what else –?'

Lewis was silent for a while, then he began softly, 'I'd have said – whatever happens, whether I am destined to get out of this or not, I shall never forget you. And even if it comes to – well, even then, I shall think of you at the end. I shall remember you in your straw hat when we first met outside the Victoria Hotel, and you were so scornful with me; and how bright it made your eyes.' His voice was low and soothing, and she snuggled closer beneath his arm. 'I would have said, I shall remember how I teased you, and you would become uncertain and confused. I loved you for your confusion. I love you for your transparency, your honesty. You can never have a false emotion. And I've spent my life dealing in false emotions. Your honesty, and then, well –' he paused '– of course, I remember you by the bathing pool, asleep. How could I not love you? You were just so beautiful. And when you woke up and were confused and angry with me, it only made me love you more.'

She slipped down, until her head lay in his lap.

'I never thought I was beautiful till you told me.'

Despite all her fears, despite her terrors, she was very tired and could feel herself falling into a light doze.

She lost all sense of time, but at some point the door was opened and Katie brought in a tray with bowls of stew. It was growing dark outside. Katie looked at Anne but said nothing.

They talked, then they were silent. She had no idea what the time must be. Then she slipped into a doze again.

Suddenly she was being shaken awake. As she opened her eyes, she saw the flicking of an acetylene torch on the ground by the door.

'Anne! Lewis was whispering. 'Get up!'

She struggled to her feet, dizzy with sleep, and he had to hold her to steady her. She realised now that the door was open and someone outside held a torch pointing at the ground.

'What is it?'

Lewis took her arm and guided her to the door.

As she passed out into the night air, she heard a voice, whispering, 'Get you gone now! Quick!'

She turned. It was Mrs Donnelly's voice.

'What?' She was confused still. Lewis had her arm and was guiding her. She looked back and saw Mrs Donnelly in her nightgown, with a shawl round her shoulders, the torch shining at the ground.

'Go on!'

'Mrs Donnelly –'

'Don't say anything, Anne.'

She had a last glimpse of the older woman as Lewis pulled her forward. There was a moon, though low now in the sky; the night was far gone. In a daze she was led through the darkened garden into the lane.

They hurried away.

'What's happened?' Anne whispered to him.

'Don't ask me. Mrs Donnelly unlocked the door and told us to go.'

'But why?'

'How should I know? Hurry!'

'Where are we going?'

'No idea.'

'Lewis! What did Mrs Donnelly say? Why has she let us go?'

'I told you, I don't know.'

'I don't understand...'

They walked quickly for a few minutes, then Lewis stopped. 'Anne, wait. We must think.'

She was still reeling from her abrupt wakening but the cool night air refreshed her.

'We can't go to your house. And I don't think we should head towards Macroom in case they overtake us. You know the country better than me. What do you think?'

'We could take the road over towards Dunmanway. It's

about twelve or fifteen miles. I don't think they would expect us to go that way.'

Soon the lane came into a wider road, and Anne led him away to their left as the road climbed towards the mountain ridge.

Lewis chuckled in the darkness. 'Sure you know the way?'

'Of course. What's the time?'

'No idea. I can't read my watch.'

They set out, walking at a stiff pace. After some minutes, he said, 'Anne, are you up to this?'

'Never mind me. Only hurry.' She shivered.

'Here.' He pulled off his overcoat and put it round her shoulders.

'Thanks. Only let's keep going.'

The moon hung low in the sky and threw a ghostly light across the mountain sides, making strange unnatural shapes of the rocks and boulders. The hedges cast long frightening shadows. Nothing looked as it did by day. Elation and excitement sustained Anne for a while, but slowly, as they wore off, she could feel weariness coming on.

There was no chance of stopping, however, and after another twenty minutes she got a second wind and began to relax into a regular easy pace. The moon finally set, and as they climbed higher and were passing over the mountain ridge, the sky above them was crowded with stars glittering brilliantly against the velvet blackness. They stopped to breathe, and stared up at the stars for some minutes. She had never seen the night sky so bright, filled with magnificence, shimmering and twinkling.

They had been silent for some time, standing and gazing upwards, when Lewis began to speak, and after a moment she realised it was in a foreign language. His voice was low and musical, and the words flowed on. She liked it. It had an exotic sound, un-English and strange. When it was finished, she said, 'Is that Arabic?'

He chuckled. 'Homer. *The Iliad*. Did they never teach you any Greek at school? One of the few useful things they ever did at mine was to make me learn a few bits of poetry by heart.' He began to translate: '"So they sat, night through, great of heart by the gates of battle, the fires burning numberless around them. Like the stars in the night, glittering bright round the gleaming moon in the still air. When every mountain top, every promontory, every valley is seen, endless bright air breaks open from the depth of the heavens, and the shepherd is glad in his heart. Just so burnt, between the ships and the flowing Xanthus, the watch-fires of the Trojans towards Ilium. A thousand fires burned on the plain and by each sat fifty men in the blaze of the fire. And the horses stood each by his chariot eating the white barley and oats and waiting for dawn to break."'

He paused. 'Some things don't change anyway, eh? The stars, I mean.'

# Chapter Thirty-Six

'Lewis.'

She was almost dead on her feet, walking like a sleep-walker, mechanically, not looking where she was going, stumbling over ruts in the lane, stubbing her toes against stones. He took her hand then put his arm around her shoulder.

'Do you want to stop?'

'No, let's get on. Only, Lewis –'

'Yes?'

'Why do you think Mrs Donnelly let us go?'

'At this minute, I haven't a clue, my darling. My brain is numb, number than my feet.'

'Yes, but I know her. I've known her for ever. She's said to me, over and over, that it will be a fight to the finish.'

They stumbled on in silence until she tripped again and Lewis had to catch her.

'I think it must be because of Vere. I said to Cathal he couldn't kill you because of Vere –'

'Don't talk. It's all right. We can ask when it's all over.'

'But I want to understand. Why? After everything she said.' A new thought came into her mind. 'Unless it was because of you.'

'Hmm?'

'You. When you saved Cathal's life that time. Perhaps it was because of that.'

'Perhaps. We can ask her one of these days.'

They stumbled on in silence. The dawn was now beginning to show the merest vestige of a pink flush across the sky ahead of them, and they could see the landscape appearing around them. They were descending from the mountain now. The walking was easier, and there were fields to either side. As the light strengthened she saw, in her half-waking state, a ghostly layer of mist across the field and cows standing in it, still, silent, marooned up to their shoulders.

Anne was swept by a wave of giddiness, and lurched suddenly out of her way. Lewis steadied her.

'There's a town up ahead,' he said.

'Dunmanway.'

The dawn had broken as they walked into the town but it was still very early, and the houses stood still, silent, deserted. They stood in the empty street, dazed, and she tried to think but her brain had ceased to function. She saw only a haze of tiredness. Every bone in her body ached. She weaved again on her feet, and Lewis caught her.

'We must go to the cottage,' she said.

And then, thinking harder, concentrating to make sure the words came out in the right order, 'We have a cottage near Bantry. That'll be safe.'

They were still standing in the deserted village street when they heard the rumbling of a lorry in the distance behind them, and instinctively pulled to one side into a shop doorway. But, as they saw it turn into the village and come towards them, Lewis stepped into the road, waving it down, and the lorry slowed to a stop.

'Are you heading for Bantry?'

'I am.' The driver nodded up behind him, and in a moment Lewis had helped Anne up on to the tail-end, and they were sitting on a pile of old potato sacks, as the lorry picked up speed and passed through the empty village.

An hour later, Lewis banged on the roof of the cab.

'Thanks, this'll do.'

Anne had been asleep in his arms most of the way, but she had woken in time to signal that they had arrived.

To their left, the sea glittered in the morning light. The breakers dashed in among the rocks, over them they heard the harsh cry of gulls, and there was the heavenly smell of the ocean.

As the lorry disappeared round the bend and they stood on the deserted road, she pointed up the rocky slope to the old fisherman's cottage, and he took her hand as they made their way up the narrow path, between clumps of broom and gorse and bleached white rocks. Peering through the windows, it appeared untouched. Anne went round to the back and fished out the key from beneath the rock where it was kept.

The kitchen had a frowsty smell from long disuse. Swaying with tiredness, she pushed open a door. Inside stood a bed, the blankets in a neat pile on top.

'Do you mind making it up yourself? I'll be in there.' She indicated the other door.

'Sleep well,' he said.

She went to the other room, and crossing to the window, opened it to let in some fresh air. Then kicked off her sandals, pulled the blankets over her and was asleep at once.

When she woke she lay staring up at the rafters, and for a second could not think where she could be. Then memories came back, horribly jumbled: herself and Cathal shouting, then being locked in the darkness with Lewis and how gentle and patient and brave he had been, then the extraordinary sight of Mrs Donnelly with her torch. Anne still puzzled in her mind for a reason for that. She still felt desperately tired, but restless too.

And there were things to be done. She pulled herself upright, shook her head and went out into the kitchen. She knocked gently on the other door and looked in. Lewis was still under the blankets.

'Are you awake?'

She tiptoed over to him and looked down. He was asleep. As she looked down he had never seemed more precious to her.

He stirred.

'Lewis,' she whispered, 'I've got to go into the village, to get some food. And I must send a telegram to Father. Have you got any money? I'm awfully sorry but I never thought to bring any yesterday.'

He pulled himself up. He pointed to his trousers which were hanging over the end of the bed.

335

'You'll find some there.' As she fiddled with them, burrowing into his pockets, he went on, 'Funny thing, the gallant lads never searched me – once they'd got my gun, I mean.'

Anne found some money. 'Oh – and water. There's a spring just above the cottage. I'll get a bucket now in case you want to wash.'

'Wash?' He fell back into the bed. 'That's putting it mildly. I feel as if I haven't washed in a month.'

'Nor me.'

She took the bucket and climbed the rocky path to the spring a hundred yards above. All about her it was glorious afternoon, a light breeze flickering the clumps of gorse. The sea spread out, glittering where the sun caught the wave caps, and with long streaks of an intense aquamarine, or cobalt blue. She stood as the bucket filled beneath the spring, looking about and breathing deeply. When she had filled the bucket, she knelt and undid the upper buttons of her dress. She eased it and her chemise over her shoulders to her waist, splashing water over herself. The refreshing coldness was heavenly. Buttoning herself up again, she took the bucket down to the cottage.

'I've brought some water,' she called. 'I'm going into the village now.'

Across the room Lewis watched her from the bed, smiling.

She walked along the deserted road into the village, with the sea on one side and the rocky mountainside on the other, and couldn't help her heart lifting. She was sure they must be safe now, and was able to shake off her tiredness a little.

But when she was in the post office making out the telegram, doubt struck her. The telegram was for her father, Colonel Hunter. It was very probable that any mail for him was opened and scrutinised before it reached him. Miss Burke would read the telegram. Suppose it was passed on to Cathal or one of the others? He had told her that was a common practice. If her telegram were read by the IRA they would be able to track Lewis here to the village. She chewed the ancient bit of pencil for minutes until she came up at last with a formula she hoped would fool anyone: 'Having a relaxing time. Hope to get over soon. Cristabel.'

Reading these few words over and over, they seemed innocuous.

She called into the butcher and the general stores, and bought food – a loaf of bread, a pat of butter, some meat and vegetables, eggs and bacon – just went on filling up her basket. She wanted to cook Lewis the biggest and best dinner he had ever eaten – she who had only the very sketchiest idea of how to cook.

But as she carried the basket back along the road it seemed to get heavier and heavier, and by the time she climbed back up to the cottage she could barely carry it. And at last when she came into the kitchen and heaved it with a thump on to the table, she just slumped down in a chair. Her body felt hollow, rubbery, without strength.

Lewis, who had changed into one of the old beach dressing gowns they kept in the cottage, was washing clothes in a tin tub on the table. He had shaved and combed his hair. He appeared to be completely recovered. He looked down at her.

'There's another dressing gown behind my door. Why don't you slip out of those things and I'll give them a wash?'

She looked up in a daze of tiredness. And at last said stupidly, 'Yes.'

In her room she undressed and wrapped herself in the voluminous old beach dressing gown of her father's.

'You're a genius, Lewis. I was dying to wash my clothes. Is there no end to your talents?'

'I have barely begun,' he said gravely. 'Why don't you go back to bed? You're done in.'

'I've got to prepare the dinner. You must be starving. We haven't eaten since last night –'

'Go to bed. Let the dinner worry about itself.'

'I can't –'

'As I said, leave it to Lewis.'

'What do you mean?' she said weakly.

He chuckled. Then as she stood dazed in the doorway, he wiped his hands, took her by the arm, led her back into the bedroom, turned back the blanket and made her lie down. He arranged the blanket over her, and closed the thin old frayed curtain at the window.

'I'll wake you when it's ready.' And he kissed her lightly on the forehead.

She fell asleep.

When she eventually returned to consciousness it was dark and she lay for some minutes feeling deliciously relaxed, as if her limbs were flowing through the bed, blurring at their edges, as if she no longer had a fixed outline but just merged into the bed around her. She lay happily for a long time, drowsily listening to sounds from the kitchen, seeing the slit of light where the door was not quite closed, and hearing Lewis humming and then sometimes half-mouthing the words of a song, and the sounds of saucepans moving on the range. She could smell dinner.

Twisting in bed, she stretched her arms above her head, and snuggled against the old tick pillow without its cover, feeling the odd sensation of the dressing gown against her naked body, happy just to be there, comfortable, relaxed, and knowing Lewis was only a few yards away, knowing he was safe now. And happy too, as he hummed and sang and rattled the saucepans.

All of a sudden she was out of bed, and tying the dressing gown around her, she pushed open the door.

The paraffin lamp was lit and hung over the table, where plates were set out. Lewis was at the range.

He turned. 'Have a good sleep?'

She nodded and smiled.

'I didn't know you were a cook,' she said at last, leaning against the doorframe, happy just to watch him.

'Well,' he adjusted the frying pan, 'I am a little constrained by our limited ingredients. But I'm doing what I can.'

'What's for dinner?'

'Cutlets.'

'Hmm?'

'You bought them, remember?'

'Did I? I don't remember anything. I think I just pointed things out to the butcher and hoped for the best.'

'Take a seat. Cup of tea?'

'Please.'

'Sorry I can't offer you a glass of wine. Still, once we get home. Condensed milk all right in your tea?'

She nodded. He frowned slightly as he poured the condensed milk into her cup.

'An acquired taste, condensed milk. One I haven't actually

managed to acquire myself, just yet. I'll take mine straight.'

He raised his cup, looking down at her.

'Here's to us, Cristabel.'

As he raised his cup and they drank, he leant over where she sat at the table, by the light of the paraffin lamp, and kissed her lightly on the lips. 'And many more to come.'

He turned again to the range, deftly opening the fire door with the poker, and pushing in some bits of broken driftwood. As she watched him she saw that one of the saucepans contained soup, and soon afterwards he set out two bowls and filled hers for her. The smell made her almost dizzy with hunger.

She dipped her spoon into the soup and tasted it.

'Lewis, it's divine.'

She went on spooning up the soup. It was almost too delicious; at that moment her hunger was a raging physical appetite she could barely control; at that moment she could have absorbed soup through her pores.

Lewis watched her with a professional eye.

'Plenty of butter. That's the secret of a good soup.'

She looked up and caught his eye. Then, a bit later, 'Where did you learn to cook so well?'

He was again at the range, adjusting the fire beneath the frying pan.

'Comes of being a bachelor. It makes one too self-reliant. A very bad thing.'

'Is it?'

'Decidedly. The most successful husbands I know can become very helpless when need arises.'

Already she could feel strength returning, and the heavy fog in her brain beginning to clear. She looked up, amused.

'What do you mean?'

'Work it out for yourself.' He took up the bowl which he had set down as he adjusted the fire, and took a mouthful of soup. 'Got to leave the wife something to do; it stands to reason.'

He set down his bowl, and turned again to the cutlets, now frizzling in the pan.

'Oh, I see. So once we're married, you'll be –'

She stopped, conscious of what she had said. After a

moment, as the silence began to lengthen, he turned, looking at her seriously. She became uncomfortable. 'Sorry. Perhaps I shouldn't –'

They stared at each other and she could feel herself begin to redden. He still hadn't said anything.

'Sorry, I wasn't thinking,' she stumbled.

'Hmm.' He turned again to the cutlets, and adjusted their position with a fork. 'Beginning to take me for granted already, eh?'

'I'm sorry. Tactless, I know.'

'Tactless? I don't know whether that is quite the word I'd use.'

She was terribly alarmed.

'What do you mean?' She was staring up at him.

He turned and looked down at her, a serious, almost severe expresion on his face now.

'What do I mean?' He leant across the table, his face close to hers. 'I mean, I don't know what your father is going to say when he hears that his daughter proposed to me.'

She was utterly confused. 'Lewis, you don't mean –'

He shook his head as he set out two plates with a clatter, and began to arrange the cutlets on them. 'Modern girls these days, they ride rough-shod over all the formalities. Make a mockery of tradition. Think they can take you for granted...'

He set out dinner for them both, and at last sat down opposite her.

'*Bon appétit*, wife.'

Now a smile spread across her face, and without thinking, she half stood and leant across the table to kiss him. 'Oh, Lewis, I do love you.'

'I love you too.' He cut into the dinner in front of him. 'Hmm. Glad we've got that sorted out anyway.'

Anne laughed with relief, and picked up her knife and fork. But then, after a little, as they ate their dinner, she began to feel nervous, a strange trepidation, an anticipation of something that now seemed inevitable, something that loomed before them in the little cottage. Lewis seemed quite relaxed, eating his dinner, making small talk. He set out a dish of strawberries between them, and they took it in turns to take one, but she was now almost unable to meet his eye, nervous, constrained, and beginning to worry about all sorts of absurd irrelevant details, like which bed it should be, and what Lewis wanted or intended. He had made no sign yet she knew with absolute certainty that it was to be tonight and within a very short time too.

The feeling of trepidation grew in her until it swamped her, and she could feel her hands and legs trembling, and didn't know how much longer she could hold out if he didn't do something soon.

The conversation finally came to a complete stop, and they were sitting facing each other, beneath the lamp.

They were looking each other full in the eye. Lewis looked fearfully serious.

At last in absolute silence he rose carefully, not fast, and took her hand, and she rose with him, and he led her towards the room he had slept in. As she passed through the door behind him she saw the bed had been straightened in the semi-dark room, barely lit by light from the kitchen. He turned to her, and took her head in his hands, and kissed her very gently and slowly.

As he did so all her body seemed to lose its strength, she had difficulty breathing, and could feel the trembling in her legs getting worse.

'Cristabel,' he whispered, kissing her face, running his lips over her cheeks to her ear and down her neck.

Then he sat her gently on the side of the bed, and was about to reach for the girdle of the dressing gown, but her own hands were there first. She undid the girdle, and he was able to ease the dressing gown over her shoulders, so that it fell about her. His lips found their way down to her breasts and she felt a terrible thrill as they grazed across her nipples. Gently she was laid across the bed and he was beside her, his hand moving across her belly, up and across her breasts as he kissed her again. She found he was looking into her face as she opened her eyes for a moment, her lips slightly parted and puffy with desire. She gasped very slightly as she felt him touch her *there*, in the centremost point of her being, touching her gently, and as she felt his hand moving there she wanted him more than she knew it was possible to want anything.

Now his lips had moved down, caressing her breasts, her

341

belly, nuzzling and kissing her there in that secret place, and she arched her back instinctively, opening, spreading, inviting, pleading with him to come into her. Then, at last, after it seemed his hands and lips had been moving over and round her forever, till her skin was flayed with desire, she gave a gasp as she felt him entering her. Very slowly, his eyes looking down into hers as he gradually and gradually came into her, further and further, in and in, until she was absolutely clamped round him, as if she were filled by him. But her whole body was just flowing away out and round him as she tightened her legs round his back, and as he moved again, and then again, deeper and harder, she couldn't help it, she gasped again, cried out, an inarticulate, half animal noise, as if from some deeper part of herself than she had ever been aware of.

At first it was tight, and a little painful; but she could never have imagined anything could be so wonderful. And now he was moving in her so deeply she cried out again, a harsh, inarticulate cry, no words could say what it felt like, only a heavy shuddering swoon through her. And she knew that all her life had been leading to this, and whatever might come after didn't matter, because they had this now, and were for ever together. So she clung to him as she felt herself losing all control, her head thrown back as she seemed to dissolve in the inmost centre of her being, all liquid, flowing outwards, merging into Lewis until they were floating together, her head thrown back, and at last she shuddered to an utter cosmic standstill.

Much later, she opened her eyes, and turning her head, lay, empty, weightless, wondering at the man in her arms.

# Chapter Thirty-Seven

She was awake. There was light outside and she turned slightly in bed. Lewis was asleep, his back to her, and she was aware of them naked beneath the coarse blankets and the old bare mattress beneath them.

She propped her head on one elbow and studied the skin of his back and shoulders where he lay beside her. She reached out her hand, laying it against his warm back, and ran it down to his hips and back again, down and up, needing to touch him, touch his skin, the realness of him warm and alive beside her. She wanted to absorb the reality of them together, and the preciousness of him. He moved slightly in his sleep as he felt her.

But thinking this, thinking of his preciousness, she was reminded of how nearly she had lost him, and a shaft of fear ran through her. Were they really safe now? She looked round the room, and through the open door into the kitchen. Who had seen her yesterday in the village? Lots of people knew her. Was it possible anyone had sent a message to Lisheen?

She sat up with a start. Why had she been so foolish? At any moment someone might come for Lewis.

She steadied herself. Stilled her breathing. No. It must be all right. Half a dozen people had seen her, but no one had remarked anything. She had certainly noticed nothing suspicious. She had been seen there often. And no one had seen Lewis; that was the main thing.

Surely Cathal would believe Lewis had gone to Macroom for safety? He would never associate Lewis with Bantry. In any case – she tried to think about it – Cathal knew nothing about the cottage. She was sure of it and felt relieved.

In her relief she felt stronger, sat up and pulled the dressing gown round her shoulders. Lewis was fast asleep so she tiptoed into the kitchen. Their dinner plates still stood where they had finished eating the previous night. As she looked down at the end of a meal, everything just where it had been left, the memory of that inevitable moment when he reached over and took her hand and led her to the door of the bedroom, and the memory of their love-making, flooded into her mind, and she stood still for a moment just to let it flow through her. Why had she been singled out for such stupendous good fortune?

She opened the little fire door of the range and, squatting before it, prodded with a poker at the ashes. Then looking about her at the heap of old driftwood that Lewis had brought in the previous afternoon, she arranged some twigs and dried heather as kindling, and got the fire going. Once she felt sure it was under way she took the bucket and walked up the hillside to the spring. It was early morning yet and cool, though the sky was clear. As the bucket filled she stretched her arms and breathed deeply, taking in the little clouds in the fathomless blue of the sky high above, the bony, bare mountain behind her, and below her the wide sweep of the rocky coastline; the beauty of the morning, and the great emptiness of sky all about her. And there near below the little cottage where Lewis lay still asleep.

When the bucket had filled, she threw off her dressing gown and, shivering, splashed water over her face and chest. Huddling quickly back into the dressing gown, she took up the heavy bucket and made her way down the uneven little path to the cottage.

Lewis was still asleep, but the fire had taken well. She filled the kettle, set it over the range, and went out again to where her clothes were hanging on the line running from one corner of the eaves to a post a dozen yards away. Washing clothes was not something they had ever done much of at the cottage and the line was in fact only for wet bathing costumes. There were plenty of women in the village willing to take in washing for a small sum. As she ran her hand over the still damp clothes moving in the mild breeze, a smile spread across her face as she remembered Lewis, so neat and orderly at the tub on the kitchen table, washing out his underwear. And hers too, she thought, as she checked it on the line. She loved him for that. But she loved him whatever he did. She loved him when he cooked her dinner. She loved him when he smiled at her, but then she loved him when he was serious too. She loved him when he told her stories; she loved him when he teased her. She loved him awake; she also loved him asleep. What had she ever done before she had met him? How could she have lived without Lewis? She was nothing without him. She felt she had been married to him forty years already.

The kettle boiled and she made some tea. Glancing into the bedroom, she took in a cup of black tea. I must get some fresh milk today, she thought.

She leaned over him.

'Lewis?' she whispered. 'I've brought you some tea.'

He turned and at last opened his eyes.

'Did you sleep all right?'

He nodded sleepily. 'Best ever.'

Much later he got up and wrapped himself in his frayed old beach gown, and they made breakfast together and ate it slowly, sitting opposite one another at the old table and sometimes talking, sometimes joking, sometimes just silently looking at each other.

When the sun had got up higher they walked down to the beach and stared for a long time at the sea, the waves crashing down over the clean sand and dashing in among the rocks which made little promontories at either end of the miniature bay.

Lewis walked into the water up to his ankles.

'Cold,' he remarked.

'Mmm. It never gets very warm, I'm afraid. Still, we've always swum here, cold or not.'

He looked round at the mountainside stretching up behind them to the road, and the little cottage alone among the great white outcrops of rock, the patches of heather and broom. Then he turned back, and dropping the dressing gown on the sand, strode naked into the sea. He dived in and swam out, appearing briefly as he breasted the rollers which lifted him, then falling out of sight in the troughs. As he was swept upwards he waved to her as she stood and watched.

'What's it like?' she called.

'Freezing. It's lovely. Coming in?'

She threw down her own dressing gown and ran quickly into the water. It was icy and she felt that horrible tight clutching at her chest as she dived under the water.

She gasped as she came up, but immediately a big roller overwhelmed her and she was submerged again.

Then, gasping and spluttering, she managed to right herself, and to strike out a few strokes to sea. She could see Lewis not far away, turned now towards her, his feet up before him. He grinned.

'Just what we needed,' he called. 'It's woken me up.'

And then, not long after, because the sea was too cold to endure long, they made their way back to the beach, taking up their beach gowns as towels, and wiping their faces.

Although the sea was cold, the sun had now become hot and they spread out the beach gowns and sat side by side staring out to sea. The cold had invigorated her and she felt the blood tingling in her veins, the sun on her skin, and the light sea breeze, gave her a wonderful feeling of zest and energy.

'Lewis –'

But as she turned to him, he kissed her gently; his mouth was salty. Then he looked up towards the road.

'By the way, we aren't likely to be disturbed here, are we?'

She shook her head, waiting for him.

'One wouldn't like to be disturbed, would one?'

'Oh, one wouldn't,' she murmured as she lay back on the beach robe. 'One wouldn't. Not at all.' She reached her arms round his neck and closed her eyes as he leant over her.

The day passed in a dream; sometimes they were clothed, sometimes naked, it seemed to make no difference; sometimes Lewis was cooking, and they were eating – what was it this time? Bacon and cabbage? Or was he baking potatoes in the oven and serving them with omelettes, and teasing her as he served the plate to her with a flourish as if he were the maître d'hôtel of some elegant French restaurant? Then they were making love again, she lost count how many times, it was as if they were making love continuously, as if they had made love all their lives, instead of barely twenty-four hours. But then everything they did together was a love-making – only the means varied.

Late the following morning, as she dressed, her clothes had that delicious smell of things that have dried in the sun and wind. She took her basket and walked into the village to do some shopping. This time Lewis had given her a shopping list. It included fresh milk, but not wine. 'Frankly,' he had said, 'I don't trust any shop in that village to stock a drinkable wine. Get a couple of bottles of stout, if you like.'

She had just finished her shopping and was walking back through the village with her full shopping basket on her arm, when she heard her name.

'Miss Hunter!'

Rosheen came running across the street towards her. The sight of the slatternly girl, in her thin flowery print dress and socks falling round her ankles, took Anne by surprise.

'Hullo, Rosheen.' She was thinking fast as the girl came up with her. 'We're only down for a few days and managing very well, thank you. I think – that is – I think we'll be able to manage on our own this time –'

'Oh, Miss Hunter, what a terrible thing!'

Anne stopped. 'I beg your pardon?'

'The house – burned! 'Twas in the papers.'

'What?' Anne still could not understand her.

'Who could have done such a thing, Miss Hunter? We all said it was such a terrible thing –'

'*Rosheen*! What are you talking about?'

'Your house, miss, 'twas in the paper, burned to the ground!'

Anne put her basket down. Her mouth was dry. 'In the paper?'

'Yes, miss, yesterday.'

Anne stared round for a moment, unable to focus. She picked up her basket and ran back down the pavement towards the stores.

'The paper –'

'Which paper, Miss Hunter?'

'Oh, which paper?' Her mind was in a fog. 'I don't know. *The Cork Examiner*?'

347

The shop assistant picked up the paper. ''Tis the last one.' She smiled. 'You're in luck.'

Anne snatched at it, laying it out across the vegetables, and began ripping it open, spreading the pages everywhere, her eyes racing up and down the narrow columns of print.

*Arson Attack in Lisheen*. She gave a strangled cry. Her eyes could not take in the blur of print.

'Last night, during the early hours of Saturday 9 July, Lisheen House, the home of Colonel Hunter, late of the Ninth Lancers, Resident Magistrate, President of the Irish Kennel Club and well-known personality in the county, was the subject of an unprovoked incendiary attack by persons unknown. Fortunately there were only three servants in the house beside Colonel Hunter and all four were able to escape to safety. Less fortunately the house was most thoroughly destroyed, some few pieces of furniture and a quantity of personal items, some porcelain and a few paintings, being rescued from the blaze. The fire brigade from Macroom arrived approximately an hour and a quarter after the fire was started, but could do little, as the blaze had by this time taken a firm hold on the house...'

'Oh!' She seemed to choke. 'Oh, Lewis!'

Turning, she snatched up her basket and ran up the road, her mind a blur, seized by the horrible, frenzied necessity only to be there; just to be there, to know her father was safe, to do whatever she could.

By the time she reached the cottage she had a tearing stitch in her side. Her heart was beating so hard she felt the pounding of blood in her face, in her temples, and finally she burst into the kitchen.

'Lewis!'

She threw herself into a chair, fighting for breath as she rested her face in her hands. 'Lewis!'

He was there above her. 'Take it easy. Get your breath back. What is it?'

She looked up, still unable to speak, fighting to draw breath.

'Oh, the house! Our house – burnt!' Her face was buried in her hands. 'Burnt. Lewis, I must go. Now. I must. I must go.' She was still fighting to breathe.

He sat opposite her. 'They lost me,' he said thoughtfully, 'and they've taken it out on your family.'

She was just beginning to think straight. 'I have to go now. What are we going to do? You can't leave here.'

Lewis reached across to her. 'You're quite right. You must go home now. We'll just give you a little lunch –'

'I couldn't!'

'You must. You'll be no use to your father if you're fainting from hunger when you arrive. Can you get a taxi in the village?'

'I suppose so.'

'That's the best thing. Just sit there, and I'll put something on the table.'

An hour later she was in a taxi on her way to Lisheen. It was agreed Lewis must remain at the cottage for the time being. He had given her the money for the taxi ride.

As they drove up the long *bohreen* from the village she saw already the blackened walls of the house, and as the car pulled at last on to the gravel sweep she could take in the full extent of the devastation. The roof was completely gone, the walls and chimney stacks standing black against the sky. Even now there lingered the strong, hateful, acrid smell of burning, and a wisp of smoke still rose to be wafted by the afternoon breeze.

About her on the gravel stood some pieces of furniture. She recognised some chairs and the sideboard from the drawing room standing gracelessly where they had been set down in haste.

As she paid the taxi, Leary came round the side of the house.

He saw her and came over and for a moment they both surveyed the terrible scene. Leary shook his head.

'A sad sight, Miss Anne,' he said at last.

'Where's my father?'

'He'll be back later. He's gone over to Mr Archer, to arrange about this stuff. He'll be glad to see ye well. He was worried for ye.'

They stared at the furniture. Then she said stupidly, 'About this stuff? In case it rains?'

349

He nodded. 'We managed to get a lot of it in the stables. Mr Archer has offered to store it for the time being. The colonel's coming over with a cart.'

'Are the horses safe?'

'We got 'em away quick enough, don't worry.'

'Worry?' She was still trying to take in the reality of the ruin before her.

She wandered round the house to the west lawn. The French windows into the drawing room stood open, and looking in she saw a dismal scene of blackened devastation, everything drenched in water, large puddles on the sodden carpets, fallen beams lying across the room. One painting still hung on the wall, blackened and charred. She knew that painting; she had known it ever since she could remember.

Some other pieces of furniture stood on the lawn; the old sofa, and an armchair.

After a while she sat in the armchair and stared at the house, looking up through what had been the ceiling of the drawing room at the afternoon sky, and then up at the window of what had once been her bedroom. She felt inert; the destruction was complete. What was an armchair now? A sideboard? Meaningless relics; they had no significance outside the house they had occupied.

She stared up at what had once been her window, and remembered all the times she had sat and stared out of it at the mountains, her mind far away. All her life had been in that room, in this house. What she was had been fashioned here. Who could say what she was or could be apart from the house where she had been made?

Restless she got up again and wandered down through the garden, across the west lawn, beneath the oaks, and down to the old stone seat against the wall at the bottom. She had half sat but rose again, and as she came up once more towards the house she was struck afresh by the ugly deformity of its destruction.

Later, sometime, she lost count, her father arrived with a man on a horse and cart. Leary and the carter started loading up pieces of furniture.

Both Hugh and Anne seemed empty of feeling. He embraced her.

'Did you get my telegram?' she asked after a while.

He nodded.

'I took Lewis to the cottage. He's there now. It was the best I could think of.'

'How did you escape?'

'Mrs Donnelly unlocked the outhouse where we had been locked up. I don't know why. Then we made our way down to Bantry. And now this. Did anyone see who did it?'

'No.'

'Don't need to.'

'No.'

After a long silence, as Hugh stood with his arms round her shoulders, he said at last, with a weary sigh, 'The Archers have been very decent. They've offered us a room and space to put the things.'

'We go there tonight?'

'Mmm.'

That night, Sunday, she slept at the Archers', in a strange bed. As she was getting into it she remembered she had slept in this bed once before, after an all-night ball for Teddy Archer's twenty-first.

What were they to do? There was nothing left. Absolutely nothing. Their few pieces of furniture had been stored against some possible future home, when one should be sorted out. But at that moment there seemed to be no future.

And she must get back to Lewis, soon, be sure he was safe.

At about midday the following morning she was in the drawing room of the Archers' house when the newspaper arrived.

Matthew, the youngest boy, came into the drawing room holding it, and abruptly let out a shout.

'Hey!'

All heads turned.

'Not so loud, dear,' his mother remarked.

'Not so loud?' he shouted. 'Mother, Father, listen!'

They all swivelled in their chairs.

'There's been a cease fire!'

Anne was silent. It was not possible.

Matthew could see the incredulity on everyone's face. He

351

read out the text with laboriously pedantic pronunciation.

'A cease-fire has been agreed between representatives of His Majesty's Government and the Republican forces. As of midday today Monday July 11, all military activity will cease on either side.'

There was a second of stunned silence, then everyone leapt into the air, shouting and cheering. Matthew seized Anne and whirled her round the room. Then she disentangled herself, snatched up the newspaper and looked down the column. She saw the words, half mouthed them to herself, but still could not properly take them in: 'Military and Sinn Fein pronouncements; Mr de Valera's Proclamation; curfew and other restrictions lifted. . .' Then clutching the newspaper to her, she gazed round at the others as the realisation sank in: it meant they were safe. Lewis was safe. Everything was all right.

# Chapter Thirty-Eight

They stood in front of the house again. There was nothing more to do, but still they stood, unable to tear themselves away, yet still empty of feeling. Even the cease-fire had had little effect. Hugh sighed.

'I know this is a useless thing to say, but if it had been only a couple of days earlier –'

'The house might be still here.'

After a silence, Anne said, 'Father, this may sound callous but frankly I don't mind about the house, now that I know Lewis is safe. The one thing that gives me nightmares is to think that he was so nearly shot. Father, suppose they had shot him, and then the next day the cease-fire had been announced –'

Hugh put his arm around her shoulders, and she rested her head against his chest. There was a long silence between them. Then her father heaved a sigh.

'Thieves have been through it already, you know.'

'What?'

He shook his head. 'Silly things. Trifles. Knives and forks, saucepans, anything that wasn't quite destroyed has gone. Even some of the furniture that was only slightly damaged, or else soaked by the hoses.'

'When is Mother coming down?'

'This afternoon. We've got to discuss what to do. I must admit, at the moment I haven't the faintest idea.'

'Do you suppose Lewis has heard of the cease-fire? He is keeping as much as possible out of sight. And I had bought in a lot of food. He won't go out for two or three days in all probability. I must go down.'

'I would drive you only I've got to go and meet your mother at the station.'

Late that afternoon, Mr Byrne drew up below the cottage, and Anne ran up the path and beat against the window.

'Lewis!'

There was no reply so she went round to the door. It was locked. She found the key beneath the stone and let herself in.

Everything was neatly tidied up and stacked away. She looked into their bedroom. Blankets were folded on the mattress. The beach robe hung behind the door.

She ran out again, scanning the beach below the cottage. It was deserted. She looked up the mountain slope.

She ran down to the taxi again. 'Drive back into the village, Mr Byrne, please.'

There were several bars in the village. She went into every one. There was no sign of Lewis.

'Drive back to the cottage. Perhaps by this time he's come back.'

But when they got back, everything was as they had left it.

The confusion in her mind was transforming itself gradually into a nameless dread; it was impossible. Where could he have got to? Did he know there had been a cease-fire? If he had been near a newspaper he did. If he had been into a bar he did. If he had been into a shop, or on a bus or train. If he had spoken to a living soul...

Or had the IRA found him somehow before the cease-fire had been announced? She was able to calm herself when she considered that if this were the case, the cottage would not have been left in such good order.

The long shadows of evening lengthened over the sandy beach beneath them as she stood with Mr Byrne beside the car and thought furiously, trying to decide what to do.

'It'll be dark in an hour, Miss Hunter. There's no more ye can do here.'

'We'll wait a little longer.' The sun crept lower in the sky till there was a path of beaten gold across the waves and the sun itself was a flaming ball balanced on the edge of the ocean. It was after nine o'clock. Tears smarted in her eyes, and she turned abruptly to the car.

'Very well, we'll drive back.'

All the way, as it grew dark, she racked her brains. Where coud he have gone? They had certainly not passed each other on the road coming down. It was impossible he had somehow got to Lisheen first or he would have come to the house. But if he had not come up that road, which had he taken? Where was he? She wanted to wail, like a lost child. She wanted Lewis. *Where was he*? She bit her finger as tears forced themselves against her will into the corners of her eyes.

It was after midnight when she arrived at the Archers'. Her mother had arrived, and had been waiting up for her.

'Darling, where *have* you been?'

Anne could scarcely speak. 'I'm sure he's all right. I expect he's –'

She was silent. At last Claire said uncertainly, 'Lewis?'

Anne nodded.

'He's gone?'

She nodded. Her parents looked at one another.

'There's bound to be some perfectly simple explanation,' Claire said briskly. 'Go to bed now, darling, it's after midnight. We've got to have a talk tomorrow. About the future.'

Anne did not sleep for a long time. She could see the cottage too clearly, see through the window the pile of plates neatly stacked on the table, the pile of blankets neatly stacked on the mattress. Everything neatly ordered. And the house empty. As if Lewis had neatly ordered himself right out of sight. Tidied himself away, as if to say: Thank you very much for your hospitality, and now goodbye. They've made a cease-fire, my job's over, so I'm off.

What else could it mean?

Unless he had gone to the house and found no one there and did not know where to find her? She started up in bed in the darkness. But a moment later she slowly lay down again, her heart beating. He had only to ask anyone in the village. Anyone at all.

But why had he gone? They were so happy together! She just knew they were made for each other, it was destined, written in the stars. She drew a long breath, and turned in the darkness.

It was like before, when Vere was killed; Lewis the Master Illusionist had just vanished, shimmied out of sight, performed his last great vanishing trick.

After breakfast the following morning she sat with her father and mother in the Archers' drawing room and began to talk about the future. But they had barely begun to speak when she heard the sound of a motor car outside, a large, familiar car – in fact, only one car in the whole world had ever sounded quite like that – and going to the window was in time to see the Old Beast swing round before the door and come to a stop. Lewis got out, but she was through the front door and into his arms before he reached the step.

'I thought I'd lost you,' she gasped into his jacket front. 'Oh God, Lewis, you gave me such a fright. Where on earth have you been?'

He chuckled. 'Let me get through the door, old girl.'

His arm round her shoulders, they returned to the drawing room. The others were all on their feet.

'Crawford. We wondered where you'd got to.'

The Archers had come in at that moment, and Hugh introduced him.

'Yes,' said Lewis, 'I'd love a cup of coffee. Thank you.'

He threw himself into an armchair. 'Decent of your friends to put you up like this,' he said, looking round.

'*Lewis!*' Anne almost screamed. '*Where have you been?*'

'Hmm? Oh, yes. Well, it was about the Beast. Just went to pick her up; make sure she was safe and sound.'

'You went to Martin's farm?'

He nodded, and looked up as Mrs Archer came in with a cup of coffee and passed it to him.

'Thank you very much.' He stirred the coffee and took a sip. 'Mmm, delicious. I must say, I do like a cup of decent coffee. Freshly ground beans and just a pinch of salt, that's the secret of good coffee.'

'Lewis! *Please!*' It was more of a wail this time.

'What? Oh, yes. Well, as you can imagine, it wasn't going to be very easy. Not after everything that had happened, and

356

needed more than a little tact. But, by great good fortune, I remembered I just happened to have a case of Hocks and Mosels in the boot, safely locked up. They had never tried to force it open or anything. So I suggested we toast the cease-fire. The Martins didn't have an ice-box unfortunately, and I must admit we were at a loss there for a moment – not much fun drinking Hock warm, as you know – until Martin's eldest son, Rory – smart lad – suggested we suspend the bottles in the bucket and lower it down the well. Of course it made an ideal cooler. Now I had to think quickly, as you can imagine – I thought I'd better not take any risks – so we opened the batting with an Oppenheimer Krotenbrunnen Kabinett. A nice dry white wine, very drinkable in the afternoon, lies not too heavy on the stomach. Then, since that seemed to be satisfactory, I suggested we try a Riesling and opened a bottle of Eitelsbacher Karthäuserhofberg – an old favourite – and followed it up with something a little more select, a Schloss Böckelheimer Trockenbeerenauslese Kabinett, pre-war vintage. That went down pretty well too, I must say. By the way, I was keeping a bottle of Tokay up my sleeve in case things got sticky. I still couldn't be too sure, and didn't want to leave my flank uncovered. But in the event I needn't have worried. We worked through the Hocks, and went on to the Mosels.' He paused, and then drew a breath. 'So I didn't get away last night as I'd intended.' He thought for a moment. 'Decent enough fellow, Martin.'

'And the Old Beast was safe and sound?'

'Yes. Rather the worse for wear, though. I shall have to have a bit of work done on her once I get back to London.'

Anne looked at him for a moment, shaking her head.

'Lewis, is there *anything* you take seriously?'

'One thing anyway.'

'The Beast?'

'You.'

# Epilogue

Anne stood, her arms crossed, looking down. Below, the traffic had now come to a complete standstill and taxis began hooting. Glancing along the street she saw that a coster-monger with his fruit-barrow was the source of their frustration. He seemed to have got stuck at the street corner and was arguing with a man in a car. She gazed up at the sky, one low leaden expanse, the smoke from tall brick chimneys flicking this way and that in the rain. In the street people hurried past, cowering beneath umbrellas, which would be caught by sudden gusts of wind. A newspaper man, uttering incomprehensible little squawks, could be heard over the noise of the traffic. Across the road the shop had its lights on, though it was barely the middle of the afternoon.

She shivered and touched the radiator beneath the window. It was faintly warm and made rude gurgling noises. She adjusted the cardigan around her shoulders, and crossed to turn on the electric fire – disguised as a log fire – to warm the room. Lewis had had to complain to the janitor about the heating before, but the staff here in London were another breed. She thought fondly of Mrs Deasey and Bridget, Leary and Costello. Ireland seemed a long way from Mayfair, and it was one thing to live in a so-called 'service flat' but where was the service? The janitor maintained the heating wasn't his responsibility. 'I suppose it works by divine command,' Lewis had said.

Turning to the room, she pulled a cover straight over the back of the sofa, and plumped up a cushion, then wandered into the passage to their tiny kitchen. Mrs Carter had left everything ready and had promised faithfully to be back in time for dinner at eight-thirty.

She stretched; at four months she was suffering terrible back pains. It came of being tall, perhaps. She returned to the window, looking down for her parents' taxi. The rain beat steadily; at the corner of the street the newspaper man was still uttering his guttural squawks.

The bell rang, and a moment later she was in the passage and opening the door.

'You found your way, then?'

'Darling, the ogre at the door didn't want to let us in! How are you?'

Claire took her in her arms.

'Fine.'

'You look pale.'

'I'm fine. Father, it's lovely to see you. Do come in, and I'll make tea.'

Hugh embraced her, and she led them into the sitting room.

Once Anne had put on the kettle, Claire insisted on being shown over the flat. 'Darling, it's very smart, very compact. And so convenient. And fearfully glamorous being right in the heart of the West End. I do envy you.'

'We go everywhere. Lewis loves to go out, and we have hundreds of friends. People are always dropping in.'

She made tea and they sat down in front of the imitation log fire.

'How's Torquay?'

'We're well settled in now,' Claire was very cheerful. 'And I've started to get the garden in order. Gerald's been tremendously helpful, made lots of introductions. Of course the house is much smaller than Lisheen, but now there's only the two of us it makes sense. Hugh's joined the golf club.'

'How are the dogs?' Anne turned to him. 'You can't imagine how I miss them.'

'Don't suppose you're allowed to keep dogs here?'

'I shouldn't want to. Poor things – they'd go mad, being cooped up all day.'

'Hmm.'

'Have you been able to do any more work on the *History*?'

Hugh raised his eyebrows, 'Don't you remember about the Customs House?'

'The IRA burnt it out.'

'And amongst other things, all the Births, Deaths and Marriages were destroyed. It's made the *History* very difficult.' He shook his head. Then, after a moment, as if this had prompted a thought, 'I had a letter from Canon Blenkinsop last week.' He paused. 'As a matter of fact, Anne, a bit of bad news.'

Anne looked up.

'It's about young Donnelly.'

'Cathal?'

'You haven't heard?'

She was alarmed. 'I haven't heard anything. What's happened?'

'Well.' Hugh ran his finger over his moustache. 'He's – er – I'm afraid he's been killed.'

'Oh –' Her hand flew to her mouth.

'It all happened after you left. You probably read that after the Treaty was signed last December, some of the IRA held out against the new Free State government. Cathal was one of the die-hards apparently. And it seems about a month ago he was killed in Dublin, in a skirmish with Free State troops. In broad daylight in O'Connell Street. He's buried in the village, and Blenkinsop had the story from his mother.'

For a moment Anne was unable to speak, but after a moment she said softly, 'I'll write to Mrs Donnelly.'

'I always liked him,' Hugh went on. 'He was a fine lad. I'm sorry it had to end like this.'

'Poor Cathal.' Anne was staring down at the carpet. And then vehemently. 'What a stupid waste!'

Claire roused herself and changed the subject. 'When's Lewis coming in?'

'He should be in around six.' Anne pulled herself up straight. 'By the way, we're going to Bordeaux, did I tell you? To tour the vineyards, look at the new harvest, tasting, and so on.'

'Lucky you.'

A bit later, when Claire and Anne were together in the tiny kitchen, Claire said, 'Darling, you can't have a baby in a flat, you know.'

Anne smiled. 'It's all right. We've been looking at houses. Lewis thinks Surrey.'

'Why don't you come down and live near us, darling?'

'Lewis has to be near town, Mother. But I'll get down whenever I can.'

'I wish you would. Your father misses you and Pippa badly. He puts a brave face on things, but you know sometimes he gets very low thinking about everything. Losing his job, and the house being burnt, and ending up in Torquay in a villa. Don't misunderstand me my dear, for myself, I'm perfectly happy; but it would do your father good to see you from time to time.'

Lewis came in at six, and mixed them all cocktails, then Mrs Carter arrived and cooked dinner, and they had a pleasant evening reminiscing, and hearing all Lewis's plans for the firm.

Anne hadn't thought about Ireland in the sixteen months since she had left. After everything that had happened she was determined to put it behind her and make a fresh start with Lewis, but that night for the first time, she thought about Lisheen.

Sleep would not come; the news of Cathal's death had brought everything back. After the cease-fire she had with some trepidation gone to see Mrs Donnelly, but the lady would not receive her. They had exchanged two stoney sentences at the door before Anne was dismissed. What Mrs Donnelly was thinking Anne had no means of knowing, and she was left disturbed and confused to make her way slowly home. She had not seen Cathal since that last bitter scene between them.

Her last duty, before she left for England, was to thank Katie. After giving this some thought, she had gone to Katie's parents' house in the village and left her a parcel containing a length of fine Limerick lace 'for her bottom drawer', ostensibly as a memento on leaving the village.

When she did finally drop into sleep she found herself again wtih Cathal, but in earlier times, on one of their expeditions across the mountain, Cathal with an old shot gun beneath his arm, and the dogs bounding through the heather. The two of

361

them, standing in the great sweep of the mountainside staring up into the emptiness of the sky, tracing the path of a hawk as it circled lazily on a current of air. Or staring across towards the mountains opposite, blue-grey or lavender in the shifting afternoon sunlight as the clouds moved over them, closing in or opening suddenly to reveal a brilliant splash of emerald green between the bare grey-white rocks, and hearing the cry of a curlew far away, or the song of a skylark high, high above her.

# PROMISES TO KEEP

## Anne Griffiths

War drove them apart, but love would reunite them ...

Misha Martin is half-English, half-French and madly in love with Philippe Constantin. He sees the sixteen-year-old as a little sister, not a lover, and her heartbreak is complete when Philippe agrees with her parents that Paris in 1939 is no longer a safe place for Misha. Packed off to stay with her English cousins, Misha feels exiled and alone.

Seizing her first opportunity to return to France, she finds her beloved city in a mood of defiant gaiety as the Germans advance towards Paris. Despite danger, hunger and fear Misha's heart lifts as she throws herself into the fight against the invaders: for she is home.

And she promises herself that Philippe will find a woman, not a child, waiting for his return . . .

Through occupation, resistance and retreat, *Promises to Keep* is a poignant story of separation, heartache and love.

The very best of Piatkus fiction is now available in paperback as well as hardcover. Piatkus paperbacks, where *every* book is special.

☐ 0 7499 3064 0  Water's Edge            Connie Monk      £5.99
☐ 0 7499 3025 X  Promises to Keep        Anne Griffiths   £5.99
☐ 0 7499 3076 4  Only Love               Erich Segal      £5.99
☐ 0 7499 3057 8  Dreaming of Tomorrow
                                          Doreen Edwards   £5.99
☐ 0 7499 3058 6  The Turning Tides       Elizabeth Lord   £5.99
☐ 0 7499 3002 0  Under The Rowan Tree
                                          Una Horne        £5.99

The prices shown above were correct at the time of going to press. However, Piatkus Books reserve the right to show new retail prices on covers which may differ from those previously advertised in the text or elsewhere.

Piatkus Books will be available from your bookshop or newsagent, or can be ordered from the following address:
Piatkus Paperbacks, PO Box 11, Falmouth, TR10 9EN
Alternatively you can fax your order to this address on 01326 374 888 or e-mail us at books @barni.avel.co.uk.

Payments can be made as follows: Sterling cheque, Eurocheque, postal order (payable to Piatkus Books) or by credit cards, Visa/ Mastercard. Do not send cash or currency. UK and B.F.P.O. customers allow £1.00 postage and packing for the first book, 50p for the second and 30p for each additional book ordered to a maximum charge of £3.00 (7 books plus).

Overseas customers, including Eire, allow £2.00 for postage and packing for the first book, plus £1.00 for the second and 50p for each subsequent title ordered.

NAME (block letters) _____
ADDRESS _____

I enclose my remittance for  £ _____
I wish to pay by Visa / Mastercard          Expiry Date: _____

| | | | | | | | | | | | | | | | | | | |
|---|---|---|---|---|---|---|---|---|---|---|---|---|---|---|---|---|---|---|---|
| | | | | | | | | | | | | | | | | | | | |